NOT THIS TIME

What Reviewers Say About
MA Binfield's Work

One Small Step

"I really loved this book and the gradual way Iris and Cameron's relationship builds. It feels very authentic as they both gain confidence from their genuine care for one another. The author takes time to carefully build something real between the two of these women. This book kept me intrigued."—*Bookvark*

"I lost myself in Iris and Cam's growing feelings and doubts in a very enjoyable way. They're both endearing characters, and the web of friends and teammates around them is full of interesting people."
—*Jude in the Stars*

"The author crafts a deeply emotional romance that is as grounded in stark reality as it is elevated by the ethereal nature of love. …*One Small Step* is a tremendous romance début. MA Binfield's portrayal of a couple in search of the courage to fight for the love that they deserve is written with sheer honesty, humor, and heart."
—*All About Romance*

Visit us at www.boldstrokesbooks.com

By the Author

One Small Step

Not This Time

NOT THIS TIME

by

MA Binfield

2020

NOT THIS TIME

ISBN 13: 978-1-63555-798-5

This Trade Paperback Original Is Published By
Bold Strokes Books, Inc.
P.O. Box 249
Valley Falls, NY 12185

First Edition: December 2020

CREDITS
EDITOR: CINDY CRESAP
PRODUCTION DESIGN: SUSAN RAMUNDO
COVER DESIGN BY TAMMY SEIDICK

Acknowledgments

Huge thanks to my fantastic editor, Cindy Cresap, for the improvements she made to this book. Cindy corrected my writing errors with wit and patience, but more importantly, helped me tell a better version of this story.

Thanks to Bold Strokes Books for making the authoring process so easy for a newbie like me. The support and encouragement we get is awesome, and I'm proud to be a part of the BSB family.

Thanks to Amanda for being my advisor on all things American. She helped make sure that my Miami setting never inadvertently turned into Wolverhampton.

Thanks to Helen Lewis for feeding me, encouraging me, and always listening patiently to my writing woes, even the really boring ones. Having Helen by my side is a strength and a comfort.

Finally, *Not This Time* is my tribute to all the girl bands I've loved (and there are many!), and it was a lot of fun to write. It's inspired by my imagination, my ridiculously romantic soul, and my love of a happy ending.

Dedication

For Mila

Prologue

S top ignoring me, Maddie. Please. We need to talk. I need to see you."

Sofia paused, not sure what else to say, not sure what would make Maddie react and stop ignoring her texts and calls. She sighed. This was turning out to be the worst day of her life.

"Mads, please. You know how much you mean to me, how much our relationship means to me. Please call me back. Or just come back to our room." She paused again. "I'm leaving the band, Maddie, I'm not leaving you." With tears in her eyes, Sofia ended the call.

She couldn't understand why Maddie was so upset. They'd talked about going solo so many times. They'd moaned about the shitty songs they were forced to sing and talked endlessly, lying in bed late at night, about what it would feel like to release their own albums as individual songwriters that people would take seriously. To Sofia, leaving the band was the start of all that. For her, yes, but also for Maddie, for all of them. She might be the one to go first, but someone had to, and maybe one day they'd all thank her for it.

But Maddie hadn't been happy about it. She'd called her selfish and dishonest and said that she'd been stupid to think they had something special when Sofia was walking out on her. Sofia had cried and Maddie had left, not giving her the chance to explain. If she had, Sofia would have told her that the two of them had something amazing, and she didn't intend to let that go for a minute. In fact, in Sofia's version of their future, her leaving the band was the thing that would save them.

"Fuck it, Mads, I'm doing this for us." She spoke out loud, swiping a hand across her cheeks as the tears started falling again.

More than a solo career, more than the approval of her management or their fans, she wanted Madison Martin in her life forever—without the pressure and insanity of being side by side in one of the biggest girl bands on the planet, tied into a contract that didn't allow either of them to be who they wanted to be.

There was a knock at the door. Sofia ran to answer it, before swinging it open with more force than she intended.

"Hey." Felix's voice was deep and always contained a hint of amusement, as if he was in on a joke that no one else understood. "How are you doing?"

Sofia knew he meant well, that he understood that deciding to leave the band had been hard for her. As her manager, she had to believe he had her best interests at heart in pushing her into going solo.

"Maddie won't talk to me. She's ignoring my calls and I don't know where she is. Have you seen her?"

"You told her?" Felix frowned.

"I had to."

"Dammit, Sofia. You agreed not to say anything—we haven't even signed the contract yet. You only had to keep it quiet for three more weeks." He started pacing. Sofia could tell he was trying not to be angry with her. "How are you going to do the rest of the tour with them knowing you're leaving? Did you stop and think about that?" He sounded more exasperated than angry. "It's going to be really fucking awkward."

"I didn't tell them all. I only told Maddie." Felix's pacing was making her anxious. "I had to tell her once I knew it was definitely happening. She's my girlfriend. I know you'd all rather she wasn't, but she is." Her voice cracked and she felt the tears building again.

"And you think she hasn't gone off to tell the other girls? Of course she has. And I'm guessing from how upset you are that she didn't exactly congratulate you."

"She didn't believe me at first, and then she got upset, called me some horrible names, and walked out. And now she's ignoring me, and I need to see her, I need to explain."

Felix stopped pacing and pinched the bridge of his nose with his fingers, like he always did when he was stressed.

"Look, Sofia, we're doing this because you've outgrown them, because you're going to be a big star. They can all have their own careers without you. You're the one taking a risk, not them. You're too good to be singing other people's songs. You've done your time in the band and you're ready for this. Maddie knows that really, they all do. They'll come around. It would have been easier for you, for them too probably, to get to the end of the tour without them knowing, but whatever happens, you need to remember that you're entitled to do this, as any one of them is. Just because you're doing it first doesn't make you the bad guy, it makes you the brave guy."

It was the longest speech Sofia had ever heard Felix give, and for a few seconds, his words made her feel better, but then she remembered the hurt, angry look in Maddie's eyes as she walked out on her. She looked down at her phone. Still nothing.

"Are they all gonna hate me for this?" Sofia looked up at Felix, willing him to reassure her.

"Probably," he said. "But not forever."

Not forever was no comfort to Sofia. She loved Maddie with everything she had, and she couldn't do any of this without her. She needed Maddie to not hate her right now.

❖

Sofia had gotten into bed twice but couldn't settle. She riffled through the minibar wondering if she could stomach the small bottle of brandy in an attempt to take the edge off her anxiety. She unscrewed the cap and sniffed the amber liquid. Something about the smell reminded her of Maddie, of the time years ago that Maddie had made them try every bottle in their minibar, laughing herself stupid at Sofia's disgusted expressions each time she tried one and then spat it out. Maddie had ended up tipsy. Sofia stayed sober and she remembered, with a flush, that Maddie had climbed into bed with her that night for the first time and wrapped herself around Sofia possessively, breathing the sweet boozy fumes into Sofia's neck as she slept. Sofia had stayed awake as long as she could, marveling at just how good it felt to have Maddie that close to her, to be wrapped gloriously in Maddie's arms and legs. In the morning, they'd shared their first incredible kiss.

A shiver ran through her at the memory. From that first kiss, Sofia had been convinced that Maddie—her bandmate and best friend—would be hers forever. Now she wasn't sure. Maddie's reaction to the news that Sofia was leaving the band—the hurt and disbelief in her eyes, the tension in her jaw that only Sofia would recognize as Maddie trying not to cry—was awful. The sight of Maddie as she walked away, ignoring Sofia's calls for her to stay, played on a loop in her mind.

As she sipped at the brandy, Sofia looked again at her phone. She couldn't stop herself from rereading the messages she had sent, knowing they had sounded increasingly more desperate as the night wore on. She didn't care, she was desperate. She'd already decided that she wouldn't leave the band if it meant losing Maddie, and she didn't care what Felix or anyone else thought about it. A solo career could wait.

Sofia put her phone down with a frustrated sigh. Next to her was Maddie's bed, covered in their clothes and half packed suitcases. As usual, they had slept in Sofia's bed last night. In the beginning, they hid their relationship and used to make both beds look slept in, but in recent months they hadn't bothered. The people close to them knew they were lovers, even if they weren't entirely happy about it, and Sofia had gotten tired of pretending they were just close friends. It was nobody's business what they did with their private lives, and the record company's constant interference was just one more reason why them both going solo would be good for them.

She looked again at her phone. It was ten past one. She had to accept that Maddie had decided to sleep somewhere else. She lay down and tried to stop tormenting herself with the thought that she had ruined everything. The solution was simple—she would see Felix in the morning and tell him that she had changed her mind. She'd stay on for the next album, longer if Maddie needed her to. Sofia had to hope it would be enough for Maddie to forgive her.

As she climbed under the covers, she heard a muffled thud out in the corridor. Her heart beat rapidly as she crossed to the door, using the peephole to see who was outside, needing it to be Maddie. The corridor looked empty, but then she caught a flash of a dark jacket and dark hair moving across her field of vision, and she jerked open the door and leaned out, seeing Maddie's back retreating from her, her steps a little unsteady.

"Maddie," Sofia called after her.

Maddie turned around to face her, and Sofia felt her breath catch. Maddie's dark hair was tousled, her eyes were smudged with mascara, and even at a distance of five yards, Sofia could see the look of hurt defiance. *God, she's beautiful.* She felt her heart beat faster in her chest.

"Why? What's the point?" She sounded a little drunk. Her words suggested there was nothing to talk about, but she remained still, facing Sofia.

Sofia badly wanted to go to her, to cross the space between them and wrap Maddie into a hug, to nuzzle her neck, stroke her beautiful hair. Her heart hurt and she knew that only by making it right with Maddie would it stop.

"Come inside, please. We're going to wake people out here." She didn't know what else to say.

Maddie looked around as if realizing for the first time where she was. She looked at Sofia and then looked down the corridor toward the elevators, seeming to weigh her options. Maddie moved toward her, and Sofia felt her breath leave her body. She allowed Maddie to pass into the room and let the door close gently behind them. She moved to switch on the main light.

"Don't." Maddie whispered the word, her voice sounding low and husky. Sofia moved away from the light switch and stood in the middle of the room, a few feet away from Maddie, never being less sure of what to do or say. Maddie stared at her. The look in her eyes was guarded, even a little hostile, and to see it there was awful. Maddie had never looked at her that way before. Sofia took in another deep breath, steeling herself. She could do this, she could fix them.

"Do you want a drink?" Sofia pointed at the fridge. "Everything's there, except the brandy, I drank that. I couldn't sleep. Obviously. Or I could order something. Coffee maybe?" Her anxiety was making her ramble.

"You trying to sober me up?" Maddie took off her jacket and tossed it onto the pile of clothes before sitting on the edge of Sofia's bed. "You sound like Daya and Suzy. I told them you were leaving, and they spent the last hour trying to make me drink coffee and come and see you." She took off her boots and kicked them under the bed. "Like you, they seem to think we have things we need to talk about."

Maddie had not taken her eyes off her, and Sofia was transfixed by the attention. She wanted to look away, to compose herself and find the words she needed, but Maddie's gaze was like being captured by an SUV's headlights.

"It's funny how people wanna talk when they wanna talk but manage to not say very much at all when they've got secrets to keep." Sofia could hear all of the feelings from earlier—the upset, the anger, the hurt pride—and then Maddie looked her up and down and her eyes flashed with something else, something Sofia understood well. She told herself that above all else they needed to talk, but her body betrayed her by reacting to Maddie's gaze. She felt the gentle thrum of arousal between her legs and knew there was nothing she wanted more than to taste Maddie's mouth, to feel Maddie's hands on her. But it wasn't the way they were going to fix things between them. She made herself speak.

"I thought you weren't going to come. I called so many times. You didn't—"

"I think you knew I was gonna come." Maddie cut her off. "I'm stupid enough to be in love with you. You wanna talk, let's talk. Maybe you can explain to me how you leaving the band is anything other than you turning your back on us, on me. Anything other than you deciding you're too good for us, too good for me." The last four words came out a little choked and Sofia couldn't help but move toward Maddie. If she couldn't find the words to tell Maddie how much she loved her, maybe she could let her kisses make it clear.

"Don't." Again, the single word, this time accompanied by a palm held up in her direction. Both stopped Sofia in her tracks.

"I'm sorry. I just want to hold you. I'm scared. I didn't mean to ruin anything. I just thought it was time. I thought we both felt that. And I thought we'd be happier, that we'd finally be able to have our relationship without them interfering, without them watching every

move we make. You always hated the way they made us hide it."
Sofia spoke in a rush, tears forming in her eyes. Waiting for Maddie
to come back to her today had taken its toll.

"So you're leaving the band for me?" Maddie spoke with
something close to a sneer. "The lucrative solo career, the high profile
collabs you've probably already got planned, the deal on your first
album. All for us? That's sweet, Sofi. Completely fucking deluded
but kind of sweet."

"Don't be like this. I know you're hurting, but I did do this for
us, and yes, I also did it for me." Sofia knelt on the floor in front of
Maddie. There was no point in pretending that she was doing anything
other than throwing herself at Maddie's feet and hoping she would see
sense.

"We've hated this past year, you know we have. The songs they
give us are embarrassing, they treat us like puppets. We both want
to write and perform our own music. We've said it so many times."
She was struggling to get her words out in the right order, to make it
sound as right as she knew it was. "We knew the band wasn't forever.
We didn't even think it would last this long, and this is our chance to
move on." She willed Maddie to understand.

"This is your chance, Sofi, not ours. Don't kid yourself. Felix is
buying out your contract so you can get out now. But he's doing that
for you, not for the rest of us. They'll expect the three of us to just
carry on without you. It'll be worse for me, not better. And that's not
even the worst thing. You agreed to a fucking solo contract, without
telling me, without really discussing it with me. Can you imagine how
stupid I feel right now?" Maddie leaned forward, looking at Sofia, her
eyes full of sadness. Sofia almost couldn't bear it. "I thought we had
something special, that we were in this together." She faltered. "I let
you in. I know you know that I worshipped you."

Sofia hated hearing Maddie using the past tense about them. It
terrified her.

"You always made me feel so special, but now…" Maddie waved
a hand into the space between them as if to suggest that, whatever it
was, it was gone.

Sofia got up onto her knees, leaning toward Maddie. She took
her hands. Maddie tried to shake her off, but Sofia held on to them
tightly and Maddie relented.

"I'm not leaving you, Mads. I'm not. I know it'll be hard at first because we're used to being together all the time, but it'll be better for us I promise. We won't have to deal with the hypocrisy of them telling us we can't show each other the smallest amount of affection because the fans are 'too young to handle it,' while making us pretend to have boyfriends they want us to be hanging all over. This way, we can do and be what we want, without the record company saying it's against the terms of that fucking contract we signed when we were too young to know any better. I want to write and sing my own songs, but I'm also sick of them controlling our lives, and I know you are too." She looked at Maddie, wanting her to believe it would be better, that it was a start and not an end for them.

Maddie pulled her hands away, but Sofia didn't move. She put her hands on Maddie's knees, needing to be touching her somehow.

"You didn't talk to me about it, Sofi. That's not what people in a proper grown-up relationship do. And it makes me feel like a fool to have trusted you."

"I told you as soon as I decided to do it. It's just all happened so quickly. Felix is mad that I told you at all. He wanted me to wait but I couldn't." She wanted it to count for something. "You can trust me, you know that. I will never hurt you and I will always love you." It was time for her to lay it on the line. "I love you, Maddie. So damn much. I did this for me—of course I did—but I honestly did it for us too. You have to believe me. Tonight when you didn't come, when you didn't call, was the most unhappy, the most heartsick I have ever felt. The idea of losing you is terrifying." Sofia rested her head on Maddie's knees, letting the tears fall finally.

Maddie tensed beneath her, and Sofia waited for her to push her away. But then she felt Maddie's fingers in her hair, stroking her head gently, soothing her as she wept. Sofia felt the relief in her body replaced with arousal as Maddie's fingers moved from her hair to trail across her bare neck, across her bare shoulders.

"I was always gonna come. I think we both know that." Maddie's voice was barely above a whisper. "I don't know how to be without you."

Sofia's breath caught in her throat as Maddie's nails raked down the top of her spine, feeling like someone had plugged her into an electric socket. Jolts of arousal pulsed from Maddie's fingertips and landed between her legs. Maddie's fingers kept moving, overloading her senses. She lifted her head to look up at Maddie. Her brown eyes were almost black, her lips full and red. She stared at Maddie's mouth. Normally, she didn't wait, had never waited, to be kissed by Maddie. It was her favorite thing, and every moment they had alone meant Sofia would go to her, claim that mouth, kiss those lips. But as Sofia knelt in front of Maddie, her face tilted upward, she understood that, this time, she had to wait. Maddie's gaze moved from her eyes to her mouth and back again, and Sofia was mesmerized by it. Then, briefly, Maddie closed her eyes. When she opened them, she seemed to have decided something because she reached one hand to the back of Sofia's neck and the other to the small of her back, pulling her closer and capturing her mouth in a hard, possessive kiss.

Sofia moaned, heat coursing through her body at the taste of Maddie's lips, the feel of her tongue, the urgency of the kisses. She could taste tequila and coffee mingled together in Maddie's mouth and it was the sweetest thing she had ever tasted.

Maddie pressed Sofia closer to her, pulling her in between her knees, the kisses hard and passionate, and when Maddie used the arm around Sofia's waist to lift her up from her knees and pull her into her lap, Sofia let out a soft moan of desire. She had her hands in Maddie's hair and moved her lips from Maddie's mouth to her neck, tracing kisses down behind her ear, and biting her neck softly. Maddie shifted underneath her, letting out a soft curse.

She worked the buttons on Maddie's shirt and pulled it open, dipping her head to place kisses across her shoulders, across her collarbone, stopping only when she felt Maddie's hands slip under her tank and her nails scratch slowly down her back. Sofia arched her back toward the touch, feeling herself get more and more aroused. When Maddie stopped, looked at Sofia for a few seconds, and then lifted off her tank top and tossed it on the floor, Sofia took in a breath at the anticipation of Maddie's hands on her breasts. As Maddie caressed them, softly at first and then more roughly, pinching her nipples, Sofia whimpered with want. She clamped her eyes shut, her ass grinding into Maddie's lap, feeling as if she was on fire. She wanted this, needed Maddie, didn't want her to hold back.

Maddie took a nipple into her mouth, and Sofia moaned, feeling the sensation of arousal travel down her body to her center, now wet and throbbing with need. She took hold of Maddie's shirt and tore it open completely, revealing Maddie's breasts in a low cut, deep purple bra. She clumsily helped Maddie out of the shirt, wanting her own hands, her own mouth on those breasts at least as much as she wanted Maddie to keep tasting her own.

"You are so fucking beautiful, Mads. I don't have the words right now, but please know that you're everything to me." Sofia tried to say what she was feeling. Maddie was silent in response. No smile, no words, just a look of utter wanting.

"Take off your shorts." Maddie's voice came out low and hoarse, and Sofia got up from her lap immediately.

Sofia took them off and kicked them across the floor, not once taking her eyes off Maddie's face, seeing her eyes widen as Sofia stood in front of her naked now. She felt all the blood, all the heat in her body rush between her legs. Maddie's gaze was so intense and all Sofia wanted was Maddie's hands on her to give her the release she needed. In the past, she might have grown uncomfortable under such scrutiny, but tonight, for reasons she couldn't untangle, Sofia wanted Maddie to look at her, wanted to be seen. However their management and their families treated them, they were grown ass women who knew what they wanted, not children who needed to be constantly told to stay away from the fire. And right now, Sofia wanted to stand close enough to Maddie to be burned.

Without taking her eyes off Sofia, Maddie stood and then reached out a single finger to stroke it gently across Sofia's naked shoulder as she slowly walked around her.

"Maddie, please." Sofia wanted Maddie to touch her properly, to kiss her, to lay her down and fuck her. Maddie's response was to trail the same finger upward until it rested on Sofia's lips in a silencing gesture.

Maddie continued to move slowly until she was behind Sofia. Sofia could no longer see her, but she could feel Maddie's breath on her neck. In seconds, Maddie was pressed against Sofia, gently brushing Sofia's hair to one side so that she could kiss Sofia's neck. As soon as Maddie's lips made contact with Sofia's skin, Sofia gasped slightly and pushed herself backward to increase the contact her body had with Maddie's. As Maddie snaked a hand around to lay it flat on Sofia's stomach, pulling her even tighter into the embrace, Sofia's body tensed in expectation as Maddie's other hand reached around Sofia's body to close over her breast. When the hand on her stomach moved so that Maddie had both hands on Sofia's breasts, Sofia closed her eyes, losing herself to the blind arousal now coursing through her body as Maddie caressed both breasts, pinching the nipples between finger and thumb. Every touch of Maddie's hands sent currents of pleasure to her center, making her wet and ready.

"Please." Sofia made no attempt to disguise how desperate she was. When she opened her eyes, Sofia saw that Maddie had turned them both and they were in front of the large mirror. Sofia was surprised to see herself standing there naked with Maddie's chin resting on her shoulder and Maddie's hands on her breasts. She watched as Maddie glanced down to the area between Sofia's legs, before looking back up at her. For a second, she felt exposed and vulnerable, but then she locked eyes with Maddie's reflection, and the arousal written across her face sent sparks of desire to Sofia's already molten core. She nodded, unable to form actual words. In response, Maddie stopped caressing Sofia's breasts and moved a hand slowly down her body, over her ribs, past her navel, pausing to trace light feathery patterns along the dark stripe of hair covering Sofia's aching wet center. The anticipation of what was coming made her close her eyes. She had never wanted Maddie's fingers inside her as much as right then.

"Open your eyes." Maddie whispered the words into her ear, and she found them impossible to ignore. She opened her eyes and looked past herself to Maddie, her arousal matching Sofia's own, her eyes the darkest that Sofia had ever seen them. She was breathtakingly beautiful.

"Watch." The single word came out of Maddie with a rasp. She cleared her throat. "I want you to watch."

Sofia couldn't have said no to Maddie in that moment, whatever she'd asked, and she couldn't stop looking at Maddie's hands on her body, the fingers of one hand softly stroking her between her legs, and the other closed possessively over Sofia's breast. The sight was intoxicating.

"Uhhh." Sofia's thoughts were interrupted by the feeling of Maddie turning her body to capture her mouth in a hard, wet kiss at the same time as she entered her with her fingers. Maddie's tongue pushed into Sofia's mouth and she pulled Sofia closer to her. Sofia rode her fingers, the thrusts making Sofia cry out with pleasure. Maddie encouraged her with soft murmurs into her mouth. Her world, her whole world, was reduced to the feeling of Maddie's fingers deep within her. She had no words, her vision had gone, and she couldn't even tell if her feet were on the floor. The only feeling was the consuming blackness of the desire, the desire to be filled over and over by Maddie, to never be without her, to have this, to have them, go on forever.

Sofia felt Maddie sink her teeth into her neck and she shivered at the feel of her skin being marked and then she tensed, close to the edge. She wanted the release, but she didn't want Maddie to stop. Maddie's hot breath was on her ear as she began to move her thumb in short soft strokes across her clitoris. It was all it took to push Sofia over the edge, and her orgasm came with a burst of color and light, her whole body shuddering as wave after wave of pleasure moved through her. Her legs felt like liquid and only Maddie's arms around her kept her from sliding to the floor.

"I love you." Sofia found the words to go with the cry that she let out, and then swallowed, as the orgasm hit. Her muscles had tensed around Maddie's fingers and Maddie waited before gently withdrawing them, not moving away but holding Sofia close until she came back down to earth, stroking the goose bumps on her arms and pressing Sofia to her, nuzzling her neck, before kissing her lips over and over, sweet, soft kisses now, much less demanding.

Sofia's eyes were still clamped shut as she waited to be reunited with the rest of her senses. When she opened them, the intensity of the way Maddie was looking at her almost made Sofia step back. Then Maddie gently turned her around so that they were both facing the mirror, in the position they had started in.

"Look at yourself, Sofi." Maddie put a finger under Sofia's chin, tilting her face upward, making her look at herself in the mirror. Sofia, released by the orgasm from the grip of her desire, was now embarrassed at standing there naked. She hated her body. The constant comments about her weight had gotten inside her head.

"You are so fucking beautiful. I want you to look at yourself and see yourself the way I see you and never forget how beautiful and perfect you are, no matter what anyone ever says to you. Or whatever you might think about yourself." She tapped Sofia's forehead. "I would not change a single thing about you."

Sofia began to speak, but Maddie gently clasped a hand over her mouth. "Not a single fucking thing." She moved her hand. "Okay?" She smiled at Sofia and the smile made her feel that, despite what she'd done, Maddie still loved her.

"Okay." Sofia nodded at Maddie's reflection before turning to her.

"Now take off your clothes and lie down on that bed. It's my turn." She put out a hand to push Maddie backward toward the bed where she had been sleepless and full of sorrow just fifteen minutes ago. Maddie had come back and it was all going to be okay.

Maddie's left arm had long since gone numb under the weight of Sofi's body, but she didn't want to move, didn't want to wake her. Their desperate lovemaking of the past two hours had wiped them both out. Maddie flushed now at the memory of it all. Sofi had always driven her wild, her appetite for sex was almost endless. But this time had been different, more intense, and more desperate. The two of them holding nothing back, not being careful with each other at all, and Maddie ached all over, with a couple of new bruises on her neck that she'd need help covering up before they performed in Portland tomorrow.

The thought of having to keep rehearsing and performing and pretending everything was fine while knowing Sofia was leaving the band was not a good one. She fought to stop herself from panicking. Maybe she wouldn't lose her straight away, because maybe Sofi meant it when she said she intended for them to stay together, but if her schedule was anywhere near as hectic as the band's, Maddie just couldn't figure out how they would ever see each other. The band had brought them together, enabled them to fall in love, and without it she feared they'd fall apart.

"You're awake." Maddie looked down to see dark eyes gazing up at her, Sofi's voice thick with sleep. She started to shift position, but Maddie reached down to stop her.

"No, don't." The words came out sharply. "I mean, it's fine, stay like that, it's nice. You're keeping me warm." She tried for a laugh as she said the last few words, but it came out more like a soft sob.

"Hey, what's wrong?" Sofia reached up and stroked Maddie's cheek softly.

"This, whatever you say, it feels like an ending." Maddie shrugged. "I don't think we can survive you leaving the band."

"That's not—" Sofi started to speak. Maddie cut her off.

"Sof, listen to me. You're a good person, but you're naive sometimes. It's one of the many reasons I'm in love with you, but…" Maddie didn't want to finish the sentence, "when you go solo, it'll be impossible for us to see each other. We never get time off as it is, but if you're not in the band, we won't even have this." She gestured around the room. She hated the way they had to sneak around, but the idea of not seeing Sofi at all was much, much worse. "You'll be building a new career, trying to attract a new set of fans. They'll work you into the ground. I doubt if we'll ever be in the same time zone, let alone the same hotel. I don't know how we can have a proper relationship if we never see each other." She sighed deeply. She felt fearful, could feel actual dread in her stomach.

"I won't work as hard." Sofi gazed at her. "I already told Felix that I need more freedom, that I'm not just going to write my own songs but I'm going to want to be in charge of my scheduling. I'll make sure I can have time off to see you. And, if you go solo too, you can ask for the same freedom. It can work, I promise." She smiled a shy smile. "I even told him that, this time, I need to be able to date, be in a relationship with, whoever the hell I want and they won't be able to prevent it."

Maddie was surprised to hear Sofi say it. She had always been the private one, the one who had been scared of showing their relationship.

Sofia climbed on top of Maddie and put her hands on either side of Maddie's face. "I love you, Maddie—so damn much—and if you don't want me to leave the band I won't. I'd choose you over my first solo Grammy any day." She leaned in and planted a soft kiss on Maddie's lips. "But when we finally go solo and one of us is Grammy nominated," Sofi raised her eyebrows, "I'll expect to go with you and show everyone that I'm the luckiest woman in the world for being able to walk the red carpet with you. I'm proud of loving you, and I don't want to do any of it without you."

Maddie opened her mouth to Sofi's kisses. She traced her tongue alongside the inside of Sofi's bottom lip, marveling at the feel of Sofi on top of her. She lifted her hips off the bed and pushed against her as she continued to claim deep, warm kisses from the woman she loved. Sofi pulled her mouth from Maddie's and moved it to her ear, nibbling softly and then stopping.

"I can wait for a solo career until we're both ready. I'll talk to Felix today and tell him." Sofia moved her head back up to face Maddie and peered at her waiting for a reply.

"Let's sleep and talk about it later." Maddie wasn't sure it'd be that easy now that the genie was out of the bottle. She pulled the covers over them both, settling Sofia's head back on her chest, willing the awful churning feeling in her stomach to settle.

CHAPTER ONE

Five Years Later

Sofia stood with a towel around her neck, her hair damp and her face flushed. She tossed the water bottle she'd just finished into the trash and went to get another.

"Why doesn't this place have a cooler? It's ridiculous. I mean, look at all those empty bottles. I feel bad, but I have to stay hydrated so what can I do?" She waved a hand in the direction of the trash can.

Sofia was taking a break in the large lounge that was part of the downtown dance studio they'd booked for the month. She was midway through the day's rehearsals and she was thirsty, hungry, and tired. And if she was being honest, feeling every kind of grouchy. This was their fifth straight day in the studio, and the constant repetition of the choreography was taking its toll. Only the fear of forgetting the moves, of the performances being anything less than perfect, gave her the mental and physical energy to carry on. Worse, she knew from experience that she had several more days of this. Once she'd nailed her own choreography, the dancers would join her until the group dances were worked out to perfection too. And then she'd perform the same choreography for sixty nights across the globe until she was exhausted and bored of it all. She loved performing her music, but dancing to it, not so much. She yawned and popped the cap on her water.

Felix and her mom were on the couch, the long comfy couch that ran across the wall opposite—the one that she loved to stretch out on, the one she really wanted to lie down on right now. They were looking at an iPad, their heads together, scrolling and murmuring, neither of them listening to her. Neither of them seeming to care that her thirst was destroying the planet.

"I thought I'd stop halfway through the show, get some girl out of the crowd and do some naked salsa dancing. I mean, it might not go down that well in Nashville, but I think it adds a bit of variety to the show. Sounds good, huh?" She raised her voice on the last three words, causing her mom and Felix to finally look up at her, realizing that she'd asked them a question. Though Sofia knew damn well they hadn't heard what it was.

"Sound good?" She pushed them to either agree with her or admit they hadn't been listening. She was thirty-two years old, but sometimes still felt like the rebellious teenager she had never really had the chance to be. And she was enjoying the fact that they were both staring at her now, unsure of what to say. She made sure her face was a picture of innocence.

"She wants you to agree to let her do naked dancing on stage and also to kinda save the planet from disposable water bottles." From his chair in the other corner of the room, Noah spoke up, his voice showing gentle amusement, though he was still staring at his phone. "Oh, and she's annoyed that neither of you are listening to her." He looked over at Sofia and blew her a kiss before turning back to his phone.

"At least my fake boyfriend is half listening to me." Sofia curtsied in his direction. "Though it seems you'd all rather interact with your devices than with this exhausted, real life human in front of you." Sofia was joking—but she was also not joking at all. For someone whose music videos were watched by millions of people, she often felt invisible.

"I'm sorry, cariño." Her mom spoke first. "We're just trying to see how we can fit everything in." She waved her hand at Felix. "He has all the European dates figured out, but we can't seem to get as many dates in South America as the promoters want and still fit in all the big end of year shows here at home. Unless…" Her mom lowered her eyes a little guiltily before looking at Felix, clearly willing him to speak.

"Unless what?" Sofia wanted one of them to speak, she didn't care which. She could already tell that, whatever it was, she wasn't going to be happy about it.

Felix stood up and stretched. "Your mom knows all about the options, Sofia. I'll leave you guys to talk about it. I have a meeting with the promoters. But we can't miss the Grammys—whatever else you decide, that has to be on the list." Without waiting for a reply, he disappeared out into the corridor, letting the door snap shut behind him. Her mom turned back to her.

"It's Argentina, Sofia, we missed it altogether last time and we promised them dates this tour, but we can only do it if we run their shows on either side of the Grammys and you fly in and out for them." She spoke hesitantly, her voice pleading, like she already knew how Sofia would react. "It's an important market for us and you can sleep on the plane both ways. The time difference works in your favor too." She looked at Sofia hopefully.

For a long time, Sofia had been happy that her mom played such an important role in her career. She had liked having her along on tour, felt better when she was involved in decision making, but lately…well, lately, Sofia felt that her mom was more of a manager than Felix was. That she was more of a manager than a mom.

She looked at Noah, who had finally put his phone down and was now staring at her. She looked at her mom, who was still waiting for her response, and then, from nowhere, she started to cry. She didn't know why the tears were falling right then rather than yesterday when she'd twisted her knee or the day before when she'd realized she was going to miss her niece's birthday again, but here the tears were. And they kept on falling. Tears of frustration and exhaustion, and underneath both of those things, tears of sadness she couldn't have explained even if she'd wanted to.

Both Noah and her mom came to her side, but Sofia waved them away. She didn't want comfort from either of them, and maybe crying was just what she needed to do. But as quickly as the tears came, they stopped and Sofia used the towel around her neck to blow her nose.

"Babe, it's okay." Noah put an arm around Sofia's shoulders, but she shrugged it off. It was bad enough that she had to let him do that in public, she didn't want him touching her in private.

"What's okay, Noah?" Sofia looked him in the face, while stepping backward slightly. "Is it okay that I'm so exhausted I can barely function? Is it okay that my mom seems to think she has a machine for a daughter, a machine that doesn't need rest or days off? Or is it just okay that somewhere along the way I forgot how to be a person who loves to make music and let myself turn into this thing that exists just to sell records?" She looked from one to the other. "Because it doesn't seem okay to me." She made herself swallow her frustration, not trusting herself to say anything more.

"I know you're tired. I am too. But this is what the business is, what we have to do to stay at the top. And I know that you wouldn't swap it for anything else so let's not get too dramatic, babe." Sofia knew that Noah had only tacked "babe" onto the end of the sentence to make it seem less harsh.

"Sure. Let's see if you're still saying that five years from now." She tried to keep her tone even, despite her rising annoyance. "I've been doing this for ten years. I've been on tour, rehearsing for a tour, or locked in a fucking recording studio for ten years, Noah. I've done every interview with a smile on my face, answered every stupid question. I've had to laugh off every unflattering photo, every insult, and every review that isn't kind. I'm tired and I need a rest. But I can't stop because I'm told that the minute I do they'll all forget me and move on to the next big thing, but you're right, I should totally be more grateful. What was I thinking?" The sarcasm was something she hated but couldn't resist. Noah had no idea. He was just starting out.

"Sofia." Her mom said her name sharply. "I know you're tired, but there's no need to take it out on Noah. He's come all the way here to have lunch with you."

"Lunch, Mama? It's a photoshoot. Call it what it is at least. We're going to have a salad and have some paparazzi we tipped off take pictures of us fake dating and pretending we care about each other so that we both sell a few more records."

"I do care about you."

"You care about sales of your new album, Noah. And Felix and my mom care about maintaining my profile in the run-up to the tour. And faking this relationship helps us both. Let's not pretend otherwise."

It was cynical but it worked. The magazines and websites gave them so much more coverage when they were together. And every time she felt shitty about the lying, she reminded herself that everyone did it. She was playing the part of Sofia Flores, and having Noah, the perfect pop star boyfriend, was as much a part of the show as her choreography.

"It doesn't mean I don't also care about you." He was pouting now and sounding upset. He'd been like this more and more often lately, acting like they had something that was real. Her mom patted his arm. She was actually comforting him. Sofia wasn't surprised. Her mom always treated him like he was her dream son-in-law. It would be funny if it didn't all make her feel so sad.

She took another water bottle from the fridge. "Now, in case you've forgotten, my tired ass has a show to rehearse for." She stopped at the door and turned back to them. "I'm supposed to be enjoying this y'know. This was supposed to be my dream come true." To her annoyance, she was close to tears again. "And I don't care whether we nail this routine today or not. I am taking tomorrow morning off so I can meet the designer. It's my fucking house and I should be the one who decides what they do to it."

Her mom had arranged to see the design company without her, but Sofia didn't want that. She wanted to meet them, to make sure they were right for the project. She was finally going to fix up her new house and spend some time there. She just needed to finish the tour and get that third Grammy everyone was so focused on. After that she would take a break. She needed one. She tried to ignore the voice that told her she'd promised, and failed, to give herself some real time off in every one of the last five years. She left the room before more tears fell.

CHAPTER TWO

Maddie stood next to Daya, leaning back against the wall. They had been passing a cigarette back and forth. Maddie closed her eyes, wanting to be somewhere quiet and cool, rather than an alley behind a gay bar in Miami Beach on a sweltering hot August night. Her new shoes had given her blisters and she was suddenly in desperate need of food.

"Do you wanna go and eat?" She pushed herself off the wall. "I'm starving."

"You're gonna bail without saying good-bye to tequila babe in there?" Daya comically put a hand on Maddie's forehead as if to check whether she was running a temperature. "Are you sure about that? She was hotter than these temperatures, and you, honey, already admitted you are in the middle of a pretty big dry spell." Daya laughed.

"She's cute," Maddie shrugged and lifted her hands, "but I guess I'm not feeling it tonight. Sorry to be such a disappointment."

Despite Maddie not buying a single shot, the tequila girl—with her big brown eyes and her skimpy cowgirl outfit—had been paying her a lot of attention and Maddie had promised not to leave before they swapped numbers. The attention was nice, but the connection had been nonexistent, and since having Mateo, she'd given up on meaningless hookups.

Her sister and Daya had conspired to force her out of the house tonight. Ashley had played the auntie card and insisted on taking Mateo for the night, and Daya had forced her into a gay bar, with the stated intention of getting her a woman. She tried to enjoy the dancing, the music, and the beautiful women, but the truth was that she couldn't stop wondering how Mateo was and had spent most of the night wishing for her bed and a good book. In the days when she was thrashing around after the band split up, Maddie would have gotten drunk and taken tequila girl home, but that version of her was someone she hadn't known in a very long time.

"Let's find pizza. Pizza is what I need in my life right now. I need it more than I need tequila girl." Maddie pulled Daya along with her, toward the cabs lined up at the curb outside the club.

"Okay, okay. I'm down with that." Daya linked her arm. "Pizza is definitely less awkward to deal with in the morning." She laughed at her own joke.

Maddie was relieved they were leaving. She had always hated these clubs, the dressing up, the trying to be seen, the people whose motives couldn't be trusted.

I started feeling tired the day you left
The day after, the day after
I stopped trusting anyone at all

Maddie felt the words of the song pop up unexpectedly inside her brain, the tune maddeningly catchy, the lyrics always hurtful. Where the hell had that come from? She couldn't remember the last time she'd listened to the song. It was from Sofi's first album. The album Maddie had listened to a hundred times, in grief and in anger, before eventually making herself stop.

She tried not to overthink the fact that this song was in her head now. Being out with Daya reminded her of Sofi—of course it did. They'd been out together here so many times back when they were all in the band. And being back in Miami meant she was bound to think of the band…and of Sofi. She reminded herself it was a long time ago and the memories no longer had the power to affect her. She let herself believe the lie and focused on the pizza she wanted to eat.

Despite it being two a.m., the pizza place was full. Of course it was. This part of Miami was full of hungry clubbers just like them who wanted to eat before going home. Maddie didn't want to wait in line and was just about to suggest that they go back to Daya's and order in, when she felt Daya tug at her hand and march them to the front door. While Maddie was focusing on just how much her new shoes hurt, Daya was chatting animatedly to the tall bearded man who was gatekeeping the entrance. Within seconds, Daya tugged at her hand again as the man unhooked the rope that was strung across the doorway so they could pass through. A flash from the line suggested that someone was taking their photo and Maddie reflexively put up a hand.

Inside, a waiter showed them to a table at the back of the room.

"How the hell did you manage to get us in here?"

"I told them who we were, about our millions of Instagram followers, and that we'd give them a big shout out if they let us in." Daya sounded pleased with herself.

"For fuck's sake, Daya. That's not cool." Maddie shook her head. "I hate you doing that. Apart from the fact that I haven't used that account in three years, and nobody cares anymore which pizza place I'm eating at, what makes us any better than those other people waiting out there?" Maddie stood up. She would go home and order something in rather than jump the line on the basis of her so-called celebrity. Since she'd given up music, she barely ever got recognized. And thank God. When she set up her design business, she'd used only her first name precisely so no one could say she was riding on her past to get clients so there was no way she was going to use it to jump the line in a pizza restaurant.

"I'm sorry, I thought you were hungry. I was trying to help." Daya sounded contrite. "But sit down, honey. We might as well eat while we're here. It'll be embarrassing to leave now."

The waiter arrived and set down a jug of iced water and two tumblers, and Maddie sat back down and poured herself a tall glass. She was thirsty as well as hungry.

"What can I get you?" The waiter had his fingers poised over a tablet, ready to take their order.

"We'll have the extra-large four cheese pizza, thin crust, and two side salads to go." Maddie looked at Daya across the table, daring her to object. "And we can wait at the bar while you're getting it ready. Please go give this table to whoever's next in line." The waiter looked from Maddie to Daya not sure if he was being messed with.

Daya sighed and raised her eyebrows. "Sounds like the lady has decided we're going home." She picked up her bag and walked across to the bar. Maddie poured another glass of water for herself before following.

At the bar, Daya leaned in and kissed her cheek. "Sometimes you remind me just why I love you so much." She nudged Maddie playfully. "This just isn't one of those times."

They laughed and Maddie felt happy all over again that she'd moved back to Miami. She'd moved with Mateo so that they could be closer to her family, but Daya was here too and Maddie was pleased to have her back in her life. She'd spent years living in hotels and on tour buses, but at thirty-three, with a three-year-old son to think about, she was happy to finally put down some roots.

I thought you were sent to save me
But our roots didn't hold
And I stopped trusting anyone at all

Sofi's song again popped into Maddie's head and she sighed deeply and shook it away.

"You okay?" Daya regarded her closely.

"Yeah. Sorry, just worrying about Mateo." It was half a white lie. She had worried about being away from Mateo all night, but she also didn't want to tell Daya she was thinking about Sofi.

"He's fine, he's happy with his auntie." Daya put her hand over Maddie's. "You're allowed a night off, you know."

"I know. It's not just that." Saying it out loud was hard. "It's just that being back here reminds me of the old days. And of Sofi." She decided to say it and then tensed, waiting for Daya to tell her how stupid she was being.

"It's funny, but I was thinking about those days too. About us going out together and getting mobbed by fans. Sometimes it seems like yesterday, not five years ago."

"Maybe the day before yesterday." Maddie made herself sound lighter than she felt.

"Remember that time we were in that club and I had to pay that girl five hundred bucks to delete those pictures of you and Sofi off her phone? Sofi was terrified she'd caught you guys kissing and you'd get outed and our record company would go apeshit."

"They would have." Maddie's stomach knotted at the memory.

"Maybe they'd have just given you a fake pregnancy and an extra boyfriend each as damage control."

"Let's not go there." Daya's joke was too close to home to be funny.

Maddie chased away the memories and made herself focus on the mouthwatering smell of the pizzas coming from the wood-fired oven to the right of the bar.

"It's just good to be back. To be close to Mom and Ashley and you. And soon, I'll forget all about how Miami reminds me of the past," she hesitated, knowing that even all these years later, thinking about losing Sofi brought her nothing but sadness, "and I'll make a new set of happy memories. Mateo already loves the house. He's been paddling in the sea every day and I'm having a new dock built this week so I'll be able to get a little boat or maybe a couple of Jet Skis. He's a water baby, just like me." Maddie couldn't keep the pride out of her voice.

"Well, amen to that. I missed you. You guys all abandoned Miami. I was the only one that stayed here." Daya leaned a head on her shoulder.

"I had good reasons for leaving." Despite her best intentions, Maddie couldn't stop thinking about the past. She had to hope that it would fade.

"Yeah, I know." Daya squeezed her hand softly.

"Do you ever miss her?" Maddie hated herself for asking, for wanting to talk about it at all.

"Sort of. The four of us were so close, we spent all that time together, had so many experiences. And they were mostly good ones. But when she left and you guys broke up, it wasn't hard for me to choose sides. It was bad enough she used us the way she did, but to then act like a victim, I can't forgive that."

Maddie nodded. She didn't want to be reminded of how Sofi had tossed them aside. Something poked at the corner of her mind. A voice mail from Sofi, a message that had turned out to be her last attempt at contact. It was months after the band split, after all the blaming and recriminations had been played out. Sofi was asking—begging—Maddie to call her back, to meet her, to give her a chance to explain. She'd sounded drunk and so unhappy. Maddie had played it to Daya and Daya had told her to just ignore and delete it. It was good advice, and she followed it, but it was something that she had always regretted.

Two boxes were placed on the counter in front of them. The smell of the cheese and the warm dough was mouthwatering. Maddie pushed herself off the stool. She would save a slice for Mateo's lunch. Mateo loved cold pizza almost as much as she did. Tomorrow she'd go early to Ashley's and collect her son. He was the light of her life, and right now, she didn't need anything or anyone else but him.

CHAPTER THREE

Maddie got out of her jeep. She checked the address on her phone and then looked up, taking in the neighborhood. She whistled softly under her breath. This was a very nice house. Probably the nicest she'd been asked to work on. Two stories. No close neighbors and a sweet spot on the ocean at the swankiest end of North Coconut Grove. And Maddie's own house was barely a twenty-minute drive away, meaning it would be easy for her to go home to Mateo whenever she wanted to. She couldn't have hoped for a better gig.

She smoothed down her dress, grabbed her briefcase from the front seat, and walked up to the front door. She was never without butterflies when meeting a client for the first time. No amount of singing live in front of millions of people had prepared her for this.

"Hello." The greeting slipped out before Maddie registered who had answered the door. She held back the smile she'd been intending to offer. *What the actual fuck?*

"Madison." Rosa said her name incredulously, telling Maddie that she was just as surprised as she was to see her. She was no longer famous, not the kind of fame that made people stop and stare, but right then, Sofi's mom was staring at her as much as any starstruck fan. Though maybe with more of an "I'm going to close the door in your face" expression than a request for a selfie.

"I'm here for the design meeting. About the house." Maddie held up her briefcase as if it would somehow help. "I didn't know it was yours. They didn't tell me whose house it w—"

"Mama, is that them?"

Maddie stopped speaking as she heard a familiar voice from inside.

"Show them in and tell them I need a few minutes. I'm on a call."

Maddie wanted to turn, get back in her car and forget the fact that she'd worked hard to get this commission. She wouldn't have worked so hard for it if she'd known it was a house belonging to Sofia Flores. If the universe had brought her back to Miami for this, then the universe had a sick sense of humor.

As panic started to creep in, Maddie took several deep breaths. The part of her that knew how much her company needed this job, needed to build its reputation in the city, told her to grow up. Sofi was a huge star and doing this job would mean she could pull in other clients. But the part of her that had taken months getting over the heartbreak of Sofi leaving her urged her to run and not look back.

Rosa looked over her shoulder into the house, and then back at Maddie. For a second, Maddie thought she was going to close the door. Instead, she swore softly under her breath in Spanish—a language Maddie knew well thanks to Sofi—and opened the door wider, nodding for Maddie to go in.

"Through there." Rosa eyed her coldly and pointed at a door to the left of the hallway. As she entered the house, Maddie wondered if Sofi's "welcome" would be just as unwelcoming. Regardless of Sofi's reaction, she should just suck it all up, have this initial meeting, and then assign the actual work to another designer. How bad could one meeting be? They hadn't spoken to each other in close to five years. Everything had to be water under the bridge by now. And if Sofi wasn't prepared to have her work on the house because of things they'd done or said in the past, then she couldn't do a thing about that.

"I'll be back in an hour," Rosa called into the house. Maddie noticed the bag on her shoulder for the first time. She was leaving. Whatever it was she was doing must have been important because Maddie couldn't imagine it was an easy decision for Rosa to leave her alone with her precious daughter.

Maddie walked slowly through the door and into a cavernous room, sparsely furnished, neutral colors, no real personality. A kitchen took up one end—designer, expensive, the cabinets a light gray color. In the middle of the space was a large glass dining table surrounded by twelve high-backed chairs, and immediately in front of her were two cream sofas, each with a matching armchair and side table. Everything looked so clean, so unused. It felt like a show house.

The floor to ceiling windows were the best feature by far, running the length of the room, and wrapping around both corners, letting in a breathtakingly panoramic ocean view.

"Maddie?"

Sofi's voice saying her name made Maddie's insides tighten with anxiety. She made herself move slowly, putting down her briefcase and running a hand through her hair before finally turning toward the voice.

"Sofi." She paused. "Hi."

"What are you doing here? I mean, how come you're…" Sofi didn't complete the question. She seemed as shocked as Maddie felt. She was also jaw-droppingly beautiful. Her hair was tied up in a messy bun, her chocolate brown eyes were staring at Maddie with suspicion, and her cheeks had a flush to them that Maddie knew was a sign of anxiety. In the flesh, she seemed more beautiful than her recent photos, but she also looked very tired. It was a cliché, but to be near her again made Maddie feel light somehow, like her feet weren't quite on the floor. Nothing about seeing her felt real.

She made herself focus, took a breath, and leaned down to pull an iPad from her briefcase. It was enclosed in a case that had the "Madison's" logo emblazoned across it. She held it up and gestured around the room with her hand. "Your interior designer, believe it or not."

Sofi was still staring at her, looking a lot like she'd seen a ghost.

"Your people interviewed me, made me send in my portfolio. They've asked me to do your remodel. I didn't know who you were. I mean, I do obviously, I just didn't know whose house it was. They didn't say. I didn't know you'd be here." Sofi's silence was making her even more nervous.

"It's my home. Why wouldn't I be here? I've got to live in it, not them." Sofi sounded annoyed.

"Look, they just told me to come by here today for an introductory meeting because the client—you—were going away. It was all a bit

last minute. It was only when Rosa answered the door that I realized."
Maddie gestured toward the hallway. She'd been there two minutes
and the tension between them was already unbearable. This was
impossible for them to do. They had far too much history.

"I wanted to fit the meeting in before I left. I'm going to Atlanta
tomorrow for the Video Music Awards and then I go on tour. I'll be
away for months. Europe, Southeast Asia, Australia, South America."
She sounded unhappy about it.

"Sounds tough, I'm sorry." Maddie had no idea why she was
apologizing, this was the life that Sofi chose.

"You're back in Miami?"

Sofi hadn't offered her a seat, and she hadn't stopped staring at
her.

"Yeah." Maddie wasn't sure whether to elaborate. She took in a
slight breath, trying to be friendly and professional. "Setting up this
company gave us an opportunity to come home finally." Mentioning
the company, her company, put Maddie back in touch with why she
was here. Sofi's house, not Sofi. She cleared her throat.

"The company's not large, but all my designers are hand-picked
and very talented. I always meet the client at the start of any project,
but it doesn't necessarily have to be me doing all the work."

She'd found her stride again. She wasn't going to let Sofi throw
her off. So what if she was looking like a goddess, even dressed in
frayed shorts and a T-shirt. And so what if her never-quite-recovered
heart was telling her that she should turn and run. This was business
and she'd surprised even herself by how good at it she was. She
would take this meeting, give the work to someone else, and then
take herself as far away from Sofi as possible.

"As long as I understand what you want, I can match you with
the right designer and—"

"Who's 'us'? Who did you come back to Miami with?"

"Me and Mateo." Maddie answered without thinking. She owed
Sofi nothing by way of information about her life. But somehow she
found herself responding. "He's my son."

"Your son?" Sofi raised her eyebrows in surprise. She hadn't
known then. Maddie was disappointed for some reason. She had

kept tabs on Sofi, despite telling herself not to. She'd listened to the albums, watched the videos. She'd even kept track of the Grammys.

"I didn't know you had a son. How old is—" Sofi stopped. "Never mind, not my business, sorry."

They looked at each other for a few seconds. Sofi seemed sad as well as tired. Maddie had spent a lot of time looking into those eyes, and it was hard not to ask her if she was okay. She just wanted them to be nice to each other, to be friendly. Just that. It didn't seem like a lot to ask after all this time. She could do this.

"He's three. We moved back about six months ago. I wanted to be closer to Mom and Ashley, and I needed a hand with the childcare really. I wanted to work, to have a career, but I didn't want to leave him with strangers. And I missed Miami." Maddie was talking more than she should, more than she wanted to. She made herself stop.

"Does he look like you?" Sofi's question surprised her.

"He does." She couldn't help smiling. His father had been a one-night stand, one of many mistakes she'd made when the record company dropped her and she was in a partying hard, pity spiral. It was a source of constant happiness to her that Mateo took after her and not his absent father.

"Lucky boy." Sofi said the words almost to herself as she moved into the kitchen and took a pitcher from the refrigerator. She poured iced tea into two glasses and handed one to Maddie without even asking.

"I'd like you to do the redesign personally rather than match me with another designer. I'm not going to be here and I want to know that I can trust whoever is doing the work." Sofi stumbled slightly over the word "trust," and Maddie felt an unexpected rush of feelings, shame mixed with sorrow. "It's important to me. This place is important to me."

Maddie was annoyed at Sofi's arrogance, but more than that, she was annoyed that Sofi didn't seem to be finding this difficult at all. She'd assumed Sofi had moved on and never given her a second thought, but to have it confirmed like this was hard. Suddenly, the idea of them working together was ridiculous.

"That's not how it works. There's usually multiple projects going on at once so it's impossible for me to dedicate myself to just one." It wasn't true. Before realizing who owned the house, she had intended to do this job personally.

"Make it possible. I'll pay extra if needed. I don't want one of your people working on it. I want us to agree what's needed and then you do it. Yourself." Sofi sounded so serious and so like someone used to getting what she wanted. She held Maddie's gaze as she spoke, and Maddie hated herself for the way her body reacted to those eyes. The color, the depth, the intensity. She'd never been able to say no to Sofi. Not until she'd been forced to. She shook the memory away.

"I can't promise that, I'm sorry. It doesn't matter what you offer to pay. I make my own decisions about scheduling and who works on what. If that isn't what you want, then maybe this won't work." She wanted to do the work, but she didn't want to cave in. Sofi had treated her like a fool in the past, but this Maddie wasn't someone she could boss around. She braced herself for Sofi telling her to leave and getting some other company to do the work.

"Okay." There was a slight pause, and a very familiar biting down on her bottom lip. Sofi had more to say but she was choosing not to. Maddie hadn't really expected her to give in so easily.

"Let me start by giving you a tour. No shoes please."

Maddie bent down to remove her shoes, happy to escape the intensity of Sofi's gaze. She was still completely stunned by the fact that she was in Sofi's house, and that Sofi—the woman who had broken her heart and stomped all over it—was standing in front of her, looking a lot like she had never been away.

The house was beautiful—bright, spacious, and built to a high-spec. On the upper floor, just like downstairs, there were the same amazingly panoramic views of the ocean thanks to the way the architect had been so generous with the windows. But it had little by way of a personal touch, or even much of a human presence. Maddie couldn't pretend she knew the Sofi who had bought this house—they hadn't seen each other in so long—but nothing about it reminded her of the Sofi she had once loved and understood so well.

"How long have you lived here?"

"I bought it in March." Sofia frowned. "But I don't think I've spent more than a couple of weeks here. When I get time off, I come home to see my family and I think I imagined them coming and hanging out here, making this seem more of a home." She waved a hand into the space around them. "But usually I go and stay there. It's easier somehow. This place feels so soulless." She ran a hand through her hair and sighed in a way that was very like the Sofi she had known. The familiarity unsettled Maddie.

"It's a beautiful house. It's a shame you don't get more time here." It sounded trite but Maddie meant it.

"I imagined sitting here reading." Sofi pointed at the window seat that ran the length of one of the side windows. "Or playing my guitar on the deck, with the ocean in front of me. Maybe having friends over, grilling outside, listening to music and watching the sunset with a glass of nice pinot gris."

Maddie thought it sounded perfect. Her own house was much more modest than this one, but it was on the ocean and she'd had all the same dreams when she moved in. She almost said it but managed not to. She felt herself blush.

"Like I say, it's all imagined." Sofi shrugged and sat on a stool next to the breakfast bar. "Aren't you supposed to have color charts or drawings or something like that to show me?" The confiding tone had disappeared.

"That comes later." Maddie pulled out one of the dining chairs and sat down. She made herself look directly at Sofi. It was hard. The tight hot feeling in her chest was not a good thing.

They had spent years together, barely ever separated. They'd been bandmates and best friends. They'd celebrated every award, every chart success. And they had fallen in love, desperately and madly. It had been beautiful, until Sofi had shown her that it had all been a lie. And Maddie had spent the last five years trying desperately to forget her. She closed her eyes, willing herself to stop visiting the past and to focus on the here and now. This was one meeting, maybe two hours, and then they could go their separate ways again.

She opened her eyes to find Sofi staring back at her intently, her perfect eyebrows raised, a question clearly written on her face.

"I don't understand. What comes later?" Sofi glanced at her watch and then reached into her pocket to pull out her phone. She cursed softly. "And can we go a bit quicker? I have to get back to rehearsals."

"I just mean that we usually get a sense of what the client wants in terms of ambience and feel and an understanding of planned utilization, that sort of thing, with the colors and the design options coming later." Maddie tried to get back into her stride again.

"Utilization?"

"Who lives here, how you intend to use the space, does it need to be child-friendly, that sort of thing." She opened her iPad. "Can I ask you a few questions?" Maddie logged on as she spoke, not looking up at Sofi.

"Is one of them going to be whether I ever missed you?"

Maddie dropped her iPad. It clattered to the floor and she leaned down awkwardly, almost tipping herself off the chair as she retrieved it. She righted herself, feeling like a klutz, her reaction a complete betrayal of how much Sofi's question had affected her.

"What?" Maddie had heard her; she was buying herself some time.

"I said—"

"Don't." Maddie put up a hand. She swallowed and made herself look at Sofi, holding her gaze. "This is awkward enough, Sofi." The nickname slipped out and Maddie wanted to face-palm herself. Actually, she wanted to leave. Sofi could find another designer. This was Miami, it wouldn't be difficult. There'd be a dozen other companies willing to take on this project, and Maddie would rather lose the job than her sanity and self-respect.

"I'm sorry. I thought maybe you'd want to know, but okay, let's stick to your questions about 'utilization.'" She said the word like it was distasteful.

Maddie let out the breath she'd been holding and sat back down, planting herself more firmly onto the chair. She should just leave. She couldn't understand why she was still sitting there but she was. She cleared her throat, willing herself to stay focused.

"Okay, question one—is this a space where children live or regularly visit?"

"You really don't know the answer to that?"

"It's easier, and quicker for you, if you just answer." Maddie frowned at her screen, her tone sharper than she intended. Sofi had a reputation for being a hard ass, but Maddie wasn't going to let herself be pushed around.

"No. No kids." Sofi seemed pensive for a minute. "So any drawing on the walls is me when I'm drunk and feeling artistic." A sad smile appeared and was quickly put away.

"Question two—is this going to be a primary residence or a seasonal one?"

"I'd like it to be primary. I'd like to live here. To live somewhere for once. You know what it's like, I'm touring half the year and I'm in LA for the other half, but no, it's not seasonal. I intend it to be my home."

"Is anyone else going to be living here?" Maddie knew about Noah—pretty much everyone knew about Noah. Sofi and Noah were pop music's power couple. The singers who'd collaborated on a hit single and fallen in love. It had been hard to read the stories about Noah being the love of Sofi's life, as if Maddie didn't count. But she didn't—not as far as the public was concerned and maybe not as far as Sofi was concerned either. She rolled her shoulders, willing the tension away. This whole thing was a really bad idea.

"Not really, no. There might be people staying sometimes but no one 'living' here." Sofi wrapped the word in air quotes and Maddie again felt the intensity of her gaze. It was something she hadn't been subject to for years. She couldn't believe it still held any power over her, but right now, the tension in her body was telling her something different.

"You haven't changed." Sofi spoke out loud, but to Maddie it sounded like maybe she hadn't meant to. "Your hair's a little shorter, your arms look stronger. You work out now I guess." Sofi sounded so casual, like Maddie was a cousin she hadn't seen since last Thanksgiving. Was it really this easy for her? Had Maddie really meant so little? She ignored the comments and carried on.

"Just a few more questions and then I'll have someone come and take some photos if that's okay? He can be here in ten minutes. I told him to wait at that coffee place on the corner." Maddie had wanted some quiet time with her new client before Greg barreled in with all his equipment and noise. Now she wanted him here, wanted something to break the tension between them.

"Sure." Sofi nodded.

Maddie typed out a text to Greg and went back to her questionnaire.

"Is it a place to hide out, a place to entertain, or a place where you want to be creative? Tell me a little about how you see yourself living here."

Sofi pulled her knees up to her chest. It made her seem younger, and a little vulnerable. Maddie knew it was something she did when she was feeling exposed. The urge to cross the space between them and wrap Sofi in a protective hug was surprisingly strong. And completely absurd. Sofi would laugh in her face.

"Like I said, I might have friends over to hang out sometimes. I might also have more formal dinner parties, music people I need to meet, that sort of thing." Sofi waved the significance of her comments away with a hand.

Maddie smiled. The idea of Sofi having a dinner party amused her. The Sofi she had loved couldn't even make a grilled cheese sandwich.

"Wow." Sofi spoke softly. "I really missed that smile."

Before Maddie could figure out a way to respond, Sofi spoke again.

"Mostly I just imagine hanging out here by myself. I want to feel relaxed and at home. In a space that feels like mine, surrounded by things that make me happy. My books, my music, the ocean. You know those cheesy films where the heroine sits looking out at the ocean, an oversized sweater pulled over her knees, a hot chocolate in one hand, a book in the other, and a dog snuggled alongside her on the sofa? I kinda want that."

Maddie wasn't writing down what Sofi was saying. She didn't need to. She knew this was Sofi, this was what she needed, what she had always needed. They had talked about it often.

"After the Grammys, I'm going to try to maybe take some time off and spend it here." She didn't sound convincing. Maddie knew from bitter experience there was always another album, another tour, another pound of flesh to give someone.

Sofi's phone rang, interrupting the silence they had fallen into. She looked at it and rolled her eyes. "And make sure there's no Wi-Fi or phone signal. Line the walls with aluminum foil if you have to." She spoke as she stepped out onto the deck to take the call.

Maddie watched as Sofi seemed to be arguing with someone and saw the moment she gave up—the slump of her posture giving it away. She stepped back into the house.

"I'm sorry. I have to go and get changed. There's a car outside. I have to go do something, something I don't want to do, on a morning I'd arranged to take off to do this. But since when does that count for anything?"

"Sure, sorry, of course." Maddie stood up quickly, shoving the tablet into her bag. "I'll cancel Greg. Get someone to call me when things are less hectic and we can—"

"Things are never less hectic. After the VMAs, I'll be touring right through till January." There was a tremor in her voice, and for a second Maddie thought she was going to cry.

"It's okay, just get someone to call me and I can wrap it up with them. It's possible to do some of the color and fabric choices remotely. The software we use can build a virtual version of your house that we can decorate online so we can show you what it looks like." This was her chance to get away. She could maybe even do the work herself if Sofi wasn't going to be around. She tried to feel happy about it, but she couldn't. Sofi's unhappy mood was affecting her too.

Sofi stopped on her way to the stairs, a frown on her face. "Could you come back tomorrow morning? I don't leave till the afternoon. We can finish your questionnaire thing then and maybe we could..." She seemed shy suddenly. "Maybe we could just catch up a little bit too. It's been years, obviously. It'd be nice. Totally weird I know but nice maybe." She smiled hesitantly, and in that moment, she looked a lot more like the Sofi she had loved all those years ago.

Tomorrow was very short notice. Sofi couldn't possibly expect her to be free. And she'd already told Sofi that she was handing the project off to someone else. She could say she was busy and let Sofi and her people work on the house with one of her other designers. She could avoid the past, avoid the memories, and avoid any chance of revisiting the heartache.

"Sure. I could be over by nine. I'll drop Mateo at preschool first if that's okay?" Maddie wasn't sure where the words came from, but she was most definitely the one speaking.

"Cool." Sofi smiled at her again. "See you then. Let yourself out, Mads." Sofi disappeared upstairs and Maddie was left with a lingering disquiet from the way her heart had skipped a little when Sofi had smiled at her.

Maddie walked up the drive back to her jeep. She'd had the chance to walk away and decided not to—it was possibly the worst decision she'd made in a really long time.

Chapter Four

Sofia sat on the couch in the corridor outside the studio. She'd put her earbuds in to avoid talking to her mom, to escape her constant questions about Maddie. She'd told her mom the truth. Mostly. Maddie was back living in Miami. She had a son and a new career as an interior designer. She had been professional and perfectly friendly, and they were going to have one more meeting before Sofi went on tour. What she hadn't said was how hard Maddie had tried to avoid doing the design work herself and how Sofia had practically begged her to stay involved.

Since Maddie hadn't loved her enough to fight for her, Sofia wasn't surprised that Maddie wanted to stay away. But what had surprised her was her own willingness to put herself in the way of Maddie again, even if only for a few hours. She'd spent years getting over the heartbreak of losing Maddie and less than ten minutes deciding that she wanted Maddie, and only Maddie, to work on her house. And more than that, wanted a way to be able to talk to her some more. She couldn't have explained it to her mom even if she'd wanted to.

She was passing time answering questions from her fans on Twitter. A tweet caught her attention. It was a thread of pictures of her on stage with the hashtag #fatflores. She scrolled down and saw unflattering close-ups of the cellulite on her thighs, the slight paunch of her stomach, and pictures that made her look like she had a double chin.

"Why are people so mean?" She slipped an earbud out of one ear and held out the phone for her mom to take. "I mean, I know I need to lose some weight, but I'm not really fat. And I'll work it off when I'm touring. I always do." Sofia wished she wasn't always so upset by the comments, but she was.

"Not good." Her mom sighed as she scrolled through the images. "Maybe we need to get the dietician to tour with us again. Start counting the calories again, maybe fast a little before the tour starts." She handed the phone back to Sofia. "Some of them are even saying you're pregnant." She made a curving motion across her own stomach.

"You're supposed to tell me I'm beautiful and I shouldn't listen to them, not tell me to start fasting."

"You are, of course, cariño. But extra weight is not good when you're photographed from every angle every day." Her mom shrugged. "I don't make the rules. You want them talking about the album not wondering about whether your bump has a baby in it."

Her mom was direct to the point of callousness sometimes. Sofia pushed her earbud back in. Suddenly, everything about today was annoying—her mom, this interview, tonight's meet and greet with her fans, and the fact that some dumbass in her management team thought that sending Madison Martin—with her perfect body and take it or leave it attitude—to work on her house was a good idea.

Sofia called Felix.

"Who chose the designer for the house?" She didn't bother to say hello.

"Anna I think. She had a few of them send in their portfolios, got some recommendations. Is there a problem?"

"And Madison's was the agency she selected?"

"Yeah. They came with good references. What's going on?"

Sofia was spinning it out. She didn't like herself for it, but ten years in the business had left her with some prima donna tendencies.

"Madison's is run by Madison Martin. She came to my house today. To help me redecorate my house. Because you sent her there. Do you have any idea what seeing her again like that did to my stress levels?"

Sofia made herself sound stern, but she wasn't angry. Not really. She was mostly mad at herself for the feelings that had surfaced when face-to-face with Maddie. For the shameful, pointless jealousy she'd felt on hearing about Maddie's happy little family life when all she had was this—managers, PR people, dieticians, and a fake boyfriend.

"Fuck." Felix didn't often curse. Sofia was glad he felt that this situation warranted it. "I'll call Madison's and we'll get you a new designer. I'm sorry, I'm really sorry. I'll make sure they get an apology and a payoff for the loss of the contract. And rest assured I'll have a serious word with Anna about this."

"You don't need to get rid of Madison's. We've said we'll make it work—I'm leaving tomorrow anyway—and it's just one more meeting." Sofia hadn't been sure what she was doing when she'd asked Maddie to come back tomorrow, but in that moment, she understood that she simply wanted the chance to see her one more time.

"Are you sure?" Felix had seen the impact of her breakup with Maddie up close. She had been a mess for months and even he had struggled to create a new superstar out of the wreckage. All the big plans they'd made to launch her solo career had been pushed back, and her first album was agonizing to write and record.

"I'm sure."

"We can easily get rid of—"

"I said I'm sure. I just would have liked a heads up. I'm hardly going to be there anyway, because of this bullshit schedule you've committed me to." He had to take this shit from her. It was her way of pretending she had some control over her life when in fact she was locked in a cage. A cage she had agreed to live in because it was the price she paid for her success and—she made herself face up to the unpleasant facts—because after Maddie turned her back on her, her career was all she had.

She hung up, leaned back, and closed her eyes, knowing that the day wasn't going to get any better. Behind the studio door was Eduardo, Vibe FM's most popular deejay. Sofia had been interviewed by him many times before and he was an asshole. Nowhere near as funny as he thought he was and someone who went out of his way to try to be controversial.

She felt a shake on her shoulder and opened her eyes to see her mom pointing at the studio door. She sighed, sat up, and removed her earbuds. Her mom made a smile shape with her fingers and pointed at her. Sofia gave her an exaggerated fake smile and stepped toward the door. She had thirty minutes to survive with Eduardo, how bad could it be?

❖

"So, the album doesn't have as many sad songs as the last one? Are we to assume that's because Noah is making you happy? I know your fans are hoping for wedding bells. Do you have an exclusive for us, Sofia?" Eduardo gave Sofia what he clearly thought was a charming smile.

God, she really hated this guy. She took in a deep breath before replying, willing herself to be a pro. The show was filmed and live-streamed on the website, so any eye roll, any flash of annoyance would be seen and commented on. And she was Sofia Flores—sweet, patient, and always happy—so she got into character and looked back at him pleasantly.

"That's a lot of questions." She did her best to keep smiling. "The inspiration for the songs on the album comes from a lot of places. I'm sure that's true for all songwriters. Not all of it is obvious. It's part of the mystery not to spell it all out. It lets people put their own meanings onto the songs." She believed in what she was saying, it was what she'd always loved about making music, but she knew he wasn't even listening. He just wanted to talk about Noah. She was so tired of talking to people who didn't give a shit about her. For some reason, the cursing voice in her head reminded her of Maddie and her complaining about the endless interviews about fashion and boyfriends the band had been forced to give.

"And the wedding? You and Noah are, like, eighteen months in now. It must be something you've talked about." He waved at her mother standing at the back of the room. "And I'm sure your mom is like any good Latina mama and can't wait to help you plan a wedding." He laughed at his own joke.

"I'll make sure you're the first to know, Eduardo." Her voice was a little clipped, but she kept the annoyance from showing on her face. "But don't hold your breath. I'm still very focused on my music." It wasn't a lie. Her career was still her priority, even if lately she had felt tired of so much of it, and more and more aware of time passing her by.

Across the room, Sofia could see her mom making a face and lifting her shoulders, urging Sofia to smile a bit more, to be a bit more upbeat.

"I'm going to play your last single now. We all loved it here at Vibe. It's an absolute bop." He pushed a button on the console in front of him and pulled off his headphones, giving her a silent thumbs up.

"Thanks, Eduardo." Sofia gave him her best and brightest smile and then turned to her mom as if to say that she could do fake cheerful with the best of them. Her mother simply shook her head at Sofia.

As the song played, Eduardo tried to make small talk and Sofia was saved by the beep of her phone. She'd never been happier to have a distraction. Mouthing "sorry" at him, she looked at the text from Noah.

Wow, I forgot how much of a jerk this guy is

Sofia typed out a quick reply:

I know. he's spent the last 10 mins basically telling me that this album isn't as good as the last one and you and I should be getting married to give my mom a good excuse for a party

She sent it and then sent another:

But since when do you listen to Vibe?

I'm at the gym. you're keeping me company. and they play good tunes sometimes. like now. this one's by Sofia Flores, dunno if you know her. she's my girlfriend and she's fucking dope

Before she could reply and tell Noah for the hundredth time she wasn't his girlfriend, he sent another text.

Wanna have dinner?

She'd already had to endure a painful lunch with him yesterday, Sofia couldn't really believe he thought she'd want to have dinner as well.

I can't. i've got a meet and greet. i told you

I know. Felix arranged for me to drop by and "surprise" you. lots of fans, lots of cameras. and, since I'm about to go off on tour, it'll look like i can't bear to leave you, which i can't <3. i was thinking afterward.

"Fuck," Sofia said. Eduardo shot her a look, and she held up a hand in apology.

I don't want dinner, i'm too tired. and i don't really want you to "drop by and surprise me" either but I guess I don't have a say in that. i better go, the song's finishing. sorry.

Okay babe

Please don't call me babe. I don't like it

Okay...baby!

The song was finishing, and Sofia put down her phone with a sigh. She had ten more minutes of this torture left. And after she was going to talk to Felix about Noah. They had all agreed to keep things going till after the Grammys, hoping the extra buzz the two of them were creating together would be helpful. But Noah just wouldn't keep to the boundaries they'd agreed and he was driving her crazy.

And it didn't matter whether she liked admitting it or not, seeing Maddie today had reminded her what it was like when she'd had someone in her life she actually loved. Before she'd chosen lies and record sales over her own happiness. Not that Maddie had given her much of a choice in the way she turned her back on her.

She tuned in to Eduardo just as he asked her about her upcoming tour and hopes for the awards season. This was something she could talk about for hours. She leaned back in her chair and told him how excited she was about all of it. It was part truth and part lie. Like everything in her life these days.

❖

"Mateo, sweetie, don't do that." Maddie had bought him a toy ukulele in the hope of encouraging his love of music, but right now, that love of music had him bashing the instrument against a pillow like a drum. In the background, the radio played and—to be fair to Mateo—his bashing was mostly in time to the beat of the music.

Her sister had taken advantage of Maddie's abandoned meeting to go shopping to restock her fridge, and they were all going to have lunch before Maddie took Mateo home. His preschool teacher had been out sick today, and Ashley had stepped in to take him at the last minute. She had come so close to having to cancel the meeting at Sofi's house. Given the agitated state of her mind since seeing her, she couldn't stop wishing that she had.

"Mommy." Mateo reached up for her and she pulled him onto her lap, smoothing his hair. He seemed tired today. She leaned back on the couch and settled Mateo against her chest, hoping he might nap. She would have been happy to join him, but her own brain felt so full of Sofi that she was pretty sure sleep wouldn't come. Along with everything else they'd talked about, Sofi had been cocky enough to ask her if she wanted to know if Sofi had missed her. If she'd said yes, what would Sofi have said? She seemed like she was living her best life, and Maddie doubted she had given any of them much of a backward look.

She cursed softly as one of Sofi's songs came on the radio. It was one of her biggest hits—a Latin-infused pop song that had sold millions. Maddie tried not to listen to her music but always failed. This was a very catchy song, but she couldn't help but be disappointed by it. It was too light, too safe, and contained none of the raw emotions of that first album.

She tuned in properly for the first time. The song was finishing and her ears picked up Sofi's voice, thanking the deejay for having her. This must have been what they called her away for. Maddie rested her head on the sofa and let Sofi's voice wash over her. The deejay was complaining about the lack of sad songs on the new album and suggesting it was because Sofi was happy with Noah.

"I know your fans are hoping for wedding bells. Do you have an exclusive for us, Sofia?"

Maddie felt herself tense slightly, waiting for Sofi's reply. She hated herself for caring.

"Don't hold your breath. I'm still very focused on my music."

"Of course you are." Maddie said the words out loud and Mateo sat up, rubbing his eyes. She took advantage of him moving to reach across and turn off the radio. Sofi had always been "very focused" on her music. It had been the thing that had ruined them after all. She settled Mateo back into her lap trying to focus on her annoyance with Sofi and ignore the crazy sliver of happiness she felt at the news that she wasn't considering marrying her perfect pop star boyfriend.

❖

"He's sleeping." Maddie pointed at Mateo and whispered the words to Ashley as she came into the room with the groceries.

Ashley tiptoed across to the kitchen and began to quietly unpack.

"You didn't tell me what happened with that new project today." Her voice was not much louder than a whisper.

"It was okay. Nice big house. Nothing's been done with it. It's like a blank canvas really. Funny thing was it belonged to someone I knew. I was so surprised." She aimed for nonchalance, knowing she felt anything but.

"Oh yeah? Who?"

"Sofia. Sofia from the band. It's her house."

Ashley stopped making unpacking noises. Maddie waited.

"Someone you knew? Sofia Flores. Are you joking? You'd better be joking, Maddie."

Maddie couldn't imagine ever joking about it.

"I'm not."

"Maddie, you can't do that. You can't work for Sofia. Are you crazy? She literally broke your heart. I know, I was there. I peeled your sobbing drunk self off the floor so many times, sis. You can't seriously be considering taking the job, to be putting yourself in the way of her again." She had her hands on her hips. Maddie was two years older than Ashley, but Ashley had inherited all the bossy genes.

"I'm not 'putting myself in the way of her,' jeez. It's just my job. She needs a designer. The house is, like, fifteen miles from here. The job pays well, and I'll be able to spend a lot more time with Mateo. And she won't even be there after tomorrow. She's going on tour and she'll be gone for months." Maddie was talking to herself as much as to Ashley. Hearing herself say it was good—it made so much sense for her to do the work. "And it was such a long time ago, it's all in the past." That part sounded way less convincing.

"Yeah, and it was a lot of hurt and it took a long time for you to recover. I'm not sure you ever have to be honest. Who have you dated since? I mean seriously dated, not people you've gone home with when you're drunk."

"I dated Lara." Maddie didn't need to explain herself to Ashley, but she wanted this chance to talk, for herself, to be sure she knew what she was doing.

"You didn't 'date' Lara. She was a fuck buddy. And she was all ready to sell you out to the gossip websites until you got there first. I'm not sure she's the one you should be using as an example of how well you've moved on."

"Low blow, sis."

Ashley sighed and sat next to her.

"I'm sorry. I'm just worried that's all. I thought being back here was a fresh start for you guys. I don't want the heartache to follow you back here." She lifted an eyebrow. "And, yes, by heartache, I mean Sofia."

Ashley was right. This was meant to be a fresh start. She'd go tomorrow and tell Sofi she couldn't take on the project and offer her another designer to work with. It was the right thing to do, but she couldn't help but feel sad about it. It wasn't just that she needed the work. She'd agreed to meet Sofi tomorrow because she held out the hope of them talking about what had happened. She had so much she wanted to say, so much she wanted to know—but stirring it all up now wouldn't do either of them any good. She stroked Mateo's head tenderly. And she didn't just have herself to think about now. There was Mateo. He needed stability and a sober, sane mama. Not one who chased after long gone dreams.

"Okay, you win. I'll resign the commission." Her chest felt tight. She shook her head, trying to shake away the sadness that had settled in. "Tell me you got us something cheesy for lunch. I need the comfort right now." She made herself smile.

"I got us pizza from that new place on Seventh." Ashley squeezed her hand. "There might be a little cheese involved."

Maddie nodded. Ashley might be bossy, but she had always had her back and Maddie was damn lucky to have her.

CHAPTER FIVE

This time, Maddie parked on the driveway and not on the street. She was thirty minutes late and looked a wreck. It was bad enough that she was going to let Sofi down by pulling out of the project. She had at least wanted to seem professional while she did it.

Mateo woke complaining of a tummy ache. He was too sick to go to preschool. She gave him medicine, waited a while for him to go off to sleep again, and then decided to settle him in the back of her jeep. She would leave him there for the few minutes it would take for her to humiliate herself with Sofi by quitting. As she tossed and turned all night, practicing the actual words she'd say, she couldn't escape the fact that pulling out would mean admitting she wasn't quite over what had happened between them. Why else couldn't she spend a couple of hours with Sofi prepping for the work that she had been contracted to do, the work she really wanted to do? That Sofi seemed so able to rise above their past and be so casual about it all just made her feel worse.

She leaned in and placed a soft kiss on Mateo's cheek, holding her hand against his forehead and feeling happy that he felt cooler. She fixed her hair as best she could using the side mirror.

"You're not gonna leave him in there, are you?"

She turned toward Sofi's voice.

"I was gonna cuss you out for being late with one of my 'don't you appreciate how busy and important I am' speeches, but I'm guessing you definitely don't need to hear that this morning." Sofi spoke quietly, her eyes showing kindness.

She walked toward the jeep and Maddie felt herself tense. She hadn't ever imagined Sofi meeting Mateo.

"He's not well. He has an upset stomach. I couldn't take him to preschool and I didn't have anyone to leave him with so I'm sorry. I wasn't going to leave him here for long. Just for a few minutes, while I—" She couldn't make herself say what she'd been planning to say while they were out on the driveway.

"Why don't you bring him inside? He can sleep on the couch under a blanket while we talk. I've got peppermint tea. If he wakes, I'll make him some. It's good for digestion."

Sofi was close to the jeep, peering in at her son, at the most precious thing in her life. And her face looked full of wonder. "Please. I don't mind. Not at all." She gave Maddie an earnest, hopeful look, and Maddie shivered a little.

"Okay."

Sofi took the two coffees she had made out onto the deck, clearly expecting Maddie to follow her. Two cushioned Adirondack chairs sat side by side facing the ocean. Maddie cast an eye back at her sleeping son before following Sofi outside.

"He's sweet. And the spitting image of you like you said." Sofi settled herself onto the chair, pulling her feet up under her.

"He's even sweeter when he's awake." Maddie couldn't help but smile. She wasn't one of those moms that insisted her kid was special. All kids were special to someone. But Mateo was a champ. He was funny and patient and cute.

"I bet. I didn't know about him. I mean, you kind of dropped out of sight. I didn't know what happened to you after they…" Sofi hesitated. "After you stopped with music, I mean."

"After the record company dropped me? You can say it. It's not like it's a secret." It had hurt at the time, but Maddie no longer felt any bitterness about it.

"I'm sorry." Sofi cast her eyes down.

"I'm not."

"Really?"

"Really. I'm happier now. I think it was all a bit too much for me, being watched, judged, controlled. I like my privacy. And being able to do the things I want to do. And I have Mateo now so it's good to be doing something more stable." She shrugged. "I mean, it's a good career for some people. It's obviously been great for you, but I don't think it was ever good for me. Daya says it took her a long time to decide to give it up, because she didn't know what else to do. Getting dropped by the record company made the decision easy for me."

"You still see Daya?" Sofi sounded surprised.

"Now that I'm back in Miami. Not so much before I came home."

"I saw her and Suzy a couple of years back. At an awards show, Suzy was performing and presenting in a category I was nominated in. We all said hi, but it was obvious they still weren't ready to talk to me. It was awkward as hell. I don't know what I expected, but I guess I hoped after so long that we—" She shrugged and her expression closed suddenly. "Do we have things we need to do? Questions you need me to answer. Samples, photos, whatever else. I only have till noon." She was all business now, the softness gone.

Maddie had come to tell Sofi she couldn't do the project. But as Sofi gazed across at her expecting an answer, she just couldn't seem to find the words.

"Sure. Let me get my stuff."

Sofi was leaving today and wouldn't be back for months. She could be finished before she got back. How much hurt could they cause each other in a couple of hours? She went to fetch her briefcase from the jeep.

Sofia felt the news that Daya and Maddie had stayed friends like a small stab in her heart. The four of them had been close when they were in the band. Daya was the first person they'd told about their relationship and she and Suzy had covered for them so many times in the beginning when they were hiding being together. And so many other times when they weren't hiding being together well enough. Leaving the band had meant losing Maddie, but she'd lost Daya and Suzy too. And the way they'd all banded together against her, to tell the world lie after lie about her, had hurt her so damn much.

She caught movement inside the house. Mateo appeared in the doorway. He had hold of the blanket and looked sleepy and confused.

"Your mama has just gone outside to get something. She'll be back soon. Want to sit in this big chair and wait for her?"

Mateo eyed her warily before shuffling across to climb onto the chair.

"I'm Sofia. So-fia." She held out a hand for him to shake. "Would you like a drink, sweetie?"

"Fia." He said her name, sort of, and nodded. He was adorable.

"And maybe you want to watch some Peppa Pig while you're waiting?" He nodded even more vigorously at that. Peppa Pig had been her niece's favorite cartoon at his age.

She played the video, handed him her phone, and headed into the kitchen.

"He woke up. He's outside watching a cartoon." Sofia spoke as soon as Maddie came into the house, not wanting her to panic.

"Oh God, I'm sorry. This is not very professional of me. Maybe I should go and come back another time."

"I only have today. You can come back if you like, but you'll have to do it with my mom if you do." Sofia hoped the mention of her mom would encourage Maddie to stay. "Maybe it's better if we just try to do what we need to. He seems happy watching cartoons." She pointed at the cup in her hand. "I was gonna do that peppermint tea." Sofia couldn't understand why, but she wanted them to stay, wanted it more than anything she'd wanted in a very long time. She turned away, waiting for Maddie to say no and leave. Like she had done before.

"Okay."

"Was it the idea of working with my mom that made you say yes?" Sofia was happy that Maddie had said yes. She and her mom had never gotten along. Her mom hadn't wanted Sofia to be gay, and it didn't matter how often Sofia made it plain it didn't work that way, she had blamed Maddie for it.

"Mostly that." Maddie smiled back at her, and Sofia felt something inside her shift. She needed to be careful. She told herself it was just one morning, it was a chance for closure, but she didn't believe a word of it. She was enjoying being close to Maddie, enjoying seeing her with her son. It was a dangerous game she was playing.

Mateo had settled back on the couch under the blanket. He had the cartoon playing on the phone in his lap. Sofia watched Maddie as she returned to the deck and sat down. She really was beautiful.

"Will you and Noah have kids do you think?"

The question was completely unexpected. Maddie's expression was completely neutral. But Sofia couldn't believe that Maddie, of all people, thought that she and Noah were a real couple. Sure, she'd dated guys before they got together, but she was young then, she didn't know herself. And Noah was an empty-headed jerk. Surely Maddie knew her better than to think he was at all her type.

"No, not really." She didn't know what else to say. The contract she'd signed with Noah meant both of them had to keep their arrangement confidential and the penalty for breaching it was eye-watering.

"You don't want kids?"

"It's not that. It's…" What could she say? I'd love to have kids, but Noah is one of those PR stunts I swore I would never lower myself to do after leaving the band and I haven't had a real relationship since you left me. It was the truth, but it was a completely humiliating truth. "I guess I'm just very focused on my career right now." It was the same pathetic sounding answer she had given Eduardo, but it felt a lot worse saying it to Maddie.

"Yeah, of course you are." Maddie's tone wasn't as harsh as the words suggested, but Sofia still felt defensive.

"What does that mean?"

"Nothing. Just that you always were very focused on your career."

"I like working, what's so wrong with that? I've had some great experiences, some really great moments, my fans have been so loyal. I'm lucky to still be doing this." It was mostly true. She had been happy to work hard, to chase chart success. But she had also done all that because she had nothing else in her life after Maddie had turned her back on her. She didn't need to explain herself to Maddie.

"There's nothing wrong with it. You knew what you wanted, you went for it. And you succeeded. Good for you. Not everyone has that single-minded focus."

The words were unmistakably double-edged.

"You sound like you've got something you want to get off your chest." Sofia tensed. There were a lot of things they'd never had the chance to talk about, a lot of hurtful things they could say to each other.

"I don't. I didn't come here to talk about the past. I like living in the present. I find it more reliable and a lot less painful." Maddie sounded tense. Sofia had been naive to think they could simply catch up like old friends.

"I'm pretty sure none of us want to live in the past. It wasn't good to me either." Sofia wanted to be angry, to tell Maddie all the ways she had caused her pain. But face-to-face, it was hard, and all the things she'd imagined saying wouldn't come.

She saw a flash of regret pass across Maddie's face.

"Look, I'm sorry for even bringing it up. It's got nothing to do with me, and my opinion doesn't matter one little bit. Maybe we should just get back to my questionnaire." Maddie pointed at her iPad and ran an anxious hand through her hair before continuing. "If you want the truth, I came here to tell you that I couldn't do the work, because of the past...because of all this..." She used her finger to point into the space between them. "I was gonna lie and say that something else had come up, recommend a different designer."

"And I almost got Felix to fire you and find me a new designer. I didn't think spending time together was the best idea either."

They looked at each other.

"So what do we do?" Maddie spoke first.

"I'm not going to be here. I leave for Atlanta today, and I'll be gone for the best part of four months."

"I'm assuming there's nothing structural you want to change?"

"No. Just décor and furnishings I think. I mean, unless you think something needs to be changed."

Maddie shook her head. "If it's just interior design work, I could definitely make sure I get it finished before you get back."

They fell back into talking then—formally, professionally—about the house, about what Maddie would need to do. They were talking about the thing they were supposed to be talking about and Sofia wanted to feel relief, but instead she just felt sadness, wondering just how they had managed to ruin something that had once been so good.

"Let's finish the questionnaire and have another walk around." Maddie looked at her watch. "I've got color charts and fabrics in the trunk, and we should go through them too if there's time."

"I'll make time." Sofia meant it. She would take the time to do this right. It mattered to her. She should have more things in her life that mattered to her.

"Maddie?"

"Yeah." Maddie looked up from the screen. Sofia had spent so many hours gazing at that face, in want and in wonder. Always amazed that she was allowed to touch it, to kiss it, amazed that sometimes the smile that lit it up was for her and her alone. She shook her head slightly, shook away the stupid memories. She made herself remember that she had also spent a long time in too much pain to be able to look at Maddie's face, not able to hear her voice even. Today had proved that it wouldn't do her good to romanticize the past.

"I love kids. Really love them. I have a niece. She's eight and she's adorable. I haven't given up hope of having kids of my own." Maddie looked at her with surprise. "And just because I probably won't get the chance to say this to you again, I know we hurt each other but I've missed you these past few years and I can't think of anyone I'd trust more to know what I want for my house than you." Sofi let out a breath. She faked pretty much everything in her life these days, but something about Maddie made her want to be real.

"I don't think there's anyone we know who would think me doing this was a good idea." Maddie lifted her eyebrows. "But I guess I feel the same way. I want to do this for you." She shrugged. "There is one thing though."

Sofia leaned in. "What?"

"Do you think we can get someone other than your mom to oversee things while you're away? She still terrifies me."

Sofia laughed and enjoyed seeing Maddie's eyes light up.

"Are you kidding? She's coming to Atlanta and then on tour, of course. She never leaves my side. That much hasn't changed." Sofia was joking, but something about admitting it made her feel pathetic. "I'll ask Anna to stop by sometimes, but I'll give you my number if you need to ask me anything important. And I'll get you some spare keys so you can come and go."

Maddie studied her for a moment, looking like she had something to say, but she simply nodded.

"Question four. Let's concentrate."

Sofia suddenly hoped the questionnaire was a long one.

Maddie poured herself a large glass of red wine and sat at her dining table. Though it had taken two more stories than usual, Mateo had finally settled down to sleep. And now she really wanted to try to work.

The day had been a strange one. She smiled to herself at the understatement. She'd gone to Sofi's house intending to restore the distance between them and had come away feeling a desire to be close to her that she hadn't felt in years. And she was feeling this way at just the time that Sofi was leaving to spend four months on the road. The timing was going to save her from herself and she should have felt more grateful.

It had taken a supreme effort not to give in and talk about the past in the way that Sofi obviously wanted, in the way that she realized that she too wanted. She had so much she wanted to ask, so much she wanted to say. When Sofi left the band—left her—she had coped by ignoring all of Sofi's attempts to get in touch. She hadn't wanted to hear the excuses, to face up to Sofi's betrayal, but it meant that neither of them had ever had the chance to talk about any of it.

She sipped the wine and sighed at how good it tasted. She had her iPad open and in front of that, a large sketch pad and a set of colored pencils. She wanted to make some sketches while Sofi's words and feelings about the house were still clear in her mind. She swiped the screen, looking at the photos she had taken. Greg would do a proper job of photographing and measuring everything tomorrow, but for now, she could work off these.

She stopped at a photograph she'd taken of the kitchen from the other end of the room. Sofi stood to one side, perhaps believing she wasn't in the frame, and Maddie expanded the image with her fingers. Sofi was looking in her direction with a small frown, her fingers pulling at her bottom lip, her hair tousled from the wind on the deck. She looked nothing like the put together pop star that Maddie had seen hundreds of photographs of online and in magazines. Yet Maddie preferred this version of her—softer, serious, real. She stared at her face. For someone at the top of her career, with everything she wanted in life, Sofi seemed surprisingly sad and unsure.

Maddie picked up her pencil and began to lightly sketch the layout of the main living area, wanting walls and floors and furniture that she could label with some of the colors and fabrics that Sofi had liked.

If someone had photographed her that morning, maybe her face would have shown the same uncertain frown. It would be a lie to say she hadn't thought of Sofi in a while. She had. Being in Miami had brought a lot of memories to the surface, and it was hard to avoid thinking about her because she was everywhere. On the TV, on her radio, in the gossip magazines she hated herself for reading. But today was the first time in a long while that she had thought about what had happened when Sofi left and every awful thing that followed. In the past, she'd been so wrapped up in her own feelings about being left, her own envy about Sofi's success, that she hadn't really ever thought of things from Sofi's point of view. But Sofi had lost everything when the band split and they hadn't exactly been kind about her afterward. She probably had a lot to say about it all. Her phone buzzed.

How'd it go and how's my best boy feeling?

Ashley, checking in. Of course she was.

He's better. Thanks. I'm unwinding with a fat glass of merlot and doing some sketching

How'd she take you pulling out?

Ashley was too smart to let her avoid answering questions. She slowly typed out a reply.

Actually, we decided to give it a go. She left today for four months. I need the job. She needs a good designer. I can get it finished before she comes back. No big deal

A long pause. Maddie cracked first.

Sis?

What do you want me to say? It's crazy, you're crazy. I guess she must be crazy too. But you're a grown ass woman, and you'll do what you wanna do

Another text arrived immediately.

You always did

Maddie was happy to see the rolling eyes emoji. Maybe Ashley wasn't that mad at her.

We avoided talking about it. Mostly. It was okay.

Sure. And it was "okay" enough that you're needing to unwind with a fat glass of wine

Maddie sighed. Ashley was stubborn and smart and, Maddie had to admit, cared about her more than anyone.

It's okay, honestly. We both have a lot we could have said about the past. But we didn't.

Maddie hesitated, not wanting to lie to her sister.

But I'm not gonna lie and say it didn't affect me to be close to her again. It did. But I'll probably never see her again so I don't have to worry about any of it.

The thought made her sadder than she expected.

If you say so. Enjoy the wine. And just know that I'm the kind of sister that will definitely say I told you so x

Again, the eye roll emoji. Ashley used that far too much.

Oh, I know that. Good night sis x

Maddie pushed her phone away. Damn Ashley for always saying the things that were better left unsaid. She scrolled past the photo of Sofi and considered the ones she had taken of the living area as she built up her sketch. She told herself to focus on the job, to focus on the fun part of spending someone else's money. She sighed. This job already didn't feel like that—her focus was on Sofi, on giving Sofi a place to live in that she would love, that she deserved to feel relaxed in. She already cared too much. Ashley was right, she was crazy for doing this. And maybe Sofi was just as crazy for wanting her to.

Chapter Six

What the hell? Jeez, sorry. They said this frickin' room was empty." Sofia almost shouted the words, quickly picking up the pantsuit she had just dropped to the floor and using it to cover herself, shocked to see a man emerge into the dressing room from the bathroom in the far corner. She looked for somewhere to go and a way to hide her dressed-only-in-her-underwear body.

"Don't worry, sweetheart. You don't have to apologize for standing there looking so fine." He openly appraised Sofia, a smile playing on his face, making no attempt to look away.

The surprise at his appearing from nowhere had stopped Sofia from recognizing him for a few seconds, and then the realization hit her.

"Danny. Holy crap. Hello." Sofia relaxed slightly but still felt weird under his gaze. "Jeez, Danny, look the other way or something will you? Give me a break here." She pointed down at herself, shrugged, and lifted her eyebrows. "My pantsuit split. I need to get into this dress within the next five minutes or I'm going to be late on stage." She pointed at the midnight blue dress draped over the back of the couch next to them.

Almost on cue, the door opened and Ronnie stepped inside looking as stressed as Sofia felt.

"You're not ready?" Ronnie said the words before taking in the scene in front of her. Sofia dressed only in her underwear, Danny a few feet away, the two of them face-to-face. "Oh, wow, okay, sorry." Ronnie made to back out of the room, giving Sofia a look that said it was absolutely her job never to notice when the stars she wardrobed for got naughty with each other.

"No, no, don't go," Sofia called out to her. "This isn't at all whatever you're thinking. Obviously. I was getting changed and Danny—"

"Came out from the bathroom to find that the Lord had sent him an early Christmas present." He smirked as he spoke, still making no effort to look away.

Under his continuing gaze, Sofia suddenly felt awkward. She had shown far more skin to people in the past, when the record company had the band performing in the skimpiest of skimpy outfits, but the dressing room was small and the feeling was much more intimate.

"Use the bathroom back there if you want to dress without me seeing even more of your treasures." Danny nodded toward the back of the room.

Sofia looked at him for a moment. She had hated him for a very long time after he and Maddie had hooked up. He was supposed to just be one of the fake boyfriends Maddie had been given when the record company decided that she and Sofia looked too cozy together, but when Maddie decided to date him for real, it had hurt. Sofia didn't care if it was months before she and Maddie had got together, or that it was just a two-time thing. She was not going to be charmed by him now.

"I would like that very much."

He smiled at her, his blue eyes crinkling. He was handsome. She could see why Maddie had chosen him. The jolt of jealousy that she felt land in her stomach didn't feel almost a decade old. She was surprised by the strength of it. The surprise brought her back into the here and now. She picked up the dress and moved toward the bathroom.

"I'll need some blue panties, Ronnie. Nice ones. The ones I'm wearing were supposed to be hidden under the suit and they're far too nasty to wear with this dress." She rubbed her temples. "Can you get me some more Tylenol too please? I have a killer headache." She grabbed the energy drink that Ronnie had brought for her. She was tired, the rehearsals had been a struggle, and now a fucking wardrobe malfunction minutes before she had to perform. The universe wasn't being kind to her today.

"C'mon, cariño, you're on in ninety seconds. Talk about cutting it close." Her mom was standing in the doorway to the dressing room. Sofia used the last of the energy drink to down the pills that Ronnie had found for her. She smoothed her hands over the dress, over her stomach—growling at the lack of food—and she closed her eyes. She tried to go through the choreography in her mind, to run through the lyrics, but all she could focus on was the throb throb throb of her headache and the rapid beating of her heart. There was no way the pills would kick in on time. She shivered and then forced her mind back into the room.

"Sorry for the interruption, Danny, and thanks for letting me change in here. Sorry I have to rush off before we catch up." She wasn't sorry. Sofia looked from Danny to her mom and back again, feeling slightly nauseous as she moved her head.

"No problem, girl. Go slay them in your new panties." Danny laughed and fist-bumped Sofia as she passed by. "And say hi to Noah for me. He and I go way back. If it wasn't for the fact of you being his girl, and him being so jealous, I'd have given you my number so we could have a proper catch-up." He smirked as he stressed the words "his girl," and Sofia felt shame flood through her body. He had played Noah's part with Maddie in the past, and maybe that meant he knew all about her and Noah now. She knew Noah couldn't have told him— he was stupid, but not stupid enough to risk a half a million dollar penalty clause—but maybe Danny had guessed. She should have worried about it, but instead she wondered if Maddie would guess too. That Sofia really wanted her to was something she couldn't face up to right then. The thumping in her head grew worse. Her thoughts and memories knocking against each other.

She headed into the corridor and walked briskly toward the stage with her mom on one side and Ronnie on the other, now messing with her hair. The VMAs didn't have the prestige of the Grammys, but the TV audience ran into the millions and Felix always arranged for her to perform. Usually she was nominated for an award, but this time she'd been overlooked. None of them had said it, but it wasn't a good sign.

"Remind me why we're here, Mama. Why I've come all the way to Atlanta to perform a song they didn't like enough to nominate and to hand out the award to someone else whose video they liked better than mine." Sofia's chest felt tight. She felt almost breathless. "And we rehearsed for two solid days on that stage so the routine would be perfect, but right now, I can barely remember any of it. I'm going to make a complete fool of myself."

"You'll be fine once you're up there. You always are, Sofi. It'll come back to you when you hear the music." Her mom tried to sound reassuring, but even through her headache, Sofia imagined she could hear the doubt in her voice.

The intermittent beeping was the first thing Sofia heard. And then, as she pulled herself more into consciousness, she could make out the low murmur of voices.

"I told you she needed a rest." Her mom.

"They said the fasting was just as likely to have caused it as exhaustion." That was Felix.

"She'll never cope with the schedule if she's carrying too much weight. What's she supposed to do? You want her to cancel halfway through?" Her mom's voice grew louder the more annoyed she got.

"I don't want her like this either." Felix kept his voice low.

She wanted to open her eyes, but even with them closed, the room seemed too bright. She lifted a hand to cover them, to block out some of the light.

"Cariño?" Her mom's voice sounded closer now. "Are you awake? How are you feeling?"

Sofia tried to lift her eyelids, but the light made her head hurt more so she closed them again. "It's too bright."

"Hold on." Felix spoke and then the room went a lot darker and she figured he'd turned off the main lights.

She opened her eyes slowly and looked around the room. Her mom and Felix were on either side of her bed. Her hospital bed. She could see a machine covered in blinking lights and changing numbers. It was the source of the beeping and she was hooked up to it via a little contraption clamped to the end of her finger. A port in the back of her hand connected her to a bag of clear IV fluid hanging from a pole next to the bed.

"What the hell?" Her voice sounded raspy. Her throat was dry.

"Here." Her mom passed her a carton of juice with a straw sticking out. She drank it greedily.

"What happened?" She strained to remember.

"You collapsed. Don't worry, it's not serious. They've run tests and you're fine. They figure it's a mixture of exhaustion, dehydration, and caffeine. They don't seem to know exactly what happened, but they do know you're okay. They're giving you saline." Her mom pointed at the bag hanging from the pole.

"I collapsed? I was about to perform. I remember going on stage." A shiver ran through her body. "Don't tell me I collapsed on stage." She made herself sit up a little straighter in the bed.

Her mom nodded. "It's not as bad as it sounds. The lights hadn't come up. You were in position with the dancers. They were just about to introduce you, and well, you just fainted."

"Hit the floor with quite a thud. It was kinda dramatic," Felix chipped in.

"Felix." Her mom shot him a look. "It wasn't that dramatic. No one saw. Not really. The camera wasn't on you then so only those people in the audience that were close enough to see you without the lights being up could see what happened."

She took Sofia's hand. "You're okay. That's the main thing. Doctor says plenty of fluids, no more fasting, lots of rest, and definitely no more energy drinks."

"I can't rest. I'm about to go to on tour for chrissakes."

"We know." Her mom looked sideways at Felix. "But doctor's orders are doctor's orders, Sofi. Felix has already canceled the week of promos in England and we can see how you are, but we might have to postpone the first few dates of the tour too."

"No. I don't want that. I need this tour to sell the album and I've worked hard to get ready."

"I know. We sent out a press release. Check Instagram later. You'll see all the get well wishes. No one blames you, no one at all. And as soon as you're better you can hit the road." Her mom sounded so cheerful about it all, but Sofia had been around long enough to know what a disaster this was. One look at Felix's face was enough to confirm it. The album was under-performing, and this tour was important to create some buzz around it, especially overseas.

The headache kept pulsing behind her eyes. She closed them, suddenly wanting to sleep again. "Can I get something for this headache? And maybe something to eat? I'm starving."

Her mom nodded, hurrying from the room.

Sofia beckoned Felix to come a little closer. "How bad is it?" She understood that he wouldn't sugarcoat it. He never had. In that moment, she remembered clearly him telling her that the rest of the band would hate her for leaving. She hadn't quite believed him, but she should have. He'd been right.

"It's okay. It's happened before. There'll be a lot of coverage, a lot of speculation. You're lucky that your image is so wholesome—no one's going to think it's an addiction." He smiled at her with affection. "There's a video though, there's always a fucking video. Someone near enough, and with a camera phone good enough, to capture the moment you..." He made a toppling motion with his arm. "It's already out there. Websites, entertainment channels. But the coverage is mostly sympathetic. Blaming the pressures of the business, the punishing schedules. A few snarky comments about you working too hard to try to stay at the top, saying you were crash dieting because you're overweight, blah blah." Felix waved his hand dismissively.

Sofia nodded, her eyes closing involuntarily. She had been working hard to stay at the top. What else was she going to do? Her career was all she had. She was too tired to feel sad about it, to feel sorry for herself. She felt sleep drifting in and let herself give in to the welcome blankness of it.

Maddie had the TV on in the background as she reworked her sketches, now accompanied by hyper realistic 3D diagrams of the house on her laptop screen. At the stroke of her touchpad, she could move around the inside of Sofia's house without leaving her chair and paint the walls any color she wanted at the touch of a fingertip. She always preferred to do the actual designing with pencils and paper, but seeing the house in this detail was helpful. It didn't take away the need to go back there and try out the actual materials on site, but the technology made things easier.

She lifted her eyes from the sketchpad in time to catch a close-up of Sofia's face on her TV followed by a picture of a large hospital. She grabbed the remote and turned up the sound just in time to hear the newscaster talk over a badly lit video clip of someone seeming to fall over on a stage.

"We're told Ms. Flores will be kept in Atlanta General Hospital overnight for observation and hopes to be released tomorrow. Her representatives aren't talking to the media, but they have put out a statement asking for privacy and making clear that Ms. Flores is fine and simply had an allergic reaction to some painkillers she had taken."

Maddie put down the remote as the channel moved on to something else. She picked up her phone. All the entertainment websites were running the story of Sofia collapsing onstage at the VMAs and being rushed to the hospital.

She felt a wave of panic wash over her. She tried to take comfort from the news report suggesting Sofia was fine and was being kept overnight for observation only. But she knew that her management would say that regardless of whether she was okay or not. The thought pricked her into action. She had Sofia's number—they had exchanged a couple of very business-like texts about the house—so maybe it wouldn't be all that intrusive to send her a message asking if she was okay. It was the kind of thing an old friend would do.

She typed out a text. Short, nothing that would require much of a reply. Letting Sofi know she was thinking about her. She almost deleted it. And then she figured that, if the situations were reversed, she'd be happy to get a text from Sofi. She'd feel cared for, feel seen. She tried not to think about the absence of that in her life as she pressed Send.

She crossed to the kitchen to get a drink and heard the ping as a text hit her phone. It was from Sofia and she was happy that she was well enough to text right back.

This is Rosa. I have Sofia's phone. We're trying not to stress her with all the messages she's been getting. It's kind of you to text but she doesn't need to hear from her decorator right now. I'm sure you understand

Ouch. It wasn't quite a "back the fuck off" because Rosa was far too polite to use the words, but the sentiment was pretty clear. And calling her the decorator was a nice touch. Maddie sighed. Rosa was right though. Sofia didn't need to hear from her. She shouldn't try to act like a friend when they were practically strangers. She went back to her work with a heavy feeling in her chest.

Chapter Seven

L ying on her couch, Sofia checked social media for the hundredth time that morning. The video of her fainting was everywhere, and while the coverage was mostly sympathetic, she'd been annoyed to see the hand of Felix behind several stories claiming that Noah was going to interrupt his own tour to fly to Miami to care for her. That was the last thing she needed. But of course they would turn even her illness into a PR opportunity. Why was she surprised?

Except it wasn't even an illness. It was self-inflicted stupidity. She was driving herself too hard because she didn't know how to stop, and she hadn't been eating properly because she hated being called fat. And she'd replaced the sleep she wasn't getting while worrying about it all with caffeine-loaded energy drinks. She was a cliché.

She turned on her TV and tuned in to a music video channel. As well as bugging her to make a decision about canceling the opening dates of the tour, Felix kept stressing her about the need to find a video concept for the new single. She decided to cozy up under her blanket, watch TV, and call it research. As she focused on the screen, Suzy's latest video was playing. She was singing from the front seat of a car. A handsome guy sat next to her, smiling. It was a good song, and it had done okay. Suzy hadn't had Sofia's success, but she had a career that most singers would be proud of. It was the career that Maddie could easily have had. In fact, Maddie could have been a huge star. Her voice was better than all of them, and she'd written some amazing songs. They could have performed together. They could have written together. If only she'd stayed with Sofia, if only she hadn't come out and got dropped. She felt her eyes closing as the "if onlys" carried on running through her mind.

The clatter of a set of keys being dropped onto a table jolted Sofia into consciousness. She sat upright, startled and still sleepy, to see Maddie looking at her like she'd seen a ghost.

"Jeez, you scared me." Maddie spoke first. "I didn't think anyone would be here. Anna gave me the keys. I thought…actually, I didn't think, I just came. I'm sorry." She ran a hand through her hair anxiously. "I just wanted to test some colors, but of course you're here, I saw what happened." A tender look appeared on her face. It was a look that Sofia hadn't seen in such a long time.

"How are you?" Maddie moved toward the couch and surprised Sofia by sitting next to her feet and placing a hand on her blanket-covered shin." The gesture was sweet and kind of intimate. It was almost too much for her. She rubbed her face vigorously with both hands, half checking this wasn't a dream.

"I'm okay, thanks. Sorry to startle you. I'm not supposed to be here. Anna probably thinks I'm at my mom's. But I couldn't face the way she was fussing over me so I told her I needed to be alone. I can do diva when I absolutely have to." She put the back of her hand against her forehead like an old Hollywood actress and was rewarded with a small smile from Maddie. The sight of it was like a glimmer of sunshine poking through dark clouds.

Maddie stood.

"Yeah, of course, I should leave you alone too. I'm sorry. I wasn't thinking. I can come back in a few days or leave the colors for you to try. Just paint a few really wide stripes on the bedroom walls and see which one works best. I can leave instructions, if you're up to it." Again, she seemed concerned. It was nice.

"I'm just tired, really. I'm not sick. I can do that no problem. But please stay. Do what you were going to do. To be honest I'm bored out of my mind and the company would be really nice. I just wanted my mom to leave me alone because she was driving me crazy."

Maddie was looking at her uncertainly.

"Stay. It's fine, honestly. I want you to." Sofia tried to sound reassuring. She really wanted Maddie to stay, not just to do her work. She wanted the chance to spend more time with her.

"Okay."

Sofia felt her heart lift.

"Wanna sit and have some coffee with me before you start work?" She wasn't sure if she was pushing her luck. Maybe Maddie wanted to work, to just do what she needed to and leave. She had only agreed to continue the project because she thought Sofia would be on another continent by now. She waited for Maddie to say no.

"Okay. But only if you stay there and let me make it." Maddie gazed at her and Sofia felt a flutter in her belly. "And only if you have unleaded. I read all the stories. I know that you overdosed on the hard stuff." She emphasized the last words with a wry smile before putting down her bag and heading to the kitchen.

Seeing Maddie there, busying herself with the coffee maker, Sofia felt unexpectedly happy feelings. But the dehydration had left her feeling a little delusional in the hospital, so she was probably right not to trust her feelings right now.

"You know what?" Sofia spoke hesitantly. "How about you take pity on me and we go to that diner on the corner for brunch?"

Maddie was looking at her like she'd said something crazy. Had she?

"I don't have any food. If you don't believe me open the fridge. I sent my mom away but was too stubborn to ask her to get me some groceries first. The doctor said I need to rest and drink and eat so I don't see why I shouldn't go to a diner that's a five-minute walk away. A diner where I can rest and drink and eat."

Maddie was still silently staring at her.

"I just think croquetas would aid my recovery." Sofia raised her eyebrows.

Finally, a smile from Maddie, but her dark eyes were more serious.

"Croquetas, huh?"

Sofia nodded. They'd eaten croquetas together so many times. For some reason, Sofia wanted Maddie to be remembering those times. The good times.

"If I let you eat some croquetas, then you'll lie down and rest like you're supposed to and let me work?" Maddie's tone was light, teasing. "And stop being a diva?"

"All of that, I promise."

"Okay." Maddie switched off the coffee maker. "But it's only because I want the croquetas as much as you do. I skipped breakfast because Mateo somehow lost his shoe between the house and the car and I didn't notice and had to go back for it." She shrugged as if embarrassed. "Mom life. A bit less glamorous than yours."

"Collapsing on stage isn't glamorous. Especially when some people are suggesting it was because I was crash dieting on the instructions of my record label on account of me being so fat."

"Social media is a cesspool of lies and gossip. Even now I stay as far away from it as I can. And in case you need to hear it, you're not fat, not at all." Maddie shook her head. "But even if you were, I'd still go get you croquetas. Life's too short for dieting."

Sofia was ridiculously pleased to get the reassurance from Maddie. She slid out from under the covers.

"I don't think so." Maddie pointed at her feet. "You're not coming. I'm getting takeout. Back under the blanket, please." She blushed. To Sofia it was adorable. "Sorry I pretty much only hang out with a three-year-old these days. It makes me bossy."

"You're not with anyone? I thought you were parenting Mateo with someone...I kind of assumed." Sofia couldn't believe she'd asked the question out loud. It deserved the internal face-palm she gave herself.

Maddie waited a beat.

"Nope, just me."

Another pause. A longer one.

"It was always just me. He's the light of my life, but he wasn't planned, and his father didn't stick around. Thankfully." The frown was not hard to miss. "And there's no one else." Maddie pointed at Sofia's feet again. "Now, back under the blanket, or no croquetas."

Sofia did as she was told. Maddie was single and she was willing to stay for some food. Her mood lifted more than it had a right to.

Watching Maddie eat had always been one of Sofia's pleasures and she couldn't help but enjoy the satisfied expression on her face as

Maddie sat back having cleaned her plate. Growing up in Miami, as they both had, it was impossible not to love Cuban food.

Maddie had stripped down to a simple black tank top, the skin of her neck and shoulders looking as pale as ever against the dark material. She looked in great shape, and Sofia couldn't help but feel a little frumpy by comparison. Whatever Maddie had said about her not being fat, she'd been eating too much comfort food lately and it had started to show. She sipped at the giant-sized iced tea that Maddie had brought back from the diner, trying not to think about the sugar. At least no one could accuse her of not taking the order to hydrate seriously.

They were talking, but it wasn't easy. Nothing was easy about them being together again. And it was like they both understood it the same way, both of them avoiding any talk of the past. They had been talking about the house, as Maddie ran through her ideas, and now they were talking about Sofia's tour and what was going to happen.

"I'm not bothered about missing the interviews and TV appearances. But I hate the idea of canceling the shows. I still love singing the songs I've written, and it feels crappy to let people down. And to be honest, I need this tour to go well." She didn't want to admit that she was feeling the pressure, that she was worried she hadn't quite got the same drawing power as before, but it was true.

Maddie reached across and stole one of the remaining papas from Sofia's plate. It reminded her of old times. Everything about them eating together did. It wasn't sensible, but it felt great.

"It can't be helped sometimes. The fans will understand that you need to rest. We canceled those shows in Australia when Suzy got sick, do you remember? And we were bummed because we'd never been before and we all really wanted to go and we begged them to let us play without her but they wouldn't." Maddie looked down, perhaps realizing what she'd said.

"I remember." Sofia couldn't keep the sadness from her voice. Those rearranged dates in Australia were the first big tour the band had played after she'd left, and they'd made a really big deal of the fact that it was just the three of them now, that they were stronger and happier without Sofia, and the media had lapped it up. It had hurt, really hurt. Her shoulders tensed. There was so much she wanted to say.

"I was gonna play this big festival in London. Felix had arranged for me to perform with Little Boy. He's that huge new rapper who—"

"I know who he is, Sofi. He's pretty cool. I might have a three-year-old, but I still listen to music."

"Of course, sorry." Sofia felt stupid. "I just mean it would have been a good move. He's so hot right now and the exposure to his fan base would have been good for me if I'm going to take the edges off how wholesome everyone thinks I am. We're trying to make a collaboration happen and we were gonna talk about it while we were both there. It's not till Friday, and I might feel better by then so I told Felix not to pull me just yet."

"Are you serious?" Maddie's eyes flashed with concern.

"What?"

"You just collapsed and you've been told to rest. A long flight, jet lag, the stress of performing—it's hardly resting. Surely your recovery has to be more important than a festival."

"It's a really big deal. The exposure is exactly what the album needs right now. This is my job, Mads, I have to take it seriously. It's not easy to stay relevant after all this time." She hated having to spell it out, but surely Maddie, of all people, understood.

"Maybe you should worry more about being healthy than relevant." Maddie muttered and shook her head, and once again, Sofia felt judged.

"Look, I stayed in this business when you didn't. This is what it looks like up close. It's unforgiving and it's relentless. Maybe you've forgotten or maybe you just never cared as much as I do."

"No one could care as much as you. You've always put your career ahead of everything, ahead of everyone." She stressed the final words and Sofia felt the sting as she was supposed to.

"That's not fair."

"Isn't it?"

"You know it isn't." She took in a breath, wanting to control her words carefully. "You know I offered to stay, to put my career on hold for you. But you made sure that option was taken away from me. You guys leaked the news of me leaving and made it seem like I'd been conniving to leave for a long time. I couldn't stay after that. You turned your back on me—no matter what the world thinks."

"I wasn't trying to get into that." Maddie cast her eyes downward. "You're not well, Sofi, that's the point I'm making. You clearly need rest. I don't think—"

"I wasn't well then either. I didn't eat for weeks. I couldn't sleep the night through for months. I don't remember you caring about me then." Sofia had to say it now that she had started. It was like a lid had come loose. "And even when I thought I was doing better, hearing a song, seeing a clip of you guys on TV, going to any place we'd ever been together, killed me all over again." Sofia paused to try to compose herself. "You walked away from our relationship and left me with nothing. And now that this career is all I have, you're judging me for being too committed to it? Well, you've got a lot of nerve."

She walked from the dining table to the couch and sat, trying to calm herself, wanting some actual distance between them. It was ridiculous to think they could have a chat and some food and none of this would surface.

"You really think you're the victim here? There was no 'relationship' for me to walk away from, Sofi. You'd already betrayed everything we had. You spent months planning to leave without telling me. Registering your face, your name as a trademark, setting up the websites, even having merchandise made. And all of that behind my back, while pretending to my face that you loved me, that you were going to stay for me, that we would have something even if you left." She stopped and closed her eyes. "I didn't want to believe it, I wanted to think better of you, but when they showed us the proof, showed us that you'd just used us, biding your time until you were ready, I just felt so fucking stupid."

Sofia had heard all this before. It had been in the press release the band had issued about her leaving. It had been easy to deny because it wasn't true. But she'd had no idea that it was what Maddie actually believed.

"So yeah, I walked away and we pushed you out, but you deserved it. And our record company made it clear that the only way the band would survive was if we went public straight away and blamed you for leaving. Every time I felt bad about it, every time I thought about calling you, I remembered how you'd used us." Maddie sat down next to her. "I didn't care if the band survived—I didn't care about much at the time—I just felt pathetic for ever trusting you."

"Felix did do some of those things—the trademark, the merchandise—but he did them without my permission, without my knowledge. I can't make you believe me if you don't want to, but everything I said to you was true. Before you guys announced I was quitting the band, I'd already told Felix I wasn't going to leave, that I'd wait till you were ready." Sofia needed Maddie to know. "I meant it when I said you meant more to me than a solo career, and I couldn't understand how you could just walk out on me, ignore me, and then hate on me the way you all did." Sofia hesitated for a second and then decided they'd only have one chance to say this to each other. "I figured I must not have meant very much to you for you to let them stab me in the back and walk away like that."

"I didn't know it wasn't true. And it didn't feel like I was the one walking away." Maddie sounded like she was fighting to keep her composure, and Sofia had the impulse to reach for her, to hold her. It was crazy.

"How could you think I'd lie to you like that? After everything we'd been through. You believed them and you didn't even give me a chance to explain."

Maddie put her head in her hands, when she looked back up at Sofia, she had tears in her eyes.

"I just didn't know what to do. It all happened so fast. They told us all this stuff you'd done, they already had the press release ready. They said we had to strike first, and they made it clear we shouldn't have any contact with you. And I was a mess. I wasn't thinking straight at all. I just kept thinking that you and I had been a lie and I hadn't even realized. It hurt. I felt like I'd been hit by a truck."

"Maddie." Sofi didn't know what to say. She'd felt exactly the same way.

"When I listened to your album, it was the first time that I really thought maybe I'd gotten it wrong. Every song made it clear how hurt you'd been, how let down you felt. I don't know what I was expecting, but I wasn't expecting it to be so raw."

"I had to write about it. It was all I could think about."

"I felt so ashamed of myself for letting you go so easily, and hearing the album made me want to speak to you, to at least say I was sorry. But then I heard you telling everyone it was about some guy who had broken your heart, heard you telling all these stories about the songs that I knew couldn't be true and it made me doubt you all over again. Daya told me I shouldn't assume the album was about me, that maybe you were just writing an album that you thought would win you a Grammy. I didn't want to believe her, but it's what happened." Sofia could see the set of her jaw as Maddie fought to keep her composure.

"That album wasn't about winning a Grammy. It was all I could write, all I could think about. I couldn't write anything else, and everyone was so impatient for me to release something. In the end I stopped fighting it and let it all out, poured everything I felt about losing you into those songs. They hated it, but they couldn't stop me from releasing it."

Maddie's forehead creased. "But why tell everyone it was about some guy? It made what had happened between us feel even more like a lie."

"What did you expect me to say?" She hadn't expected to ever have this conversation, but now that they'd started she wanted to say what needed to be said, what they should have said all those years before. "I wrote about being left, about being hurt. How could I have told the truth about who it was about without dragging us both out of the closet?" Sofia held Maddie's gaze, challenging, pushing her. "And we'd always said we didn't want that, that we didn't need people knowing about us." She had wanted to say this so many times.

"We couldn't have said anything, even if we had wanted to. They wouldn't let us."

"They wouldn't have let us while we were in the band, but I was leaving. I was signing a new contract. I had asked for more freedom. Maybe we could have found a way, especially if you'd gone solo too. I offered to stay for you, Mads, but I thought that, even if we'd both gone solo, we could have found a way to keep going, to maybe even love each other out in the open. I thought love was enough and I would have accepted whatever loving you did to my career. It took me a long time to realize it, but eventually, I had to accept that our relationship just didn't mean enough for you to stay with me."

"That's not true," Maddie blurted out the words. "I thought—"

"That I was a calculating bitch who'd used you until I was ready to cast you aside. I know, I get it." She rubbed her temples. The headache was coming back.

"You have no idea what listening to that album did to me." Maddie was close to tears.

"Do you have any idea what writing it, performing it over and over, did to me?" Sofia's voice cracked as she spoke. She waited before continuing, wanting to compose herself. "I wanted to tell people about you, about what had happened. I hated pretending it was about someone else. But I knew you'd hate me if I did. And I really couldn't bear the idea of you hating me any more than you already did. So I lied, and I haven't stopped lying since. It's pathetic." She wiped the tears from her eyes and slumped back in her seat. Sofia had lost all her courage when she lost Maddie. And she'd willingly climbed into a different cage as a result. It was easier to live that way.

"Can we start again?" Maddie said the words quietly. "I mean, can we try at least?"

"What would starting again look like, Mads?" She kept her tone neutral not daring to let Maddie see the hope that bubbled up inside her.

"I don't know. I just know I don't want to argue. And I don't want to have to avoid you, and I definitely don't want to see us both getting upset talking about the past. I quite liked the eating croquetas together part."

There was sadness in Maddie's eyes, and Sofia appreciated her trying to find a way for them to stop and get past this. She had another impulse to hug her, wanting to be held.

"Neither of us got it right. Both of us got hurt. But it was a long time ago and we've both moved on. I've got Mateo and you've got Noah and we've got a house to refurbish. We could try not to talk about it and just be nice to each other." She offered a small shrug.

Not even the mention of Noah, which pricked at her like the shameful secret it was, could ruin the moment for Sofia. Maddie was offering her an olive branch, a chance to be in her life again, however fleeting and however difficult. She should have retreated, should have been worried by just how much she wanted it.

"I would love that." She had never grabbed at anything so fast.

Maddie smiled at her and it was like she had been plugged into a power pack. She felt the charge in every corner of her body.

"Now get back under the covers," Maddie lifted them and pointed, "and let me go and paint stripes on your bedroom walls."

Sofia couldn't stop herself from yawning deeply.

"You still seem wiped out." Maddie's voice was calmer now and the cadence of it washed over Sofia like a soothing hot shower.

"I am. I'm not sleeping well. I'm always not sleeping well, you know me." She shrugged, unable to stop herself from remembering the times they'd been on tour when she'd found it hard to sleep and Maddie would soothe her by stroking her hair, letting her fall asleep on her chest. The memory made Sofia feel warm in her core but also a little sad for what they had lost. Maddie was gazing at her intently. Her expression suggesting she might have been remembering the same thing.

"I should get to work." Maddie stood. "I only have an hour before I have to collect Mateo." The change of mood was abrupt. Sofia almost heard the shutter come down.

"Sure." She couldn't help but feel a little sorry. "I'll be the sad sack dozing on the couch if you need me."

"You'd better be." Maddie gave her a half smile before picking up her materials and heading up the stairs.

Sofia watched her go, shaking her head at how upside down her life felt. She'd been bored, tired, and lonely a week ago. And now she was what? Confused. Conflicted. Contemplative. She lay down wondering if counting "c" words was a better way to sleep than counting sheep.

Chapter Eight

Maddie was waiting to be served and watching Mateo wading through the ball pit, a huge grin on his face as he picked up and threw to one side every yellow ball he could see. Daya was sitting on the side, encouraging him by pointing them out. There were thousands of balls in the pit, and hundreds of them were yellow. She wondered how long it would take the two of them to get bored.

She carried the tray to their table and couldn't help but laugh as Mateo, inspired by the sight of the ice cream, began clumsily clambering toward their side of the pit, all thoughts of separating out the yellow balls erased by the idea of chocolate fudge ice cream. Yep, he was definitely just like her. Daya lifted him out when he got close enough and sat him next to her, tucking a napkin inside the collar of his T-shirt.

"You're getting pretty good at that. Maybe you should get one of your own." Maddie sipped her coffee.

"I told you, my brand is super cool auntie. No sleepless nights, no stretch marks, just being cool and idolized." Daya spoke in between mouthfuls of bright green pistachio gelato. "And I'm too busy. I just know this business will turn its back on me the minute I squeeze into a maternity smock."

"You sound like Sofi." Maddie regretted the words as soon as they left her mouth.

Daya licked her spoon, looking at Maddie with confusion.

"You talked to Sofi?"

She nodded.

"Damn." Daya clasped her hand over her mouth as Mateo looked up at her. "Sorry, for the curse word, buddy."

"I think he stops hearing words when he's in the vicinity of ice cream." Maddie leaned across to stroke Mateo's head.

"When and how the actual heck did that happen?" Daya leaned forward.

"I'm redesigning her house."

Maddie waited for the barrage of questions. When Daya said nothing, she filled in the space.

"I didn't know it was her house when I pitched for it, obviously." She paused. "Did you see what happened to her?"

"The fainting? Sure, it's a good bit of PR. Everyone's talking about the tour and whether she'll make it. Of course she will, but there's a buzz about it now that wasn't there before, so good job her PR team."

"It's not like that. She's genuinely exhausted. She hasn't had any time off for years. You know what that's like. And now she's talking about going to Europe in three days and that's not what the doctors advised. And I feel like I'm the only one who thinks that's crazy."

"So you saw Sofia—the woman who broke your heart—for the first time in a hundred years, and you already talked about her not daring to have babies and decided you're the only one who cares about how tired she is." Daya frowned. "And all this in the two weeks since I last saw you?"

Maddie sighed. Put like that, it did sound a little crazy.

"It's weird, I know."

"It's weird all right." Daya leaned over and wiped ice cream from Mateo's face. She really was a natural with kids. "And not good at all." She fixed Maddie with a skeptical gaze. "She's really not well? I honestly assumed it was a PR stunt. Suzy said that her PR people wanted her to pretend to go to rehab last year, but she persuaded them to let her do *Dancing with the Stars* instead. This is a sick business sometimes."

"She's all right. But she needs to rest. She really does. And…" She made herself not say it, knowing Daya would think she'd really lost it.

"And?"

"She seems unhappy. I don't think it's just because of me. I mean we talked about the past, it wasn't fun, not at all. But it seems like something else. Like she's a little lost."

"Sure you're not just seeing what you want to, babe? You always tried to protect her, always saw the best in her."

"And you always saw the worst. There were so many times when I almost called her in those first few weeks and you told me not to, and sometimes I wish I hadn't listened to you quite so much. If I'd called, if she'd explained the way she explained it to me this week—" It was too painful to think about could-have-beens. "I'm not trying to protect her. I'm just telling you what I saw. Whatever else happened between us, I know her pretty damn well and she's not in a good space."

"Babe, I was the one who protected you from her, from more lies and more hurt. But if you want to think I cost you a chance at happiness with her, I can't stop you. Whatever she said to you, whatever she hoped, you guys were never going to make it. The focus groups would have told her what a PR disaster being with you would be, and we both know that she'd never do anything that would come between her and her precious career. At best you'd have been her dirty little secret." Daya shrugged.

Maddie couldn't think of a thing to say. Daya was being harsh, but she couldn't really say that she was wrong. Apart from that first album, Sofi hadn't made a risky move in the last five years and now she even had the perfect pop star boyfriend. There would have been no place for Maddie in a life like that.

"But since you're in Miami and she's in Miami and you're working on her house, should I be worried that you're gonna get sucked in again?"

"No. It's not like that." Maddie tested the truthfulness of her response in her own mind. She thought it was mostly true. "She just seems a little bit like she needs a friend. She seems lonely. And Noah…" She almost stopped herself from continuing but decided this was Daya, and it didn't matter if she sounded a little stupid. "Noah seems mostly absent. He's not living with her and he hasn't even been to see her. If that was me, and she'd collapsed, I wouldn't have left her side."

Maddie pulled Mateo onto her lap, but he wriggled away, clearly anxious to get back to his yellow ball quest. She lifted him into the pit and he toddled off happily. When she returned her attention to the table, she found Daya frowning at her.

"Number one, it's absolutely not your job to be worrying about the state of Sofia's relationship. I saw them on some Mr. and Mrs. quiz show thing the other week and they seemed very happy together. And number two," she ticked the points off her fingers, "you sound to me like you need to be careful with your feelings. I get that you want to do the work, but you can't seriously be thinking of letting her back into your life?"

Maddie had seen the same show. At least, she'd seen some of it, before the laughing and flirting between them had made her turn it off. And she wanted to defend Sofi, believing that, despite everything, she was a good person. But she really didn't want to hear Daya remind her of all the reasons why she wasn't.

"I'm not letting her back in. I'm hanging out with her because I'm working on the house. I'm just saying that Noah is away touring and she seems like she could use a friend right now. That's all. I guess it doesn't even have to be me."

"Well, it ain't gonna be me." As Daya muttered the words, a yellow ball skittered across their table and almost took out both their coffee cups.

"Mateo," Maddie and Daya called his name in unison.

"Don't make me come in there and dunk you." Daya reached down to remove her shoes as Mateo chuckled and let himself fall backward into the balls.

"You're taking this cool auntie stuff kinda seriously." Maddie laughed as Daya stepped into the pit.

"On the contrary, babe, I'm not taking it seriously at all." She knelt down and pretended to swim through the balls toward a Mateo who was now squealing with delight.

Maybe Daya was right to be worried about Maddie being around Sofi again. Maddie threw the yellow ball back into the ball pit. She wished it was just as easy to throw away her worries about Sofi.

Chapter Nine

M addie didn't see the group of photographers until she had pulled up outside of Sofi's house. They descended upon the jeep without warning. She hadn't been ambushed by paparazzi in a very long time, but as they pointed their lenses in her direction, the clicking and shouting brought back the familiar feeling of being invaded—except this time she had Mateo with her, and the desire to tell them to piss off and leave her alone was even stronger. She considered fleeing, forgetting all about her impulsive mercy mission, but she wanted to check on Sofia, and—she let herself admit it—she simply wanted to see her.

She picked Mateo up and settled him on her hip. "It's okay, sweetie, they're just taking our photo." She kissed his cheek before scooping up the large bag of groceries and slamming the door shut with her foot.

"Here to see Sofia?"

"How's she doing?"

"Who are you?"

"What did you buy for her?"

"Who's that kid? Is he related to Sofia?"

The questions came thick and fast. She ignored them and walked steadily toward the front door.

"Madison? How come you and Sofia are hanging out again?" One voice cut through the noise, someone who had recognized her. She turned slowly toward the voice. It was a woman, wearing a beanie and a flannel shirt. It was unusual, photographing celebrities out on the street like this was almost exclusively a man's game. "Are you guys discussing a reunion? Is the band reuniting? Is that your kid? Can I get a picture?" She might have been a woman, but her rude questions and nonstop snapping were every bit as annoying as the men.

Maddie turned away from the voice and pressed the doorbell with her elbow, trying to ignore the knot in her stomach that the woman's questions had caused. Back when they had been together—in the band and as a couple—the questions about her and Sofia had been persistent and unnerving. At first, they had laughed the speculation away, played up to it even, with flirting and hints. But when they had started their relationship, and when the record company found out and made it clear they had to hide it, Sofia had gotten spooked. She had stopped flirting with Maddie, stopped sitting next to her even, and she'd even taken on one of the fake boyfriends they'd arranged for them, despite swearing she never would. The tension had caused arguments between them, with each of them thinking the other was ashamed of the relationship and neither of them having the courage to do anything about it. Maddie wasn't ever ashamed of loving Sofi, but being together out in the open just wouldn't have been possible while they were in the band. The vultures outside Sofi's house proved that.

"Maddie. What are you doing here?" The cameras burst into action as soon as Sofi opened the door, still dressed in the sweatpants and T-shirt that she'd been wearing earlier in the day. She looked pale, with dark half circles under her eyes. Maddie felt a rush of affection for her. And a jolt of unexpected attraction. She made herself try some words.

"I brought you some food." She tilted her head in the direction of the groceries.

"Come inside quick. Those guys just arrived. They don't normally bother me here. I thought we'd kept this place off their radar, but obviously not." She waved a hand toward the photographers, looking stressed before ushering Maddie and Mateo into the house and slamming the door shut.

"I just thought..." She handed the bag to Sofi. "You said your fridge was empty. And I was passing by." She lifted a shoulder in a half shrug. "Kind of."

Sofia looked at the bag and then back at Maddie. "You didn't have to do that." Her eyes clouded slightly. "But thank you." Maddie could hear the upset in her voice.

"Hey." Without thinking, she put a hand on Sofi's arm. "Are you okay?"

"I guess. Too much time to think maybe." Sofi forced a smile. "Hey, buddy. Want something to drink?" Mateo nodded.

Maddie followed Sofi into the kitchen and watched her unpack the groceries before she handed Mateo a carton of juice.

"Want some adult juice?" Sofi held up a half empty bottle of white wine. "Doc told me to hydrate, I figured this counted." She pulled a sheepish face and Maddie couldn't help but smile.

"Small one." She pointed at Mateo, now wandering along by the window looking out at the sea. "He refuses to be the designated driver. So selfish. And anyway we should let you rest. I just wanted to drop some food by, not disturb you."

They were awkward together. Careful, formal. It was sensible in the circumstances, but it bothered Maddie in a way she hadn't expected.

"You're not disturbing me, not at all. I needed company. I was driving myself crazy trying to figure out what to do. Felix said he needs to let people know if I'm gonna cancel dates." She handed Maddie a half-filled wine glass and crossed to the couch.

Maddie followed and so did Mateo. Surprising her, he sat next to Sofi happily. He usually took longer to get comfortable with new people.

Sofi stood, lifted the lid on a small chest next to one of the pristine armchairs near the far wall, and pulled out a box of colored bricks. She emptied them out onto the rug in front of them.

"My niece visits sometimes. My sister left these last time. Are they okay for Mateo?"

Maddie nodded as Mateo clambered off the couch and onto the floor. Sofi joined him, her legs stretched out and her back against the couch, and she had no choice but to sit back and watch her son and the woman she had once imagined loving for the rest of her life, building a colorful rectangular tower together. The universe was throwing her one hell of a curve ball.

"What did you decide?" She found her voice. "About the shows."

She wanted Sofia to cancel them, to cancel some of them at least. To stay home and rest properly. Because she cared about her health. She wasn't prepared to face up to the fact that at least part of it was because she also wanted to see more of her, didn't want this new connection between them to end before it even got started.

"I didn't. I want to go—I need to go—but I still don't feel great. And I realized today—" Sofi turned a blue brick over and over in her fingers, facing forward, avoiding Maddie's gaze. "I'm sorry. You don't need to hear me griping about my first world problems."

"I asked, Sofi."

Sofi turned her head to look up at her. "I realized it's not just that I'm tired—I mean I am tired obviously, but nothing a few more days of rest and sleep wouldn't fix. It's not that." Her expression was a questioning one, as if she was deciding whether to continue. Maddie got down on the floor, mirroring Sofi's position. She reached across and stroked the back of Mateo's head.

"Go on."

Sofi took a big swallow of her wine. "It's like I'm tired of being me. I'm tired of the photographers, I'm tired of answering the same questions over and over, and I'm tired of talking about myself, of the bullsh—" She clasped a hand to her mouth and mouthed a "sorry" in Maddie's direction. Maddie waved the apology away. She wanted Sofi to continue, wanted to hear her thoughts.

"I'm tired of talking BS, saying things I don't even believe, acting all dumb and cutesy because it's what everyone wants to see, because it's my 'persona.' And this is the crazy part, I'm tired of not having any of the things I really want." She raised her eyebrows and pulled a face. "Says the millionaire with two Grammys who has the career she always dreamed of. I know it's ridiculous, but I can't help feeling I've lost my way and that maybe this whole falling down thing is a wakeup call, a chance to feel less lost."

Mateo chose that moment to knock over the tower and Sofi busied herself replacing the bricks that had come loose. Maddie wanted to say something, something reassuring and affirming, but she didn't know what. She didn't know what Sofi meant, not really. She didn't know this Sofi at all. The vibe she was giving off was an unhappy one, slightly bitter and, yes, kinda lost. It seemed like exactly the right word for Sofi to use.

"I think you need a lot more rest. And I definitely don't think you should do that festival. I can see how tired you are, how pale. Your eyes..." Maddie felt nervous, stupid even, she didn't know if she even had the right to say it, "they don't have their usual sparkle." She shrugged. "I don't know about the rest of it, but maybe taking a bit more of a break will give you the chance to figure it out. Maybe it won't feel so confusing then." Maddie picked up one of the yellow bricks that Mateo had separated out and piled up next to her knee. Her son really hated the color yellow.

Sofi nodded at her, an earnest expression on her face.

"What did it feel like? When you walked away from the business?"

"I didn't walk away, Sofi. I was dropped—from a great height. And nothing about it felt good. I didn't have music, I didn't have Mateo then, I didn't have anything really." Maddie didn't like to think about it. "I wasn't ready for it to stop as soon as it did, and I didn't exactly handle it well. Don't tell me you didn't read about that." Maddie's downward slide had been well documented, her stumbling out of clubs with a different woman, or man, on her arm, was an embarrassingly regular feature of the entertainment websites.

"I saw some of it." Sofi drained her glass. "I felt responsible somehow."

"You weren't." Maddie's response was immediate. "I made my own mistakes. It was hard to accept that I'd failed, that I'd misjudged things so badly, but it didn't turn out too badly for me. I've got a job I love and a son I adore. I'm home finally and I feel settled."

"It doesn't look like you failed to me. I mean, like you say, you seem sorted, happy. It makes me think that, despite everything, I don't really have a clue what 'success' looks like."

Sofi chewed her lip anxiously and Maddie wanted to say something wise and reassuring, but everything she tried out in her head seemed wrong. Sofi seemed successful to her—she had Noah, she had her career, and everything she wanted at her fingertips.

"I saw Danny, I forgot to tell you. In Atlanta, right before I fainted. I ended up getting changed in his dressing room. My pants split. Not my best day." Sofi rolled her eyes. "Do you ever see him?"

"No. Not since we worked on that video together."

"He's friends with Noah. I didn't even know. He acted like a jerk. I think I always thought he was a jerk, but maybe it was just the jealousy because you guys hooked up before we got together, when I was crushing on you hard, but couldn't find a way to tell you. And I hate the idea of him and Noah being friends." Her voice was a little slurred around the edges.

She got up and began to open a new bottle. Maddie wasn't sure it was a good idea.

"Is it okay if I make some tea? And Mateo might like a lemonade." She couldn't help acting like a mom. She drove herself crazy with it. "Why don't you join us?"

"Trying to manage my drinking, Mads?"

"Not exactly." She had been, Sofi was right to call her on it. "Maybe a little bit. Sorry." She held up her hands.

"Don't be. I kind of like it. Shows you care." Sofi held her gaze and Maddie felt a little warm. "I just want to drink tonight. It's been a weird week. I'm not going to develop a problem. Don't worry, I'm far too sensible for that. Don't I always do the sensible thing? I bore myself constantly. I never had your rebellious streak."

"Well, I never had your courage." Maddie hadn't meant to say it out loud. Whatever else she felt about Sofi leaving the band, it had been gutsy to be the one to get out first.

"Courage?" Sofi scoffed at the word. "I don't feel very courageous right now. The opposite actually. And anyway, I wasn't the one who came out as bisexual to the whole world with an open letter attacking the president of the United States for his stance on LGBTQ rights. You got so much flak for it, but I was so proud of you." She poured herself another glass of wine and returned to the couch, sitting with her feet underneath her. "Though if I'm being white-wine-honest, I was upset that you were willing to come out for Lara but not for us."

"Are you serious?" She couldn't believe Sofi had said it. "I didn't come out 'for Lara.' I had no choice. She was about to out me—she had pictures of us, texts, and a website ready to run the whole story. I had to get ahead of it. I didn't want to come out, but I had to. So I tried to do some good with it. I was terrified, I assumed it would be the end of my career. And I suppose it was, in a way. It was definitely the end for me and Lara. I was mad as hell at letting myself get played by her. And the only silver lining was that the record company paid her to go away."

"I didn't know that. I just thought you and she broke up." The way Sofi was looking at her made Maddie pause.

"What?"

"Nothing."

Maddie didn't believe she had nothing to say, but Mateo chose that moment to turn to Sofi. "Peppig?" He placed his tiny hands on her leg. "Peppig pleeezey." Sofi looked at Maddie and raised an eyebrow.

"He wants to watch a show."

"I know that. I wanted to check it was okay."

Maddie looked at her watch. "He should eat soon, but sure, he's okay for a while. If you don't mind."

"I don't mind." Sofi reached down the side of the couch and pulled out a small tablet. She found a video and held the tablet out for Mateo. Rather than taking it, he climbed onto her lap. Maddie saw her surprise and was going to ask Mateo to climb down, but Sofi settled them into a comfortable position before pulling a blanket across them both. Maddie couldn't help the swelling in her heart. She was happy that Mateo liked Sofi and happier still that Sofi liked Mateo. She didn't know what it meant but she knew it made her happy.

"I would have, eventually I mean."

Sofi looked at her with confusion.

"I would have come out for you if we'd stayed together after the band split. I know it's what you wanted. It was just so hard to do it while we were in the band—and not just because the record company wouldn't let us. We were constantly watched. Every look, every gesture was examined, analyzed. I couldn't stand it. But, after I came out, I realized people were not even all that interested. It was the discomfort, the lies, the secrecy that got them excited—once it was out in the open, it was no fun for them and they moved on to the next sucker."

"Did it really cost you your career, do you think?"

It was something Maddie had thought about often.

"That's pretty much what the record company told me when they dropped me. They said I was 'no longer marketable' to my intended audience," Maddie wrapped the words in quotes, "and they weren't willing to wait around to see if I could grow a new set of fans. They said they'd tried. I'm not so sure." She shrugged. "I was a nightmare to deal with then to be honest. I wasn't working hard, I was drinking too much, and I resisted singing what they wanted me to sing. I won't ever know what really made them give up on me, but, since I didn't have anything like the kind of freedom in my solo contract that you managed to get in yours, it was probably for the best."

Sofi looked pale and Maddie had the feeling she'd said the wrong thing again. A beat passed between them, and Maddie waited for Sofi to finally say what it was she was trying not to say. She'd never been good at not saying things.

"Hey, look." She felt Sofi's hand grab at her thigh and then point at the TV. Sofi grabbed for the remote to turn on the sound as Maddie found herself looking at her own image, hearing her own voice. It was her final single, the one that hadn't sold well, the one her manager had told her wouldn't sell but which she'd wanted them to release anyway.

"I love this song." Sofi still had her hand on Maddie's leg. She felt the heat of it. Sofi was singing along to the video, not getting a word or a beat wrong, captivated by the TV. "You sound so good." Sofi didn't look at Maddie, even when she spoke. It was like she was talking to the TV. "And this video is amazing. I was so blown away with it at the time."

She watched Sofi watch the screen. The song was nearing its end and the video had an ending that some music channels wouldn't show. Maddie, wearing just her underwear, under a long leather coat, in a passionate clinch with a woman dressed head to toe in biker leathers, the two of them kissing before cutting to Maddie being driven off into the night on the back of the woman's motorcycle. She held her breath, not sure if she wanted the station to cut off the ending or show it so she could see Sofi's reaction.

On the TV, she saw herself framed in the doorway of a house in sexy underwear. She looked pretty good, but it was impossible not to feel embarrassed. She had tried, and failed, to find a more adult audience for her music.

Next to her on the couch, Sofi shifted slightly, her gaze moving from the TV to Maddie. She raised one eyebrow and let out a soft "damn" in Maddie's direction, holding her gaze for just an instant before looking back to the TV. She felt the temperature in the room rise by about twenty degrees.

As TV-Maddie moved into the arms of biker woman for their kiss, she moved her own gaze to Sofi again. Sofia's bottom lip was now caught between her teeth, her eyes wide, her body still, and her breath held. As the kiss deepened, Sofi swallowed, and as the tracking shot showed Maddie riding off into the night on the bike, the commercials intruded. Sofi exhaled and turned to Maddie, her eyes darker than their normal shade. She waited. She wasn't sure for what. They held each other's gaze until Sofi lowered her eyes.

"I might learn to ride a motorbike." Sofi said the words quietly, sounding serious, but then she raised her eyebrows and smiled. "I could give rides." She tilted her head as if she was giving Maddie time to think about it. Maddie couldn't help but laugh. The tension of the moment was gone.

"Is that the sweet innocent Sofia Flores flirting with me? While she has my child on her lap." Maddie clutched a hand to her chest.

"Not necessarily." Sofi's eyes were shining. "I mean, I might just really want to learn to ride a motorcycle and it might have nothing to do with that video, with the idea of you sitting behind me." She muttered the words "in your underwear" into her hand as she pretended to cover a cough. She grinned. "Maybe I'm just someone really in need of a new hobby."

Maddie was enjoying the banter, the alcohol-fueled flirting, and low down in her center was a tension, a wanting, that she recognized from times past. She tried to ignore it.

"I can't see you on a motorbike. I guess it's just hard for me to forget how much you squealed with terror when we all went go-carting that time and I don't think you went over five miles an hour the whole way around. Suzy lapped you twice, and she can't even drive." She laughed. The memory was a happy one.

Sofi was looking at her intently with a serious expression on her face. The intensity of her gaze made Maddie feel things she hadn't felt in a long time, things she didn't want to feel sitting this close to Sofi, things she desperately missed feeling at the very same time.

"What?" She dared to ask Sofi the question.

"What what?" Sofi lobbed the ball right back at her, her eyes containing a challenge. She took a long drink of her wine.

"What are you thinking when you look at me like that?"

Sofi's eyes widened in surprise. She had clearly not expected Maddie to ask that question. She didn't know why she had. It wasn't like her, and she didn't even have the excuse of the alcohol.

"I was just thinking about how beautiful you are when you laugh." Sofi didn't continue until Maddie met her eyes. Maddie felt her insides liquefy—she couldn't stop her body from reacting to Sofi's comment, to her gaze. "And I was thinking about just how long ago it seems that we went go-carting."

"It was." Maddie felt a sadness about the loss of those days.

"But you're right. I'm too terrified to ride a motorbike—whatever the motivation. Hell, who am I kidding, I'm probably still too terrified to drive a go-cart."

They sat quietly for a few moments, Maddie willing herself to stop reacting every time Sofi looked at her. She was just being friendly, just teasing her, and she needed to get a grip.

"Was she a good kisser?" Sofi nodded at the TV screen where Miley Cyrus was now singing a ballad.

"I've never kissed Miley Cyrus." She wondered if Sofia had heard a rumor that she hadn't. "I've never even met her."

Sofi turned to Maddie, her eyes dancing with amusement. "Not her, dummy. The biker woman in your video. That looked like a hot kiss."

Maddie could see Mateo's eyes closing. He was comfortable enough with Sofi to fall asleep in her lap.

"Was it your idea to put the kiss in the video or the director's? Did you choose the woman yourself? Did you already know her?" She felt pinned to the couch by Sofi's earnest gaze and her questions.

"I forgot how many questions you ask, and how damn personal they always are." Sofi's curiosity had always appealed to her, and the way she looked expectantly at Maddie, so open and intense, was impossible not to respond to.

"We shot that kiss about twelve times so I don't think hot is the word I'd use. And that woman was so straight." The memory was so clear to her. "I don't know where they found her, but she was so freaked out at having to kiss a woman. I swear that she must have told me she had a boyfriend about ten times." She raised her eyebrows. "And I'm pretty sure I heard her ask the lighting guy to lower the lighting a bit so she'd be less likely to be recognized. Not exactly good for the ego."

"You should have gotten rid of her, Mads. Told her that there'd be dozens of women willing to take her place. Hundreds. Jeez, you looked so good, you had even me contemplating buying a motorbike."

Maddie blushed at the compliment. She let herself enjoy the feeling of Sofi saying something nice to her, even as she understood it was the drink talking. Sofi looked at her then while biting her bottom lip, her eyes moving from Maddie's face to her mouth. The gaze was unmistakably familiar, and Maddie felt the ground shift a little beneath her. The space between them was definitely feeling smaller than it had when they sat down.

"I directed it myself. Kind of." She made herself keep talking, to keep answering the questions. She focused on the face of her now sleeping son, anything but the way that Sofi was staring at her. "I had help with the technical parts, but the story, the concept, the design was all mine. I drew all the storyboards. I loved it. As much as making the music. More actually." She couldn't help but feel proud.

"Wow. I had no idea."

"Why would you?" Reality came barging in. Sofi had moved on, without ever really looking back, without wondering what Maddie was up to. Yet she had watched every move of Sofi's, listened to every song, watched every video. She felt pathetic for staying so interested.

"I knew you'd directed that video of Danny's. And that you'd done that documentary short on the Million Moms march—I loved that by the way—but I didn't realize you'd made this video too."

Maddie felt a lightness in her chest, a fluttering. Sofi had cared enough to keep track.

"Can I tell you something maybe I shouldn't?" Sofi leaned closer, putting a hand on her arm. Maddie could smell the wine on her breath.

"Maybe not, I mean if you shouldn't."

"I mean, the people who want me to keep keeping secrets would tell me I shouldn't, but I think I should. Though I need you to promise me something."

"Not to tell anyone? Goes without saying." Maddie shrugged. Sofi had been drinking and she should really put a stop to the conversation, take Mateo, and go home. But she couldn't, she wanted this. The closeness, the intimacy, the confiding.

"Nope, I need you to promise not to judge me. And not to hate me." Sofi closed her eyes briefly and tilted her head. "Please."

Maddie nodded. Looking at Sofi, seeing how nervous she seemed, how beautiful she was, Maddie felt giddy. But unlike Sofi, she was stone cold sober.

"I hated you calling me courageous because I'm not. I'm a coward and a liar." As she said the words, Sofi pulled her hand away and Maddie snaked out a hand to stop her, holding on to it.

"Sofi." Maddie had no idea what to say.

"No judgment, you promised. I'm in a mess. And I need to put a stop to it, but it's harder than it seems and I know you're gonna hate me for it, you should, I kind of hate myself. But I promised myself that I was gonna be braver and more honest and I'd rather you heard it from me. Even if it ruins things, I need to stop doing things that make me unhappy, stop making decisions just because of my career. But I don't know how, not really." Sofi looked tense and she had turned pale.

"Are you okay? You don't seem good." Maddie reached for Mateo, taking him from Sofi and settling him on the adjacent armchair. She didn't know if Sofi was going to be sick, but she wasn't taking any chances. Sofi moved from the floor to the couch, her breathing now seeming a little erratic. Maddie moved to sit next to her, recognizing the signs.

Sofia felt the wave of panic moments before it hit. She leaned forward, putting her head down closer to her knees, taking in breaths as deeply as she could. Her chest felt like it was folding in two and her heart was racing, the sound of it whooshing in her ears. She couldn't feel her hands or her feet. Maddie shuffled closer and Sofia felt Maddie's hand on her back as she began to stroke it firmly and evenly, from the top of her spine to the bottom and back up again.

She tried to focus on the feel of it, on the up and down movement, to breathe in time with the stroke. Maddie took her other hand and turned it over so that it was palm up on her thigh. She began the same rhythmic stroking movement, tracing her fingers from the center of Sofia's palm, up her wrist and back again.

"Breathe, Sofi, just breathe. It's okay, it's all okay."

Despite the pulsing in her head, she could hear Maddie telling her over and over that it was going to be all right. She gave in to the soft soothing sound of her voice, letting herself breathe in time with Maddie's stroking. Sofia had had panic attacks back when they had been together in the band. And Maddie was doing everything she had done then to calm her down.

Slowly, she felt the crushing feeling in her chest lessen, her breathing became easier, and her vision and hearing cleared. She concentrated on the feel of Maddie's fingers on her hand and wrist as she kept murmuring reassurances, not stopping the movement of her hands.

"It's settling. But please don't stop." Sofia managed to squeeze out the words, wanting Maddie to know that what she was doing was working. Maddie kept on, and Sofia felt the tension, the panic, slowly dissipating. She felt able to lift her head and look at Maddie.

"Thank you."

"It's okay." Maddie's eyes contained tenderness and Sofia felt the warmth of it flood through her body.

Maddie moved to lie down on the couch and Sofia felt the loss of her touch like a chill.

"Come here." Maddie patted the space next to her. Sofia didn't hesitate. She lay side by side with Maddie on the couch. The panic had left her body; now she just felt tired and fragile.

"Turn on your side." Maddie spoke softly and Sofia did as she was asked. The remaining tension in her body drained away completely as Maddie pressed herself along the length of her back, reaching her arm across Sofia's body and taking hold of her hand, this time stroking it softly with her thumb.

Sofia nestled herself against Maddie, wanting to get as close as she could.

"Just relax, sleep if you can. Just for a little while." Maddie murmured into her ear, her lips pressed close enough for Sofi to feel the words as well as hear them.

"Mateo?" Sofia felt so sleepy, she was surprised she remembered. "He's okay. He's watching his cartoons." Again, Sofia felt the welcome vibration of the words as Maddie's lips brushed her ear as she spoke. "Just relax, baby."

Sofia relaxed into the feeling of Maddie's body pressed against her, at the wonder of Maddie calling her baby. She could feel the in and out movement of Maddie's chest against her back, the gentle grip of her fingers, the movement of her thumb. She was alive to all of it.

Lying together like this felt strangely familiar for something they hadn't done for so long. Maddie unlaced their fingers and moved her hand to gently brush away the wisps of hair on Sofia's cheek. Sofia couldn't stop her senses from responding to Maddie's touch. She willed her body to calm down. The panic attacks she'd had in the past were when she was overloaded and not facing up to things. And Maddie had always been the one who helped her figure out where exactly the stress was coming from and how to deal with it. This time though, Maddie couldn't help. Sofia had to find a way to end it with Noah and tell Maddie she'd been lying about him all along for the sake of her career. She'd told herself that the lie wouldn't harm anyone, not really. But she didn't expect Maddie to understand, or to approve. She felt her chest tighten. She concentrated on her breathing again.

"Wanna talk about where that came from?" Maddie spoke softly.

"No." Sofia spoke quietly.

"It might help."

"This is helping. This is what I need." She pulled Maddie's arm around her, wanting the closeness.

"Sofi."

"I thought you of all people might guess, that I wouldn't have to spell it out. I mean, we never labeled ourselves I guess, what we were, what we weren't. It was illerivant…irrevelant…" The alcohol, mixed with the panic still buzzing in her brain, meant that Sofia couldn't get the word out. "When we were together, I guess it didn't matter. And it shouldn't matter now either. But I just don't want to tell lies any more. Especially not to you." She stopped, too scared to say it, even with the alcohol. It wasn't just that she'd signed a confidentiality agreement. She thought Maddie would think she was ridiculous and pathetic.

"I don't understand."

"Noah is a good guy. He really is. He's sweet sometimes, and sometimes he's really annoying, but that's not my point—"

The chime of the doorbell sounded throughout the house. Sofia and Maddie both sat up. Mateo, startled by the noise, jumped off the chair and went to Maddie. She pulled him into her lap as Sofia went to answer the door. As soon as she opened it, the photographers began their chorus of shouts, their cameras clicking and whirring.

Noah reached for her and wrapped her in a big hug on the doorstep. She felt his lips on hers and she pushed at his chest, but his grip was too strong. In a shameful corner somewhere deep in her brain, she registered the photographers and the fact that they were being photographed and she stopped fighting him. But his kiss was not the kiss she wanted. He broke the embrace, put an arm around her waist, and steered her into the house, slamming the door behind them. Sofia let him lead her, not quite believing his timing.

"What are you doing here?"

He ignored her. "I need a key you know. I shouldn't have to ring the bell and wait for my girlfriend to let me in. It's not very conv—" Noah stopped talking as he caught sight of Maddie, now standing with Mateo in her arms next to the armchair.

Despite the awkwardness, the insane mess of it all, Sofia couldn't help but be attracted to her. She remembered the feel of her fingers brushing her cheek, her breasts pushed against her back just moments ago. The arousal flooded her senses. She really was losing her grip on reality.

Noah looked from her to Maddie and back again.

"Madison Martin." He said Maddie's name in a way that sounded accusatory. "Well, I definitely wasn't expecting to see you here."

"Noah." Maddie nodded, her expression guarded.

"Who's this little guy?" He crossed to Maddie and patted Mateo on the head. Sofia watched as Maddie ever so slightly turned her body, and Mateo, away from him.

"This is Mateo, my son. We were just leaving, I just dropped by to bring some food for Sofi."

"I didn't know that you guys were back in touch." Noah turned to her. "How did I not know that you're hanging out with the band again?" He didn't sound happy.

"Not the band. Just Madison. She's working on the house. Her design company is doing the interior design while I'm away." She didn't want to explain herself to him, but with Maddie standing there, she didn't want him to get angry enough to blurt anything out that she wasn't ready to explain.

"At eight thirty with wine and her kid in tow? I wish that was the kind of 'work' I got paid for."

"I'm heading out." Maddie put Mateo down and took his hand.

"You don't have to." Sofia stepped closer. She didn't want Maddie to go. She didn't want their evening to end like this, and the idea of an evening with Noah brought the tension back into her chest. He would have to stay the night. The photographers had seen him arrive.

"Stay and have some tea. You said you wanted some. Eat some of that food you bought for me. It's not late. Or we could go get takeout maybe." Even as she said it, she understood how ludicrous she was being. How did she imagine an evening sitting between Noah and Maddie would unfold?

"I think you should let her go, babe. You need to rest." Noah took a step toward the door, clearly expecting Maddie to follow, but for some reason, she didn't move. Noah moved back to Sofia's side, threading an arm around her waist. She couldn't stop herself from stiffening. It wasn't just his touch, it was Maddie's gaze. "And I didn't come all this way to see you, just to spend the night with these guys." He turned to Maddie. "No offense meant."

The look on his face was hostile. The offense was meant.

"Say good-bye to Sofia, Mateo." Maddie moved closer to Sofia and Mateo held out his arms. Sofia gloried in the feel of his hug and placed a soft kiss on his cheek. The tenderness in Maddie's eyes, coupled with the care she had shown Sofia earlier, made her feel emotional.

"I'll see you tomorrow maybe. Call me if you need anything." Maddie held Sofia's gaze before heading for the door without a backward look at Noah.

As the door closed, Noah turned to her.

"Really? You're hanging out with Madison again. That's insane. Should I be worried about you two?"

"I told you, she's working on the house." Sofia walked to the fridge and opened it, needing something to get her away from him. She felt too fragile for an argument but too annoyed by him to offer the reassurance he wanted. If they had actually been dating, the anger she felt toward him for ruining the intimacy of her evening with Maddie should definitely worry him. But they weren't, and he had no right to question her. She took several breaths. "I wasn't expecting you. Usually someone lets me know." She tried not to say anything that would inflame him.

"I know." He smiled, looking pleased with himself. "This visit was totally my idea and I didn't even tell Felix. I wanted it to be a nice surprise. Your mom knew, no one else. You're sick. I wanted to be here for you. I mean, that's what I told the photographers on the way in, but it's the truth as well. I'm worried about you."

She gripped the fridge door a little harder to stop herself from reacting to his words. He had no right to just turn up and he knew it.

"Maybe you could go and get us some Chinese food. I'm starving, and all this," she waved at the inside of the fridge, "needs to be prepared and I'm too tired to cook." She wanted to eat the food Maddie had bought for her, but she wanted him gone more, if only for a short while.

"Sure." He smiled at her. "I'd be happy to. Anything for my best girl."

She was too tired to challenge him again. She would eat the food and use her "illness" as an excuse to go to bed early. And tomorrow she would speak to Felix about calling the whole thing off. Her anxiety about it was off the charts. It wasn't just Noah's behavior, it was Maddie. She made her call into question everything that she'd felt certain about. She felt more and more like she was on the edge of a cliff. She didn't know if she was going to jump or fall, but either way it was terrifying.

CHAPTER TEN

Maddie woke up to the sound of her phone ringing. She picked it up. It was Daya. She'd spent the night tossing and turning, but even her sleep-deprived brain understood that a call from Daya this early was unusual. She was not an early riser.

"What's up?" she answered as she forced herself out of bed and headed downstairs for coffee.

"I got the job. After that second audition. Obviously, they couldn't believe how amazing I was the first time around and needed another look to be certain." Daya's excitement sounded even louder this early in the morning. "I start in six weeks and I'll be filming in Vancouver for three months. Three months in the rain." She groaned comically. "I'm letting you know so you can start to prepare for life without me and," she paused dramatically, "start arranging my fabulous going away party."

"You got the hospital drama thing?" Maddie couldn't stop smiling. Daya deserved the break.

"Dr. Marianne Theron, distinguished but slightly kooky psychiatrist, reporting for duty." She laughed.

"That's amazing. I'm so proud of you. But, damn, I'm gonna miss you. So is Mateo. Who's he gonna eat ice cream with now?"

There was a pause on the other end of the call.

"He doesn't look like he's short of playmates to me." The excitement disappeared and Daya sounded a little snarky.

"Huh?"

"I'm just saying maybe you'll both be too busy hanging with Sofi to miss me." She sighed. "I honestly don't get why you're so eager to be back in her orbit. It seems kind of masochistic."

"I'm not back 'in her orbit'—whatever that means—I'm redecorating her house, I already told you. I have to go there. I have to see her."

"In the evening, with Mateo, and a big bag of fucking groceries. That didn't look like a working visit, babe. Not unless you're now moonlighting as a chef to the stars."

"I just…" Maddie started to respond and then the penny dropped. "How did you know we hung out?"

"TMZ, Just Jared, Pop Crave, Daily Mail. Photos of you heading into her house on every entertainment website I looked at this morning. Most of them expressing more joy than they should at the idea of you two burying the hatchet, several wondering if this means the band is getting back together."

Maddie typed her name into the search engine on her phone and cringed at the series of photos and stories that appeared.

"Dammit." She'd assumed no one would be interested in running photos of her. Most of the photographers hadn't even known who she was.

"You can see Mateo's face."

"Yeah. He takes a good photo. Gets that from his mama." Daya still sounded pissed, but her tone was a little softer.

"I don't want this." Maddie kept scrolling through the stories. All very similar versions of each other. Same photos, same blurb. She stopped at one that had a picture of her arrival at Sofi's house next to one of Noah and Sofi kissing on her doorstep. The kiss looked passionate, and the photo made her feel every kind of stupid for imagining that Sofi had been flirting with her with any kind of intent. She hated herself for clicking on the link. The story was short and highlighted the fact that Noah had interrupted his own tour to fly back and spend the night with his sick girlfriend, who was apparently being cared for by her "old friend" Madison Martin. Farther down was a photo of Noah carrying a bag of takeout food that was captioned #couplegoals.

She was annoyed. She told herself it was nothing to do with seeing them kissing and everything to do with the fact she'd taken the trouble to fill Sofi's fridge full of healthy food. The article contained all kinds of guesses about whether Sofi would have had the energy for the kind of night that Noah might have been expecting. She felt tension in her body. This bullshit was exactly what she'd been happy to get away from when she left the industry—the endless innuendo, the intrusion, and the scrutiny—and she hated seeing herself, and Mateo, splashed across websites writing that kind of trash.

The unmistakable feeling of jealousy buzzed like a wasp at the back of her consciousness. Sofi had been complaining of loneliness, but here was Noah coming to her side like a knight in shining armor.

"Babe?" Daya's voice reminded her she was on the other end of the phone.

"Yeah. Sorry. Went down the rabbit hole."

"Be careful."

"What?"

"Be careful with her. I'm not stupid, I know you guys left things unfinished, and I can imagine it's hard not to want to talk about that, but I just don't trust her and you don't need her playing games with your heart again."

"That's not fair. We're both sorry about what happened. I told you. We've talked and she's explained. I feel like a lot of what we blamed her for wasn't even anything she did. And I feel bad that we treated her so badly." Maddie felt tired, like she wanted to crawl back into bed. She didn't want to defend Sofi to Daya. "It's just not anything you should worry about. And I'm not going to get my heart broken, it's not like that." Though, if Daya had asked, Maddie couldn't have explained what it was like. She shook her head, trying to shake away the uneasy feeling that had settled in.

"Okay." Daya spoke softly. "I don't believe you, but okay. Just know that if you want to talk, or ever think you're going to do anything stupid, I'm here."

"Is that offer from Dr. Theron or Daya?" She tried to lighten the conversation.

"Me. I don't think you could afford the good Dr. Theron, shrink to the stars."

They said good-bye with a promise to meet for lunch later in the week and Maddie carried her coffee to the couch, wanting a quiet half hour before Mateo got up.

She was loving the project at Sofi's house, but if she was honest, she had all kinds of feelings about seeing Sofi again. Daya was right, there were a lot of reasons to be careful.

Sofia had a headache. She didn't know if it was the stress of the night before, a simple hangover, or linked to how badly this meeting was going. She didn't care really. She just knew her head hurt and she wanted to be in bed.

They'd moved the meeting to her house, in recognition of her "need to rest," but it hadn't helped. She wasn't in the mood for it at all and was starting to feel anxious as well as grouchy.

At one end of her living room, Rick stood next to a portable display screen, flanked by his far-too-excitable assistant, Carly. He was the video director that Sofia had worked with most often, and he'd spent the last hour talking through possible themes and visuals for the video to her new single. The single they were all worried about. The one that needed to do well to give the album a boost. They'd found fifty different ways to say how important it was that it sold well without really saying it directly, but she understood the euphemisms and she certainly felt the pressure. On top of that, the questions everyone asked about her health as they arrived were clearly loaded with worry that she might need to cancel more tour dates. She was just as focused on her career as they were, but sometimes she really needed the concern to be for her and not just for her sales figures.

She was on the couch. Her mom and Felix sat side by side on the couch across from her and two of the dining chairs had been pulled into the living area for Justin and Krissy. Both of them looked stiff and uncomfortable at having to meet outside of the record company offices where they usually insisted on doing business.

The meeting had started badly and gone slowly downhill. Justin's opening contribution had been to ask if the decision to release "Not This Time" could be revisited. Sofia hadn't expected to have to defend the song again, and she'd been annoyed that neither Felix nor her mom had helped her stick up for it. She loved the song, and when she sang it she felt like she was saying something that mattered, something that moved her. It was all about taking chances, about not allowing yourself to have regrets. And with Maddie suddenly appearing back in her life, the song meant a whole lot more to her now.

"It's my choice to make. There's no debate to be had." She didn't hide her annoyance.

"Yeah, obviously, no one's disputing that. It's just that the focus groups seem to have a strong preference for "De Nada." We showed you the feedback."

Sofia wasn't stupid. She knew that the record company wanted her to endlessly release songs that were just like her mega hit single—a Latin-infused sugary pop song. They wanted a sure thing. And usually she'd done exactly what their focus groups recommended. But for once, she wanted to try something a little different, something that she felt more connected to.

"I know what the focus groups said. But I think this song could do just as well if we promote it properly to the right audience. And since that's exactly why we're here, we should get on with it." Sofia had drawn a clear line. But then they'd spent the last hour looking at Rick's ideas for the video and Sofia didn't like a single one.

"Can we take five minutes and get some air?" Sofia stood and headed toward the deck as she asked the question, not really expecting anyone to say no.

"Good idea. This room's like a fishbowl." He smiled. "Write that down, Carly. New video idea—Sofia trapped in a giant fishbowl." He was trying to lighten the mood and Sofia appreciated it. She wasn't feeling his ideas today, but he was much too good at his job to take it personally.

Sofia stood at the railing and let the ocean breeze wash over her. She looked at her watch. Though the wine had made her memory hazy, she was sure Maddie had said something last night about coming by this morning to decide on which fabrics to use. She smoothed a hand down her yellow sundress. She had already kicked off the shoes that matched the dress perfectly, feeling stupid wearing them for a meeting in her own house and knowing she had dressed for Maddie, who not only didn't seem to be coming but who probably didn't even care what she was wearing.

Sofia sighed at her own stupidity as the door behind her slid open. She turned to see her mom.

"It's so nice out here." Her mom joined her at the railing.

Sofia nodded in reply.

"You okay, cariño? You seem not so good today." Her mom looked at her with concern.

"I'm tired."

"Yeah, I saw the bottles in the recycling."

"Really, Mom?"

Her mom held up her hands. "I wasn't checking, I just saw them."

Sofia turned back to the ocean. Below them, at the shoreline, one of her neighbors was walking his dog. He waved at Sofia and she lifted a hand in response.

"I saw the photos too."

Sofia was surprised her mom had waited so long to raise it with her. She kept watching the waves rushing toward the sand and then sliding away again.

"You said it was going to be all business. That you wouldn't even see each other."

Sofia turned to her mom. "She brought me food. It was nice of her. She has no one to leave Mateo with, so she had no choice but to bring him." She hated explaining things to her mom. She didn't really understand why she was. Maybe she just needed to say it to herself. "She was a really good friend once. I just want…" She stopped herself. This wasn't something her mom would understand.

"Noah came all this way to see you. We made sure that the photographers were there to see him, but today the stories are all about her, not him. They're talking about you wanting to bring the band back together. It's not helpful, Sofia." Her mom was not a monster and Sofia sensed her awkwardness, understanding that she had drawn the short straw in being the one to talk to her about this.

Sofia shook her head. Of course that was why the photographers were there. Her mom and Noah had sent them. This house was her only refuge from all the madness in her life, and they'd ruined it for another photo op with her fake boyfriend. Did she really need the publicity that badly? The whole thing was so unbelievably fucked up that she didn't trust herself to respond reasonably. She swallowed down the words she wanted to say.

"Let's just get this meeting done. I still need to rest." Sofia spoke through gritted teeth. "I'm sure the one thing we all agree on is how much me not touring would cost us in album sales." She pushed away from the railing and moved back toward the house. Her mom leaned in and placed a gentle hand on her arm.

"She's not good for you, she never was." Sofia heard genuine concern in her mom's voice and couldn't help but be moved by it. But she shook away the feeling, wanting to stay mad at her mom, at Felix, at Noah, at all of it. She needed the anger. She just didn't know what for yet.

❖

"I just think the song is a lot darker, a lot edgier than the vibe this is giving me." Sofia spoke as Rick nodded and skipped to the next storyboard. "It's about someone confronting the fact that they were too timid in the past, too willing to accept second best. It cost them a whole lot, and this time, they're going to be braver and just go for what they want, regardless of the consequences." She trusted Rick and loved working with him, but he just didn't "get" the song yet.

The front door chimed and her mom went to answer it. Moments later, Maddie walked in ahead of her mom, looking hesitant, a backpack in hand. She offered Sofia a small self-conscious wave. Sofia's pulse quickened at the sight of her. Hadn't it always? She was in shorts and a long-sleeved T-shirt. The sleeves were rolled up to the elbows and the neckline was artfully torn to reveal her collarbone. Sofia couldn't stop the tug in the muscles low down in her belly that the sight of her produced.

"Hey, Maddie." She lifted a hand and was rewarded with a nervous half-smile.

"Sorry for disturbing you all. I didn't know there was a meeting today." She swept the room with a hand as she spoke, sounding unsure. "I could come back tomorrow."

"No, stay. We're almost done. Come sit down a while. It might be good to have your perspective on something." Sofia indicated the vacant space next to her, ignoring Felix's quizzical look and the murmuring from Justin and Krissy. Maddie hesitated.

"Please." The plea worked and Maddie crossed the room to sit next to her.

"You know 'Not This Time'?" Sofia was making a big assumption.

"Yeah, I love that song."

Sofia flushed at the knowledge that Maddie still cared enough to listen to her music.

"Describe it in three words." Sofia was putting Maddie on the spot, knowing that all eyes in the room were focused on them.

"Wow, only three? That's tough." She chewed the inside of her cheek self-consciously and Sofia found it wonderfully familiar. "Okay, I'd say dark, sexy, and kind of mean." Maddie smiled at her as she spoke and Sofia felt the room get a little warmer, felt her skin tingle. She held Maddie's gaze for a beat and then turned back to Rick.

"Exactly that and that's the vibe we need for the video." She had always felt so sure of herself with Maddie at her side. They might not get her, but Maddie did.

"But I'm not sure the fans expect 'dark, sexy, and mean' from you, Sofia." Krissy spoke up for the first time. "I mean, it might not go over well. Your usual vibe is a lot lighter." She looked from Sofia to Justin and back again. "Maybe we do need to look again at the song choice. We all know the choice of second single is going to make or break this album."

Sofia checked herself, getting hold of her frustration. There was no need to upset anyone, no need for angry words. They weren't listening to her and they didn't understand the song, but that didn't matter because she was in charge. She might not always act like it, but she was.

"I totally agree with Krissy. I mean, I love the song, but maybe it's not right for you, babe." The voice came from the bottom of the stairs, where Noah—dressed only in boxers and one of Sofia's tour T-shirts—was now standing.

"Hi, guys." He addressed the room before crossing to sit in the space on the couch between Sofia and Maddie. He smiled the smile his fans found so irresistible. "Sorry for oversleeping. I'm on a different time zone. Just came to see my girl yesterday, to offer a bit of TLC in her hour of need." He threw an arm around her shoulders and rested his head against hers. Sofia tensed. She hated him touching her when it wasn't absolutely necessary. And the little performance he was putting on definitely wasn't necessary because everyone in that room, with the exception of Maddie, knew that their relationship had been constructed entirely for PR reasons. She felt the weight of the lie yet again.

"You again?" Noah turned to Maddie. "Delivering groceries and now sitting in on creative meetings. That's a pretty wide set of responsibilities for a decorator." The sarcasm was obvious.

"Noah." Sofia said his name like a warning, removing his arm from her shoulders and patting his hand. "Why don't you go get showered? We're nearly done and I think we're going for lunch soon." She wanted him gone, wanted him away from Maddie.

He looked like he was going to say something but then seemed to decide against it.

"Okay, sweetheart." He leaned across and kissed her cheek, and it took Sofia a lot of effort not to slap him. She took a moment to compose herself, not daring to look at Maddie, knowing how close she'd come to telling her last night that she and Noah were faking it. He was such a jerk. However good they'd gotten at faking it, she couldn't believe Maddie would think for a minute that he was her type. She waited till he had padded back upstairs before continuing.

"Whatever you all think, the problem is not the song. And we're not going to change it, okay?" Sofia kept as calm as she could, despite the churning in her belly. If this went wrong, if the album tanked, it would all be on her.

She turned to Rick. "Can we try again with some themes that are a bit darker? A lot darker actually."

"Absolutely." Rick nodded. "I get it, Sofi. Give us a few days and we'll come back and pitch again." He began to pack up his laptop and notes.

"Thanks, Rick, you too, Carly. See you guys soon." Sofia shook their hands. She could feel the tension in the room. It wasn't just her asserting herself over the song, it was the fact of Maddie being here.

"Shall we go and do what we need to?" She spoke softly to Maddie and was rewarded with a nod. She waited for Maddie to stand and headed out onto the deck.

❖

Maddie sat, her backpack on her lap and her mind a whirl of conflicting thoughts. As fast as Sofi had spirited her outside, she had disappeared inside again to get them some drinks. Maddie didn't know what to feel first—embarrassment that she had stumbled into a meeting that no one wanted her at, anger that Sofi was still refusing to rest properly, or shame that, despite everything she'd told herself about guarding her heart, seeing Sofi's relationship with Noah up close made her feel things she shouldn't. There were a lot of reasons why she needed to be careful, but the depth of her antagonism toward Noah, for his infuriating grin, and for wearing one of Sofi's T-shirts in bed was chief among them.

"Coffee?" Sofia pointed a cup in her direction.

"Sure."

"I'm sorry." Sofi sat next to her.

"What for?"

"For Noah. His idea of a joke isn't always funny. And sorry for putting you on the spot like that. I just thought if you knew the song, you'd get the vibe, and they were driving me crazy. You definitely helped. Thank you."

Her expression was serious. Maddie simply nodded.

"And thank you for last night too. You were sweet for coming by. I'm sorry if I got all off the wall with the wine and the big panicking thing. I hadn't eaten and I was feeling a little stressed. It hasn't happened for a while, and I'm sorry you got caught up in it."

Maddie felt the distancing, knowing that Sofi was rowing them back a little. She should have been relieved, but instead she felt a disappointment that she had no right to feel.

"I was happy to help, and Mateo had fun." She wanted to say more about last night, but Sofi was making it plain she didn't want to talk about it. "And, yeah, I wasn't really expecting the welcoming committee today. Not that they were very welcoming."

"Yeah, sorry about that. I think the media coverage of your visit freaked everyone out. They said they don't want people talking about me and you when they should be talking about the album. But I told them that people talking about me at all is good for the album. It doesn't really matter what they're saying as long as my name stays in the news." Sofi sipped her coffee, seeming oblivious to what she'd just said.

"Glad to be of use," Maddie muttered, unable to keep the annoyance out of her voice. Everything always came back to Sofi's career.

"That's not what I meant."

"I think it's exactly what you meant. Last night must have been a jackpot for you—me, Noah, and a 'mystery child' for them to talk about. How did we impact on your streaming numbers? I'd like to think my son was of some use to you." Maddie was hurt, but she wasn't going to say it. She took refuge in sarcasm.

"Maddie, it's not what I meant. Honestly. I just said that to calm them down. They worry about everything. And they try to make me worry about things that I don't want to worry about. Things that I feel really good about. I'm just happy you're back in my life."

They sat silently for a minute. Not for the first time, Maddie felt like she was out of her depth. She kept telling herself that they should just do what they needed to do and she should leave. But for some reason she couldn't seem to make herself listen.

"I'm sorry." Maddie meant it. It wasn't Sofi's fault she was freaking out.

"Don't be. I am obnoxiously and ridiculously career-focused, but I would never use you or Mateo in that way, though I get that you'd think that I might. It fits." Sofi sounded upset.

They sat in silence, both looking out over the ocean. Maddie couldn't help but react to Sofi's words, wanting to say something back, wanting to reassure her, but she couldn't. It still all felt too uncertain.

"So, none of them like 'Not This Time,' huh?" Maddie tried to move them onto safer ground.

"They hate it." Sofi turned to her. "But I love it—and I think the fans will too. A lot of them have grown older with me, and I think they're as ready as I am for something different. It's funny, but I wasn't sure."

"About what?"

"I wasn't sure if you still listened to my music, y'know."

"I do. I always did. And I've always loved it, but..." She wanted to be honest, but she wasn't sure how Sofi would take it. "I think you play it safe sometimes. I don't mean that in a bad way, I know how it works, but 'Not This Time' is real, more raw, and I really like it."

Maddie was pleased to see Sofi smile shyly.

"Thanks. That means a lot coming from you. You were always the one I wanted to impress."

Maddie bit back the self-deprecating comment that was on the tip of her tongue and let herself enjoy the compliment. She hadn't made a success of music, but she had learned to love some of the songs she had written.

"Well, I think it's great that you're trusting your instincts more. They were always good. It's just that no one ever listened to us back then."

"That's an understatement."

They fell into silence again, and Maddie assumed that Sofi was, like her, remembering some of the not-so-good times they'd had in the band. The stupid songs they'd been given to sing, the ridiculously cheesy videos they'd had to appear in. Going solo was supposed to liberate them from that, but Sofi, with all her success, was still having to fight to be listened to. It sucked. But it wasn't Maddie's battle. Not anymore.

"I pulled out of the festival."

"You did?"

"Yeah. And we postponed the other UK dates too. The tour starts in Paris now. And that means I get another ten days to recover properly. Last night was a bit of a wakeup call."

"Good for you, Sofi." Maddie was surprised but happy. "I'm so pleased about that."

"I think you're the only one. Felix is still going to try to get Little Boy to do the song with me, but it's going to be much harder to schedule once we're both on tour so I guess it might not happen. That was the hardest thing to let go of, to be honest. It would have been huge, and I needed it. But you were right last night, I definitely need more rest, so something had to give." She lifted her shoulders in a shrug.

"There'll be other chances. And I don't care what the rest of them said, I'm proud of you for putting your health first." It sounded trite and kinda motherly. But Maddie was too relieved to be embarrassed.

"Want to see some of the fabrics for the bedroom?" Maddie patted the backpack. It was full of samples she'd chosen. Some she wanted to use to reupholster the chairs and some for cushions and curtains.

"Yes, please." Sofi sounded genuinely excited. "Let's go and look at them next to the walls so we can match colors." She stood and Maddie followed unthinkingly. Halfway up the stairs, she stopped. Noah was upstairs. He was either getting changed or had gone back to bed. Either way, she didn't want to encounter him again.

"You okay?" Sofi looked back at her.

Maddie willed herself to damp down the ridiculous feelings of jealousy. "Sorry, no, I thought I'd forgotten something, but it's fine." She followed Sofi up the stairs and watched her push down on the handle of her bedroom door—the bedroom where Sofi and Noah slept together—and step inside. Maddie took a breath and followed her, wanting him to at least be dressed.

"I quite like the plum color. My first thought was that it was too dark, but it looks a little lighter now that it's dry, and if we had just one wall like that and the rest more neutral it might work. What do you think?" Sofi walked across to the wall behind her bed and put her hand on the foot-wide stripe of dark purple paint.

"I like it too."

Maddie looked around the room. The bed was made, the room was tidy, and there was absolutely no sign of Noah, or his things. She felt confused, and more than a little relieved. She began to unpack the samples and lay them out on the bed—on Sofi's bed. She tried to ignore the knots that formed deep down in the pit of her stomach when Sofi came and sat on the bed and let her slender fingers caress the fabrics that Maddie had laid out.

"I was thinking we could cover the chairs in this." Maddie picked up a large square of patterned linen. As she handed it to Sofi, their fingers touched and Maddie felt the contact like electricity. She swallowed as Sofi laid the square across her thigh and stroked it with the palm of her hand. Maddie felt the touch almost as if it was her own leg. She was losing her mind. She dared to look at Sofi and, when their gazes met, she saw on Sofi's face a look that was instantly familiar to her. The idea that Sofi might be finding them being together equally affecting had her shook.

At the back of the house, something clattered to the floor and smashed, and Maddie heard heavy footsteps clumping along the corridor toward them.

"Sofi. I need a dustpan and brush," Noah shouted. "I dropped my cologne, and it's gone all over my shoes. And they were both damn expensive."

"For fuck's sake," Sofi said. "He's so clumsy it's ridiculous."

"He sleeps in another room." Maddie hadn't meant to say it out loud. She wanted the bed to swallow her whole.

Sofi looked at her with a face full of something that looked a lot like panic.

"He had jet lag. I knew he'd want to sleep in. I suggested he sleep in one of the spare rooms. So I wouldn't disturb him this morning, I mean." Sofi avoided looking at her as she spoke, acting like she had things she was ashamed of.

Maddie's first thought was that they were having problems and her second thought—that maybe Sofi was tiring of him and had finally realized she could do a lot better—wasn't one she was at all proud of. If Noah was who Sofia loved, Maddie should absolutely not be wishing for a break-up.

"Hold on." Sofi disappeared from the room still holding the square of linen.

Maddie heard raised voices at the other end of the corridor and was relieved that she couldn't make out the actual words. The feeling of something not being right between Sofi and Noah—the tension, the snarky comments—made sense if they weren't as happy as the gossip websites would have everyone believe.

Maddie heard Noah say her name. He followed it up with a distinctly annoyed, "Really, Sofi?" What Sofia said in response was inaudible, but it had clearly inflamed Noah as he was stamping around and she heard him call Sofi reckless and, possibly, selfish. Maddie felt terrible about listening, but it was impossible not to. She tore a couple of sheets from her notebook and labeled the fabrics she intended to use before picking up her backpack and heading downstairs. If Sofi and Noah were having problems, she didn't want her presence to be making things worse. Whatever old feelings might have surfaced between her and Sofi, they were in very different places in their lives. Sofi needed someone willing to live their life with her in the eye of a storm, someone willing to move from country to country, and someone happy to be second to her career. Noah seemed like that person, but even if he wasn't, Maddie knew with certainty that it wasn't her.

"I just don't want to do it anymore. Why is that so hard to understand?" Sofi stopped pacing and looked from her mom to Felix. "I don't care what you tell people about us breaking up, I just don't want to have to be with him anymore. He won't stick to the rules and he's acting all jealous like he's got a right to tell me who I can and can't have in my life. I wouldn't take that from him even if he was my boyfriend."

"He already said he's sorry, Sofi." Her mom spoke first. "And he's not being jealous, he already explained that to you. He just thinks that you're going to get yourself in trouble hanging out with Madison, that people will start talking. Like they did before."

Sofia walked to the window and back again, wanting to burn off some of the tension she felt. "I don't give a damn what people are saying about us. I never did. I can be friends with whoever I want and Noah can't say a thing about it. He's not my boyfriend or did you both forget that somewhere along the way? I want to end it."

"You can't." Felix spoke quietly.

"What do you mean, I can't?"

"The contract runs till after the Grammys. You can only 'break up' if you both agree to it." He indicated the words with speech marks in the air. "And Noah is pretty clear that he doesn't want to."

"I thought the contract had expired?" Sofia felt a tightness in her chest.

"Nope, four more months. Sorry." Felix shrugged. "You guys need to sort this out though because you can't be canceling events we've arranged for you both. The press will get pissed and you both need the publicity."

Sofia couldn't care about that today. She had argued with Noah. He had accused her of getting too involved with Maddie and said she was ruining everything. And when she had gone back to her room and realized Maddie had left, she had been angry enough to refuse to go for their scheduled lunch appearance.

"He's making me stressed. I collapsed on stage. Last night I had an actual panic attack. Surely there's a medical get out clause?" She appealed to her mom, wanting someone to understand how crazy this was, how much she was hating the whole thing.

"Just see out the contract, Sofi. Do the Grammys together and then blame work commitments for breaking up like we always planned. You'll both sell better these next few months if you're together. You know that the two of you together creates a buzz. It's why we did it in the first place." Her mom cast her eyes down. It was no comfort to Sofia that she felt shame about treating her this way. But then Sofia was as bad. She'd willingly agreed to it, and then signed the damn contract which had her trapped.

When Maddie came out, Sofia had watched as her career crashed and burned. She had felt terrible for Maddie and spent weeks fighting the urge to get in touch. The younger fans they'd had in the band couldn't seem to adjust to Maddie's new out-there sexuality, and she wasn't given any time to build a fan base that was more comfortable with it. Worse than that, some of the gossip websites started to talk about Maddie and Sofia again, to look at their "close relationship" again through the prism of Maddie's bisexuality. The whole thing had terrified her, and it hadn't taken much for them to persuade her that Noah—on the same record label and just starting out—would be perfect camouflage and a boost to both their careers. But now everything felt different and she was sick of lying, sick of hiding.

"Did it ever dawn on you that I might want a relationship of my own one day, that I might be sick of living a lie? This thing with Noah is plain crazy and I want out."

Her mom and Felix exchanged a look.

"If this is about Madison—" Her mom said it first.

"It's not." Sofia's denial was instant, if not entirely truthful. "I've been struggling with it for a while. It was okay in the beginning, it felt under control, but lately it's become impossible." Knowing that lying to Maddie about Noah was what was really weighing on her. "He's acting more and more like a jealous boyfriend and I just don't feel good about it, or about the lying."

"Does Madison know?" Felix asked.

"I haven't told her, but…"

"But what?" Her mom was determined to have the conversation.

"But she had a relationship with me, Mom. For three years. I know you don't want to think about it, but over that time, we got to know each other pretty fucking well. She's gonna guess before too long. She must know that I would never be with someone like Noah."

Yet Maddie had accepted the relationship at face value. Maybe she didn't know Sofia all that well, or maybe she was simply too good a liar. Sofia felt a little nauseous.

"And when I saw Danny the other day, he pretty much made it clear that he knew it was fake too. I'm gonna be a laughingstock if this gets out—Noah too. It's got to be better to end it now before it does."

Her mom blanched at hearing Sofia spell it all out so openly, but Felix looked at her like he got it. He was shrewd. He wouldn't want this to blow up in their faces.

"Okay. I'll talk to Noah's people again. I'll make that point. I still think we should wait till after Grammys, but let's start looking at an exit strategy. We can start to plant seeds about your conflicting schedules."

Her mom looked like she wanted to object, but for once, she deferred to Felix.

"Thanks." Sofia didn't feel that grateful, but she also didn't want to keep talking about it. "Now maybe I can have some rest." She walked away, heading up to her room, dismissing them both.

"He's a good man, Sofia." Her mom spoke to her from the bottom of the stairs. "He treats you well and he cares about you. It's a shame you won't give him a chance."

Sofia wanted to go back down and scream in her mother's face that she was a lesbian, that being a lesbian meant loving women and that it didn't matter if Noah was the king of fucking England, she would never want him the way she had wanted Maddie. Who was she kidding? There was no past tense. She would never want him the way she still wanted Maddie. But her head had started to pound and she wanted to lie down right then way more than she wanted to get her mom to take her sexuality seriously.

She lay on her bed and stroked the fabric samples that Maddie had left for her. She was washed out but too wired to sleep. She tried to order her thoughts. She had lost Maddie because of deception she hadn't been guilty of in the past. But she was lying to Maddie—lying to everyone—about Noah in the here and now, so maybe Maddie was right not to trust her. She sighed heavily. If she wanted to make Maddie and Mateo a part of her life somehow, she had to find a way to come clean about Noah and hope like hell that Maddie would understand and forgive her. And hope like hell that she didn't end up paying him half a million dollars for breaching the contract she'd scared herself into signing.

She rolled onto her back, trying to control her breathing so that the tightness in her chest would lessen. And no matter how Maddie reacted, maybe it was time for her to be a bit truer to herself as well.

Chapter Eleven

"Make my video for me." Sofia waited about five seconds after Maddie had answered the phone before blurting out the thing that she'd been thinking about all night. She'd woken up in the early hours with the idea already planted in her brain, and she hadn't been able to talk herself out of it in the hours of wakefulness that had followed. It was both the best and the worst idea she'd ever had and she really wanted Maddie to say yes.

"What?" Maddie sounded sleepy and a little confused. "Make what video?"

"Make the video for 'Not This Time.' The single is out next month, and I still don't have a concept. Write it, design it, direct it." Sofia knew she sounded excited, even a little crazy, but she didn't care. "Please, Mads. You said you really enjoyed making your own videos, that you loved working on Danny's." Sofia faltered for the first time. "I want you to do it, I would trust you to do a great job, and it'll be a great excuse for us to hang out." She swallowed, not realizing until the words were out of her mouth just how much she wanted to do this with Maddie. But all there was on the other end of the call was quiet.

"Just don't make me ride a motorbike. Or a go-cart." Sofia couldn't stop talking, her anxiety getting the better of her. She didn't know what to do with Maddie's silence.

"Have you been at the energy drinks again?" Maddie's voice—low, teasing, and husky with sleep—sent shivers down Sofia's spine. She remembered this Maddie, how she looked and sounded in the mornings, how she woke with her hair tousled, her face pink, her arms and legs wrapped around Sofia possessively. It was something she'd never tired of remembering, and thinking about it now gave her serious goose bumps.

"Of course not. It's seven in the morning."

"I know. I looked at the time when I answered, wondering who the hell would be calling me this early, imagining an emergency that wasn't just you needing someone to make your next video."

Sofia could tell Maddie wasn't really annoyed.

"I also thought it might be someone who didn't know me very well, who didn't know how much I love to sleep in the mornings, but guess what, it was you." Maddie pretending to be grouchy was making Sofia's heart smile. She made herself focus.

"I'm serious, Maddie. Do the video. Do it because I need the help, but also because you'll enjoy it and you'll be great at it. And you get the song, the way I don't think other people do. They don't even want me to release it. Help me prove them wrong." Sofia was close to pleading. It wasn't cool, but she didn't care. She'd never cared about being cool around Maddie. She thought this was a great idea, and she wanted Maddie to trust her instincts for once.

Maddie yawned.

"First, I don't really have the time. I have your house to decorate in case you've forgotten."

"But that's going well. We've worked on it lots lately, and the video won't take you away from it for more than a couple of days."

"And second..." She heard Maddie take in a breath. "Literally everyone we know would say it's a terrible idea. I mean, the paparazzi are outside your house every day, and they're already on overdrive about some imagined reunion between us. They're going to have a lot of stupid stuff to say about us working together on a video. I don't want that and neither should you. It'll be an unhelpful distraction."

Sofia had guessed this would be Maddie's concern.

"We can do it somewhere away from Miami. Some location we can keep private. No one even needs to know until it's all finished. There won't be any blowback for you, I promise."

"And for you? You'd be happy for people to start talking about us again? Noah already seems annoyed about you hanging out with me. He's gonna hate this."

She wanted to tell Maddie that Noah could go fuck himself. And to remind her that Sofia was a lot older, and possibly even a little braver, than she had been when they'd been together in the band. But it wasn't the right time to say any of it. She tried again.

"You're not being very positive about my great idea. You can't see me, but I'm pouting hard right now. Come on, Mads, it'll be great. Rick can help, and I'm convinced you'll enjoy it." She added more seriously, "And if people don't like the idea of us working together, that's for me to worry about. I'm tired of doing everything I'm told. I love this song, and I want to make my own creative choices around it."

"How hard are you pouting?" Maddie sounded amused.

"It's pretty bad I can tell you. If the wind changes direction, it could be devastating for my career." Sofia held her breath.

For a moment, they were both quiet.

"Rick has made some great videos for you." Maddie broke the silence first. "Wouldn't it be easier to just work with him again?"

"No." Her reply was emphatic. "I want you to do it. I want something different, something edgier, and I know you'll come up with something beautiful. Everyone is obsessed with it selling—and I am too, don't get me wrong—but I want to do it justice too. And it'll be a great experience for us both to do it together, to have a joint project." Sofia felt weird saying it out loud. "Can you imagine how cool it'll be to see your name on the credits? People will lose their shit when they see that." She couldn't contain the excitement she felt.

For a beat or two, there was silence again on Maddie's end of the phone.

"That's not why you want me to do it, is it?" There was a tension in Maddie's voice that wasn't there before. "To create some noise?"

"No, no, Maddie, I'm sorry. That's not what I meant at all." Sofia couldn't get the words out fast enough. "I just meant that it'd be cool to have you making the video. It would be a privilege honestly. I've always liked the way you see things, the way your mind works. And I really like the way your videos make me feel." She wasn't sure she could explain. "I just feel like it's time to grow up, to show myself a bit more."

Sofia could hear movement, the noise of a running tap. But no reply.

"What are you doing Thursday?" Sofia asked.

"Working. I have to go and look at tiles and then meet with the decorators."

"Meet me and Rick instead and we can talk about the video." Sofia wasn't going to let it drop. "He's coming to pitch to everyone in the afternoon, but I asked him to meet me separately first to talk through his ideas. Please, Maddie, come and contribute, bring some ideas, bring that amazing creativity of yours that I've always loved." She hadn't meant to use the l-word, though it was true. She didn't want to scare Maddie away by reminding her of the past.

"Okay." The word was accompanied by a sigh. "What time and where?"

Sofia couldn't stop the squeal that escaped. "You won't regret it, Mads. You'll be awesome and it'll be fun. I promise."

"Can I have my coffee now?" Maddie's tone was light.

"Only if you promise to think of video concepts while you're drinking it."

"Hear that sound? That's the sound of you pushing your luck." Maddie laughed softly as she spoke.

"Okay, okay. I'm going. Thank you. I really appreciate you saying yes."

"You didn't give me much choice."

Sofia ended the call after agreeing to a time with Maddie. For the first time in several weeks, she felt like she could breathe easily, like she wasn't carrying a heavy weight on her chest.

Maddie rang the doorbell rather than using the keys she'd been given. She wasn't sure if Noah was around, and the last thing she wanted was to walk in on him and Sofi having some kind of moment together. She recognized the feeling as jealousy and tried to push it away. Trouble was, the more time she spent with Sofi, the worse it got. And the fact she'd had lunch with Daya and chosen not to mention the possibility of doing the video together said everything about how dumb she felt agreeing to do something that would mean her spending even more time with Sofi.

As soon as Sofi opened the door, the shouts of the paparazzi became more intense. They were calling Sofi's name, Maddie's name, asking them both to turn, pose, and smile.

"You came." Sofi offered her a shy smile as she spoke, leaning on the door and seeming oblivious to the photographers. "I wasn't sure you would."

Maddie couldn't help but stare. Sofi looked great. Bare feet, faded jeans that hugged her curves, and a fitted white shirt with enough buttons unfastened to reveal a chevron of smooth brown skin dipping down to her cleavage. She looked hot. There was no other word for it. At least not any polite ones. Sofi held her gaze and Maddie felt things shift a little. She couldn't deny that this feeling was attraction. She cleared her throat and held up a large portfolio folder.

"I did my homework."

Maddie caught the up and down look that Sofi gave her and felt an unwelcome throb of arousal between her legs. Sofi looked at her a moment longer and then stepped back, giving Maddie space to pass inside.

"I'm excited." Sofi reached out and touched her arm.

"Me too."

They were talking about the video, about the meeting. Of course they were. Maddie shook her head slightly, hoping to shake some sense into it.

"Want a drink? Rick's already here, but we haven't started. We're meeting the others downtown at three, so we have plenty of time."

Maddie nodded. "Coffee would be good. But can I just use the bathroom?" Her nerves were already getting the better of her.

"Sure." Sofi smiled warmly.

She stood in Sofi's bathroom trying to compose herself. Rick Wahlberg was the best in the business right now, and Maddie wanted two things—not to embarrass herself in front of him, and to make Sofi proud of her. She had struggled for hours last night to come up with something suitable, and then, after a couple of glasses of wine, she just let her instincts take over. What she'd come up with suited the song perfectly and she'd gone to bed happy. But the morning brought an awareness that the concept was far too challenging for Sofi, so she'd quickly adapted it and come up with something that was safer but still suited the song. Luckily, the sketches being in pencil meant most of the adaptations were easy to make.

Maddie toweled off her hands and ran a hand through her hair one last time before taking in and releasing a few deep breaths. As she emerged into the living room, she could see that Sofi had dragged the coffee table closer to the couch and cleared its surface. Her portfolio—still zipped shut—lay on the table, next to a white mug, and Rick and Sofi were at either ends of the couch, both of them looking at her expectantly.

Maddie sat in the space they had left between them and leaned forward to unzip the folder and pull out a loose sheaf of sketches.

"I'm excited about the chance to collaborate, Madison. I'm Rick." He offered her a hand to shake. "I had a look at the videos you worked on before." He nodded. "Very good." He put on his glasses and sat forward in his seat.

He was probably being polite, but Maddie couldn't help but be encouraged by his words. She moved her head from side to side to loosen the tension in her neck.

"Come on, Mads, show us what you've got." Sofi offered her a reassuring smile.

She took in a breath.

"So, we're in Paris, and we're shooting in black and white." She shrugged a little self-consciously and lifted the first sketch. "Sofi is a photographer. She's part of a crowd of paparazzi, but she's not like them. She's on the edge of the group, she seems more serious, and she's the only woman among them. They are following a man, an actor, around Paris taking pictures of him. He's handsome and sophisticated of course. He's at a premiere, arriving there with his wife, then we see him having coffee outside a chic little café. Then he's up early and going to the gym, maybe going to a gallery opening and whatever else we need to see him doing to understand that he's rich and his life is glamorous. The point is that he and Sofi see each other a lot—because Sofi is following him around Paris with a bunch of other photographers, intruding on his life.

"And from our viewpoint, we can see that the man is going out of his way to give Sofi the best shots, and that he sometimes waits to make sure Sofi sees what he's doing and can get a good shot. We don't understand their relationship, but we think maybe he's as intrigued by Sofi as the paparazzi are with him." She was lifting her sketches to show them the visuals that went with her words.

"We cut to the man saying good-bye to his wife. It's the evening and she's going on a business trip or something. Moments after she leaves," Maddie couldn't help but pause and swallow, her anxiety bubbling up, "a woman arrives at the house by taxi and our actor kisses her on the lips before ushering her inside. We are left to assume it's a secret lover. We see Sofi across the street leaning on her car—this time she's the only photographer there—and we see that she is easily able to capture the whole wife leaving/woman arriving scene with her camera. But rather than do that, she lowers her camera and puts the cap back on the lens. We understand that she doesn't want to hurt the man by revealing his cheating. She looks sad and we understand she also has feelings for the actor.

"Before going into his house, the actor looks back, catches sight of Sofi, and witnesses her lowering her camera, refusing the money shot. They look at each other for a lingering moment. Sofi walks off and gets into her car. The actor goes inside." She looked from Rick to Sofia, worrying about their reaction.

"Is that the end?" Rick asked.

"Not really, no." Maddie pulled another sketch from the pile, feeling less sure of herself.

"Go on." Sofi put her hand on Maddie's arm. The touch made her shiver. She cleared her throat.

"Next scene. Sofi is again outside the house. In her car with a long lens trained on the front door. It's late and she's alone. The actor comes to the door. We see him framed for a few seconds. He is holding a coffee which he takes outside, walking slowly to the car to hand it to Sofi with a longing look. Their hands brush."

She heard Sofi swallow.

"And then we cut to Sofi walking up to the front door to return the coffee cup and the actor opens the door kinda wide. They stand looking at each other, and rather than hand him the cup, we watch as she walks into the house, trailing a hand across the man's arm as she passes. We cut and our view is now that of a photographer in the street outside. We see from the street that the actor moves to the curtains to close them—basically letting us know that they are going to be getting down to something and he wants privacy."

She took in a breath.

"And then we watch as Sofi moves next to him and stops him from doing it, throwing the curtains wide open again. They are framed in the window looking at each other. They kiss passionately. And that's where it ends." Maddie put her hands facedown on the table and made herself breathe evenly, trying to seem much more relaxed than she was.

"For me, 'Not This Time' is about being in charge, about no longer doing what's expected of you and not accepting it when people offer you too little. It could be addressed to a partner or anyone in your life really. It says that I want things for me, on my terms, and this time, I'm not going to accept less. It's true for the actor who's not living the life he wants, and it's true for the photographer who wants more for herself than to just photograph, to witness other people's lives." Maddie had run through versions of this speech in the mirror last night, but it had sounded so much better, so much more righteous before she'd bottled it and changed the woman she'd originally scripted Sofi following across Paris to a man. The song was about being more courageous, and sitting next to Sofi, she couldn't help but feel the irony of her refusal to follow her own instincts for fear Sofi would think she was trying to "out" her and ruin her career.

There was a long moment of silence, and Maddie thought she'd blown it. Even without the same-sex storyline, showing Sofi as a paparazzi, falling for and sleeping with a married man was incredibly risky for someone as wholesome as Sofia Flores.

"I mean, I know it's rough and needs some work, but I didn't have much time. And I know it's a bit of a risk to portray Sofi that way, but I was aiming for something edgy, something that suited the vibe of the song. I don't expect you to go with it if it's wrong. I mean, I'm happy for you to tell me that it's not right." Maddie's confidence was evaporating, and she was speaking to fill the silence, to avoid hearing from both Rick and Sofi about how much they hated it.

"Rick?" Sofi invited him to speak. Maddie cared about his opinion—he was Rick Wahlberg after all—but she cared more about what Sofi thought.

He sat back in the seat and put his hands behind his head as if stretching. He waited a beat.

"I love it." His face broke out into a grin. "I like the vibe—the watching, the being watched. There's something dark and predatory about it. And seeing Sofia in charge like that is perfect for the song."

Maddie let out a breath, not quite believing that he liked it. She dared to turn to Sofi who, without warning, leaned over and pulled Maddie into a tight hug. Maddie let herself enjoy it for a minute before gently extricating herself and holding Sofi at arm's length.

"You haven't said anything, Sofi. Do you like it?"

Sofi looked from Maddie to Rick and back again. "I guess I'm just a little confused." Maddie felt her heart sink. Sofi didn't like it.

"I'm confused by this." Sofi reached for a sketch at the bottom of the pile, pulled it out, and placed it on the table in front of them. Maddie cursed inwardly. After she redrafted all the sketches, she'd thought she'd left the originals at home. Somehow this one must have attached itself to the pile. It showed the window to the house and, framed against it, two female figures were kissing.

"I changed my mind." She couldn't get the words out fast enough. "I thought at first that maybe it might work with the actor being a woman, but then I realized it wouldn't and I changed it." She attempted a shrug, as if to say it was no big deal.

"Oh, that's interesting." Rick sat forward. "Same story but with a woman being photographed and Sofia ending up in her house at the end?"

Maddie nodded.

"I think that suits the song even better." He turned to Sofi. "It's a little more subversive, and that thing about being true to yourself makes more sense if our lead is a woman. If it's a man, then he's just replacing his wife with a series of younger women, including Sofia, and that's meh, but if it's a woman replacing her husband with a woman, then it speaks to hiding and wanting to be seen. I like this version even more." He tapped the sketch.

Maddie felt her insides churning. Sofi was silently staring at the sketch, and she couldn't help but think she'd upset her somehow. After what felt like a long time, she lifted her eyes to Maddie's.

"This version. With a woman. We'll do this. The concept is everything I hoped for. Dark, edgy, and sexy as hell. I chose the song just so I could do and feel something different, and because it has something important to say about longing and regret and having courage. And this story is perfect for it. You nailed it, Mads, just like I knew you would. I'm just sorry that you couldn't trust me enough to show me the original idea you had." Sofi was full of emotion as she spoke, and this time, Maddie was the one who pulled her into a hug. And this time, the hug lasted a little longer.

Beside them, Rick coughed an exaggerated "ahem," and they both turned to look at him. He had an amused look on his face. "A few things before we decide that this is what we pitch to your people later." His face turned serious. "Paris is a tricky place to film, and it's going to be expensive to fly everyone over there. We can pull it off, but you could just keep the same concept and shoot it here." He waited for a response.

Maddie held her breath. She really wanted it to be in Paris, but she couldn't expect Sofi to necessarily feel the same way. And Sofi was the one who'd have to pay for it.

"It needs to be Paris. I'm going to be there anyway, and I really want to stay true to the concept. We can make it work." Sofi sounded decisive, and Maddie felt her heart lift with happiness.

"What else?" Sofi asked.

"You must already know this, but your people are going to hate this, Sofia. I can't think of a video that's more opposite to everything you've done before. It's moody, it's dark, you're playing a character that most people will have no sympathy for, and you're not singing the song to camera once." He looked at Maddie for confirmation that was the case. She nodded. "And, well, if we go with this version," he tapped the sketch of the two women kissing, "they're going to say that it's too risky for someone with your fan base." He shrugged as if to say that he didn't care but everyone else would.

"I agree, they're going to hate it. But I don't care. It's time I showed a bit more of my own truth." Sofi held Maddie's gaze as she spoke, and Maddie felt a fluttering in her belly.

"What else?" Sofi asked Rick. "You look like there's something you're not saying."

"You could play it a little safer and skip the kiss at the end. It wouldn't change the vibe entirely, and it might make it more palatable to the record company. And to your fans."

"I agree." Maddie didn't give Sofi a chance to respond. "I thought it needed it, but now I think it's too much and Sofi can't be seen to—" She stopped herself. "I just don't think the video needs a big ending like that. Maybe it's better to leave people wondering."

Sofia was touched that Maddie was trying to protect her, but she couldn't help but think this was her chance to show Maddie that she could be courageous when she needed to be. Putting out a video that had Sofia playing the part of a woman who loves a woman, a woman who kisses another woman, was a risky career move, but it was also exciting. She kept telling herself she was sick of hiding. This was her chance to be seen.

"It needs the kiss." Sofia nodded in Maddie's direction. "I think it makes it much clearer that the song is about finally stepping up and taking what you want. You can't have a song like that and then chicken out at the end."

Sofia hoped that Maddie understood what she was really saying. For all her big talk about being willing to live her relationship with Maddie out in the open, they'd never had the chance to even consider it. And, in the years since, she'd never publicly acknowledged that she was someone who loved women. In fact, for the sake of her career, she'd actively gone out of her way to hide it. But Maddie made her want to be braver. She always had.

Rick and Sofia both turned their gaze to Maddie, waiting for her to respond.

"It's not my decision." Maddie shrugged and looked away.

Sofia put a hand on her leg and Maddie looked up at her. On impulse, Sofia leaned across and kissed Maddie on the forehead. Maddie blinked with surprise.

"Thank you." She was thanking Maddie for the sketches, for the video ideas, but she was also thanking her for giving Sofia another chance to be the woman she wanted to be.

"We better get going." Rick stood up, looking at his watch. "If we're going to be shouted at and told we're lunatics who are collectively trying to ruin Sofia's career, I at least want to be on time." He laughed and headed to the door. "I'll see you there."

"Yeah." Sofia nodded as Rick headed for the front door.

"He's right. They're gonna fucking hate this." Maddie looked fearful.

"Probably. But I love it and he loves it too, so I don't care. They want me to keep being the same peppy little pop princess. But I'm sick of that person, maybe I always was. I'm ready for this, and if my fans don't like it then maybe they're not the kind of fans I want." Sofia remembered saying something like that to Maddie once before, but she'd lacked the courage to see it through. Not this time. With Maddie by her side again, she felt like she could be exactly who she needed to be.

She helped Maddie gather up the sketches and put them back in her folder. She held up the sketch that Maddie hadn't meant to show them. "You really weren't going to tell us you'd written me as gay the first time around?"

Maddie shook her head. "I guess I just got worried and decided to play it safe."

"But you kissed a woman in your video?"

"It's different."

"How is it?"

"I worry that it'll backfire, that people will think you're trying too hard to be edgy, that people will think you're—" She ran a hand through her hair. It was always a giveaway that she had something she didn't want to say.

"People will think I'm what?"

"That people will think you're a straight girl engaging in a bit of queer baiting for marketing purposes. I was already out, so seeing me kiss a woman wasn't queer bait, it was kind of expected."

Sofia blinked at Maddie. It hadn't been what she'd expected her to say.

"I'm not straight and I'm not queer baiting. You know that better than anyone. This is important to me. It's part of who I am."

"Part of who you were," Maddie said. "And a part of you that you haven't shown to anyone. The world sees you all loved up with Noah and has assumed you're super-straight, and since you've never told them anything different, it's a fair assumption. So making a video where you kiss a woman when you've never even talked about that part of your sexuality might seem like attention-seeking."

"Or me trying to come out finally." Sofia couldn't believe that Maddie didn't understand.

"Is that what you think this is?" Maddie pointed at the sketch.

"It could be my chance. I was imagining talking about it, about the song and the video and being more open about things."

Maddie had turned to face Sofia, and her gaze was more than Sofia could cope with. It literally made it hard for her to breathe.

"But I wrote the song about you, so talking about the song, the video, talking about having 'loved women,' will mean talking about you. And we never wanted that, never wanted people to know about us."

"You wrote it about me?" Maddie looked shocked.

"I'm sorry. I know it's weird to still be writing about what happened, but sometimes, the feelings don't always seem like feelings from five years ago, and I still need to write about it sometimes."

Sofia felt pathetic. Maddie hadn't been anything other than friendly. She hadn't given Sofia any indication that she wanted to get pulled into any drama. In fact she had carefully kept her distance from all of it. A voice in her head told her to slow down and be more careful. She didn't want Maddie to leave again.

"And Noah? What will he think about his girlfriend coming out about her woman-loving past?" Maddie sounded pissed. It wasn't what Sofia had intended. She thought Maddie would be proud of her for finally being more honest.

"We haven't talked about it, obviously. But he already knows. About us, I mean. I haven't hidden that from him." The deception wasn't intentional, but it was there. Every time they talked about Noah without Sofia being honest about who he was to her, she was deceiving Maddie. It didn't feel good.

"Well, he doesn't exactly seem relaxed about it, about me being around again. All this is going to freak him out. And I'm not sure I'd blame him for reacting." Maddie pushed on.

They were going to be late for the meeting, but Sofia knew this was important.

"He's like my mom. He's always been," she searched for the right word, "concerned. Said that I shouldn't talk about that part of me, that the fans wouldn't understand and would turn their back on me." They had had the conversation so many times, and more than once she had told him he was wrong, but then she continued to pretend, continued to stay in the closet. It was easier, safer, and—yes—better for her career. She hadn't been brave. She knew that.

Sofia slumped back into the couch. It was hard to face up to how much of a coward she'd turned into once she lost Maddie.

"He might be right." Maddie's voice was kinder now.

"But if I don't start being honest now, I'll be trapped in this cage forever." Sofia let out a frustrated breath. "I should have just told everyone about us five years ago. You hated me anyway, and I might have gotten a bit more sympathy when you all blamed me for leaving." She was joking but also not. "We should go." Sofia pushed herself up off the couch, not wanting Maddie's pity.

"Sofi." Maddie was gazing at her, a serious look in her eyes. "I never hated you. I wish I could have. It might have helped it all hurt a lot less." She lowered her eyes and Sofia waited, her breath held, until Maddie lifted them again. "And I'm really proud of you for saying yes to this. I'm sorry to be so scared about it. I know I should be the one supporting you the most."

Sofia couldn't say it, but with Maddie by her side, she had enough courage to take on the world. The problem was, as she knew from bitter experience, when Maddie wasn't there, the bravery evaporated.

"Let's just make a really cool video." Sofia made herself ignore the butterflies in her belly. Rick was right. They would all hate it. It wasn't going to be a fun meeting. "And hope my record company doesn't drop me when we explain the concept to them." She pulled Maddie to her feet.

"Could they do that?"

"In theory. I mean, we both have get out clauses. But I've made a lot of money for them, so it would probably take a lot more than this. They're gonna be very unhappy though. My mom too."

They stood awkwardly toe to toe until Sofia wrapped her arms around Maddie tightly. Maddie responded and they stood, holding each other for a long time.

Maddie dropped her arms first, picked up her portfolio, and ran a hand through her hair. Sofia picked up her car keys and they headed out into the hallway.

"You're really gonna do this?" Maddie asked Sofia as they stood together on the threshold of the house, looking out at their cars.

"We're really gonna do this." She turned to Maddie before pulling the door shut behind them.

CHAPTER TWELVE

"Hey. How're you doing?" Sofi sounded a little flat on the other end of the line.

"I'm okay. You?"

Maddie was happy to get the call. She'd spent the day forcing herself not to call Sofi, not wanting to seem like she was checking up. When she'd been working at the house yesterday, Sofi had seemed tense and out of sorts. Maddie still wasn't convinced that she was well enough to go on tour, but it seemed like she was the only one who thought so.

"I'm at the gym. This call is gonna count toward my goal of spending an hour here."

"The gym, huh?"

Sofi hated the gym almost as much as Maddie did.

"My mom suggested that I needed some exercise to get in shape. In that way that moms do. She's right though. I've put on weight. It's not good."

"That's bullshit." Sofi had always struggled to feel good about her shape. Her mom should know better. "You look pretty perfect to me." Maddie spoke without thinking, simply wanting Sofi to understand how beautiful she was.

They both fell quiet, and Maddie worried that she'd made Sofi feel uncomfortable with the compliment.

"I wasn't sure if—"

"Did you—"

They both spoke at once.

"Go on." Sofi let Maddie go first.

"I wasn't sure if you'd be having second thoughts about the video. After everyone was so freaked out about it, I mean." Maddie had wanted to say it to her yesterday, but hadn't had chance. Both Felix and Rosa had been around for most of the day. It had almost felt like Sofi was being chaperoned. "I just wanted to say that I wouldn't blame you. I wouldn't mind if you went with something else, something less risky. Maybe they're right to worry."

There was a long silence on the other end of the call.

"If you're having second thoughts about being involved after the way they all behaved, just say so. I wouldn't blame you either. I'm sure you're sorry you ever got involved."

"Sofi." She didn't want them to argue. "Of course I still want to do the video. I told you already how much I'm looking forward to it. I'm just giving you an out if you want one and saying I'm not going to judge you for choosing something safer."

"I know it's not the safest choice. But it's going to give me the chance to say something important about my identity. Maybe not everyone will understand it, maybe a lot of people won't want to see me that way, but it's a chance to show people a part of who I am that I've kept hidden. You know that, better than anyone, and that's why it seems so right that we do this together."

The sincerity of Sofi's words made her feel so many conflicting emotions. Fear, pride, excitement. "You could just have that part of your identity in private. It doesn't make it any less valid." She had had the same battles with herself. She was a private person. She might not have chosen to come out if Lara hadn't forced her to.

"I think it does. I think people like me have to stand up and be visible if we can."

Maddie tried to be positive for Sofi's sake. "I got so many messages after I came out. So many kids, so many young women. For every person who told me I'd rot in hell, there were five thanking me for standing up for them."

"Wow," Sofi exclaimed softly.

"Yeah. Though I felt like a fraud because I hadn't meant to come out. I'd probably still be hiding if it wasn't for Lara. At the time, I hated her for exposing me when I wasn't ready, but I probably should go back and thank her."

"Really?"

"Really. It's hard to pretend to be something you're not. It's tiring. And after I had Mateo, I vowed that I would always be honest, always be myself so that I'd be a good role model for him."

They were both quiet for a while.

"Sometimes people have to lie. Or they think they do. They can get boxed into a corner and one lie becomes another lie until you've built a house of lies to live in and you can't find a way out without the whole thing falling down." Maddie heard Sofi sniff.

"Sofi, are you crying?"

"No, no, sorry, it's nothing. Hormones maybe. Or lack of caffeine. I'm just tired. Sorry."

Maddie wasn't at all convinced.

"You can talk to me."

"I know."

Maddie waited.

"I don't suppose you want to go to the diner, eat some Cuban food with me? I'll be entitled to a plateful after all this exercise." Sofi emphasized the last three words.

"I tell you what," Maddie and Daya had planned to hang out that afternoon, "grab some croquetas to go and come over to my place." The words didn't come from Maddie's head, they came from her heart. Sofi sounded like she really needed some company. "I have Jet Skis. They're like the go-carts of the ocean. And it's about time you overcame your fear of go-carts."

"Jet Skis." Sofi sounded amused.

"Me and Mateo could give you a lesson. I mean, if you had the time, and if you're not too chicken." Maddie made herself sound more casual than she felt about Sofi saying yes.

"I'm supposed to be going through set lists and tour schedules with Felix later."

"Of course. I wasn't thinking, you're going in a couple of days. You're too busy. Sorry." Maddie felt silly for even suggesting it. Sofi wasn't likely to choose a play date with her and Mateo over things that were important for her career, but she couldn't help but feel deflated anyway.

"Tell you what, let me call Felix. I'm sure he can find something else to do this afternoon that doesn't involve me."

Maddie heard the smile in Sofi's voice and felt a tingle of happiness.

"Text me your address and I'll come over once I've finished disappointing him. Do you want me to bring anything apart from croquetas?"

"Just your own sweet self." Maddie couldn't stop the words from coming out. She felt a deep blush rise from her feet to her cheeks.

"Did I hear that right?"

"Er, no. Maybe." Maddie groaned. She used to be cool once. Was still kinda cool actually. But never around Sofi.

"I'm guessing that you're blushing hard right now." There was a smile in Sofi's voice. "I always loved it when you blushed—I still do if I'm being honest." The words were low, sultry, and flirtatious, but Maddie was pretty sure that Sofi was just playing with her. She'd probably be embarrassed if she knew the effect the words were having low down in Maddie's core.

"Come any time after midday." She couldn't wait to hang up. She needed two hands for the massive face-palm she owed herself.

"I'll bring my sweet self just as soon as I can." Sofi's parting words didn't spare Maddie's blushes.

"Damn." What the hell was she doing? This thing with Sofi was something she needed to get a grip on. However unhappy she seemed, however much Maddie was attracted to her, Sofi was in a relationship. And even if she wasn't, Maddie had spent the last three weeks telling herself that getting too close to Sofi was a bad idea. She shook her head and cursed again softly. Obviously, inviting Sofi to come hang out at her house—in her swimsuit—was not the best way to guard her heart and Daya was going to give her all kinds of shit about it.

Sofia had intended to call Felix, collect her swimsuit and some food, and head straight over to Maddie's, but it hadn't been that easy. The call hadn't gone well. He'd been annoyed with her for canceling and made things sound difficult to rearrange. Eventually, Sofia had just told him she wasn't coming and he needed to find a way to make it work. She hated arguing, but she was also sick of being told what she could and couldn't do.

Within minutes, her mom called.

"Hey, Mama. I guess Felix just called you to snitch on me."

"What are you doing, Sofi? What's gotten into you lately?" Her mom sounded concerned, but Sofia couldn't help but think that the concern was about her missing the meeting rather than anything else.

"I took the afternoon off. I felt like I wanted to. Is that too much to ask?"

On the other end of the phone, there was quiet and she felt herself get tense.

"Mama, the answer you're looking for is, no, it's not too much to ask. You work hard, you've worked hard for the last ten years, and in the grand scheme of things, an afternoon off when you're supposed to be recuperating won't matter a bit." Sofia got the words out and then allowed herself to take a breath. "In fact, an afternoon off to relax at the beach with a friend is something I should do a lot more of, for my own mental health."

"Of course you should take time off when you need it, cariño. It's just that we don't have much time before we leave and we need to plan. You can't be walking out on things we've scheduled. And—"

"And what, Mama?" Sofia made an effort to swallow her anger as much as she could. "Why don't you say what you're really annoyed about?" Sofia knew, she just needed her mom to say it. They had to have this conversation at some point.

"You being like this is because of Madison, I know it is. It's not good that she's back just when you need to be concentrating on other things. She's bad for you. She always was. She makes you lose focus."

It was pretty blunt, but it was no worse than Sofia was expecting. The effort of the conversation made Sofia sit down on the edge of her bed, amongst the dozens of tops and shorts and bikinis that she had pulled out of her closet and drawers. She'd been trying to choose something to wear to Maddie's when her mom had called. She absentmindedly picked up a red bikini that she used to look good in and set it to one side. She ran a hand through her hair, feeling weary all of a sudden.

"I was tired and needing a break long before Maddie and I got friendly again. I've been doing this for so long now and it's exhausting, and of course I know it's important, but sometimes it's just not fun anymore. I'm thirty-two, and I want a life as well as a career." She lay down backward on her bed. The strength of the feeling was a surprise even to her.

"And Maddie is not bad for me. You don't even know her. She's supportive and hardworking, and it's good for me to have her around to talk to, to spend time with. None of you understand what this is like for me, but she does." Sofia felt the truth of it like an arrow thudding into her chest. Maddie did understand her, she always had.

Sofia heard her mom make a scoffing noise, and she felt anger rising in her body.

"Did you have something you wanted to say, Mama?"

"I don't want us to argue, Sofia."

"But here we are."

"Maddie made you very unhappy. She was horrible to you, about you. They all were. I can't believe you've forgotten. I know you think she loved you, but if she did, why did she walk away and why did she treat you like that? She is not a good person and it's not good for you, or for your career, to be getting close to her again. Did you forget what people said about the two of you the first time around? It wasn't nice. And now it's going to be much worse. She already told everyone about her own private life, and now she's encouraging you to make videos where you run around Paris chasing women. She is a terrible influence."

Sofia was in no mood to hear any of it. It wasn't just the casual homophobia, it was that her mother's concern was always as much for her career as it was for her happiness. And every time Sofia realized that, it hurt.

"I don't need to be reminded that we hurt each other, Mama, I was there. And, in case you need reminding, it was me that ruined things by leaving the band. Everything that came after that was my fault, not hers. And having Maddie back in my life is making me happy for the first time in a long while, so I'm not letting her go again.

If you can't be happy for me about that, then I don't know what to say." She took in a breath. "And I've told you a thousand times that I'm a lesbian. I know you know that because you've spent the last ten years encouraging me to hide it. I'm sorry you hate it, but I love women." It wasn't even true. Sofia had only ever loved one woman.

But trying to explain any of it to her mom was pointless. She stood up. She was going to spend the afternoon with Maddie and Mateo, and she was going to enjoy it. Nothing her mom could say would change her mind about it.

"What's the point of selling records, filling stadiums, winning awards, if I'm not happy while I'm doing it? There should be afternoons where I hang at the beach with friends and don't feel weighted down by everything. There should be whole weeks like that."

The reality of it hit hard. Sofia had been so busy fighting to stay at the top that she had forgotten how to enjoy making music, and she had definitely forgotten that there was more to life than her career. It had taken Maddie coming back into her life to show her that things were missing.

"I've gotta go." Sofia ended the call and busied herself getting ready. Her choice of words when talking to her mom had been interesting. She hadn't wanted to let Maddie go the first time around either, but Maddie had turned her back on her, and on their relationship. And she hadn't been able to do a thing about it. This time, she had a chance to try for a different outcome.

Sofia hummed softly to herself as she parked alongside Maddie's house. It wasn't all that fancy by Ocean Drive standards, but it looked like it was in pristine condition and she liked the fact that this end of North Beach was quieter, with the houses more spread out. Before even getting out of the car, Sofia could hear and smell the ocean which, looking past Maddie's house, was barely fifty yards away.

She reached across to the seat next to her and picked up her backpack. She shook her head at how heavy it was. She hadn't been able to choose an outfit, not liking how she looked in any of them, and in frustration, knowing that—thanks to her mom—she was much later than she said she'd be, she'd put on the red bikini, covered it with shorts and a tee, and shoved several other items of beachwear into the bag in case she changed her mind.

She grabbed the bag of food from the back seat, walked up the path, and rang the bell. Her heart was beating as fast as if she'd run here. She tried to calm herself. She wasn't on a date. She had no reason to be anxious or afraid. This was Maddie and Mateo and they were going to have a relaxing afternoon together just hanging out and taking out Maddie's Jet Skis. *And I'm gonna see Maddie in her swimsuit.* Sofia's pulse quickened unhelpfully at the thought.

The door opened wide enough for Mateo to poke his head into the gap.

"Fia," he said his version of her name excitedly and reached out a hand for her. Her heart melted at the warm welcome. The door opened fully, and she was astonished to see Daya looking at her with a cautious expression.

"Hey, Sofi," Daya said as Mateo wrapped his arms around her legs.

"Daya. Wow. Good to see you." Sofi let herself be pulled into the house by Mateo, his tiny hand tugging at hers. Her mind was racing. She hadn't expected Daya.

"Maddie's just taking a quick shower." Daya led them into a large open living area. "She won't be long." Daya was measuring her words carefully, and Sofi felt awkward. Like they were strangers, not two people who had lived on a tour bus together for the best part of five years.

"I didn't know you were going to be here." Sofia cringed. Her choice of words sounded like she didn't want to see Daya. And she did. Leaving the band had cost her a friendship with Daya, as well as her relationship with Maddie. She was glad to see her. It was just a little weird.

"I live in Miami." Daya's tone wasn't friendly, but it wasn't unfriendly either. "I'm around sometimes."

"I know. Maddie said. It's good, it's great. That you can see each other. I just meant that I didn't know you were coming today." It wasn't her most coherent sentence.

Maddie appeared at the bottom of the stairs, and the sight of her made Sofia's mouth go dry. Her hair was still damp from the shower, and she was wearing frayed cutoffs and a white linen shirt. The shirt hung open and did little to cover the black bikini top and the beautiful creamy skin visible underneath. Sofia told herself—as she had done every thirty minutes since Maddie had invited her to the house—that they were just friends hanging out for the afternoon, but the ache low down in her center suggested that her body didn't quite believe her. Mateo released her hand and ran to Maddie. She scooped him up, gave him a kiss, and put him down again.

"Hi, Sofi." Maddie lifted a hand in greeting, and as Sofia managed a nod in response, she noticed a look pass between Maddie and Daya. Daya's raised eyebrows weren't hard to miss. And when Maddie shrugged and tied the shirt loosely at the waist, Sofia was grateful for the respite, hoping Maddie covering up a little would help her recover the power of speech.

"That's a pretty big bag for an afternoon at the beach." Maddie pointed at the backpack on Sofia's shoulder. "Tell me it's not all croquetas."

"They're in here." She held up the brown bag. "Croquetas and," Sofia crouched down next to Mateo, "coconut pastelitos." She was rewarded with a big smile.

"Oh boy. He's your friend for life now." Maddie jerked a thumb in Daya's direction. "This one too. You wouldn't guess from looking at her, but she's made of one-third water and two-thirds flaky pastry."

Sofia smiled, happy to have done the right thing.

Daya turned from Maddie and addressed Sofia properly for the first time. "Maddie figured that since you guys have managed to bury the hatchet, you and I should try to do the same. I agreed, and that was before I knew you had pastelitos."

"Sounds good to me." Sofia shuffled from one foot to the other, unable to hide her anxiety. This was weird. She was going to be hanging out with the two people who knew her better than anyone but, after everything that had happened between them, were practically strangers.

"Daya, why don't you show Sofi around while I get the Jet Skis ready and put some chairs out on the deck." Maddie reached out for Mateo's hand. "Mateo's gonna come help me."

As Maddie walked through the large sliding glass door leading to the deck, she turned back and caught Sofia blatantly checking out her ass. Maddie's eyes widened before she looked away quickly. Sofia felt a little ashamed of herself, but given how incredible Maddie looked, she wasn't surprised by the hot feeling in her body.

Daya headed over to the couch and motioned for Sofia to follow. Daya's face was much more serious than it had been when Maddie was with them, and she guessed she wasn't getting a tour. A sick feeling started in her stomach. Daya had a sharp tongue—Sofia had watched her lash out with it plenty of times—and she really hoped that this wasn't going to be one of them. They had a lot of hurtful things they could say to each other.

"It's been a long time." Daya sounded calm enough. "Probably too long. And I'm sorry about that, about all of it."

"It's—" Sofia started to respond, intending to say to Daya that it was okay, that she understood, but she didn't. She'd eventually understood why Maddie had stayed away, but Daya hadn't been heartbroken and she could have found a way to keep being Sofia's friend, even at a distance. "You and Maddie see a lot of each other?" Sofia already knew from Maddie that they'd stayed close, but she wanted Daya to say it.

"It's been easier since she moved back here. I'm away sometimes, but when I'm home, yeah. It's been great getting to know Mateo."

"I live in Miami too—when I'm not traveling." Sofia wanted Daya to know that she had been here the whole time. "I would have loved to have seen you. We were close. It was hard to lose you as well as Maddie." She made herself say it.

"I know. At first, I was just mad as hell at you for leaving, for thinking you were too good for us. But then I calmed down and figured it was an opportunity we'd all like to have been given. I even told Maddie not to hate you for it, to try to at least save the relationship, even if the band was finished. But when they told us all that stuff about how badly you'd used us, how you'd been plotting to leave for months, I was raging pretty hard for a long time. And I hated seeing what it did to Maddie, seeing how much being used by you hurt her, so I took sides. I'm not sorry about that."

"I didn't use you or Maddie. I didn't want to lose her. And I would have stayed in the band longer if they'd let me. But the record company had already decided I was a lost cause and they were going to make the band work with just the three of you. After it all happened, I was in pieces too. You think losing Maddie, losing you and Suzy, was easy for me?"

"It can't have been easy. I know that now. But at the time I just thought you were selfish and callous and deserved everything we threw at you. All that success you had while the rest of us were struggling? I resented it. And I was too naive to understand they were playing with us, happy we were tearing each other down because the feuding was good for sales."

Sofia could tell from her face that Daya had something else to say. "What?" She was tired of things not being said.

"When Maddie said she was working on your house, I told her to stay away because I didn't want her to get sucked in, didn't want her to get hurt again. But Maddie's made it clear that you're not the person they said you were, that you suffered just as much as we did, even if it didn't look like it. And I figured that if you and Maddie can sort things out, then there's no reason why we can't spend an afternoon together without it being awful."

"You told her to stay away?"

"Yeah, sorry. I reminded her that you guys had crashed and burned pretty badly once before and said I still didn't trust you."

Daya had always been blunt.

"We were good together for a long time, Daya. She was my best friend as well as the love of my life and I never stopped missing her. It's been so good to be able to spend time with her." Sofia didn't know why she so badly wanted Daya to approve of her and Maddie being in each other's lives again, but she did. She needed someone to understand why they were doing this.

"I know that and Maddie has said the same thing to me."

Sofia felt her heart race at the idea that Maddie might have missed her just as much as she had.

"But I also saw up close just how awful those months after you left were." She shrugged.

Sofia wanted to object, wanted to remind Daya that she, and everyone else, had closed a protective circle around Maddie and frozen her out. And she'd been left lonely. Lonely and brokenhearted. It had taken throwing herself into her career to feel like life had any kind of a point.

Daya put a hand on Sofia's arm, bringing her back into the here and now. "But Maddie tells me you're both doing okay with it and you're being nice to each other so I'm trying not to worry so much."

"Of course we are." Sofia couldn't imagine doing anything to hurt Maddie.

"And you have Noah now and you guys seem pretty serious and solid?" The question was a strange one, and Sofia resented having to talk about Noah yet again. She was so sick of the lying.

"Not particularly serious and not particularly solid."

"Really?" Daya's eyes widened. It obviously wasn't the answer she'd been expecting. It wasn't the answer Sofia had expected to give either.

"Yeah. It's just…" The contract he'd signed meant that she couldn't tell the truth—though she badly wanted to—but it didn't mean she had to act like he was the love of her life. "It's the scheduling. We're never together. It's impossible to make it serious. I know everyone always acts like we're about to get married, but it's nothing like that. We're probably not even going to last much longer." It was true of course, but not in the way that Daya would understand it.

"Okay, wow, I'm sorry."

"Don't be. We both got into it with our eyes open."

Daya dropped her eyes to the cushion next to her and began picking at the seam, avoiding Sofia's gaze.

"What?" Sofia couldn't help but ask.

"Nothing." Daya stood up, seeming flustered all of a sudden. "Hey, I'm supposed to be giving you a tour."

"Daya?" Sofia didn't move. "Give me the tour in a minute. First, say what you're trying not to say."

"Does Maddie know? About you and Noah not being very solid."

"We haven't talked about it." Sofia was in dangerous waters. They hadn't talked about it because it wasn't strictly the truth. She was telling Daya a lie because she was sick of telling lies. There was logic there somewhere.

Daya nodded.

"She's settled and happy here." Daya looked out to the deck where Maddie was busying herself carrying life jackets down to the jetty. Mateo trailed behind her carrying a large teddy bear that was wearing a life jacket of its own. "She doesn't need things to get complicated."

Sofia tracked Maddie and Mateo until they dipped down the steps at the end of the deck and went out of sight.

"I get that." She wanted to tell Daya to mind her own business, but at the same time, Daya was probably the only person in her life who really understood just how much she had loved Maddie. "But we bumped into each other so randomly that it's impossible not to think the universe meant to give us another chance. I wouldn't ever have had the courage to contact her myself after all this time, and especially after the way it ended. But I missed her for the whole of that time and I'm really glad that we found each other again. It's not my intention to make things complicated."

Daya tilted her head as if deciding on something.

"You don't think taking Maddie to Paris to direct a video in which you're playing a lesbian is complicated? She's already in deep with the house, with you and Mateo spending time together. People are gonna have a lot to say when they know you're working together again on a video like that."

The challenge was clear. Daya thought it was a bad idea.

"She's a grown woman, Daya, and she wants to do the video. And the lesbian thing was her idea not mine."

"I'm not saying you're not grown women, and I'm not saying you shouldn't be friends. Just be careful with her. She has a kid she needs to stay sane for this time around." Daya held her gaze, before setting off toward the stairs, lifting the gate, and going upstairs. Sofia felt the weight of the past in her words. She wanted to tell Daya she wasn't the same person this time around, but sometimes even she wasn't convinced it was true.

Sofia followed her. The tour didn't take long. The house wasn't that large, but it was beautiful, and as Daya showed her around, Sofia could see Maddie's design touches throughout, the color choices, the way the furnishings and fabrics complemented and added to the ambience and character of each room. If Maddie did half as good a job on her own house, she'd be delighted.

Daya finally led her outside and they stood on the deck watching Maddie messing with the Jet Skis at the other end of the long jetty that led from Maddie's deck to the ocean. There wasn't a cloud in the sky, and the sea behind Maddie was a perfect turquoise color. Mateo was sitting in a large swing chair on the deck, snoozing adorably in the arms of his teddy bear.

"And Noah honestly doesn't mind you guys spending all this time together? I'm sure my man wouldn't be all that keen on me hanging out with my ex, especially if we weren't all that solid." Daya raised an eyebrow.

"Daya." Sofia sounded a warning. "My friendship with Maddie has nothing to do with Noah." It was the truth for more reasons than she had let Daya know.

"Okay, okay, I'll leave it." She held up her hands defensively. "Let's go get some vitamin D and try not to get sunburned." She headed for the recliner angled to face the sun in the opposite corner of the deck, a few yards from where Mateo was sitting.

Sofia looked down the jetty and saw Maddie looking back toward the house. She lifted a hand and waved. She noticed that Mateo had shifted position and dropped his teddy bear. She picked it up, tucked it back next to him on the seat, and, without thinking, leaned in to place a soft kiss on his forehead. When she straightened, she noticed Daya watching her with a quizzical expression. She shrugged. She wasn't going to let Daya make her feel bad about being fond of Mateo. She opened the gate and picked her way down the steps.

As she approached the end of the jetty, she could see the two Jet Skis tied up along one edge, but Maddie was nowhere to be seen. She looked back to the house, not understanding how Maddie could have passed her, before the sensation of cool water hitting the back of her legs made her realize that Maddie was down in the water and splashing her with a silly smirk on her face. Sofia grinned back at her.

"C'mon, slowpoke, get ready. We're going go-carting, and we'll be going faster than five miles an hour this time, so no screaming."

Maddie leaned her arms and elbows on the jetty, letting her body float in the water. "You just need to strip and put on a life jacket."

Sofia's eyes widened and Maddie laughed.

"Don't worry, we're not skinny-dipping. I'm assuming that you were smart enough to wear a swimsuit underneath those clothes." Her eyes flashed and Sofia wondered if Maddie was also remembering the time they had bathed naked together on a secluded beach in Puerto Rico.

Sofia nodded and swallowed, her throat full of feelings, her head full of memories. She watched as Maddie pulled herself up out of the water and sat on the edge of the jetty, running her hands through her hair before getting to her feet. The sight of Maddie in a black bikini, her body perfectly toned and slick with water, her breasts filling the bikini top in just the way they were supposed to, made Sofia's insides turn to Jell-O and caused a feeling between her legs that she couldn't deny was flat out arousal. If this was a movie, Maddie would be moving in slow motion, the screen would be in soft focus, and romantic music would be playing.

"You coming in?" Maddie turned away from her to call in Daya's direction, giving Sofia time to recover her composure.

"No way," Daya called back. "Last time, my thighs cried with pain for a week. Me and my boy are just fine sitting here chilling." She slid her sunglasses over her eyes and dismissed them both with a wave of her hand.

"Just me and you then," Maddie said quietly. Sofia could see something like disappointment in Maddie's eyes, and it hurt. Did she really want Daya to be going out with them? Sofia wasn't dangerous. They didn't need a chaperone.

"If Daya's not coming then we can take one each." Maddie picked up a life jacket, pulled it on, and fastened the clips securely. Sofia felt a sliver of regret that half of Maddie's body was now pretty much hidden from view.

Maddie watched Sofi watching her fasten the life jacket. She hadn't moved, or gotten undressed, or done anything other than stare at her. And now she was chewing her lip and had a slightly upset look on her face and Maddie had no idea why.

Maddie was trying to hide her own disappointment. Daya not going out with them meant that they had no excuse for sharing a Jet Ski. Maddie had spent the last hour imagining the two of them on the same machine, Maddie wrapping herself around Sofi from behind, the two of them pressed close. The thoughts hadn't made her feel like a very good friend, and it was probably for the best that it wasn't going to happen, but she couldn't help but feel sorry.

In front of her, Sofi had started to move finally. She looked across at Maddie shyly before slipping off her shorts and folding them neatly before placing them on top of her sandals. Maddie almost laughed. She knew that Sofi being tidy like that was a sign of her nervousness, and when she caught Sofi looking at her timidly from under her eyelashes, Maddie's protective instincts kicked in.

"You can leave your T-shirt on if you want." Maddie's body reacted with regret even as she said the words. "Though if I had a body like yours, I wouldn't be hiding it from anyone." She stopped the loud curse from slipping out of her mouth at the surprise that she'd said the last part out loud. *Nice move, Maddie. I'm sure Sofi's not a bit nervous about undressing in front of you now.*

Maddie wanted to say she was sorry, to explain, but really what could she say? That she paid her friends compliments about how good they looked all the time? She honestly did, but they both knew that wasn't what that was. She simply shrugged and pulled a rueful face in Sofi's direction. She was rewarded with a slow smile spreading across Sofi's face.

"Well, if that's how you feel..." Sofi didn't take her eyes off Maddie as she lifted her T-shirt over her head and tossed it to the jetty.

Touché. The sight of Sofi in a deep red bikini, a brazenly flirtatious look on her face, was enough to make Maddie's mouth dry and other parts of her a lot wetter.

"And while we're paying compliments," Sofi looked Maddie up and down slowly, "that bikini on you is just sinful." She whistled softly. "You're in great shape, Mads. Honestly. You make me insecure enough to give up croquetas." Sofi placed her hands over her stomach self-consciously.

Maddie stepped closer to her and reached out to take Sofi's hands, moving them away from her stomach. "Don't say that, don't even joke about it." She waited until Sofi lifted her gaze from their joined hands. "You're perfect. And don't listen to anyone who says any different, including yourself." She batted away the memory of the last time she'd said something similar to Sofi, the last night they'd spent together, before it all went so wrong.

"Are you guys going to get into the water at any point? We want to watch you fall off," Daya shouted down the jetty breaking the tension. Maddie stepped back, treading clumsily on the life jacket that Sofi hadn't yet put on. She picked it up, feeling flustered, and handed it to Sofi. It was big on her and covered the whole of her top half, making it a lot easier for Maddie to look at her.

"The green Ski is a little smaller. Might be easier for you to handle. If you climb onto it, I'll show you how it works." Maddie was speaking in a rush, happy to do something that wasn't simply staring at Sofi with what was obviously a raging thirst. The fact that she sometimes imagined seeing something of that same want staring back at her just made it harder. She was single and had nothing to lose, but Sofi was in a steady relationship, and Maddie was not the kind of person to get involved in that, however much of a jerk she thought Noah was.

Inside her head, a voice taunted her. *Nothing to lose? What about the way you're gonna feel when she discovers your feelings and walks away again?* Yeah, that wouldn't hurt at all.

"Hey, where'd you go?" Sofi waved a hand in Maddie's face, an amused look on her face. "Have you been drinking tequila? I'm not sure you're allowed to drink tequila and be in charge of a go-cart Ski thing." Sofi seemed happy and playful, and Maddie had to get a grip on her feelings or she was about to spectacularly ruin this beautiful new connection between them.

"Sorry. I was just imagining how much fun it's gonna be dunking Daya in the water later." She said the first thing she could think of. "Did you say something?"

"I said that I'd rather we went out together if you didn't mind." Sofi sounded a little unsure of herself. "I mean, I've never ridden one before and I know you think I'm a wuss, but I'd feel happier if we shared."

Maddie looked at Sofi and smiled and Sofi smiled back at her sweetly. Maddie had no idea if Sofi knew how much her lack of courage had made her day.

"Come on then." Maddie took Sofi by the hand to the bigger blue machine and helped her get on it, showing her where to sit and where to put her feet. She slipped onto the seat behind Sofia. There wasn't a lot of room, and Maddie edged as far forward as she could, having no choice but to press herself against Sofi's back, to wrap her thighs tightly around Sofi's. As she settled into position, Maddie felt Sofi take a big breath in and then, unmistakably, gently lean back into Maddie while she let out the breath. For a long moment, they sat there, closer than they had been in many years, their bodies pushed up against one another, the life jackets between them acting as a barrier, making it seem like what they were doing was not as intimate as it might have been.

Maddie's thighs being wrapped around Sofi's meant her now aching center was next to Sofi's ass. It was completely intoxicating to be so close. As Sofi dropped her hands from the handlebars to her side, her forearms rested briefly on Maddie's thighs and the feel of Sofi's skin on hers made Maddie flush.

"Don't let me fall off." Sofi took both of Maddie's arms and used them to pull Maddie even closer. Maddie closed her eyes, letting herself enjoy the moment, letting her cheek rest against the back of Sofi's head. She felt like her body was made of electrical impulses, snapping and firing and sending currents through her body. Yet, at the same time, she felt completely content. She had the urge to tell Sofi that was how she felt—in a way old Maddie would never have done—but instead she pulled herself together and freed her arms from Sofi's torso and leaned them on either side of her to turn on the engine and grip the throttle. She leaned back and untied the rope tying it to the jetty before speaking into Sofi's ear.

"Put your hands up on the grips and hold on tight." Maddie's voice was raspy, and she hoped that Sofi wouldn't realize that it was because she was aroused. She tried to clear her head and concentrate on the machine, on taking Sofi out for a spin. She wanted them to have fun together, like they used to, before it all got so damn difficult.

"Ready?" Another excuse for Maddie to put her lips close to Sofi's ear. Pressed against her, Maddie again felt Sofi's deep intake of breath. Then Sofi nodded and Maddie released the throttle and revved the engine to get them going. Sofi moved her hands from the handlebars and placed them over Maddie's. She snuggled closer to Sofi and got them moving, increasing the throttle and the speed as soon as they got into deeper water. She was rewarded with a squeal from Sofi and a thump on her thigh which she soon learned was Sofi's way of telling her to slow down. If her thighs weren't going to hurt enough from the effort of controlling the Jet Ski, they were going to be bruised from Sofi's persistent punching.

They traveled the length of the beach, turning for home when they reached the inlet. And when they tipped over close to the jetty, as Maddie was trying to bring them alongside while going too fast, they both tumbled into the water spluttering and shrieking. Maddie knew she had not felt this happy in a really long time.

As Maddie finished tying up the Jet Ski, Sofi swam up behind her and jumped on her shoulders, dunking her under the water and then swimming away laughing. Maddie came to the surface with a splutter and saw Sofi trying to pull herself up out of the water a few yards away. She was there in three strokes, just in time to pull Sofi by the legs back into the water. She now had Sofi trapped against the jetty, an arm on either side of her shoulder, their faces barely six inches apart. The look on Sofi's face as she stared at Maddie's mouth was one Maddie had seen a hundred times before. And in that moment, Maddie understood that Sofi was as turned on as she was. If she gave in to her own desire to let her lips press against Sofi's, the kiss would not only be thrilling but it would be exactly what Sofi wanted. The realization surprised her. She leaned in slightly and watched Sofi's eyes widen, felt her inhale deeply. She dropped her arms into the water and slipped her hands around Sofi's waist. She wanted to strip off their life jackets and pull Sofi to her so she could feel Sofi's breasts pushed against her own, the idea causing a pulse of arousal between her legs. When Sofi leaned in, Maddie tilted her head, bringing her mouth closer to Sofi's, seeing the intensity of her own desire reflected back at her in Sofi's eyes.

The huge splash in the water next to them made them spring apart, soaking them both with spray. Maddie took a second to recover her senses and realize that the splash had come from the spare life jacket, now floating next to them in the water. Looking up along the jetty, Maddie saw Daya standing a few yards away, hands on hips, making it clear she was the one who had thrown it. It was as if Daya had thrown a bucket of cold water over them both, and whatever had been about to happen a second before, Sofi and Maddie now both looked at each other a little awkwardly.

"After you," Sofi said, indicating that Maddie should climb up onto the jetty first. Maddie did just that and then reached a hand back to help Sofi pull herself up out of the water. They both took off their life jackets, picked up their clothes, and walked shyly toward Daya like teenagers busted by their parents for making out on the porch. Except they hadn't even had the chance to do anything. Maddie tried to feel grateful to Daya for saving her from fucking things up with her out of control libido, but she couldn't. The desire to kiss Sofi had been so strong. Her mind scrambled as her body reacted with arousal to the idea of it. Maddie made a mental note to spend less time with Sofi when she was in a bikini.

Next to her, Sofi whispered behind her hand, obviously not wanting Daya to hear. "That was fun, Mads." Maddie nodded in agreement. "And I mean all of it, not just the part where you agreed to climb out first so I could get a great view of your butt in that bikini." She offered Maddie a cheeky wink and stepped away before Maddie could react. Maddie watched her walk back along the jetty with Daya, feeling as confused as ever. It wasn't just her own feelings she was confused by. Sofi was definitely not acting like someone with a long-term boyfriend.

Mateo was waiting for her behind the gate as she climbed the steps up to the deck. She scooped him up into her arms and gave him a big kiss.

"Did you see Mommy on the Jet Ski?"

He nodded. "But Mommy fell down." He sounded serious.

She had been careful not to tip over the Jet Ski every time she had taken him out. He hadn't seen it happen before.

"It's okay, Mateo. The water is soft and Mommy's a good swimmer." She kissed his cheek.

Sofi appeared at her side with a couple of towels.

"Tia swim too?" he asked

"Yes. A good swimmer. Like Mommy."

Sofi offered to take Mateo, but he turned his back on her, clinging onto Maddie, still seeming worried about seeing her falling in the water. Maddie mouthed a "sorry" in Sofi's direction and was rewarded with a smile and a shrug. Sofi stepped closer and wrapped the towel around her shoulders. She put her own towel over her head and pulled it tight under her chin, making a goofy face and looking like a slightly deranged nun. Maddie giggled almost as much as Mateo did.

"Mommy got super wet." Sofi was talking to Mateo. "Shall we both dry her hair?" She offered her towel to Mateo and he suddenly forgot all about Maddie maybe-drowning and was once again captivated by Sofi. Maddie let him down and let herself be led by the hand to one of her beach chairs where Mateo and Sofi took turns drying her hair while playing a game of peekaboo with the towels. She sat back, glorying in the sun on her legs, the sound of them giggling behind her, and the sensation of Sofi's hands on her head and on her neck. She told herself to be careful, that Sofi had someone else and was leaving soon, but she didn't want to listen. This was the most relaxed she had felt in years. How could something this natural be so wrong?

The four of them had been in the kitchen eating the snacks that Sofia had brought. Sofia and Mateo had made non-alcoholic cocktails that tasted every bit as crazy as they looked, and having stuffed himself full of pastelitos, Mateo now lay on the couch watching cartoons.

Daya stepped outside onto the deck to take a call from her man, leaving Sofia and Maddie reminiscing about things the three of them had gotten up to on tour. It was dangerous to root through those memories, but Daya's presence had made it safer somehow, and despite the way things had ended with the band, there were a lot of good times to talk about.

"There were times when I hated it, but the four of us going through it together made it bearable." Sofia wanted them to keep talking. She didn't want the day to end, didn't want to leave all this behind. This felt like home somehow, how she imagined her life might have been before it all went so wrong. "It's a lot harder when you're doing it without a band."

Rather than respond, Maddie sipped her drink and seemed to be studying Sofia carefully. Sofia didn't know if that was her way of agreeing or if she was simply avoiding an argument.

"You don't have to keep doing it. Any of it. You could take a break, do something else. You don't always seem like you're enjoying it much, but you never stop."

Sofia wanted to argue, to tell Maddie that it wasn't that easy and she couldn't possibly understand, but Maddie was one of the few people who did. She had done the "something else." She had become a mom and reinvented herself as an interior designer. And made kick-ass music videos for a hobby.

"It's not that I'm not enjoying it." Sofia tried to locate the truth inside herself.

"Go on." Maddie gazed at her and Sofia was captivated. The sun was causing Maddie's pupils to contract, making the irises even bigger, even more noticeably brown than usual. She had honestly never seen more beautiful eyes.

"I just feel this panic when I do anything other than what I'm supposed to, when I even think about doing anything different. I feel like I'm letting people down—my mom, Felix, the fans—all these people who stuck with me and gave me this success, this great career. It feels like I'm being ungrateful to do anything other than keep going, so I keep doing the same things I've always done, over and over in the hope that it keeps working. But it's less and less satisfying as each year goes by. And, to be honest..." This was the hard part, the part she didn't like to admit to. "What would I do without it? It's all I know and I don't have anything else." She was horrified to hear the upset in her voice. She didn't want Maddie's pity. She picked up the cocktail next to her on the bar and drained the glass, buying herself some time.

Maddie took hold of her hands, holding them on the tabletop, stroking them gently with her thumbs. The tenderness of Maddie's touch made Sofia's heart leap and she felt unexpected tears in her eyes.

"I'm sorry you feel this way. I'm not going to tell you it's easy to make changes. I'm not going to give you advice. I spent a long time grieving for the loss of my career even though if you'd have asked me I would have told you I hated every fucking minute of it." Maddie smiled. "But it's not too late to make changes, to have different things, and some of us are going to be proud of you regardless of whether you're the Sofia Flores who's an international pop star or the Sofia Flores who isn't." Maddie still had hold of Sofia's hands and her words had Sofia unable to move, to breathe even. She had waited so long to hear this. The tears fell softly, and she didn't care.

"Maddie." She didn't know what there was to say, but Maddie put a finger on her lips to quiet her anyway.

"You need to hear this." Maddie swallowed. "I'm not proud of not standing up for you before—though I think you understand I had my reasons—but this time I'm going to be there for you. We're going to make this video and I'm going to help you be who you need to be. Without telling you who you need to be." Maddie had tears in her own eyes now. She wiped them away, seeming angry that they were there at all. Sofia wanted to reach for Maddie, to hug her, to make it all better. "I know you, Sofi, and I know you're not happy. And if you need to talk about it, I'm here. I'm older and a little braver than I was, and having Mateo has made me understand the value of things I couldn't understand before."

Sofia squeezed Maddie's hands. She couldn't find her voice right now but wanted Maddie to know that she appreciated every single word she was offering. She felt Maddie's arm around her shoulders, pulling her in, felt Maddie kiss the top of her head. Her body responded to Maddie's touch in ways it shouldn't. Whatever had happened in the water, Maddie was offering friendship, and maybe even some type of love, but she wasn't offering what Sofia's body wanted. Sofia made herself stop crying, made herself calm down. Maddie continued to rock her gently, murmuring soft reassuring noises into her hair. The feeling of being cared for by Maddie was one that Sofia had slowly had to learn to live without, learn not to crave. But if this was all there was for them, it would have to be enough.

Daya slid the door open and stepped back into the room. They pulled apart.

"My man wants to see me so I'm heading out and—" She stopped, as if just noticing that Sofia and Maddie had, moments before, been in each other's arms. She looked from Maddie to Sofia and then shook her head.

"It's kinda late, Sofia. I think maybe you should leave when I do."

Sofia turned to Maddie. She didn't want to go. Not yet.

"Sofi's going to teach Mateo some ukulele. We promised him."

They hadn't strictly promised, but Sofia was happy that Maddie seemed to want her to stay a while longer.

"If you're sure." The look Daya gave Maddie was clearly a warning. The nod in Daya's direction was her only answer.

"Don't say I didn't warn you." Daya sighed, her unhappy feelings obvious. She placed a kiss on Mateo's head and headed for the door. Sofia heard it close.

"Sorry." Maddie shrugged. "She's very protective. Even when she doesn't need to be. I told her we're okay, that we're just hanging out till you go away."

"And making the video together. She made it plain that she thinks that's crazy too. Said I'm making things complicated for you."

Maddie laughed and Sofia couldn't help but be delighted by the sound. "I think everything about us is complicated, don't you? Short of completely avoiding each other, I don't know how to make it simple. And I kind of tried that and failed." The look she gave Sofia made her insides contract with a mixture of desire and worry.

Sofia wanted to say more. She should tell Maddie that things were even more complicated than she realized because Sofia was single enough that they could make out against the jetty any time they wanted. But the panicky feeling in her stomach reminded her that telling Maddie she'd been faking it with Noah would ruin this new closeness between them, and she wanted this evening to be as uncomplicated as it could be. Two old friends, catching up, enjoying being together. She owed Maddie the truth, but it could wait. And, yeah, she was well aware it wasn't the first time she'd told herself that.

"Mommy can play," Mateo called from across the room. He had his hand on an acoustic guitar propped up on a stand. He waved at them. "Mommy, play." He repeated the request.

"I play for him sometimes." Maddie seemed embarrassed.

"Oh God, that would be fantastic." Sofia couldn't think of a more perfect way to end the evening. She leapt off her stool and went to the corner where Mateo was standing. She put her hand on top of his. "Mommy should definitely play." She winked at Maddie and was rewarded with a smile.

"Not fair."

"We voted. Two against one, it's very fair. Democratic even."

She picked up the guitar and walked hand in hand with Mateo out onto the deck. She propped the guitar against the chair and settled with Mateo into the swing chair to wait for Maddie to come and pick up her guitar.

Maddie appeared in the doorway and hesitantly made her way to the chair. She picked up the guitar and sat down with it.

"I know I'm being presumptuous, but I really really wanna hear you play, and if I have to join forces with Mateo to make it happen, I'm not gonna feel any guilt." The words were teasing, but she kept her tone serious. She wanted Maddie to know how much she wanted this.

"This is going to feel really weird. I haven't played in front of anyone but Mateo for years."

"It's me, Mads. Just me."

Maddie looked at her, her fingers fidgeting nervously with the pick. She moved her hands into position and began to strum softly before picking out the tune. It was not a tune that Sofia recognized. When Maddie eventually started to sing softly, her words were about lost love, and her voice—to Sofia—had not changed at all. She leaned back in the chair and let the bluesy soulfulness of the song wash over her. Maddie's voice grew a little stronger as the song progressed, and when she closed her eyes, Sofia took the chance to appreciate just how beautiful she looked. The sun was setting, the light was pink, and Maddie's face shone as she sang. Sofia couldn't stop watching her mouth as it moved. The song ended and Maddie opened her eyes before offering up a shy and hesitant smile. Mateo climbed onto Sofia's lap and clapped loudly.

"That was beautiful." Sofia was so full of emotion, she could barely speak.

"Thank you."

"Is it one of yours? I didn't recognize it." Sofia had listened to Maddie's album a hundred times. In the absence of any communication between them after they broke up, it had been where she'd gone to try to understand what had happened between them.

"Yeah." Maddie put down the guitar. "I still write sometimes. When I get the time, and the urge."

"You should release that. It's—"

"I write for me, Sofi, sometimes for Mateo, sometimes just for fun. Because I like to. Not everything's for sale."

"I'm sorry." Sofia wanted to take the words back. "I know not everything's for sale, it's just a really good song. Better than a lot of what's out there right now." She felt like Maddie was disappointed in her, that she'd said the wrong thing.

Maddie shrugged before leaning down and picking up the guitar. She handed it to Sofia and beckoned Mateo onto her lap. "Your turn."

Sofia wanted to object. As stupid as it seemed, she'd never had Maddie's confidence when it came to performing and she didn't have a voice anywhere near as powerful as hers. She had always been in awe of Maddie's abilities.

She settled the guitar onto her knee and began to play the opening chords of "Not This Time." The song that she had written as a wakeup call to herself long before Maddie had come back into her life. The song she had written about her regret at letting Maddie go. She sang the opening verse and got as far as the first chorus before stopping, suddenly feeling self-conscious.

I won't let you leave this time
Don't care what they say
Don't care how much it hurts
It's not over, not this time

She couldn't sing anymore of the song to Maddie. She felt too exposed.

"I have a terrible memory for words, even my own. Sorry." Sofia told the white lie. She tried to steady her breathing and concentrated her gaze on Mateo rather than looking at Maddie. She picked out another tune. Mateo recognized it before Maddie. She sang a few verses of the theme tune to Peppa Pig before seeing Mateo yawn.

"I should go."

"Yeah, he's getting tired."

At the door, they stood awkwardly. Nothing was easy between them. Sofia shouldered her backpack.

"Thanks for a great time." Sofia wanted to say so much more. She wanted to tell Maddie that it was the best day she'd had in years.

"Thanks for coming, thanks for the pastelitos, and thanks for being so good with Mateo. We don't often have fun like this with other people." She avoided Sofia's gaze, seeming bashful again. "Thanks, just thanks."

Sofia headed out to her car and flung her backpack on the passenger seat. She looked back and waved at Maddie and Mateo, framed in the doorway. She had traveled all around the world and seen some amazing sights, but she had never felt less like leaving a place than right then.

Chapter Thirteen

R emind me why I agreed to do this? I won't know anyone, and I'll feel like everyone is wondering why the hell the decorator is here drinking your beer." Maddie was standing in Sofi's kitchen helping her unwrap the various platters of delicious looking party food. One of the caterers was loading trays of croquetas and empanadas into the oven. The other was stacking beer in the fridge.

"You're here because I asked you to come." Sofi looked up from the box of glasses she was unpacking. "And because I wanted to be able to say good-bye to you before heading off. You're one of the few people coming tonight who I need to say good-bye to. Most of them are coming with me."

Not wanting to say good-bye to Sofi for almost four months was one of the reasons why, despite Mateo, Maddie had agreed to go to Paris and work with Rick on the video. It would mean she would get to see her again in a week. It wasn't much but it was something. She took a swig of the beer and tried not to feel anxious about just how much she was going to miss her.

"I guess it's a chance to say good-bye to Noah too." Maddie made herself mention his name.

"Yeah. He's bringing some friends. He likes a party." Sofi shrugged as if that was explanation enough.

The idea of spending the night with Noah lowered Maddie's mood even further. She and Sofi had hung out a fair amount the past few days—and nothing about it had been angsty. They'd been doing house stuff, making plans for the video shoot, and yesterday Sofi and

Mateo had even made pancakes together while she did some work on the house. Hanging out again felt so natural, so nourishing, and for all of it, Noah had been blissfully absent.

"Is he not worried about you handling the schedule?" She couldn't help herself. She still wasn't convinced Sofi was well enough to tour. And in Noah's position, she would have tried her hardest to persuade her not to go. Sadly, his main priority seemed to be insisting she throw a going-away party that he wasn't even helping to organize.

"He worries about me less than you do, and I told him I'm okay." Sofi smiled but the look in her eyes was hard to read.

"And are you okay?"

"I told you, I'm going to rest after. In my house by the ocean that a certain person will have made feel like a super stunning home for me." She spoke softly and held Maddie's gaze. It felt intimate. The two of them, in Sofi's kitchen, talking about the future. "And maybe the next party I'll throw will be a coming home party for just you guys. You, Mateo, Daya. People I actually want to spend time with."

Maddie was happy that Sofi imagined them seeing each other after the house was finished. Given she'd been trying her hardest to keep her thoughts about Sofi in the middle of the friend zone, she probably should have worried more about just how happy it made her.

"I might come. Will there be croquetas?"

Sofi nodded. "Of course. As many as you can eat. And there'll be Lego. For Daya." The wink and the smile made Maddie's heart melt. "Shame she wasn't free tonight."

"Yeah, she said next time maybe." It was a harmless lie. Daya had said she couldn't think of anything worse than a night with Sofi's music industry buddies. Maddie felt the same, but she had a Sofi-shaped reason to be here.

Sofi took a huge salad bowl from the fridge and began drizzling it with oil.

"Do you date?" Sofi asked without looking up, and for a second, Maddie wondered if she'd misheard. But this was Sofi. The Sofi who usually asked the awkward questions.

"I have a three-year-old and a busy job so not so much, no." Maddie ran a hand through her hair.

"You shouldn't not date because of Mateo." Sofi looked up at her. "A lot of people would be happy to date someone as wonderful as you with a kid as sweet as him." She stopped. "I'm sorry, it's not my business to give you advice." Sofi cast her eyes down, seeming embarrassed.

"I'm just not looking for anyone right now, Sofi." It didn't matter, but for some reason Maddie wanted her to know. And so what if her heart beat a little faster when Sofi called her wonderful. She couldn't help that.

"Noah said he was bringing Danny. He said Danny was still interested in you. Made a big deal about the two of you having a 'connection,' about you guys having a lot of fun when you worked on the video together." Sofi added croutons to the salad without looking up. "I just wanted to let you know he was planning on matchmaking so you'd be prepared. He's hard to talk out of things once he's made his mind up."

Maddie could have told Sofi that she was lactating and sleepless to the point of exhaustion when she and Danny worked on the video and that the connection between them had been nothing but friendly, but she didn't know whether Sofi cared enough to want the explanation.

"Did you try?"

"What?" Sofi looked confused.

"To talk him out of the matchmaking." Maddie wanted to know, wanted to believe Sofi still felt a little jealousy.

"I just didn't think he was doing it for the right reasons."

It wasn't a yes but it wasn't a no.

Sofi squeezed past her carrying the huge bowl of salad at the same time that Maddie moved to put down her beer. They bumped hips and the contact between them sent Sofi off balance. Maddie shot out her hands, grabbing Sofi to steady her. Sofi put the salad on the counter and turned to her. They were face-to-face, not very far apart.

"My fault, sorry." For some reason, Maddie hadn't dropped her hands from Sofi's waist.

"Don't be. You saved the salad." Sofi gave her a shy smile.

The air was heavy between them. Maddie gazed at Sofi's face. She wasn't smiling now. She had her bottom lip caught between her teeth and her eyes were dark and serious. Maddie felt herself being pulled in.

"I'm so glad you're coming to Paris."

"Me too."

"I have a lot of good memories of being there with you."

"Me too." Maddie could barely form words, being this close to Sofi, talking about Paris, the city where they had finally let themselves become lovers, was dangerous. Her body was telling her to pull Sofi closer, to taste those beautiful lips, but her brain was sounding an alarm. Sofi shifted a little closer, putting her hands over Maddie's, holding them in place as if realizing that she was about to pull away. Maddie's insides turned to hot liquid, and she felt a pulsing between her legs.

"I've never been able to go there and not think about you. Of all the places we went together, it's the place that most reminds me of us. When you suggested it as a setting for the video, I hoped that maybe you—" She didn't finish, but her expression told Maddie everything. They were playing with fire being this close.

Before Maddie could respond, the doorbell rang and they both dropped their hands and moved a little farther apart.

"Saved by the bell." Sofi picked up Maddie's beer, took a long pull, and then handed it to her with a rueful smile before crossing to answer the door. As Maddie watched her move, she let out a soft breath, her body resenting the intrusion while the part of her that was still capable of rational thought offered up a thanks that they had been stopped from doing something they shouldn't in full view of a team of caterers. She needed to keep her distance until she could get her feelings under control. She drained her beer and looked at the empty bottle. She also needed to try to stay sober.

Sofi came back into the living room with a group of mostly young women, all looking like they'd dressed for an evening at the beach. Maddie watched as they exchanged hugs and kisses and handed over bottles and bunches of flowers. As Sofi's hands got full, Maddie moved across to help her by taking some of the gifts and placing them carefully on the table.

As she turned back to the group, there was a familiar face grinning at her. She had barely a second to react before being wrapped in a tight hug.

"Madison. No fucking way. So great to see you."

"You too." Maddie hugged Tanya back happily. She had played guitar as part of the band that toured with them back in the day, and they had been close. But Sofi had persuaded Tanya to jump ship when she went solo so she was another lost connection, another person forced to choose sides. Maddie had been sad to lose Tanya. She'd gotten drunk with her more times than she could remember.

"Girl, you look good." She looked Maddie up and down and let out a soft whistle. "Sofia did not tell me you were coming." She held up a bottle. "But I brought tequila anyway. Maybe the universe knew I'd run into you." She winked at Maddie.

"And you're looking five years younger not five years older. Maybe I should drink more tequila."

"Thanks, babe, you always were a charmer." Tanya nudged her and smiled.

Tanya was a relentless flirt, but during all the times they'd gotten drunk together in the past, she had never once made a move. She was one of the few people they'd toured with who knew about Maddie and Sofi's relationship and she'd understood that they were both off-limits.

Maddie took Tanya to the kitchen to get a drink. Sofi was doing the same with the other women. She introduced them to Maddie. They were all singers and dancers from the show. As Sofi chatted with them, Maddie watched her. She seemed tired. She'd done her best to conceal the dark circles under her eyes, but the shadows were still visible. And her movements seemed rushed and a little exaggerated. To Maddie, she seemed stressed and strung out.

The doorbell rang again as Sofi was opening a bottle of wine. She held it up and mouthed a "can you get it" in Maddie's direction with a shrug.

Maddie moved to the door and swung it open. Noah, Danny, and three other men she didn't recognize stood staring back at her.

"Are you seriously opening the door for her now?" Noah didn't even say hello as he strode past. "There's, like, twelve photographers outside. Do you want them wondering why Sofi's former 'bestie' is more at home here than I am?"

"Maddie." Danny nodded at her and lifted an eyebrow as he walked by, clearly embarrassed by Noah's unpleasantness.

She followed them into the living area and couldn't help her jealous reaction to the sight of Noah's arm around Sofi's shoulders, minutes after she and Sofi had been so intimate. That she still felt the trembling of desire in her body while Sofi was now with Noah made Maddie feel miserable. It helped a little when Noah tried to pull Sofi into a kiss, and she pushed him away, giving him the dirtiest of dirty looks. They still didn't seem to be in a very good place.

"Hey, babe, it's been a while. How you doing?" Danny moved back to her side with a beer in his hand. "And how's little Mateo?"

"He's good. Growing. You wouldn't recognize him now."

Danny nodded.

Maddie couldn't take her eyes off Noah and Sofi. Sofi was on the edge of a group chatting happily with Tanya while Noah was watching her possessively. She was biased—she couldn't pretend otherwise—but Noah's appeal was impossible to understand. She supposed he was handsome, but his personality was disgusting. Even if he was jealous about her friendship with Sofi, there was no need to be so hostile. He had Sofi, she had chosen him. It should be enough.

"Is he always such a jerk?"

Danny laughed. "He's not always that bad. I think you push his buttons."

Maddie gave him a quizzical look. "I've barely said five words to him."

"It's not anything you've said or done. It's just that you're here, back in her life. He's very possessive about her. I tell him constantly how ridiculous it is, y'know. For kinda obvious reasons." He seemed to be waiting for her to say something, but when she didn't respond, he simply continued. "But it doesn't stop him from being jealous. He knows about before. He thinks you two are getting close and he's threatened by it, y'know." He shrugged.

"That's crazy." Maddie offered up the denial even as she remembered how close she had come to kissing Sofi earlier, how much she had wanted to. The look in Sofi's eyes suggesting she wanted the same thing. They had a lot of history and they were getting close again. Maybe Noah was right to want her to stay the fuck away from his girlfriend. Maddie told herself for the hundredth time that month that she needed to be grateful that the tour would put more distance between them.

"And how's Sofia doing?" Danny asked. "I can't believe I was chatting with her that day, a few minutes before she did the falling over collapsing thing. I had no idea. She seemed fine."

Maddie looked at him closely and could see only genuine concern.

"She's okay I guess. I think she hides it well. Personally, I think she still needs more time to recover, but I guess that's easy for me to say. I don't have to worry about her album sales."

"It is easy for you to say. And, oh yeah, let me think, absolutely nothing to do with you."

Maddie hadn't realized Noah was standing close enough to overhear.

"Noah." Danny said his name like a warning. "Be nice, man."

"I just think it's amazing that someone whose own career was such a shitshow thinks she's qualified to give any kind of career advice to Sofia."

"I'm not giving her career advice, Noah. She collapsed a month ago and she's about to go on tour for four months, and I might not have a right to say it, but I just wanna know she's fit enough." She could feel the anger building in her chest. "And maybe having a boozy send-off is not what she needs right now."

"Okay, boomer." Noah sneered at her. "You're not looking after a toddler now. Some of us can manage to stay up past nine o'clock, have a few drinks, and still function. She's not fragile, and she doesn't need another mother."

Maddie didn't want an argument with Noah. For Sofi's sake. She made herself stay silent in the face of his hostility. It took a lot of effort.

"She's a fucking pop star and you probably don't remember, but pop stars have to tour their records, meet their fans, and sell their albums. It's that simple. So we're gonna have a few drinks, take some party photos, and show the world that Sofia is better and ready to slay. And if she gets tired or needs anyone to care for her, I'm here." His voice was already slightly slurry. He must have been drinking before he arrived.

Maddie looked at Sofi across the room. She was busying herself handing out drinks to a new group of arrivals. She felt the desire to go to her, to help, to be by her side. Whatever Noah said, she couldn't help but think Sofi needed her.

"Why are you even here anyway?"

Maddie blinked, realizing Noah was still talking to her.

"I mean, you're always hanging out here, getting the photographers all excited, and now you're even doing her fucking video. It's making people wonder what's going on. Is it not enough that you killed your own career by coming out? You want everyone asking questions about you and her like that?"

There was so much she could have said to that. She swallowed it down, digging her nails into her hand to stop herself from reacting the way she wanted to.

"Sofi invited me. To be honest, I'd have been happier to pass. I'm too old to think that getting shit-faced and posing for selfies is cool, but for some reason, your girlfriend really wanted me here. Maybe you need to ask her why, not me." She turned and walked away, trying not to let him see the anger, the trembling in her body.

For a second, she contemplated leaving, and then Sofi caught her eye. She gave Maddie a warm, tired smile and her eyes contained a plea. Sofi did need her. Maddie didn't know why or what for, but she wasn't going to let Noah chase her away.

Half the party had drifted outside. Someone had moved one of the speakers to the doorway and was blasting music out onto the deck where some people were dancing, while others sat around in small groups chatting. Most of the food had been eaten, and empty beer bottles were scattered across the kitchen.

Sofia was half clearing plates and half watching Maddie chatting with Danny on the couch. It was a big couch, it could easily seat four people, but Maddie and Danny were sitting pretty close together. Maddie looked gorgeous tonight in skinny black jeans, dark eye liner, and a cut-off black T-shirt—looking a lot like the rock chick she wasn't any more. But more than being achingly beautiful, Maddie was smart, funny, and sexy. Of course Danny was interested. Sofia couldn't imagine anyone with a pulse not being interested in Maddie. She couldn't help the feelings of jealousy that bubbled up. She didn't know how Maddie felt about her, but earlier, there was no hiding the fact that they had again almost kissed, and unless she'd gotten really bad at reading Maddie, she had wanted them to as much as Sofia did. She had spent the night thinking about nothing but that while Maddie had been keeping her distance and acting as if it hadn't even happened.

"They make a cute couple." Noah appeared at her side. He handed her his empty plate. "I guess that's why you're over here looking all sad." He turned his mouth down like a clown. "Your baby girl grew up to prefer men after all. Danny, Mateo's baby daddy, that rapper she recorded with and then banged for a few months. She's not very bisexual for a bisexual. I think I'd probably stand a better chance than you with her right now."

Sofia had spent the evening avoiding him as much as possible. He was annoying sober, but drunk he was an unpleasant asshole.

"Did you want something, Noah?" She was determined not to let him see that she was bothered. They did look like a cute couple. And they had spent a lot of the evening together.

For a second, he looked at her with what she imagined was actual fondness. "I want my girlfriend to pay me some attention. You've been avoiding me all night. "I'm going away, you're going away. A girlfriend would be sad about that."

"For fuck's sake, Noah. I'm not your girlfriend. How many times do I need to say it?"

His expression hardened.

"Oh yeah, well, I've got a contract that says different. You're my girlfriend until the end of January. Longer if we both decide we want to sign up for a sequel." He laughed at his own joke.

She felt a pounding in her head. Was he really that deluded that he imagined she would carry this on for a day longer than she had to?

"You're drunk and you're acting like a jerk. Why would I want to spend time with you?"

She tensed, waiting for him to react, waiting for more nastiness and harsh words.

"You weren't always like this. You liked me in the beginning. I know you did." He said the words so quietly that Sofia had to strain to hear them. "And I miss the way it was before she came back."

Before Sofia could respond, before she could tell him how crazy he was, he picked up his beer and wandered unsteadily over to the couch, dropping into the space next to Danny.

Sofia felt a familiar tightness building in her chest. The contract prevented them both from ever talking about the arrangement, but he was drunk and upset enough to say anything. He could blow things wide open. For both their sakes, Felix had to find a way for them to end things sooner than January.

Maddie looked in her direction and smiled, moving her head to suggest Sofia should come and join her. Her face was a little flushed, and her smile was open and warm. Sofia immediately felt a wave of shame. She had lied to everyone about Noah for so long it had stopped seeming important, but Maddie—lying to Maddie—was something different. She needed to tell her about Noah before someone else did. She had so much she needed to say to her about her feelings, and they had so much lost time to make up for. And she believed that, with Maddie at her side, she would feel braver, less lost. In her head it all sounded difficult and crazy, but in her heart it felt right.

She put a pile of plates into the sink, picked up her drink, and moved across to sit next to Tanya.

"I still can't believe you're shooting your next video while we're in Paris. Very fucking cool. I assume that you'll need to cast a sexy guitarist." She raised her eyebrows at Sofia playfully.

Sofia caught Maddie's eye and smiled. She was so happy that Maddie had agreed to come to Paris. Being away from Mateo for a couple of days was not easy, but Maddie was willing to do it—for her.

"All her idea." She pointed at Maddie. "And you'll have to ask her for a part, because she's in charge, not me. I'm just going to turn up and do what I'm told."

"We had a blast doing my video," Danny said. "But you're right about the doing what you're told thing. She got very bossy." He nudged Maddie and smiled as he spoke. Sofia felt a stab of jealousy as she watched them together. She looked up to see Noah staring at her.

"Well, I think it'd be damn cool if we could be in it together." He didn't wait for a response. "The fans have been asking us to do something together and the video could be it. Easier than collaborating on a song when we're both touring. I'm sure I can make time for a couple of days in Paris."

"You don't need to do that." Sofia kept her tone neutral, not wanting to create another reason for him to be belligerent.

"I know I don't need to, babe. I'm offering. I think it would be a good move. Maybe you can tell your director to do what she's told and cast your boyfriend as your love interest. I assume there is one."

Sofia felt everyone's gaze on her, waiting. She felt her throat tighten. Maddie was looking in her direction, her eyes showed kindness and concern. Sofia couldn't help but wonder again whether Maddie would hate her for the deceit about Noah, or whether she'd understand. Either way, she just needed to start being more honest.

"There's a really good reason you can't play the love interest, sorry."

"Sofi." Maddie said her name softly and shook her head, lifting her beer bottle to her lips and angling her head toward Noah. She was warning Sofia off the conversation, suggesting Noah was too drunk to handle it.

"Why not? I told you, I can get time off. And it's not like I haven't acted before. The fans would love having me in the video. It'd blow up for sure then."

"You'd need to be French." Sofia was annoyed that he imagined the song couldn't sell without him in the video.

"I could do an acc—"

"And you'd need to be a very beautiful woman." Sofia cut him off.

She watched his face as the penny dropped. His mouth moved but no words came out.

"Really, Sofi?" Tanya laughed and held up her hand for Sofia to give her a high five. "Hot damn. You dark horse, you. Well, that's gonna get people talking." She turned to Maddie. "Was that your idea?"

Maddie looked uncomfortable rather than proud. Sofia didn't understand. She was taking a risk, and a big part of it was to show Maddie she'd finally found some courage to be herself.

"It was." Sofia answered for her. "She came up with the whole thing. Rick loved it. I loved it. It's awesome and exciting." She tried to sound confident, but Maddie's doubts were still written across her face, and they made Sofia worry.

"You're doing a video where you're in love with a woman?" Noah had found his voice. "Are you fucking kidding?"

"Yes and no. And you need to calm down." She was so sick of him.

"Does Felix know?"

"Of course. They all know." She shrugged.

"Why would you—"

"Why wouldn't I? It's a cool concept, it's going to get people listening to the song. I think it's a power move. I'm sick of being seen as sugary sweet, of not taking creative risks."

"I think it sounds great." Danny sounded supportive.

"Me too." Tanya smiled. "I'm proud of you."

Noah sat silently with a pout on his face. Then he pointed at Maddie. "She put you up to this?" He didn't wait for a response. "It's obviously the kind of video I'd expect her to want to make, but I don't get why you'd agree to it. She's obviously trying to fuck up your career to get you back for the way you fucked them over before. She's probably been waiting years for this chance."

"Don't be that guy, Noah." Danny put a hand on Noah's shoulder, urging him to calm down.

"No, someone has to say it. This is a disaster for you, Sofia. Your fans will hate it, the song won't sell, and you're gonna do this why? Because she suggested it and you want to look cool in front of her? You're losing your mind. They'll think you're queer. I helped you put all those rumors behind you. That was the whole fucking point."

This was her house. She didn't care how drunk he was, or what her contract said, she wasn't going to let him behave that way.

"I think you owe Maddie an apology." She was annoyed to hear her own voice waver, the upset obvious.

"I'm not apologizing to her. No fucking way."

"Then you should leave." She stood and pointed at the door. "Get out, Noah."

"I'm sorry, babe." He held up his hands in a conciliatory gesture. "But it's crazy, and she's insane for encouraging you to do this. You're not thinking straight."

"Get the hell out of my house."

Sofia turned her back on him, on all of them, and went upstairs. She sat on the edge of her bed and willed her heartbeat to return to normal. She closed her eyes and concentrated on her breathing. She had come so close to telling him that, since he wasn't her boyfriend—and hadn't even been behaving like a friend lately—he had zero right to have an opinion. But that would have meant letting Maddie know that the whole thing was a sham. She had told Maddie to trust her, said that they'd be honest with each other second time around. What a joke.

"Hey." Maddie stood in the doorway, feeling hesitant, not sure if Sofi wanted company.

Sofi nodded.

"Noah's leaving."

Sofi nodded again.

"And Tanya and Danny are clearing people out."

"Thanks." Sofi sounded like she could barely manage to speak, and the tension in her body worried Maddie. She didn't want her to have another anxiety attack. Noah's behavior, his humiliating comments, would certainly have justified it.

"Are you okay?" Maddie sat next to her on the bed, putting a hand on Sofi's back and stroking gently. She was close enough that Maddie could smell the beer on her breath, see the upset in her beautiful brown eyes. Despite everything, she felt a tightness low down in her belly.

"It's just—"

Maddie's phone beeped. She fished it out of her pocket.

"Danny. He and Tanya are heading out. Everyone's gone. They said sorry for not cleaning up." She smiled.

"Don't you wanna go with him?" Sofi looked at her quizzically. "You guys seemed pretty close tonight."

"Are you serious?"

"Maybe." Sofi frowned, and then shrugged. "I don't know. I've lost the ability to think straight apparently."

"We're not like that. He's just a friend. I told you, Sofi, I'm not dating right now."

"I'm sorry. It's just that Noah said the two of you were—"

"Yeah, well, Noah said a lot of stuff tonight that's bullshit." Maddie hesitated. "I mean, whatever might have happened before, I would never do anything to harm you or your career. You know that, right? I didn't even want the woman in the video, remember. And I know he's drunk and he probably doesn't even mean it, but I want you to know that he's wrong. I only want the best for you. I want you to be happy and healthy." She stopped, not wanting to make things worse. "And sometimes I worry that Noah doesn't always have your best interests at heart."

She kept stroking Sofi's back, wanting to give her comfort but—she couldn't lie—also needing to be touching her somehow.

"That feels really good," Sofi murmured the words, closing her eyes briefly. She put her hand on Maddie's arm and the touch heightened all of her senses. "I know you're not trying to hurt me. It took me a long time, but eventually I think I understood that you hadn't meant to hurt me back then either. And I don't care what Noah thinks. I don't care what any of them think about anything, I do want to try to be happier."

"You deserve that." Maddie wanted that for Sofi.

"We all deserve that. Life is too short not to be happy. I don't think I've let myself think that way until now." Sofi took Maddie's hand and placed it on her thigh, using her fingertips to trace a path from her palm to her wrist, and back again, in the same way Maddie had done when Sofi had needed calming days ago. Sofi's touch was so exquisite, so needed, that it made her want to forget all about the words she had come to say to Sofi about the way Noah was treating her.

Maddie took in a breath as Sofi slid her other hand around her waist, her fingers touching her skin in the gap between her T-shirt and her jeans. Sofi left her hand there for a few seconds, before reaching up under Maddie's T-shirt to rake her nails across her back. Maddie let out a soft moan, feeling a hot ache between her legs. She couldn't help reacting, couldn't help wanting more. They had been together for three years, but they had never grown used to being around each other in that way that some couples do. Being close to Sofi—whether she was awake or asleep, whether they were alone or in company—Maddie had always found her impossible to resist, always felt the physical pull of their attraction. And right then, the power of it was as strong as it had ever been, despite their years apart.

She tangled her fingers in the hair at the nape of Sofi's neck and pulled Sofi closer. She angled her head and gently grazed her lips across Sofi's before pulling back slightly. Sofi gazed back at her, the hungry look telling Maddie everything she needed to know.

This time her kiss was more certain, more demanding, and the feel of Sofi's lips—soft, warm, yielding—ignited sparks inside her core. When Sofi kissed her back, her kisses showing the same wanting, Maddie gave in to her desire. She gloried in the taste of Sofi's lips, the feel of their tongues touching, Sofi's fingers now digging into her back, their mouths greedy for each other. Sofi pushed Maddie onto her back, her kisses urgent and wanting. When she dipped her head to kiss Maddie's neck, trailing kisses down to her collarbone and then biting the skin softly, Maddie let out a soft groan and pulled Sofi closer. She kissed her hard, her tongue deep in Sofi's mouth. Sofi reached under her T-shirt and caressed her breasts through the soft fabric of her bra. Maddie felt her nipples harden against Sofi's palms, wanting Sofi's mouth on them. Maddie grabbed for her, moving her own hands underneath Sofi's shirt touching her in the same way. They had wanted this, waited for this, for too long. Something poked through the desire, through the wanting. They had waited for a reason. They weren't together, they hadn't been together for a long time, and they shouldn't be doing this.

As Sofi moved to lift off her T-shirt, Maddie reached for her hands and held them.

"Sofi, we can't."

"What's wrong?" Sofi's face was flushed, her lips a dark pink, her eyes full of arousal.

"We just can't." Maddie's throat was thick with feeling. She couldn't make herself speak. She didn't really want to say the words.

She wanted them to keep kissing, to undress each other, to make love and never stop. But they weren't together anymore, and Sofi wasn't even single.

"We can." Sofi kissed her again. The kiss was hard and passionate, and Maddie responded, opening her mouth to let Sofi's tongue inside, her hands on Sofi's ass. Her desire was overriding her thinking, she was so close to the point of no return. She put her hands on Sofi's shoulders and pushed her away.

"We can't." This time she sounded more emphatic, pulling herself up from under Sofi and into a seated position, leaning against the headboard. She willed her mind to clear.

"I don't understand." Sofi sat up on her knees, facing Maddie, her eyes clouded with desire and confusion. She was so beautiful and Maddie's longing for her was so strong that she almost reached for her all over again.

"We can't do this. We can't. Maybe you and Noah are having problems and maybe he was a jerk tonight, but he doesn't deserve this. No one does. And I'm not that person anymore, the person who fucks things up. And I don't want to fuck this up. If we haven't already I mean." She tried to make it make sense, but she couldn't. Her brain wasn't working properly.

Sofi stared at her with an expression that was hard to read. She closed her eyes and took in a deep breath and Maddie thought her panic had returned. She moved forward, ready to do something, but then Sofi opened her eyes and offered her a hesitant smile.

"You're not fucking things up and neither am I. We both want this. I know we do."

"It doesn't matter what we want. You have Noah. We shouldn't be doing this." Maddie felt the truth of it land like a stone sinking in water. *What the hell was she doing?* She moved to the edge of the bed, away from Sofi—not trusting herself.

"I don't 'have' Noah." Sofi spoke softly, but Maddie could see the tension in her body. Her hands fidgeting with the bedclothes. "We're not together. We never were. It's just PR. You know how it goes. We're with the same record company. It's good publicity for people to think we're together. And I know it's pathetic—to still be pretending at thirty-two, to not have anyone of my own, but I don't."

She reached for Maddie's hand. "I'm sorry I didn't tell you, but he isn't any kind of reason why we can't have this. If we want it."

Maddie's mind was a complete whirl. She had seen the two of them together, so many times. On television, in magazines, in this house even. Kissing, touching, eating together, telling everyone how much they loved each other. It hadn't been easy to see. And worse than all of that, she'd had whole conversations with Sofi about him, about the two of them.

"You lied about all of it? You lied to me."

"I didn't lie to you. I just didn't say everything I should have. I tried to tell you that night when I had that panic attack, but I couldn't. I signed this ridiculous contract that says I can't tell anyone." Her voice sounded shaky, betraying how upset she was. "I thought you'd just guess that it was fake. I've never really liked guys, you know that."

Maddie's brain was screaming at her to ask more questions. Everything she had assumed to be true was unraveling in front of her, and she felt fearful and stupid at the same time. "But when you left, you said that they couldn't make you do this anymore, that your contract gave you freedom to love who you wanted, so I assumed that the two of you were the real deal. Why wouldn't I?" She needed some kind of explanation.

Sofi cast her eyes down.

"They didn't force me, I agreed. It seemed harmless. It was just going to be while we had that single out, but it was easy to just keep going. People liked us together. The buzz it created was good for us both. We agreed to carry on. Felix asked me to sign a contract to make sure there were rules and it was confidential." Sofi finally met her gaze. "But I'm trying to end it. I knew as soon as you came back that I couldn't carry on. It just seemed so lame to still be doing it. And I wanted to show you I had more courage. To do the video, to be more open, to be without Noah. I thought that after all that, maybe it would mean we could try to have something. I want—"

"Are you crazy? You honestly think that you can end it with Noah and I'm gonna be happy to pick up where he left off?" She stood. She wanted to go. She didn't want to be anywhere near Sofi right now. "You're lying to the world about him, talking about a wedding that'll never happen, pretending he's so worried about you that he's flying home to be by your side. Your fans honestly believe you guys are together. It's worse than lame."

"It's no worse than we both did when we were in the band, and we—"

"We had no choice. They made us. But you have a choice. You don't have to do it. You're lying for sales, for streams, for the 'buzz.'" Maddie used the word that Sofi had used. "Daya was right when she said I shouldn't trust you. You're still lying to me."

"I didn't want to lie. I wanted to tell you. I tried. It wasn't just the contract that stopped me. I knew it would be like this, knew that you wouldn't understand. Don't hate me, Maddie, please don't hate me. I'm trying to be braver." Sofi was upset. Her voice was shaking. But Maddie couldn't afford to care.

"I should go." She didn't have anything else to say. She had let her guard down, let Sofi in again and she had done exactly what she always did—put her career above everything, not caring who she hurt along the way. Maddie just couldn't believe she had been stupid enough to let herself get drawn in.

"Maddie, please don't go."

She ignored Sofi's plea, walked down the stairs, and headed for the front door.

"You always leave."

Despite herself, she turned to Sofi. She was standing on the bottom stair.

"I'm sorry I didn't tell you. I wanted to. I should have. And I know I haven't been brave, but neither have you. As soon as it gets difficult, you walk away. From me, from your career. It's what you always do. Maybe I wasn't enough for you then and maybe I never will be, but let's not pretend you're any braver than I am."

Maddie wanted to say something in response, but she couldn't. She was disappointed, she was angry, and she felt like a fool. It didn't matter whether Maddie loved her. Sofi hadn't changed, not really. It was Maddie's wishful thinking that had made it seem like she had. She watched as Sofi tried to find the words she wanted to say. Even now, even after all this, the sight of her struggling and upset made Maddie want to go to her.

"And you can hate me for this, you can even pity me, but my career is the one thing that has always been good to me."

They stood for a beat, just looking at each other across the room. To Maddie, the distance between them now seemed like a chasm. She didn't know how to bridge it, or even if she wanted to.

"I don't hate you." The effort of holding on to her own upset was immense. She had opened herself up to Sofi, given in to her feelings, despite promising herself she wouldn't. But Sofi had made it crystal clear she still couldn't be trusted to do anything but put her career first.

She opened the door and walked outside without looking back. The flashes of the cameras surprised her. Of course they were still there. This was Sofi's crazy life. She was naive to think she could ever be a part of it. It didn't matter if they wanted each other—she let the reality seep in—and it didn't even matter if they loved each other. This wasn't a life she wanted for her or her son. She had been stupid to even try.

Chapter Fourteen

Despite the fact it was almost midnight, Sofia was wide awake. It wasn't the adrenaline of the show—that had long passed—it was the way her mind was whirring. Tomorrow they were going to start shooting her "coming out" video. She couldn't think of it any other way. She had been bullish about it with everyone—she'd had to be in the face of everyone's continued unhappiness—but she wasn't without her own doubts. And since Maddie hadn't been in touch at all since the night of the party, she'd had to deal with those doubts all on her own.

She hadn't imagined that Maddie walking out of her house in anger would mean Maddie walking out of her life for good. But that was how it seemed. Sofia had sent Maddie one text, a short but heartfelt apology for the deception, but there'd been no reply in the days since. And according to Anna, the work on the house had stopped too.

Sofi signaled to the bartender for another brandy. It was a drink she always turned to when she needed something to damp down her anxiety, and right now it was creeping around at the edge of her consciousness and she was trying not to let it take hold. When Rick had arrived at the hotel earlier that day, she'd told him Maddie wasn't coming to Paris, making up some excuse about Mateo being sick. But she hadn't told her mom or Felix yet—not able to stomach how happy they'd be. She sighed. She couldn't stop tormenting herself with what she could have done differently—how she should have told Maddie about Noah sooner, how she shouldn't have reached for her, or kissed her—but whatever else she'd gotten wrong, she was right about one thing, Maddie always walked away. And it hurt to know that Maddie had never cared enough to stay when things got difficult.

She sipped her drink. She had no choice but to make the video and try to take comfort from showing her fans something that was closer to the truth of who she was. It might mean some of them turning against her, it might hurt album sales, and according to Felix, it might even put some of her sponsorship deals in jeopardy. But she was finding it harder and harder to care about any of that. She'd spent so long obsessing about those things only to discover that none of them made her happy. What she wanted most was to make Maddie proud of her and have her understand that however deceitful Sofia had been about Noah, she was ready to be more honest about things. And if Maddie didn't care as much as she'd hoped, it didn't mean she shouldn't do it for herself.

Across the lobby, Sofia watched as Tanya entered the revolving doors, dropped her phone, and cursed loudly while struggling to retrieve it as the doors kept turning. Sofia couldn't help but smile. After a couple of rotations, Tanya emerged and Sofia waved to catch her attention. If she wasn't ready to sleep, then she was going to make Tanya come and drink overpriced French brandy with her for a while.

"So-fi-a, So-fi-a," Tanya said her name like a chant, hands raised above her head, as she walked across to the bar. She looked every inch the rock guitarist she was—leather jacket, ripped jeans, and boots—and judging by her walk, she was somewhere between tipsy and drunk.

"It's late, you're drinking alone in a hotel bar, and you're calling me over. Don't try telling me this isn't that thirsty booty call I've been expecting all these years." She swayed slightly as she crossed to the armchair opposite Sofia, sitting down heavily with a big sigh. "Well, I'm sorry, babe, but I'm too tired to tap that beautiful ass of yours." She winked and then closed her eyes and Sofia wondered if she was simply going to sleep.

"Tanya?"

She opened one eye. "So-fi-a."

"Are you awake enough to give me relationship advice?" Sofia asked hesitantly.

"I think I'm better at it when I'm asleep, but sure, let's talk. Or you talk and I'll make noises that I imagine are helpful until I fall asleep."

"Hey." Sofia prodded Tanya with her foot and she sat up with a start.

"Okay, okay. I'm listening." Tanya rubbed her face vigorously and slapped her cheeks a couple of times. "Are we talking fake relationship or real relationship?"

"Funny."

"Sorry, Sof, I'm being a jerk. Come on, talk to me." Tanya didn't say anything else, giving her the space to say what it was she needed to say.

"You know Maddie was coming to make the video with us." Sofia stretched out the question, speaking slowly, not really wanting to get to the point.

"Yeah, and I know you're real happy about that."

"I was. But she's not coming."

"How come?"

"Something happened between us."

"Let me guess. You told her you've developed feelings for her, but she doesn't feel the same way so she's running in the opposite direction."

"Why the hell would that be your guess?" Tanya had spent one evening with them. And Maddie had pretty much avoided them being together all evening, until—Sofia swam in the memory—they had kissed almost to the point of no return.

"Oh, come on, babe. I've seen you together and I've heard the way you talk about her. And I was there before, remember. When you were together—and when you weren't. I know that you loved her, and I know that you never really got over her."

Sofia didn't want to think that she was that obvious, that she was that hung up on Maddie. But of course she was, she always had been.

She took in a breath. "We kissed after the party. It was amazing." Maddie wanted her, Sofia knew that much. But, as much as Sofia didn't want her to be, Tanya was right. "But, yeah, then she ran away. Like she always does. And I don't know what to do. I spent so many wasted weeks trying to get her to come back to me last time. It was pathetic and it consumed me. And it didn't work. I don't wanna do that again."

"But?" Tanya was listening intently now.

"I'm not ready to lose her."

"What happened? What made her leave?"

"We kissed. It got heated. It felt like it was what we both wanted, but she stopped us. She was worried about Noah, about me having Noah, said it was wrong and we couldn't, shouldn't, but when I told—"

"Don't tell me that's the moment you chose to tell her about Noah?" Tanya put her head in her hands. "Jeez, Sofi. Way to go, babe. 'Oh don't worry about me cheating on my boyfriend. He's not real, even though I told you he was. Now let's fuck.'" Tanya lifted her voice an octave mimicking Sofia. "And you're surprised she left?"

"I know, I know. It's bad." Sofia hadn't been able to stop remembering the disappointed, angry look on Maddie's face. "I tried to explain, but she didn't really want to hear it. I thought—I mean, I know it sounds crazy right now—but I thought that maybe she already suspected, that maybe she'd be happy to know I was single."

"Honestly, Sofi, sometimes you can be a little dumb." Tanya sat forward in her seat. "Let's say that's she's interested and she's happy to know you're single. And let's say she even forgives the lying about Noah part. What happens then? Your life is chaos, and you're never home. She has a kid to think about, she needs stability, and to live in one place. She ain't exactly gonna go on tour with you."

Sofia sat silently. She needed to hear this.

"And let's just pretend that, despite all that, you guys did try for some kind of relationship. You're either gonna have to try to hide it—which is probably impossible—or tell the world. Forget all the homophobic shit for one second, how do you think Noah's fans, your fans, and all the nasties on social media are gonna treat Maddie when they realize she's the one who wrecked the whole Noah-Sofia fairy tale thing? It's not gonna be pretty. I mean, I guess if you told everyone that the Noah thing wasn't ever real that would take the heat off her, but—"

"I can't do that. The contract doesn't allow us to tell anyone about it. It's got some crazy half a million dollar penalty built in." Sofia drained her glass. Tanya was being harsh, but it was hard not to think she was right about all of it. She felt her heart sink in her chest.

"Even when she didn't have Mateo, she never wanted anyone to know about us. It wasn't just that she was scared of the record company, she just never liked the idea of living her private life in public." Sofia felt reality bite. What the hell did she have to offer Maddie and Mateo?

"Exactly." Tanya sat back. "Sorry, babe, but running away seems like the sanest option for her. There's a ton of reasons why she won't want to step into Noah's ugly shoes." She shrugged. "Now, let's have another one of those and try to think of something positive we can celebrate. Tomorrow is my acting debut. Let's start with that." She waved in the bartender's direction and held up two fingers, pointing at Sofia's glass. Sofia wasn't sure she could drink any more, but she definitely wasn't ready for bed now that Tanya had completely crashed her mood. She tried to find something positive of her own to drink to.

"Little Boy said yes to the collaboration. He loved the rough cut we sent. I've got a day off when we finish here so I'm going to go to London for the recording. Everyone's happy we managed to get it organized. Felix says it's going to be 'the thing' that creates enough of the right noise to win the Grammy—which is also his way of letting me know he now thinks 'Not This Time' is a write-off." Sofia shrugged.

"That's great, Sofi. Nice job."

"It's going to help me grow a more adult audience, to leave the last of that ex-girl band energy behind. They're even talking about Glastonbury and me maybe guesting with him there. I'd never get that without him. I'm not edgy enough."

"Or edgy at all." Tanya rolled her eyes and laughed.

The excitement about Little Boy lasted for as long as it took to tell Tanya. She was desperate for the album to do well, and she'd even let herself get caught up in Felix's obsession about her winning a third Grammy. But what did any of it really mean if she couldn't have Maddie in her life? She sighed.

"Should I call her? Should I try to explain or should I just let it go?"

"What do you want to do, Sofi? Forget what you think you should do. Try to get in touch with what you want to do. It's gonna sound lame, but close your eyes, inhale slowly, and try to feel what it is you want rather than thinking too hard about it."

Sofia was desperate enough to try anything. She closed her eyes. She made herself push past the guilt she felt about lying about Noah, past the panic she felt when she thought about what everyone would say, past the fear she felt about being hurt by Maddie again. She made herself push past all of it and try to get in touch with her feelings, with what she wanted. And all she could see was Maddie. Maddie kissing her, Maddie making her laugh, Maddie sitting with Mateo asleep in her lap, and Maddie caring for her when no one else seemed to. She realized she could only imagine being truly happy with Maddie and Mateo in her life.

"I want Maddie. I want us together. And I don't care what I have to sacrifice to get it." Sofia said the words out loud and blinked in surprise at her own response.

"Ladies and gentlemen," Tanya announced to no one in particular. "I think we have our answer."

"But what do I do?" Sofia pleaded with Tanya, feeling the panic, the fear, overwhelm her just as fast as she had allowed herself to acknowledge what it was she actually wanted.

"I don't know. I guess you need to figure out if she feels the same way and find a way to show her she can trust you this time." She raised an eyebrow at Sofia. "I only pretend to have the answers. Have you not noticed just how single I am most of the time?"

"I try not to notice, just like you never made me feel bad for pretend-dating a moron like Noah." Sofia managed a half-smile. She had a lot of thinking to do, but she appreciated Tanya being there for her and for believing in her and Maddie.

"How's he been since the party?"

"A real jerk. His management sent a letter threatening action if I do anything to damage his reputation." She shrugged. "I guess they think I'm gonna tell everyone the relationship was fake."

"Why would they think that?"

"I made Felix call it off. We sent them a doctor's letter saying his unreasonable behavior was damaging my health and used the medical clause to get out of the contract." She lifted her eyebrows. "He is pissed like you wouldn't believe."

"Wow." Tanya lifted her glass to Sofia's. "Good for you."

"We're going to tell people that it's a mutual decision because we can't find time to be together, but he's worried because he knows I'm going to use the video release to tell people that I'm not straight, and he's trying to stop me."

"You're really gonna do it?"

"Yeah. It's scary but it's time, and this time, I'm going to show Maddie that I do have the courage to stand up and be who I am, to not always put my career first."

"Well, I'm damn proud of you." She yawned and stood. "I'm going to bed. You should too. But I will say one thing though. Life is way too short not to kiss the girls we wanna kiss."

"Did you just quote *Supergirl* at me?"

"I did." Tanya laughed. "I steal all my best advice from TV."

"I love you." Sofia meant it. Tanya was a good friend.

"You too, Sofi." Tanya ruffled her hair on the way past. "You're doing good. See you at stupid o'clock for all the croissants we can eat."

Sofia heard her stomach growl. It was the noise of a skipped meal. She didn't want any more of her outfits splitting, and she was keen to limit the number of snarky comments from her mom. She stood up, needing to get to bed. This life had been what she wanted once, the thing she'd have done anything to hang on to. Now she was doubting everything because of Maddie. But Maddie was in Miami, and just like last time, she didn't seem to want what Sofia was offering.

French bread, French toast, French cheese, French fries. All things she loved that were French. Maddie was playing word games with herself in the elevator to distract herself from the tension she was feeling about seeing Sofi again.

French kissing.

It was not helpful of her brain to add that one to the list. She'd stayed busy over the last few days precisely so she wouldn't think about kissing Sofi. She felt a flush spread through her body—it was two parts shame and one part desire. The ratio had been changing slowly with every day that Maddie spent away from Sofi.

But then she'd decided to come to Paris.

The elevator door opened, and she checked her reflection in the mirror before heading out, past the reception desk and the Hermes boutique, and into the dining room. The smell of freshly baked pastries hit hard. She'd arrived barely two hours ago, getting the only direct flight that got her here in time, and the time difference had cost her a night's sleep. In Miami, it was not yet one a.m., and while she was desperate for strong French coffee, her body was definitely not ready for buttery croissants.

As she waited to be seated, Maddie spotted Sofi in the far corner, sitting alone at a window table. She had her phone in one hand and a coffee cup in the other. Two tables away, Rick sat with Carly and someone she didn't recognize. He lifted a hand in her direction. She returned the wave. She'd texted him she was coming only as she'd boarded the plane the afternoon before, not convinced she wouldn't back out. Not convinced that Daya and Ashley wouldn't appear to bundle her into a car and lock her up for a few days till she saw sense.

"I'm joining someone," Maddie spoke to the maître d' and pointed at Sofi before crossing the room. She had just a few seconds to feel the nerves that being in the same space as Sofi brought before Sofi looked in her direction. Her surprised expression made it clear that Rick hadn't told her Maddie was coming.

"Can I join you?" Maddie felt so uncertain about being here, about what she wanted to say to Sofi, about how Sofi would react. But her heart couldn't help but react to Sofi's anxious gaze. Maddie wanted to hug her, kiss her, and tell her everything was going to be okay. Except it would be a lie.

"Sure. Please. I wasn't expecting you. I mean, I didn't think you were coming." Sofi blinked at her.

"Neither did I." Maddie sat down. Within seconds, a waiter in a crisp white shirt appeared at the table with a pot of coffee. She pushed her cup toward him.

"When did you get here?"

"Couple of hours ago. I'm sorry if it was a problem that I didn't travel on the flight I was booked on."

They were awkward and formal together. If this was going to work at all, they had to clear the air. Maddie had spent nine hours on a plane figuring out what she needed to say, but sitting opposite Sofi, she couldn't find the words. But neither could she take her eyes off her. It was like Sofi was a puzzle Maddie just couldn't figure out, and her head and heart hurt from trying.

"I'm glad you came. But I already told everyone that you weren't. I assumed that, when you weren't on the flight, you'd had second thoughts. Because of, you know?"

Sofi looked like she had more to say. Maddie leaned in, wanting the chance to explain why she was there and what she wanted.

"You were right about me doing the walking away thing. It's not a good habit."

"It was all my fault. I'm sorry. I came on too strong. I didn't think. I let my feelings take over and I'm sorry for not telling you about Noah. Maybe on some level I knew it would make you leave."

"It's okay. It's all okay. We both have things to be sorry for. I just didn't want to walk away from this. I made a promise to you, to Rick, to help with the video. I take that seriously. It's important to you and I know how difficult it's going to be." She was trying to stay focused on what she'd come to say. "I promised I would do it, and as a professional and as a friend, I wanted to keep that promise."

Sofi looked like she wanted to say something, but the arrival of the waiter prevented it. He placed an omelet in front of Sofi. Maddie was happy to see her eating proper food—the fasting was ridiculous. Sofi would never be skinny, but she had always been perfect to Maddie. She stopped herself from thinking that way and took in a breath.

"I should never have let things get so out of hand after the party. I'm not gonna blame the drink, but maybe it was a bit of that and a lot of us just spending too much time together. We said we wouldn't get close but—" She stopped. This was harder than she had imagined. Sofi's gaze was hard to cope with.

"Please don't act like this is something we can just brush away as a mistake." Sofi spoke quietly. "I know you have feelings for me."

"It doesn't matter. We can't do anything about it. We said we wouldn't get close enough to hurt each other, but look at us. We can't seem to stay away from each other and the closer we get the greater the chance we're going to do things that hurt each other."

"I'm sorry I didn't tell you about Noah. I know that's a big part of why you're saying this."

"It's not because of Noah." Maddie sipped at her coffee, willing herself to stay calm and to find a way to say the things that they both needed her to say. The things that would allow them both to walk away, with not too much harm done. In a parallel universe somewhere, she would declare herself to Sofi, tell her she had never loved anyone else and ask her to give it all up and stay with her and Mateo in Miami for the next hundred years. But it was a pipe dream, and right now, in this breakfast room in this hotel, she needed to say something else.

"Sofi, your life is crazy and you live it in public. Mine is boring and private, and I like it that way. I was mad at you for lying about Noah, but I shouldn't have been, not really. What you guys have been doing isn't even out of the ordinary. I just forget that because it's not my world anymore. Touring till you drop—ordinary. Photographers following you everywhere—ordinary. Fake boyfriends—ordinary. It's all so crazy. You're beautiful, but this business has you doubting it. You're successful but no one in your life will let you enjoy the success. It's relentless and it's toxic, but it's what passes for ordinary in your world. I wish it wasn't but it is."

"Maddie."

"But I can't handle it. Your crazy life will always make me doubt you and doubt your intentions. I don't want that. It's too hard for me and I have to think about Mateo." Her own voice cracked slightly, but she carried on, making herself sound brighter and lighter than she felt. "So, let's just enjoy being in Paris and make an awesome video we can both be proud of. And then you'll go on tour and I'll go finish your house, and in a few months, when you eventually get some time off, bring Mateo some pastelitos and we can spend the afternoon catching up, like old friends."

"Old friends?" Sofi echoed her words. She still hadn't picked up her fork. "I don't want to be an old friend. Look, Mads, my life might not always be crazy." She reached across and took Maddie's hand, her voice thick with emotion. Maddie should have pulled away, but she couldn't. "I want to find time for you and Mateo. And I'm not just talking about an afternoon 'catching up.' I feel like we've been given a second chance, and I promised myself that this time I would make the most of it, but we can only do that if you want it enough, if you trust me enough."

"It's not about wanting or trusting, it's about you making promises you can't possibly keep." Sofi imagining a life for them was hard to resist, but she'd been disappointed before. It was better that she leave things with Sofi as clear as possible. "There's nothing wrong with being an old friend. It's easier for all of us. And it seems to me like you need more people in your life that are rooting for you, that care about you the way that friends do. Maybe that's what the universe meant us to have this time around."

They were still holding hands and Maddie waited a moment longer before pulling her hand away. She picked up Sofi's fork to steal a forkful of egg.

"I might join you. It smells great. Eat it before it goes cold. We have a long day today." She forced herself to sound okay, handed the fork to Sofi, and then signaled for the waiter and ordered her own portion. It was a pause they both needed.

Sofi began to pick at the food. She was avoiding Maddie's eyes now and clearly seemed upset.

"Did you get that actress you wanted?" Maddie wanted to get Sofi talking about stuff that wasn't difficult for them, and she was curious. Before the party, before it had all gone so wrong, they'd spent an agonizing couple of hours with Rick searching for the woman to play opposite Sofi in the video. They'd watched dozens of show reels sent over by a French agency. And, of course, Maddie's jealousy meant that she found fault with all of them, and she especially found fault with all the ones that Sofi expressed any kind of liking for. Sofi had eventually settled on an actress called Claudine who was tall, with long dark hair and expressive blue eyes. Maddie hated how at ease with herself she seemed, how poised and elegant, how she spoke impeccable English with a strong French accent that both Rick and Sofi pronounced as "very sexy." It was left to Maddie to point out that, since she wasn't going to say a word in the video, it didn't matter what her accent sounded like. She knew she sounded jealous. Watching Sofi fan girl over beautiful French women hadn't been her ideal way to spend a morning.

"Yeah, we did. She said she was delighted to do it," Sofi replied. "Though it was pretty clear she had no idea who I was." Sofi lifted her eyebrows. Her eyes gave away how upset she was despite them trying to keep things friendly. She yawned and rubbed her face.

"Tired?"

"Yeah, not sleeping well. And not just because of this." She pointed into the space between them. "Everyone is so vexed about the video. They're convinced it's going to be a disaster. I've been worrying about that. And Noah has been a jerk since I ended our arrangement." Sofi picked up her fork again, and looked away, seeming embarrassed. "Sorry, I know you don't want to get involved. I just wanted you to know I'd ended it, properly, finally."

Maddie nodded, working hard to keep her expression neutral. It shouldn't matter. And yet she felt so happy to hear it. They sat silently for a beat or two.

"How was Mateo when you left?"

"I'm not sure he gets how long I'm going to be gone, but he was definitely a little mad at me for going away. But when I told him I was helping 'Fia' make a really cool movie, he forgave me. He likes you so it let me off the hook." Maddie smiled. She'd been so happy Sofi and Mateo got on well. Staying away would mean them not seeing each other again. It was something she hadn't thought about.

"I like him too. A lot." Sofi looked down at her plate, concentrating on her omelet, and Maddie could tell she was fighting not to be upset.

This misery they both felt was all on her. She could let them try, let them have something together. They both wanted it. She shook her head. It wouldn't work. Everything she'd said about Sofi's crazy life was true. They were in such different places in their lives, they wanted such different things. The waiter placed her omelet in front of her and she began to eat.

"Is your mom still planning to lure me to the top of the Eiffel Tower and throw me off?" Maddie tried to lighten the mood. Whatever happened after the tour, they had to spend the next two days together. "Or is it death by blunt force injury using a stale baguette?" She waited for Sofi to lift her eyes, the weak smile she offered up made Maddie's heart hurt.

"She's mad at you but maybe mad at me more. She keeps giving me this disappointed look, complete with an I-can't-quite-believe-it head shake. It's like I came home pregnant with Eric Trump's baby or something."

"She never wanted you to be gay."

"No."

"And she always blamed me."

"Well, you were hard to resist." Sofi offered her another small smile.

"I don't remember you resisting very hard." Even now it was hard not to enjoy the memories from when they were good together. They had been great together for a really long time. She stopped herself from thinking that way. "I think if your mom wants to blame anyone, she should blame Buffy the Vampire Slayer. I think Willow and Tara had you over on the dark side long before you met me." She finished the last forkful of her omelet. Sofi was still picking at hers.

"When she sees what we've come up with, she'll have to accept it's right for the song and I can pull it off in a way that none of them think I can." Sofi sounded like she was trying to persuade herself.

"Exactly that. And even if she hates it, so what. It's your career not hers."

"It's my career to ruin. That's what she said this morning." Sofi shrugged.

"It kind of is." Maddie leaned forward and put her hand on Sofi's arm. "Your career, your risk, your creative choices. They all need to realize that."

Sofi looked at her intently. "Thanks, Maddie."

Maddie frowned.

"For being on my side, for believing in this. For coming to Paris."

Maddie nodded. There was nothing she could say to that that would have helped them. The truth was, despite everything, she'd found it impossible to stay away. She stood and pushed her chair backward.

"See you back here in half an hour."

Sofi nodded at her and picked up her fork. Maddie walked away, her feelings in turmoil.

CHAPTER FIFTEEN

The house the production company had found for them was in Muette, a suburb on the western edge of Paris. It was a good pick, matching Maddie's sketch almost perfectly. The owners—a pair of thirty-something teachers who both spoke English—were good about keeping the small cast and crew supplied with strong coffee and bread and cheese, and despite trying to resist, Maddie had eaten enough Camembert to last a lifetime.

She looked at the light meter. It was only seven but already dark enough for them to set up and shoot some of the video's closing scenes. She called for action on the scene that was set. Sofi was sitting in a car at the curb as Claudine left the house, walked slowly across the picture-perfect garden with coffee cup in hand, and handed it to Sofi. Maddie felt a spark of unwanted jealousy as their hands brushed as per the script, and Claudine turned and went back into the house. Maddie's attention was not on Claudine but on Sofi, on Sofi watching Claudine walk away. She couldn't quite believe they were doing this together, that they were in Paris shooting a video, a video in which Sofi was showing a part of herself to the world that no one had ever seen before.

"What do you think?" Rick raised an eyebrow as he spoke.

"Great. Way less of the annoying swaying that time." Maddie knew she was finding more fault than she needed to with Claudine's work. "How was Sofi?"

"Also great."

She nodded with satisfaction. She couldn't see Sofi as anything other than perfect, but Rick had more objectivity.

"Okay, people, that's a wrap. Set up for next scene, please." Maddie gave the instruction to the camera crew and felt Rick pat her on the back. She was feeling more and more confident as the scenes were being ticked off.

"So, two more scenes at the house and then we can all break for dinner while we relocate." Maddie looked at the sheet in front of her, addressing the comment to Rick and Sofi. Out of the corner of her eye, she could see Rosa approaching and braced herself. Rosa had done nothing but complain since they'd started.

"We need to choreograph the last scene before we shoot," Rick said. "It's tricky. Closing the curtains, opening the curtains, and then moving in for the final kiss. And it's all got to be framed perfectly within the window. They'll need to practice positioning." He sounded as matter-of-fact as she should have been about the whole thing. And she would have been if they weren't talking about Sofi practicing kissing a beautiful French woman while she watched, a woman Maddie had scripted Sofi kissing in a video that might badly hurt her career. She tried to damp down the panicky feeling in her chest. She didn't want either the jealousy or the responsibility for hurting Sofi.

Next to Maddie, Rosa huffed. "It's ridiculous. I just don't understand why everyone's trying to make her look like a lesbian."

"Mama, please," Sofi pleaded, not for the first time, for Rosa to stop complaining.

"What?" Rosa shrugged. "It's true. None of your fans want to see you chasing a married woman around Paris and then kissing her like a lesbian and," she paused as if searching for the right word, "an adulteress."

Maddie heard Rick swallow a laugh. She didn't doubt that he hadn't heard anyone use the word adulteress for a couple of decades at least.

"Nothing is funny here, Rick. This is my daughter's career you and Maddie are ruining." Rosa glared at him and he shuffled uncomfortably from foot to foot.

"We still have the option of dropping the actual kiss." Maddie spoke up and earned a surprised look from Rosa and a glare from Sofi.

"Are you kidding me?" Sofi spoke first.

"I just mean that it would still work if we ended the video with you going into the house and opening the curtains after Claudine closes them. The meaning should still be clear and it might be neat to leave people wondering what happened." Maddie looked from Sofia to Rick and back again. "Your mom has a point, Sofi. There's a lot of risk in this for you. There's no shame in rowing back a little." She lifted her shoulders as if to say it was only a suggestion.

"No shame?" Sofi sounded annoyed and Maddie found it hard to look at her.

"Of course there's shame, Maddie. There's shame in hiding, in dodging doing the difficult things, the right things, in case we offend people. I thought you of all people understood that." Despite her anger, Maddie knew that Sofi was choosing her words carefully, that she was talking about more than the video.

"I just don't think we have to shove it down people's throats." Maddie said it without thinking.

"Right, okay." Sofi took in a breath. "Because you wouldn't do it would you? I mean you wouldn't, for the sake of argument, make out with some woman in your underwear and then get on a motorbike with her? Of course you wouldn't. That'd be shoving your sexuality down people's throats and we can't have that. Oh, my bad, Maddie, you can have that, but I fucking can't. Is that right? I mean, I just wanna be clear."

"It's different. We've had this conversation, Sofi. I was already out. And I had a different set of fans, a different career. I had a lot less to lose."

"So you're now telling me I shouldn't do what feels right, shouldn't be truthful creatively because it might be bad for my career." Sofi shook her head. She was letting Maddie know what a hypocrite she was.

"I'm not saying that, I just mean you just don't have to go the whole way. And you don't have to be so fucking anxious to kiss her." She couldn't help but blurt out the last part. She felt ridiculous.

"Rick? Mama? Can you give us a minute please?" Sofi was all controlled rage now, and Maddie remembered too late how her temper was rarely seen but not often forgotten.

"Maybe you should listen to her for once, cariño." Rick had the good sense to wander off, but Rosa couldn't help but chip in.

Sofi took her eyes off Maddie's for a minute and looked at Rosa. "And maybe you should listen to me like the grown woman that I am when I tell you I need a minute with Maddie?" Her voice was even, but Maddie knew her well, knew how close to losing it she was. She pulled Sofi by the arm, away from Rosa, away from all the eavesdropping crew members, down the path and to the opposite side of the street.

They stood face-to-face. The anger had gone from Sofi now. She just looked hurt. Her eyes were wide and confused and Maddie wanted so badly to reach out and touch her, to make it all right.

"Why would you side with my mom against me? You said you'd support me. I don't understand." The words pulled at Maddie, made her feel terrible. She couldn't help herself, she reached out and took Sofi's hand.

"I'm not taking her side. Believe it or not, I'm on your side. I just want what's best for you."

"But I want to do this. I thought you wanted me to, I thought you believed in it, believed in me." Sofi sounded so unsure all of a sudden and Maddie squeezed her hand, tried to transmit through her touch just how much she believed in her.

"I do. I really do, Sofi. It's not that. This song is brilliant, and this video is going to be every kind of awesome. It's just…" She closed her eyes and tried to locate the right words, willed herself to be as honest as she felt she could be. "It's just that I don't want this to hurt you or your career. I'm so happy that you're feeling able to be more open about everything and I so want that for you, but maybe I want it too much and maybe I just feel kind of responsible for this, for the fact that you're about to be kissing that fucking gorgeous French woman over there, and in a few weeks millions of people are going to see you do it. And maybe they won't like it." Maddie made herself calm down. Sofi really needed her to hold on to her feelings right now.

"I don't care."

Maddie frowned.

"I mean, I don't care if they like it or not. I just want to do something that feels real for me and something that shows you I'm serious about telling the truth more. My career can worry about itself for a change."

Maddie was happy to hear her say it. She couldn't stop hope from rising in her chest.

"I'm sorry. I guess I'm just freaking out about it a little, and so is your mom." She smiled and held Sofi's gaze. "Though your mom is probably not struggling quite so much with her jealousy about you kissing the gorgeous French woman as I am." Maddie bit the inside of her lip and lifted her eyebrows. She was trying to lighten the mood, but she was also telling the truth.

"You're jealous." Sofi sounded surprised. "You wrote a storyline where I get the girl—"

"The gorgeous French woman," Maddie clarified.

"And when I do exactly what you scripted, you're jealous."

Maddie nodded, unable to take her eyes off Sofi, enjoying the feel of Sofi's hand in hers. The jealousy was kind of insane.

"Well, I guess she is gorgeous. But she's definitely not the gorgeous woman I want to be kissing right now." Sofi held her gaze and Maddie couldn't stop the gentle throb between her legs that the words caused. "And, anyway, she makes terrible coffee."

They both laughed. Maddie was grateful to have some of the tension broken.

"And, to be honest, I'm having major performance anxiety about the kiss so maybe I should let you cut it. Maybe I could just gaze at her longingly. I'm kinda good at that." Sofi stared at her and then widened her eyes. They were flirting, and despite everything that Maddie had said, it was impossible to resist.

They stood looking at each other.

"I'm glad you're worried about me, Mads." Sofi sounded more serious. "But I'm okay. Believe it or not, I know what I'm doing and I'm ready for this. And I feel like it'll all be okay as long as you keep believing in me."

Maddie couldn't find the words she needed to tell Sofi just how much she believed in her so she simply pulled her into a hug. They stood like that together and Maddie couldn't help but feel that, despite everything, this was the place she wanted to be. After a minute, they pulled apart and Maddie led Sofi by the hand back across the road and onto the set. As they reached the edge of the garden, Maddie saw Rosa watching them closely. She looked from Maddie's face to their joined hands and simply turned away.

"I promise you that we'll get the kiss done in one take. I don't care what Rick says about what it looks like, I'm not going to have you spend twenty minutes making out with Claudine." Maddie lifted her eyebrows at Sofia and was rewarded with a smile and a squeeze of her hand.

Maddie put a hand on her chest, feeling her heart flutter and willing it to beat more regularly. Maybe she'd had too much strong French coffee. Or maybe it was simply being this close to Sofi. Maddie watched Sofi's eyes follow her hand to her chest and then felt Sofi place her own hand over it before heading off to the makeup chair next to where Claudine was already seated.

Rick approached Maddie.

"We're doing the kiss." Maddie answered his unasked question. "Let's just make sure we get it done in one take if we can, I'm worried Rosa might burn the set down otherwise." Maddie was only half-joking.

The French cast and crew disappeared off into the evening. They'd worked a second straight twelve-hour day and had earned their night off. And bar for a few reshoots they needed to do in the morning, they were done. Tomorrow evening, she'd head to London for her collaboration with Little Boy and Maddie would go home to Mateo. She couldn't stop the tightness that formed in her chest when she imagined not seeing Maddie for months to come.

She was sitting with Rick and Maddie in the hotel bar, wanting to be part of their debrief and just enjoying the moment, letting the importance of what they'd done with the video properly sink in. Rick poured them each a glass of red wine.

"Well done both of you. Nice fucking work. I think we've produced something amazing." He lifted his glass to them. "And we managed to do it all without Mama Flores killing anyone." Rick laughed gently. "It was touch and go for a while. I've never heard such aggressive sighing." He clinked his glass against Sofia's. "Though I'm guessing she'll forgive you when it's got a billion streams and we're all picking up the Best Video award at next year's VMAs." He smiled at her.

Sofia smiled back at him. There was a time when that would have been all that excited her, but now she just wanted to know if Maddie was imagining them still being in each other's lives then. Maddie's eyes were dark and full of something serious, and the way she gazed back at Sofia as she sipped her wine pulled at Sofia's insides, making the muscles in her core feel tight and her skin tingle with warmth. Sofia took a gulp of her own wine, trying to keep her hands steady. Maddie had said they couldn't be together, their lives were too different, and she was planning to go home to Miami and forget all about her. She didn't want to let that happen.

"Well, I'm gonna go and make some calls. See you guys in the morning." Rick stood, downed the rest of his wine, and headed across the hotel lobby toward the elevators.

"I guess I should go and call Mateo." Maddie yawned but didn't move. "Today was amazing, but jeez, we worked hard. I'm ready for a nice long bath."

"I'm more hungry than sleepy. We haven't really had any proper food today. And we haven't seen anything of Paris." She lifted her shoulders slightly. "How about we go out and have some dinner?"

Sofia wasn't hungry—she eaten so much bread and cheese that she'd happily have skipped dinner—but she really needed to try to talk to Maddie about the way she was feeling, to find out if there was any way that Maddie would give them a chance.

Maddie tensed, looking at her watch for a long time. Sofia waited for the brush-off. But when Maddie finally lifted her head, the look in her eyes—fearful, intense, and wanting—made Sofia shiver. If Maddie had anything like the same kind of feelings she did then they had double the reason not to let each other go again.

"I need to call Mateo. He's home by now."

Sofia heard the tension in her voice. Maddie sometimes seemed like a frightened deer, and Sofia knew that the wrong sound, the wrong movement, would send her skittering off deep into the forest.

"Yeah, sure, of course. But how about we meet down here in an hour?" Sofia swallowed down her own anxiety. She had persuaded herself that not saying what she needed to would be worse for them in the long run, but that didn't make it any less terrifying. "I was thinking that we could try that place in St. Germain we went to the last time we were here. I checked, and it's still open." Sofia took in a breath knowing that reminding Maddie of their past was a risk.

Maddie looked at her then, her eyes wide.

"La Grenouille?"

"Yeah. Or La Frog as we called it." Sofia shrugged and almost melted when Maddie smiled back at her.

"Okay."

"Okay?" Sofia took a second to process the reply. "Great. Fantastic. I'll see you right here in an hour. I'll book us a table." Sofia stood. "Though, let's be honest, we both know I'm gonna ask the front desk to do it. My French has not progressed at all in the past five years."

Maddie stood.

"Maybe you can ask Claudine for lessons." She raised an eyebrow to show Sofia she was joking.

"Don't tempt me. I know that she's desperate to stay in touch. I could tell by the way she completely ignored all my attempts to make small talk and spent the whole time flirting with the cameraman."

"Some women have no taste." Maddie made the comment and then looked like she wanted to snatch it back. "I'm sorry. I was just joking."

"It's okay. I know." Sofia hated the awkwardness between them. But it was better than the absence she'd felt for all the time Maddie hadn't been in her life. She should have been willing to make things easy, to accept the distant friendship that Maddie was offering. But she couldn't, she wanted so much more. It might only be a pop song, but right now, it was the anthem she needed to give her courage to make the right choices.

"See you in an hour." Maddie headed off to the elevators and Sofia watched her go. She'd said yes. It was a small shot of hope.

❖

"Hey, sis." Maddie felt her blood pressure drop a few points just hearing Ashley's voice on the other end of the phone.

"Hey. How's it going? How's Paris? Did you finish your movie?" Ashley sounded happy to hear from her.

"It's not a movie." Maddie rolled her eyes.

"Try telling that to Abuelita. She just left—she said hi by the way—she already thinks we're all going to the Oscars next year."

Despite her mood, Maddie laughed. Her grandma had always been her biggest supporter.

"It's been tough. We had so much to get through and so little time really. But Rick thinks it's gone great." Maddie couldn't help but want Ashley to be proud of her.

"I bet it has. You're a very talented woman, Maddie." Ashley gave good compliments.

"The actress we have playing opposite Sofi is a bust though. She's beautiful but has no presence. It made it harder than it needed to be. And Sofi, well, she's a natural, so she's just making Claudine look even more wooden in comparison." Maddie couldn't let go of her Claudine jealousy. Seeing them kiss had been ridiculously hard to watch.

"When do you finish? Are you going to get any time to see Paris?"

"We have some reshoots to do tomorrow morning, but then I'll be coming home. I don't want to stay away from Mateo any longer than I need to."

She hesitated, not wanting Ashley's disapproval but needing to speak to somebody. "We're gonna go grab some dinner on the Left Bank now though so we'll see a bit of the city."

"Nice."

"Yeah. Sofi's idea."

Ashley was silent for a beat.

"Just the two of you."

"Yeah. I mean, I could have invited Sofi's mom, but since she's been a bitch to me for two days, I figured maybe not." She tried for the joke, but the tiredness and the mental effort of holding onto her feelings got the better of her and her voice cracked a little.

"Hey, what's wrong?"

"I don't know. Nothing, everything." Maddie had always been able to talk to Ashley about stuff. She was so lucky in that respect.

"She hates that Sofi's doing this video. She hates that I'm here. She's spent the last two days making it clear that I'm ruining Sofi's career."

"She never was very okay about it was she?" Ashley stated the obvious. Her own mom had been great and none of her family could ever really understand why Rosa couldn't just let them get on with their relationship.

"But it's not just that." Maddie made herself talk about what she needed to. "After I found out about Noah, about Sofi lying, I told myself I needed to keep my distance and not let myself fall for her again."

"You told me that was the plan too, Maddie. You said that you had no desire to get mixed up in all the toxic crap that comes with her career. I think I'm quoting you right. Though you might have cursed a little more."

"Yeah, well, I still think that. It's just that when I'm around her I lose myself and my best intentions go out of the window. And sometimes, the way she looks at me just makes me shiver. Sorry, probably too much detail for a sister, even one as cool as you."

"Maddie, I'm sure I can cope. I've had sex. I've wanted sex."

Maddie was again struck by how lucky she was to have a sister like hers.

"I just don't know. I think we get swept up in the past sometimes. And I don't even know if she wants anything other than sex. She knows she's going away tomorrow, she knows I have Mateo, and I can't handle the kind of life she lives. It seems so hopeless. But I still want her, and if I'm really honest, I never stopped loving her and I don't know what to do about it." Saying it out loud was such a relief. Maddie felt some of the tension drain away.

"Can you talk to her?"

"I don't know if I should. There's no future for us so why put ourselves through admitting we have feelings and talking about what they are. Even if she did feel something like what I feel for her, even if she did, how would that help?"

In less than an hour, she and Sofi would be having a dinner in a place that meant a lot to both of them, and tomorrow Sofi would be leaving her behind again. She needed to figure this out.

"It's not just that we'd be apart all the time, and it's not just that I don't want to deal with the madness of her life. I don't know how we could ever be together without it ruining her career. Her mom, her people, they hate us just doing this one video together. What would they be like if we said we wanted to be together again? Her career, her music is so important to her, I don't expect her to risk it for me."

"And yet," Ashley spoke gently, "Sofia is making this video with you, despite what they all think, and despite knowing it could hurt her career, so maybe she is trying to tell you something." Ashley paused. "I can't believe I'm defending her."

"I can't believe it either."

Maddie couldn't pretend that she hadn't thought the same thing, but she'd brushed it away as wishful thinking. Hearing Ashley say it made it sound more possible. But it didn't really change a lot. However brave it was, the video would just make Sofi's life crazier.

"Mateo wants to speak to you. He was napping, but he just woke up. But let me say one last thing. She hurt you and you hurt her, but Sofi loved you once. She loved you a lot. It was awful when it ended, but I wouldn't be at all surprised if she still had feelings for you. In a way, though, whether she does or whether she doesn't isn't the issue, it's about the life she's offering and whether it's what you want. I don't want to sound like a hard ass, but love is rarely enough, and especially not when you've got kids."

Maddie knew she was right. They might want each other, they might even love each other, but neither of them were the people they were five years ago and nothing about it seemed very possible. She couldn't stop the hollow sadness that crept in.

"Mommy." Maddie felt her heart lift at the sound of Mateo's voice.

"Hey, baby. How was your day?"

She focused her attention on her son and just how great it was going to be getting back to Miami to see him.

❖

Sofia took one last look at herself in the long mirror and then reached for her phone. It had only been forty minutes since they'd come up to their rooms, but she'd showered, dried her hair, tried on three different outfits, and was now typing out a message to Maddie. She wasn't patient at the best of times, but the prospect of dinner with Maddie, of saying all the things she wanted to say, was making the wait seem unbearable. She typed out a text:

Wear something warm. I've had an idea

Sofia could see from the flashing dots that Maddie was typing a reply, but she didn't wait.

And I'm ready. If you wanna go early

I need fifteen more minutes. Gonna tell me why I need warm clothes?

Sofia's reply was instant. *Nope.*

Fifteen minutes. She could wait fifteen minutes. She reapplied her lip gloss, she brushed through her hair with her fingers, and looked at her phone. Fourteen minutes. To say she was nervous was every kind of understatement. She sent another message:

Remember the first time we were in Paris together?

Paris was where they'd first become lovers. Sofia wasn't sure she'd have dared to say it if she'd been with Maddie in person, but texting made her braver. The reply came quicker than she had expected:

Are you serious? Of course I fucking do. The reply was very Maddie.

Remember the waiter who hit on you all night?

Ugh. Don't remind me

The next text from Maddie came almost immediately:

I remember the horrified look on your face when you tried your first frog's leg. And I remember you spilling your brandy all over your beautiful blue dress. And when I think about you in the dress, I remember being surprised I was the one the waiter was flirting with

Sofia shivered. She remembered all of it too and was so happy that Maddie hadn't forgotten. She typed out a reply:

I remember you taking off that dress

Sofia's thumb hovered over the send button and then she deleted it quickly and retyped.

See you in fourteen minutes.

She needed to be careful. This was not a time for flirting. Sofia needed to know what Maddie really wanted. All she'd offered had been the chance to hang out four months from now, but that was because of Noah, and Sofia's crazy career. If Sofia offered more, would she want it?

She had fourteen minutes. She sat in the armchair in her suite, careful not to crease her dress, and laid her head back. They would have an amazing dinner and a boat ride down the Seine, and she had to hope that she could find the right things to say to persuade Maddie to take a chance on her this time.

Chapter Sixteen

The city really was beautiful lit up at night, and the view as they crossed the Pont Neuf Bridge was breathtaking. They'd walked to the bridge from the restaurant, and at some point, Sofi had taken her hand. She'd had to fight the urge to pull away, fearing the things that Sofi's hand in hers made her feel, things she absolutely shouldn't be feeling. And then she decided to let herself simply enjoy it, to enjoy Sofi being close while she could.

They stopped halfway across to look at the view, and Maddie couldn't help but explain that although the name of the bridge they were walking across translated as "new bridge," it was actually the oldest bridge in Paris. When she said it—feeling like a nerd for remembering—Sofi had simply gazed at her and smiled, and the slightly hazy look in her eyes made Maddie's heart beat a little faster in her chest. It was hard to keep telling herself this was just two old friends having a farewell dinner because every time Sofi looked at her like that, the feeling low down in her stomach and the fluttering in her chest conspired to screw with her attempts to keep things platonic.

The restaurant had changed a lot in the seven or eight years since they had last visited. The tables were more crammed together and the annoying music being piped in made the atmosphere feel a lot less intimate than Maddie had remembered. And when one of the waiters asked Sofi for a selfie, they both agreed to eat and leave as quickly as they could.

Maddie had so many things she wanted to say, but maybe the meal being a washout was a good thing. Tomorrow, Sofi would be gone from her life for at least the next four months, and then she could stop tormenting herself with what-if and if-only.

"Shall we go somewhere for a brandy?" They were waiting for the check, and she wanted to prolong their evening together for as long as possible.

"We could." Sofi leaned forward and closed her hand over Maddie's. Maddie let herself enjoy the warmth of her touch. "But, since we missed it before, I thought maybe this time you might want to do the river cruise."

The memory was ridiculously clear to Maddie. The band had been given a rare night off and the four of them had been exploring the city. They were in a bar on a floating dock waiting to board a riverboat when Sofi had feigned illness and insisted Maddie take her back to the hotel. They had spent the evening making love with all the passion of new lovers. And when Daya and Suzy had come back full of stories about the trip, Sofi had sat in bed doing her best to look like someone who had a stomach bug while Maddie couldn't stop looking at her, not quite believing that Sofi was finally hers.

"I love Paris." Sofi turned to Maddie as they stood on the bridge overlooking the boats below them. "If it wasn't so cold, I'd definitely live here." She smiled at Maddie. "I'd learn French and work at becoming chic, and I'd cook meals for you and Mateo loaded with butter and garlic."

Maddie's heart flipped more than she needed it to at the fantasy of them living together, of Sofi cooking for her and Mateo. They'd had wine with the meal but not so much that Sofi couldn't know what she was saying. And definitely not enough to justify Maddie feeling this good about it.

"And you'll direct arty French movies in black and white and come home late smelling of brandy." Sofi softly stroked the back of Maddie's hand as she spoke.

"Sofi?" The word almost stuck in Maddie's throat, the power of speech evaporating as the feelings built in her chest. "Don't." It wasn't just the touch. She couldn't handle Sofi saying things she didn't mean. It felt too much like the past.

Sofi's thumb stopped moving, but she didn't release Maddie's hand. She moved her gaze away and looked down at the river.

Maddie had ruined the mood. She had to. They couldn't do this. They shouldn't do this. It wasn't that she didn't want what Sofi was saying, it was precisely because she wanted nothing more.

"I'm sorry," Sofi said. "It's just, y'know, being here." She didn't finish. She didn't have to. Maddie imagined they were both thinking the same thing. Paris was where they'd finally become lovers, after months of waiting, months of stopping themselves. Paris had taken them in and made it possible, and neither of them had ever been the same since.

After a few seconds, Sofi turned back to Maddie with a shy smile. "Looks like the boats are still running. Shall we?"

They walked down the steep stone steps that led down to the jetty and the ticket office. The next trip was not till ten, so they bought tickets and ducked into the small bar on the pontoon to stay warm while waiting. They were the only customers, and though the next boat was the last for the evening, there was no sign of the place closing. Sofi went to the bar and Maddie smiled as she heard her try out her French on the old bartender, then without really meaning to, Maddie sat at the corner table at the far end of the bar. It was the same table they'd sat at all those years ago with their bandmates, before they'd bailed on them to go back to the hotel. Maddie couldn't stop thinking about it.

Sofi joined Maddie at the table with two large glasses in her hands. "You wanted brandy, mademoiselle." She bowed exaggeratedly as she spoke.

"When did you become such a brandy drinker? You used to hate it." Maddie took the glass and cradled it in her hands, the amber liquid looking like nectar.

Sofi shrugged. "I got older. I think I developed a lot of bad habits since leaving the band."

"Really? Want to tell me about them?" Maddie hadn't meant to sound so flirtatious. She was curious.

"Brandy." Sofi pointed at her glass. "Pastelitos, obviously. Hiding, working obsessively, lying about myself, and I guess, letting other people decide what's good for me." She laughed self-consciously. "I think that just about covers it."

Maddie hadn't expected a serious reply. She didn't know how to respond. She wanted to reassure Sofi, but it was good that she was facing up to the things that were making her unhappy.

"Seems to me like you're already giving up most of those bad habits. And I'm super proud of you even if I don't always seem like I am."

"Most?" Sofi raised an eyebrow.

"Well, not this one," she pointed at her glass, "and pastelitos are still being eaten obviously—though I personally don't count that as a bad habit." She smiled. "But I'm not gonna not say it. I still think you work too damn hard and I worry about that. You've taken the rest days Felix gave you and filled them with shooting the video and going to see Little Boy. And the days you're supposed to have off at Thanksgiving you've filled with rearranged London dates from when you were sick." Maddie was happy to be able to say her piece.

"Is this where you say I'm not getting any younger?"

"I'm serious, Sofi. Maybe no one else cares but I do. You collapsed, you're having anxiety attacks." She lifted her hands in frustration. "Take it seriously."

"I do. I am."

"Really?"

"Yeah. I'm tired, and touring is tiring. I'm not saying it's not. But the anxiety, the driving myself too hard, it's because I don't have enough in my life that makes me happy, because I'm not being myself, and a lot of it was because of that whole thing with Noah. And now..." She swallowed a sip of brandy, avoiding Maddie's gaze. Maddie waited, desperate to hear this.

"And now, I feel like I can be different. I stopped that whole Noah circus, I did this amazing video, and you're here. Having you and Mateo in my life in whatever way you feel able to let me, well, it just all feels so much more positive." Sofi finally looked up at her with a hesitant smile and an anxious look in her eyes, and Maddie ached with love for her all over again.

"I don't know what to say."

"You don't have to say anything. Just know I'm trying and give me a chance."

They looked at each other for a beat.

Maddie nodded and touched her glass to Sofi's and they both took a long slow sip.

❖

"I mean I know you're a complete nerd when it comes to music, but I still think you must have prepped for this. You're doing suspiciously well." Maddie fixed Sofia with a stern look.

"And how, bad loser, could I possibly know that halfway around this boat trip, you would start a competition to see who knew the most songs with Paris in the title? I'm a lot of things but I'm not a mind reader."

"Maybe you just guessed that I was going to suggest it and did some revision to impress me. Like when you got all super smooth and ordered that fancy French wine with the meal."

"And were you impressed?"

"Very."

Maddie held her gaze for a second before lowering her eyes, and Sofia swallowed. Her attraction to Maddie right now was off the charts.

Despite the coldness of the temperatures, they stood together at the railing at the back of the boat with their coats buttoned up. The only passengers stupid enough to brave the boat's open top deck. Paris was beautifully lit up on either side of them, and as Notre Dame Cathedral slid by, it was harder to think of a more romantic setting.

"I can't believe I'm going to say good-bye to you tomorrow until February." Sofia had to say it. It had been on her mind all night. "It feels like a long time to be away."

"It is a long time."

"I'm going to miss Mateo's birthday. And Thanksgiving." *And you.* It should have been so easy for Sofia to say it. It wasn't a lie. In fact, it was so true it hurt. But instead she stood by Maddie's side and said nothing.

After a while, Maddie turned to her, a deep frown on her face.

"You don't have to do it, y'know. You act like a passenger, and you complain as if you've got no choice, but it's your life, your bus, you can pull off the road whenever you want to." She paused. "If you want to."

"I want to, but it's not that easy."

"Why isn't it? You've got all the money you need. You've won all the awards. No one would blame you for taking some time for you."

"I never had a good enough reason not to do it before. I don't have hobbies. I don't even have friends—not really—and I never had a person to take time off and stay home for." Sofia didn't know how to say what she needed to say. "But now, four months feels like a stupidly long time to be away and that's because of you. You and Mateo. And I'm gonna miss you like crazy. And I know it's wrong and I shouldn't feel it, let alone say it, because you've already made it clear I'm not what you want, but being with you here like this just makes me so happy. And, if I'm honest, I really just want to kiss you right now and hope it means something." She couldn't keep the want out of her voice and she saw Maddie's eyes react, saw them flood with desire, watched them move from her face to her lips and back again.

"If it's so wrong, then I probably shouldn't say that I feel the same way. I've wanted to kiss you all night. All day if I'm honest." Maddie whispered the words into the space between them.

They were inches apart, and Maddie reached out a hand to touch Sofia's cheek. Sofia leaned her face into her hand and closed her eyes contentedly. She took Maddie's other hand and interlaced their fingers. She could feel the blood in her body, the pulsing between her legs. Maddie's thumb grazed across Sofia's bottom lip and she couldn't help shivering. Maddie moved her hand to the back of Sofia's neck, her fingers now playing with the soft hair at the nape.

"Sofi." Maddie spoke softly, but her name in Maddie's mouth was all Sofia needed to hear. She pulled Maddie to her and put her mouth to Maddie's. She moaned as their lips touched, softly, tentatively, both of them holding back and then both of them giving in. The kiss deepened and Maddie moaned as Sofia moved into her arms, one hand on the small of Maddie's back and the other tangled in Maddie's hair, pulling Maddie deeper into the kiss. Sofia opened her mouth to let Maddie's tongue in, and the taste of Maddie, of the wine and the brandy, the soft touch of her tongue made Sofia gasp as her body flooded with arousal.

Sofia put her hand on Maddie's ass, using it to pull them closer together. She bit down on Maddie's lower lip gently, and when Maddie reacted with a soft groan of pleasure, she pushed her hips into Maddie wanting them even closer. Their bodies fit so well together, their lips were made for kissing each other. How had they ever stopped doing this? It felt so right, so utterly consuming that Sofia stopped thinking about who they were, what was and wasn't possible, and let Maddie's dark eyes and wondrous mouth pull her in. When Maddie turned her and pressed their bodies against the railings, her mouth greedy for Sofia and her thigh pushed between Sofia's legs, Sofia felt her insides turn to liquid and she lost her ability to think, to worry, to do anything other than close her eyes and pull Maddie as close as she could, wanting as much contact as possible. Their kisses were sometimes desperate and greedy and sometimes soft and tender. All of them made Sofia's head spin and her skin prickle with want. She wanted Maddie, she had always wanted Maddie.

She felt the boat bump and pulled away from Maddie slightly, breaking their kiss. The lights seemed brighter and she realized that the boat was already docking back at the pontoon and the trip was over. She looked at Maddie, who was gazing at her with eyes clouded with desire, her lips full and her hair tousled. She looked just like someone who had been making out for fifteen minutes straight. Her beauty caused a breath to catch in Sofia's throat.

Sofia smiled at her and Maddie tried to smile back, but her expression was full of worry and Sofia could see the panic seeping in even as the ramp was being lowered, and below them, the handful of other passengers started to disembark. She leaned into Maddie, pulling her close again and planting a gentle kiss on Maddie's lips. She wanted to keep Maddie like this, to help her understand how right this was.

"I don't want to get off." Sofia could hardly get the words out.

"We have to."

Maddie took her by the hand and pulled her toward the stairs to the lower deck. Sofia let herself be led, not able to think of anything more than just how good kissing Maddie had felt. They were in a foreign country, they had been apart for so long, but kissing Maddie felt like coming home.

The wide embankment next to the landing stage for the boats was made for a late night stroll. It had benches dotted along it where courting couples and shivering tourists sat watching the river. Sofia and Maddie walked a hundred yards before coming to a bench that was empty. Sofia had not let go of Maddie's hand. She knew Maddie, knew that right now she was freaking out. Sofia had to find a way to make sure Maddie knew this was okay. It was more than okay, it was righteous and important, and they could, if they both wanted to, find a way back to each other for good.

They sat on the bench and faced the river. Both of them silent, both of them thinking. Sofia turned to face Maddie and took her hands, pulling them into her lap. Maddie looked as Sofia expected her to—lost, wary, and a little confused. She also looked so completely irresistible that it took all the willpower that Sofia possessed not to climb into her lap and start kissing her all over again.

"Want to tell me what you're thinking right now?" As Sofia asked the question, she traced patterns across the back of Maddie's hands with her thumbs. Maddie looked down at their hands, saying nothing in response. Sofia stopped the movement, and Maddie looked up at her, almost seeming hurt. Sofia watched her eyes clear, watched her swallow, and waited anxiously.

"We can't, we shouldn't do this. I'm sorry." Maddie shook her head. She was struggling to speak. She took in another breath and tried again. "This is wrong." She said the words, but Sofia could tell she didn't mean them.

"No, Maddie, it's not wrong. It's right. We both know that, we both feel that. I know we do." Sofia placed a hand on the center of Maddie's chest. Her heart was beating heavily.

"You're going away, your life is crazy. I can't—" Sofia watched a dark look pass across her face.

"You can't what, Maddie?" They had to talk about these things now or they'd never have a chance. She also knew that, right now, Maddie was ready to flee. Running was what she did, and Sofia just couldn't face the idea of losing her again.

"You mean too much to me for me to do this all over again." She said the last three words bitterly. "I can't love you tonight and lose you tomorrow. And spend months apart from you, worrying about you and whether you're healthy. And knowing that you won't listen, you won't stop, that your career means more to you—has always meant more to you—than anything else." She tried to compose herself. "I'm sorry." Maddie's face was a picture of despair.

"I can be different this time." Sofia tried to find the words that would make things better. "I am different. I'm ready to stop, to choose you and Mateo, if you want that."

Maddie was gazing at her, and Sofia couldn't help but be affected by her beauty. It made her heart hurt to have Maddie so close and not be able to just keep kissing her.

"We're not good for each other." Sofia made herself stay silent and not tell Maddie how damn wrong she was, how this was just her fear talking. She stood, and Sofia thought that was it, that Maddie was leaving. She stood to stop her, to beg her to stay, but Maddie didn't leave, she simply paced in front of the bench and Sofia sat back down.

"It doesn't matter how much I want you." Maddie spoke as she paced. "And it doesn't matter how much I might love you. Our lives are too different and we don't want the same things. And we hurt each other so much last time. I don't think I could survive that again."

Sofia felt panic rising in her own chest.

"Maddie, please. Give us a chance. Finding you again made me realize that I never stopped wanting this, wanting you. I've just been treading water. I feel like, when you're in my life, I'm the best person I can be. I stopped seeing Noah, I made this video, and I'm coming out. All because of you. I want to be more honest with my fans and I want to be happier." She paused. "And I will have a break next year. I promise you. Maybe we could take a trip with Mateo." Even as she said the words, Sofia knew they weren't enough.

"Sofi." Maddie held up a hand, motioning for her to stop. Sofia felt the hurt of it like a spear to the chest.

"Sorry, I just don't know what else to say." Sofia felt her voice breaking.

"I know you feel like love is enough." Maddie sounded defeated and Sofia couldn't bear it. "But it rarely is." She sighed. "And I've never had your courage, your belief in us, and I just don't know how we can do this."

"But you want me, you want us?" Sofia had to know.

Maddie looked at Sofia for a long time. "Yes, I want you."

Sofia stood. She wanted so badly to hold Maddie. Maddie stepped away as soon as Sofia got close enough to reach for her, but then relented and let Sofia move into her arms. They held each other. Sofia could feel Maddie shaking.

"You'll realize we're not enough for you and you'll leave again, and I'll never recover. I'm not strong enough for that, to love you and lose you again." Maddie shook her head, wiping away tears from her cheeks.

"You were always enough for me, Maddie, and I'm not going anywhere. I promise I want this. I've always wanted this. I know this is weird, and hard, and unexpected, but I know we can do this. I can put you first." She twisted her body around in Maddie's arms so that they were both facing the river, pulling Maddie's arms tightly around her torso. "This is Paris, Mads, it would be wrong to be here and not to even try to do something about this insane and beautiful love story that we've been caught up in for so long." Sofia felt Maddie relax slightly in their embrace. Hoping that she was letting herself believe, Sofia turned to face her.

"Seeing you again, spending time with you, has made me realize that I never stopped wanting a life with you, I never stopped loving you, I just lost my way. But if there's a hope, the smallest hope, that you could feel the same way and give us another chance, then I'll do whatever you need me to do to make us work. I promise—"

Maddie pulled her in for a kiss that made her senseless. She spread the fingers of one hand in the hair at the back of Sofia's neck and put the other in the small of Sofia's back, pushing their bodies together at the waist. Maddie said her name into the kiss and then moved her lips to Sofia's ear, nibbling softly on the lobe. Sofia moaned at the sparks it sent around her body.

"Take me back to the hotel." The words were whispered, and Maddie's eyes, when they looked at Sofia for an answer, were as black as the river next to them.

Sofia captured her mouth in a long, hard kiss before taking Maddie by the hand and leading them back along the embankment toward the bridge. Maddie snaked an arm around Sofia's waist and pulled her in a little closer.

❖

Maddie watched Sofi fumble slightly with the keycard to her room and suddenly understood that she wasn't the only nervous one. She closed her hand gently over Sofi's and relieved her of the card, before opening the door and standing back to allow Sofi to go into the room ahead of her.

Sofi turned to her, reaching for her hand, her eyes wide and full of want. Maddie wanted to ask her if she meant what she said, if she really knew what she was doing. Tomorrow was the last time they'd see each other in a long time, and yes, she wanted to ask if this scared Sofi as much as it scared her. But when Sofi stepped closer to her, she realized that none of her questions mattered. Having Sofi this close to her—kissing her, touching her—was intoxicating and she couldn't make herself care about tomorrow. She pulled Sofi into her arms and claimed her with a possessive, urgent kiss. Sofi pushed against her body, meeting her kiss with the same urgency, the same wanting.

"I know I won't see you for a while, but I want you to know how I feel." Sofi faltered, a cloud passing across her face. She pulled Maddie close again, pressing her lips to Maddie's and running her hands down Maddie's back before resting them on her ass and using them to press their bodies together even more tightly. Her hard, demanding kisses telling Maddie what she felt without need for words. She pulled away, leaving Maddie breathless.

"I never imagined seeing you again. I had let it go, accepted that I would only ever have this career instead of the relationship and babies thing that everyone else did. I told myself it was just as good, better even. I got a million downloads faster than anyone else, sold out my first concert tour faster than anyone else. And after spending one evening with you and Mateo, I understood just how hollow it all was. I want you to know that I have never stopped loving you. And this time I won't fuck it up. I'm not going to hide anymore and

I'm going to put you and Mateo first. If you'll let me." She gazed at Maddie, biting her bottom lip, the desperation in her eyes pinning Maddie to the spot.

"Don't say things you don't mean. I can't—"

"I mean it." Sofi interrupted Maddie with another demanding kiss. Maddie closed her eyes and then found the strength somewhere to put a hand on Sofi's chest and push her away.

"I can't be hurt again. And I can't let you close to Mateo if you don't mean it. I'm not stupid, I know it won't be easy, I know that everyone will hate this, but I need to know that this isn't just you fucking around, that you mean for us to have something somehow." Maddie felt a tightness in her chest that matched the tight, shivering feeling low down in her belly.

"I." Sofi kissed her behind her ear.

"Mean." She bit softly down on Maddie's neck and her skin turned into a sea of goose bumps.

"It." She put a hand on Maddie's cheek and looked into her eyes. And the way Sofi looked at her told her that she did mean it. And she decided it was enough.

Maddie put her hand at the nape of Sofi's neck and used it to pull her into a kiss. She gloried in the feel of Sofi's lips, moaning when their tongues touched. She moved her other hand up Sofi's leg, under her dress, and past the top of her thigh until she could cup her beautiful ass. Sofi moved to grind against her, and Maddie felt herself get even more wet.

"You are the most beautiful woman I have ever seen. And I've spent an indecent amount of time tonight thinking about taking off that dress." Maddie sounded smoother than she felt. She swallowed. Her mouth was dry suddenly and her heart was about to burst out of her chest.

Sofi smiled a smile that told Maddie she had just said absolutely the right thing. She threw her coat on the chair and bent to remove her shoes while Maddie did the same. They were toe to toe now, next to the bed.

"Sofi." The thickness of her voice completely betrayed the desire Maddie was feeling. Sofi responded with a hungry kiss, her tongue darting inside Maddie's mouth in a way that had always driven

Maddie wild. All the time, Sofi's hands did not stop moving along Maddie's body, grazing her breasts through the fabric of her dress, caressing Maddie's shoulders, running her hands up and down her back and across her ass. Maddie felt herself surrender. She was hot, she was wet, and all she could think about was getting naked and having Sofi underneath her.

She pulled Sofi to her, kissing her hard and then stepping back. When Sofi reached for her, she moved farther away, out of her reach, putting her hand up as if to ask Sofi to give her a moment. Sofi's eyes were wide and wanting. Maddie teasingly reached behind herself to slowly unzip her own dress, pausing before she allowed it to fall from her shoulders so that she could enjoy Sofi's reaction and then letting it fall down her body to the floor. She stepped out of it and kicked it to one side, then faced Sofia in just her underwear, glad that she had chosen something lacy and black.

Sofi moved to take off her own dress and Maddie stopped her. She took hold of Sofi's hands and kissed them both before placing them on her hips. They stayed there for about three seconds until Sofi moved them to Maddie's breasts, stroking them through the soft sheer fabric of her bra. Sofi undid Maddie's bra and let it fall to the floor next to the dress. Maddie leaned her head back and enjoyed the feel of Sofi's hands on her breasts, bolts of pleasure landing between her legs every time Sofi grazed a nipple and then, when Sofi bent her head to take a nipple in her mouth, they both moaned and Maddie felt her legs get a little unsteady. She was so close to just letting go, and she knew that if Sofi's hands strayed any closer to her center than their current position at the edge of her panties, she wouldn't be able to hold on.

Maddie lifted Sofi's face to hers and kissed her. Seeing Sofi's desire made Maddie even more aroused. She turned Sofi gently so that her back was to Maddie and unzipped her dress slowly, letting her fingers follow the zip, tracing a line down the soft skin of Sofi's back. She felt Sofi shiver under her touch, and Maddie let the dress fall to the floor, before gasping at the sight of Sofi almost naked in front of her. She stepped toward Sofi and unhooked her bra, then let it fall to the floor. Maddie kissed the back of her neck, gently at first and then not gently, biting her skin. She peppered kisses along Sofi's neck and shoulders, before reaching around Sofi's body, moving her hands onto her breasts, pinching her nipples gently. Sofi's moans telling her all she needed to know about whether she liked it.

She pinched harder. Sofi arched her back and pushed herself back against Maddie. Maddie dropped one of her hands, her fingers playing with the edge of Sofi's panties, darting in and out of the waistband until Sofi took hold of Maddie's hand and lowered it into her panties with a low moan. Maddie smiled and bit down on Sofi's neck as she felt just how wet Sofi was. She began to stroke the wetness, finding the spot that she knew Sofi needed her to touch and enjoying the feel of Sofi grinding her ass against Maddie's own aching center as her pleasure built.

"Maddie."

Maddie was so far gone that she barely registered Sofi saying her name. But when she did, she stopped and pulled away, worried that Sofi wanted her to stop. Sofi groaned instantly.

"No, no, don't stop," Sofi pleaded.

Maddie turned Sofi around to face her, needing to understand what she wanted. Sofi moved Maddie's hand back to where it had been, but at the same time, she moved backward toward the bed, sinking slowly onto it and pulling Maddie down on top of her. She used her hands to push down her panties as far down as she could reach.

"I want you inside me," she whispered into Maddie's ear.

Maddie kissed Sofi hungrily, never stopping her rhythmic stroking through the soft wetness between Sofi's legs. She moved her mouth to Sofi's breast, feeling Sofi react with a gasp to the feel of her tongue flicking across her nipple, Maddie entered Sofi, moving in and out slowly, and then, as Sofi responded, lifting her hips from the bed to meet Maddie's fingers, quicker and harder. Fucking her in the way she wanted, in the way they both wanted. Sofi's hands were all over her—on her breasts, in her hair, on her ass.

Maddie lifted her head from Sofi's breasts to kiss her, knowing she was close to coming. Sofi had a pleading heavy look in her eyes, her lips full and red betraying her arousal. The sight was electrifying to Maddie, and she felt the throbbing between her own legs grow even stronger. As if reading her mind, Sofi reached down and slid her fingers inside Maddie's panties, dipping them into the swollen wetness with a sigh of pleasure. As soon as Sofi touched her there, Maddie felt her body react. She lost possession of herself and, for a moment, ceased the in and out strokes that Sofi was straining for.

"No, don't. Don't stop." The pleading words from Sofi brought Maddie back into the room. She wanted to hold on. She willed herself to not to give in to the explosive orgasm that she knew Sofi's touch was about to create in her. She continued to plunge her fingers deep into Sofi, glorying in the sounds that Sofi was making on every stroke, and she pushed her own center against Sofi's hand. She wanted to come so bad but also wanted to wait, wanting them to come together.

Finally, she felt Sofi arch as she let out a soft elongated "f-uuu-ck," and Maddie knew she was coming. She let herself go in response, her own wave of pleasure taking her breath away, better than anything that had gone before and leaving her unable to do anything other than collapse on top of Sofi. Sofi bucked against her, murmuring curse words over and over as she rode out the orgasm. Her eyes clamped shut. When she opened them, Maddie could see they were wet.

"Hey." Maddie moved onto her side, stroking Sofi's cheek softly. "Are you okay?" Maddie didn't dare breathe, her own orgasm had barely subsided, her body still trembled, but she wanted, needed, Sofi's tears to be of happiness and not of regret. She couldn't bear that. She watched Sofi swipe her eyes, seeming annoyed that the tears were there.

"I'm more than okay, Maddie. That was incredible. Goose bumps everywhere." She moved Maddie's hand to her thigh to stroke her dimpled skin. She shook her head with a look of embarrassment. "It's just, I waited a long time for you, for this." She kissed Maddie softly. "And I didn't dare imagine that you would ever be mine again." Sofi's eyes were dark, watery, and full of feelings, and Maddie thought they were beautiful.

"I…" Maddie wanted to say how she was feeling. But the arousal, the orgasm, the feeling of Sofi naked next to her, all conspired to make it too hard. She wanted to say that she'd never stopped hoping they would find their way back to each other, that she was glad Sofi had brought her to Paris and had the courage to make this happen, but she was terrified about what came next. So, instead of speaking, she kissed Sofi all over again, moving her mouth from Sofi's lips to her shoulder blades and then to her breasts. They had all night to talk. Maddie would find a way to tell Sofi how she felt, but right now, she didn't have words. She felt Sofi shift beneath her, felt Sofi's hands on her ass, pulling them closer together, grinding against her. She felt Sofi bite her skin just above the collarbone and started to throb with want all over again. She had the feeling they weren't going to get much sleep in this lovely Parisian bed.

❖

Sofia woke up and stretched. She felt a tight soreness in her thighs and calves—a happy by-product of hours of making love with Maddie. The memories made her heart smile and her whole body tingle. She leaned across to kiss Maddie to find her gazing up at her, her eyes wide and full of worry.

"Hey." She placed a soft kiss on Maddie's lips, trying not to feel panic at the way Maddie was looking at her.

"We need to talk."

"About what?" Sofia needed to know what Maddie was thinking. "No good ever came from anyone saying 'we need to talk.'" She pulled herself up into a seated position and pulled the covers over herself defensively. She wasn't sure her heart would survive Maddie having second thoughts.

"I'm scared." Maddie spoke softly, her voice a little husky.

"Of what?"

"Of what comes next." Maddie moved to sit up, leaning her back against the headboard. "I never let myself imagine you coming back, and I'm so fucking happy about it that I'm terrified. I don't know how I'm going to go back to Miami and pretend this didn't happen."

Sofia didn't know what to say. She had always been more hopeful than Maddie, more optimistic somehow, but even she—with her belief that love was enough—could see that it wasn't going to be easy. But she couldn't regret any of it. They'd fought their feelings and then both accepted they had to act on them.

"I don't want you to pretend it didn't happen. Why would you say that?"

Maddie closed her eyes and then opened them again, and Sofia felt like she was standing on the edge of a dangerous precipice.

"Last night was amazing, obviously. I never stopped wanting you, my body never forgot the way you felt, how we made each other feel. But this last few weeks—finding you again, us spending time together, Mateo falling for you—well, it's made me realize just how much more this is for me than simply wanting you. I know this is maybe unexpected, but I love you, and if I'm honest, I don't think I ever stopped."

Sofia felt her heart lift. She wanted to jump up onto the bed, raise her arms in the air, and shout with happiness. But Maddie looked like she'd just delivered some devastatingly bad news.

"I don't understand. That's good, isn't it? I feel the same way. I was only ever treading water in life, waiting for you to come back. It's why I'm tired and unhappy. I had no idea that being without the person you're meant to be with was so exhausting. I love you too, Maddie. I always have."

"It's not enough." Maddie shook her head.

"How can it not be enough?" Sofi leaned across and kissed Maddie softly, searchingly. She felt Maddie respond. She wanted to make it clear with her kisses that this wasn't just enough, it was their destiny. Maddie pulled away.

"Today, you're going to be leaving for a long time, and I'm going to go home to my son. And even if I tell myself I can wait, what will I be waiting for? A week at Christmas and maybe a weekend off after the Grammys if you win and everyone agrees you deserve some time off. But only if the next-big-thing in music doesn't make a better offer. And when the focus groups tell you that coming out, ditching Noah, and hanging out with me is bad for numbers, what then?"

Maddie sounded so unhappy, but she didn't need to be. Sofia had been worrying about the same things, and she knew they could make it work.

"We'll find a way. I have lots of experience sleeping on planes. And I am home for a few days at Christmas. It's only a couple of months away. And after this tour, I promise you I will take some serious time off and live in my house. I'll even buy myself a Jet Ski." She smiled and looked into Maddie's eyes, wanting to let her know they could do this.

"And truthfully, I don't know what the hell is going to happen when this video drops, at the same time that people find out I 'broke up' with Noah, but with you by my side I know I can find a way to be brave. I'm so sick of hiding, and if Felix is right and it ruins my career, then maybe it's time to find a new one."

Maddie sat staring at her. She wasn't sure if she'd said the right thing or the wrong thing. But at least it was the truth this time.

"If I'm by your side, it's going to be worse. They're all going to come for me—not just your people but your fans, his fans. I don't want that, for me or for Mateo."

"That's what Tanya said. But she also said that if I told everyone the Noah thing was fake, that I felt like I had to stay in the closet, then maybe it'd be okay and people might not blame you."

"You can't do that. It's career suicide." Maddie's voice was small, uncertain. "You told Tanya about us?"

"Yeah. I had to tell someone. I'm sorry. I needed advice."

"And you chose Tanya?" There was the glimmer of a smile on Maddie's face. "Interesting choice. What did she say?"

Sofia chanced moving closer. She knelt in front of Maddie.

"She said that she'd always thought we were end game. And she said life is way too short to not kiss the girls we wanna kiss."

"That's—"

"I know, I know," Sofia murmured the words into Maddie's mouth, stopping her from speaking by pulling her into another kiss, deeper this time. "I don't know how this is all going to play out, but I promise you'll never regret giving us another chance." When she pulled away and looked at Maddie, the unmistakable need she saw on her face made Sofia's insides tighten. She stroked strands of hair away from Maddie's forehead and marveled at the feeling. Maddie shivered at the touch and her eyes grew wider. Sofia tilted her head and pressed her lips to Maddie's, and when Maddie parted her lips slightly, Sofia's tongue darted softly inside. Maddie moaned and opened her mouth a little wider, taking it in. The warm wetness of their kiss was so delicious that Sofia couldn't help but groan with desire. Maddie pushed her onto her back, her hands on Sofia's breasts, pushing her leg between Sofia's. Her hands moving naturally over Sofia's breasts, her palms grazing the nipples. Sofia's breathing became a little ragged.

She was mesmerized by Maddie's hands, moving across her stomach, into her hair, caressing her breasts, never keeping still. Maddie's lips moving from her mouth, to her neck and traced soft kisses across her collarbone. Sofia felt like she was made of liquid, not sure how she was still breathing.

"You're so beautiful." Sofia traced her fingers across the warm curves of Maddie's breasts, enjoying the shiver that her touch created in Maddie. She closed her mouth over one and then the other, using her tongue to tease the spot just under each nipple that left Maddie writhing with pleasure above her. Sofi flipped Maddie onto her back and moved her mouth back to her breasts before tracing her tongue down Maddie's torso and across her ribs. As she moved her mouth along Maddie's abs and into the hollow beneath her stomach, she left gentle fluttering kisses on her skin. She looked up at Maddie, seeing nothing in her eyes but want, seeing a pleading that was all the answer she needed.

She moved off the edge of the bed and knelt in front of Maddie, gently pushing her legs farther apart and leaning up on her knees to tease kisses from Maddie's navel to the inside of her thighs, allowing herself to softly graze her fingers across Maddie's center, enjoying the feeling of Maddie writhing beneath her. She felt Maddie's fingers in her hair, urging her not to wait any longer. Sofi didn't want to. She wanted to taste Maddie again more than she had ever wanted anything else in the world.

She stroked the length of Maddie with her tongue as Maddie lifted her hips, pushing herself closer to Sofia's mouth. She circled Maddie's clitoris, flicking her tongue across the swollen tip and hearing Maddie gasp every time. Maddie's breathing was rapid now, her body grinding into the bed to the rhythm of her tongue, one hand grasping the bed sheets tightly and the fingers of the other wrapped in Sofia's hair.

Sofia could feel that Maddie was close to coming. She reached up a hand to pinch her nipple, before rubbing her palm across it roughly. Sofia closed her mouth over Maddie's center, gently sucking, until she felt Maddie's orgasm crash in, heard Maddie cry out her name as she came. She felt Maddie shuddering beneath her and waited for her to come back down, for her body to grow still.

Sofia lifted her head and looked up along Maddie's body, seeing her smiling sexily back at her, her eyes still full of arousal. She moved herself slowly back up Maddie's body, trailing kisses as she went, before lying down next to her, her own body tingling and throbbing with desire.

"Wow." Maddie smiled at her. "I'm trying not to feel jealous that you're not out of practice."

"You shouldn't be. This is just my body coming back to you and remembering just how good you taste. There's no one else." Sofia kissed Maddie and snuggled in even closer. Maddie wrapped her arms around her tightly. "Unless we're including Claudine I mean." Maddie grabbed at her and Sofia laughed and struggled until Maddie had her pinned to the bed. She kissed her possessively and then moved her mouth to Sofia's ear.

"Luckily, my body remembers a thing or two about you as well and I know just the thing to help you forget Claudine."

CHAPTER SEVENTEEN

M addie woke to the sound of someone knocking on the door and calling Sofi's name softly. Next to her, Sofi hadn't even stirred. But they were in Sofi's room, and there was no way she was going to answer the door. There was no one in the hotel, except maybe Tanya, who would be happy to know the two of them had spent the night together. She lay there quietly, trying to keep the panic at bay, concentrating on the feel of Sofi pressed against her side, the soft snuffling of her breathing.

Almost as soon as the knocking subsided, Sofi's phone began to ring. This time, Maddie nudged Sofi gently and couldn't help but smile as she slowly pulled herself out of sleep, rubbing her eyes with the back of her hand and stretching like a cat. Eventually, she opened her eyes.

"Morning, beautiful." Sofi reached under the covers for her, pulling her closer, wrapping her arms and legs around Maddie's body like a koala bear.

"Someone wants you."

"I hope it's you." Maddie felt Sofi's hand on her breast as she nuzzled her neck. She laughed while lifting the hand and putting it on top of the covers chastely.

"I'm serious. Someone was just knocking at the door and your phone was ringing."

Sofi dragged herself up into a seated position and yawned. "What time is it?"

"Just after seven."

"Jeez." Sofi reached across to the bedside table to get her phone. "I'm exhausted. Someone refused to let me sleep." She smiled at Maddie and placed a hand on her cheek and a soft kiss on her lips. Maddie felt her body respond.

She pulled away and reached for the handset next to her side of the bed and pushed the room service button. She ordered a pot of coffee and headed into the bathroom. They still had a long morning's work to do on the scenes that Rick thought needed to be reshot. And then she had a flight back to Miami to catch. Without Sofi. The reality of the situation crashed in.

"Hey, Felix, what's up?" Sofi spoke into her phone as Maddie stepped into the shower and turned it on.

Minutes later, she emerged from the bathroom to find Sofi sitting on the edge of the bed, bent over her phone, unmoving.

"What's wrong?" Maddie felt a rising panic at seeing her like that. "What's happened?"

"I have to go." Sofi jumped off the bed. "Fuck, fuck, fuck." She dropped her phone onto the bed and ran her hands through her hair anxiously. "I have to get ready."

She headed for the bathroom.

"Sofi." Maddie called after her. "What's happened?"

She stopped and turned.

"I think, I mean, it seems like Noah..." She shook her head as if not quite believing it herself. "Felix said that Noah told Little Boy's people that I'm making a 'lesbian' video," she put speech marks around the word with her fingers, "and he's pulling out of the collaboration because—although he personally respects it's my choice—professionally, he doesn't want to be associated with 'that kind' of artist." She took in a deep breath. "Felix said I fucked up by making Noah mad." Sofi took in a big breath and let it out again. Her body seemed full of tension, and Maddie guessed that talking about the detail of it with her was hard.

"What did he do?" She could feel her anger building.

"The contract stops us both from talking about our relationship, from telling anyone it wasn't real, and it stops him from telling anyone I'm gay, but it obviously doesn't stop him from telling Little Boy I'm doing a video like this. I mean, it's gonna be in the public domain in a few days anyway. Felix thinks Noah told them you were making the video, that there were always rumors about us, that you already came out, that I was gonna do this gay ass video, and he left Little Boy's team to join the dots. And they freaked out."

"That homophobic little shit." Maddie moved toward Sofi. "I'm so sorry, Sofi." She wrapped Sofi in a hug. Sofi let her, but then pulled away.

"It's an absolute disaster." She pulled at her lip nervously with her fingers. "The record company wants us all on a call in thirty minutes. Felix is spinning out and has gone into full damage limitation mode. And none of us knows what Noah's gonna do next."

There was a knock at the door. Maddie took the tray of coffee and placed it on the table.

"It was never going to be easy. You knew that."

Sofi nodded.

"Everyone said I was taking a risk with this. It wasn't like I didn't know. I just thought it'd be for me to decide what was said and when, and I thought—" Maddie saw tears in her eyes.

"What?"

"It's crazy and it's going to make me seem like I'm a coward, but I always worried that I'd only have the courage to do it if you were by my side to support me. But of course you won't be."

Maddie reached for Sofi's hand.

"I have to go home. I have Mateo. You know that."

"I know, it's stupid. I just hope I can do it without you."

"You can, Sofi. You're ready for this. You said it yourself. It's time to stop hiding. It's not making you happy, and if it costs you a chance with Little Boy, then fuck him."

"That's easy for you to say." Sofi avoided her eyes.

The comment hurt. None of this was easy for her.

"It's not just something I'd say. It's something you said once. But maybe you don't remember. You said that if your fans turn their back on you for being gay then maybe they're not the fans that you want."

"I remember. But even then I thought I'd have you with me and you weren't."

Maddie stroked Sofi's hand before letting it go. This wasn't a time for the past.

"Have a shower, have some coffee, go and see how bad it looks, and I'll see you on set in a little while."

Sofi didn't move.

"This should make you angry, Sofi, not defeated. And yes, I know it's easy for me to say, but you're the one they're trying to push around. They're trying to make you live a life you don't want to live anymore. Go and tell them that." Maddie had no trouble locating her own anger. She just wished she could give some of it to Sofi.

Sofi nodded. "I'll try."

Maddie let her go into the bathroom. She poured herself a coffee and sat on the edge of the bed where a couple of hours before she and Sofi had been making love oblivious to all of this. The wonder of the sex obliterating any sense of how difficult this was always going to be. She couldn't regret it. She'd waited for Sofi for so long. She just had to hope that Sofi felt the same way.

Sofia sat in the armchair in Felix's suite and watched him pacing up and down. She could only hear his side of the conversation, but she couldn't even make herself tune in to that. Her mom had gone to get some breakfast, and Sofia had declined the offer of going along. It wasn't just that she couldn't bear to hear her mom say I-told-you-so one more time without losing her mind, it was that she couldn't imagine eating a thing. She was angry, stressed, and anxious. Mostly, her anger was directed at Noah, for being vindictive and immature enough to stir this whole thing up. But then she'd gotten mad at Little Boy for being too scared to work with an artist that might make him somehow look like anything other than the homophobic asshole that he clearly was. The stress and anxiety was all her own. They'd warned her this video was a risk, and she knew coming out might cost her, but she hadn't expected it to hit so fast and so hard.

She reached across and topped up her coffee. It wasn't helping the rancid feeling in her stomach, but it was helping to keep her awake when she'd barely had two hours of sleep. And when all she really wanted to do was go find Maddie, curl up with her in bed, and pretend none of this was happening.

Half an hour ago, she'd gone to Maddie's room to let her know what was going on, hoping to catch her before she left with Rick to set things up for the shoot, but she'd been too late so she had to content herself with a text:

We're trying to fix things. Everyone is pretty mad. But it's okay, I think. I'll see you soon. I don't know if I'm allowed to say it but I love you x

She'd added a sentence about how utterly amazing spending the night together had been but then deleted it for fear of it being too much somehow. They definitely needed to talk some more about what happened next, but this shitstorm meant they hadn't had the chance. Even from another continent, Noah was doing his best to ruin things for her and Maddie.

"Okay, okay, we get it. Noon. Definitely. No problem. Yeah, that could work. Yeah. She's with me now. I'll be in touch soon. Thanks. Okay, bye." Even when she bothered to listen, it made no sense. Felix put his phone in his pocket and sat in the armchair opposite her.

"We have until noon to do something about this. We've got two options that work. Three if you count Justin's suggestion that we ditch this song release altogether, which I'm guessing from your reaction during the call earlier is not something you're going to entertain?"

"You seriously put a question mark at the end of that sentence?"

Felix and her mom seemed like they were competing to see who could piss her off the most today.

"Just checking." He held up his hands defensively. "This is the kind of problem that might have changed your mind."

"My mind hasn't changed, Felix. What are the options?"

"Option one. We delay releasing 'Not This Time' until after we release the Little Boy collaboration. And," Sofia could tell he was choosing his words carefully, "we say nothing that might associate you with the LGBT community until at least three months after the song has been released. You both get the buzz of the collaboration, but he's long gone by the time you start talking about why you're now kissing French women in your videos." He cleared his throat. "His people think that if you guys can get it recorded tomorrow, they can have it out by the end of the month, and timing-wise, you could still release 'Not This Time' in time for the Grammys—if you still want to." Felix looked pleased with what he was saying. Like he'd just discovered a cure for something.

Not for the first time lately, Sofia wondered what the hell she was doing with her life. No one listened to her, what she wanted didn't seem to count for anything, and everywhere she turned things just seemed so fucking toxic.

"I can't wait to hear option two." She ran a hand through her hair, the tight feeling building in her chest was familiar. She put down the coffee.

"Option two is maybe better. Less disruptive anyway. You release 'Not This Time' now as we planned—so all the promo can go ahead as intended—but the video has a different theme, no kissing women, and therefore no need for you to be talking to anyone about why you might be kissing women. And you can do the collaboration with Little Boy as planned, no harm done." He sat back in the chair. "I already spoke to Rick about this. Most of your scenes are already in the can. He thinks that he'd need tonight and tomorrow to reshoot Claudine's scenes with a male actor and today should be enough time to reshoot the scenes at the house that involve you both so you can still get to London tonight." He spoke quickly. "Carly had the genius idea of using the guy whose house we were filming at. He's pretty handsome and he's the right age. Rick said he'd see if he was interested and screen test him early today. If it doesn't work, then we can go back to the agency that provided Claudine and ask them for someone urgently."

"Are you serious?" Sofia asked the question, but she didn't need to. Felix had no sense of humor. And from the way he was looking at her, she could tell he had no idea just how objectionable it all was.

"It's the best I can do. Little Boy's people are being pretty unreasonable."

"I've been fighting everyone in support of this video, in support of this song, since the beginning. I've told you all a thousand times why it's important to me. You really think I'm going to just roll over and agree to reshoot the video with a man because some rapper I've never met wants me to seem less gay? Have you listened to a word I've been saying this past month?"

"I know you're not happy about it, but it's the only way we can save the collaboration." He rubbed his face. "It might not always seem like I'm on your side, but I am. Justin's idea was to bring Noah in to play opposite you in the video. He thinks it kills two birds with one stone because it calms Noah down and gives Little Boy what he wants. He told me to talk you into it and I haven't even tried."

She stood, feeling just about ready to explode.

"Do you work for me?"

Felix blinked at her.

"Do you work for me?" She repeated the question.

"Of course I do. Look, Sofi, I—"

"You're supposed to be my manager, Felix. The person who makes things happen for me—for me, not Noah and not Little Boy. You're supposed to help me make a success of the career I want. And right now, the career I want does not involve me abandoning the song, delaying its release, or reshooting the video because Little Boy has turned out to be so fragile in his masculinity that he thinks being associated with a woman who loves women makes him look like less of a stud. Do you honestly think I would do that? That I'm that desperate for this collaboration?"

Felix looked shocked. He sat staring at her.

"And I hope you told Justin to go fuck himself at the idea of Noah being within a hundred feet of me. Not only would I never shoot a video with him, but I want you to sit down with his people and make it clear that if he does anything else to try to harm my career, I will go to the media and tell them about the whole thing and I don't care if it costs me half a million dollars to do it. It'll be worth every cent. If I have to, I'll tell everyone that I faked it with Noah because I was scared of coming out and I'll make it clear that he was an asshole who took advantage of that and caused me so much stress that I collapsed. He needs to start thinking about how he's going to explain all that because it's all he'll get asked about for the next six months."

Sofia should have been angrier, but instead, she felt all the stress and tension of earlier draining away. Somehow saying this stuff to Felix, taking control for once in her life, felt righteous and the righteousness calmed her.

"The record company won't let you do that. They're not happy with you, Sofi. You've got to know that. They didn't sign you as an angry LGBT artist, they signed you to be their very own Disney princess. A singing Latina Disney princess but still a fucking princess. They expect you to behave a certain way. This whole experiment has left them worried. I've sheltered you from a lot of what they've been saying, but..." He waved his hand as if to say he could only do so much.

She walked toward the door and back again, trying to regulate her breathing, trying to say what it was she needed to say.

"It's not an 'experiment,' Felix. It's my life. And it's a life I'm determined to live a lot more truthfully. And maybe it won't make the record company happy, but I hope it'll be good for me. I've wasted a lot of time pretending to be someone I'm not and caring about all the wrong things, and I need to find a way to stop. I need to live for me and the people I love before it's too late." She stopped in front of him. "And in case I'm not being clear enough, your options aren't options as far as I'm concerned and I can't believe you've got the nerve to even present them to me. I have a better option—one that works for me and probably works for the record company too. I want you to sit, listen, and do exactly what I say. And if you decide you don't want to, that's fine. You can issue yourself a dismissal notice. And please don't make it difficult by trying to talk me out of any of it because I'm already late on set."

She sat opposite him, and when she closed her eyes briefly, she could see Maddie sitting on the deck with her guitar on her knee in the soft shining light of the setting sun. She could feel Mateo pressed next to her as they watched Maddie sing. Her whole body smiled and she felt a lightness in her chest. With Maddie at her side, she could do this.

Maddie disconnected the call with a sigh as she reached Sofi's voice mail for the third time. She typed out a text:

I guess you're still in meetings. I hope it's all okay. I'm thinking of you (and of ways to dispose of Noah's body). We obviously need to do some talking, but I love you too. And last night was wonderfully, beautifully, incredibly...tiring! And a lot like coming home. I'll see you soon xx

She could have been self-conscious about sending it, but she wasn't. Things felt different now and she was letting herself hope. Waiting for Sofi to finish the tour would be difficult, but since it seemed as if she really meant for them to be together somehow, Maddie would cope. She'd waited for five years, what was four months?

She looked out the window on what was another fine and cold Parisian day and realized that the car had brought her back to Muette. She hadn't even noticed until they'd pulled into the street where "Claudine's house" was located.

"I don't think this is the right place."

"It is the address I was given for you, madam." Even the drivers spoke perfect English.

She peered out the window. She couldn't see anyone else, and there was no sign of any of their equipment anywhere. She was mightily confused. Even if they'd decided to reshoot some of the house scenes, they all took place at night so being here in the bright light of the morning made no sense. Another car pulled up behind hers as she stepped out, and she watched as Rick and Carly got out accompanied by a sharply dressed woman of about fifty.

"Hey." Rick nodded in her direction. "Hope we didn't keep you waiting, we had to swing by and pick up Marie. Felix found her. She's going to help us with the contract we need to get him to sign before we get started. Crazy times."

Marie held out a hand and Maddie shook it politely.

"I don't understand. What contract? And who's going to need to sign it?"

Rick looked at Carly and then back at her. "Did you not speak to Felix or Sofia this morning?"

Maddie didn't know what the hell was going on.

"I spoke to Sofi, but it was pretty early." Rick couldn't have known they'd spent the night together, but she flushed with embarrassment anyway. "She told me some of it." She didn't want to say any more, not sure what Rick had been told. They stood in silence, looking at each other.

"All I know is that we're reshooting all of the Claudine scenes."

"All of them? She wasn't that bad."

"And Marie is here to get Guillaume to sign a contract to replace her."

"Guillaume? The guy whose house we used?" Maddie rubbed her face in confusion. The lack of sleep wasn't helping. "To be honest, I don't understand what the hell is going on."

"We're reshooting the video with Guillaume in the Claudine role. Last minute decision obviously, and he's lucked out because we don't have time to find anyone else. Apparently, the woman-on-woman thing has caused real problems for Sofia and she's decided to play it safe. Felix called me at stupid o'clock and told me to be prepared to keep everyone on for another day and night. It could be a lot worse. There weren't that many scenes where Claudine and Sofia were together so reshooting them can be done today and Sofi can go to London and we can work with Guillaume on the rest—"

"We're reshooting with a man? Because Sofia had some problems?" She repeated what Rick had said.

The meaning finally sank in. Sofi was straight-washing the video. Presumably to rescue the collaboration with Little Boy. The collaboration she'd been so excited about, so convinced she needed.

"Are you sure?" She needed Rick to be wrong somehow.

"Yeah, sorry, it's disappointing to me too. But Guillaume already said yes. Marie's here to sign the contract. Felix told us to spend what we need to stay on and fix things. I thought you knew. That's why I asked you to come. If we're going to rescue this, we need to get Guillaume briefed and ready to go. We're probably going to have to use his own wardrobe too. Let's hope he has a tux." Rick was all business.

Maddie wanted to cry, scream, and shout all at once. The feelings whirled in her chest. She hadn't expected this. Sofi had left her this morning seeming like she was going to stand up for herself this time, seeming like she had decided that this career of hers was not the only thing that was important to her. She leaned forward and put her hands on her knees. The wave of nausea caught her by surprise.

"Are you okay?" Carly asked.

"Yeah, sorry." Maddie righted herself, but she was anything but okay. She tried to gather her thoughts "You're going to have to do it without me though. I can't stay. I've got Mateo to get back for. I thought we were just doing a couple of hours this morning."

"That was the plan." Rick shrugged. "Not anymore."

Maddie couldn't stop thinking about last night. She had given in, let herself feel everything she'd been fighting for weeks. Worse, she'd let herself hope. How many more lessons like this did she need?

"I get it if you have to go though. We can finish this without you. We did all the hard stuff already."

Maddie realized something.

"Sofi is staying on to do the house scenes, the kissing scene, with Guillaume." It wasn't really a question. It was just the reality dawning.

"Felix said to make sure we do those scenes as soon as it's dark enough so she can still get to London tonight."

Maddie shook her head. Sofi was going to abandon her "truth" in a suburb of Paris and then go and collaborate with a homophobe. If Rick wasn't in front of her saying the actual words, she wasn't sure she'd believe it.

"I'm sorry, guys, but I'm going to go. I'm not feeling great to be honest." She needed to get out of there before she made a fool of herself. She could feel tears pushing their way to the surface.

"Sure, sure," Rick said.

She climbed into the car without any more of a good-bye and asked the driver to take her back to the hotel. She wasn't sure if Sofi would still be there, but if she was, Maddie had absolutely nothing to say to her. She had walked out on Sofi when she found out about Noah. It was the right thing to do. The mistake she'd made was being naive enough to come back. And worse, to hope that Sofi would ever choose Maddie, ever choose her own happiness and truth, over her career.

She dialed Ashley's number, knowing it was barely three in the morning in Miami. She had to talk to someone and figured Ashley would answer. As she waited for the call to connect, she couldn't stop the tears from finally falling.

Chapter Eighteen

Sofia had made it clear that she wasn't just looking for a show to air her new video but was also offering an exclusive interview to go with it. Felix had made it clear she had something important to say, and they'd had no problem persuading several of them to agree to come to her house in Miami for the recording. In the end, she'd chosen Brooklyn Beals and her network, because Brooklyn had always been kind about her music and because Brooklyn had once been as closeted as she was. They'd even been on a date once, what felt like a hundred years ago, before deciding that they didn't have enough chemistry, or time, to do it again. But they'd stayed friendly, and Sofia believed she'd be supportive. In fact, when Sofia had sat down with her and explained exactly what was going on, she'd squealed with happiness and hugged her hard, and it was somehow exactly the reaction she'd needed to calm her nerves.

"Twenty minutes and we're good to go." Felix stuck his head into the room.

He had sorted out all the arrangements and seemed to have embraced the new strategy she'd outlined with an enthusiasm that had surprised her. He'd canceled the most imminent tour dates—to give them time for this interview—and pushed Rick to make sure the video was ready in record time. He'd also arranged several frustrating but ultimately productive meetings with the record company. All that in the few days since they'd got back from Paris.

She sipped her tea and walked over to the window to watch them finish setting up. Brooklyn was sitting in one of the two Adirondack chairs, now angled to face each other on this side of the deck, while someone put the finishing touches to her hair and she flicked through her notes. On the other side of the deck sat a stool and a microphone stand that was being taped down to the floor by a young woman in shorts and a snapback. Sofia's guitar was on a stand beside the stool. At the end of the segment, she was going to perform an acoustic version of the song. And she was going to do it for Maddie.

In one way or another, of course, this was all for Maddie, but the chance to perform "Not This Time" for her was especially important to Sofia. It said everything she had been trying to get Maddie to believe about her intentions. And since it was the only live performance of the song she was intending to do for a long time, it had even more significance.

She hadn't tried to contact Maddie. The angry voice mail she'd received that morning in Paris had, amongst a lot of other things, asked her not to. And once Felix confessed the plans he'd made with Rick to reshoot the video with a male love interest, Sofia understood why Maddie was so mad at her. She could have been upset that Maddie hadn't trusted her more, and had been quick to assume the worst, but it was a pretty reasonable assumption given her past behavior. Sofia had said a lot of words to Maddie about wanting things to be different, but now, with her actions, she was going to prove she meant it. And she had to hope that it was enough.

She heard the front door open and close. She was expecting her mom. They had barely spoken since Paris, but Sofia wanted her mom here to witness this. This was important to her, as Sofia Flores the pop star, but it was just as important to her as Sofia Flores, her daughter. And since one of the decisions she'd taken in Paris was to end her mom's involvement in her career, Sofia was determined they try to become mother and daughter again.

Her mom stepped inside the living room. She had a large Tupperware box in her hands.

"Some snacks for everyone. I wasn't sure if you'd have time." She put them on the counter.

"Hey, Mama." Sofia leaned against the couch and folded her arms. "Thanks for coming." She felt defensive and nervous.

"Your father told me I should." Her mom looked at her with uncertain eyes.

"Well, I'm glad anyway. This is important to me." Sofia held her mom's gaze. This was hard. She had so much respect for her mom, for the journey she'd made, for the family she'd shaped, for the support she'd always given her, but on this, Sofia's love for Maddie, her mom had always had a massive blind spot.

Sofia decided to just say what she had to say. There was nothing she could do to make her mom happy about any of it. "I emailed you the final cut of the video this morning. I wanted you to see it before it drops tonight. I hope you liked it. It's a great song, and Maddie and Rick did a fantastic job with the video, and I'm as proud of it as anything I've ever done. And I hope one day you'll be able to be proud of it too."

Her mom looked at her without speaking, looking like she was weighing what to say next. "And what do we tell Bella about her aunt's new video?" Sofia assumed her mom was having another dig at her, but she looked genuinely confused.

"Mama, Bella listens to a lot of music. She loves Hayley Kiyoko as well as Shawn Mendes. She knows that some songs are about women loving women, and some are about women loving men. She's—" Sofia was going to say that Bella would be cool about it, but something stopped her. Was that wishful thinking on Sofia's part?

"Bella is young, Sofia."

"I know, but she's watched plenty of movies, plenty of videos where people end up kissing. Even mine. She's seen me kissing guys before, and seeing me kissing a woman isn't going to harm her, Mama. It's who I am, it's part of what's in the world, it's natural and normal, and I'm just sorry that you don't seem to see it that way." Sofia was fighting to hold on to her temper and her tears. She closed her eyes to try to compose herself. When she looked back at her mom, she saw her wiping away her own tears.

"I'm not prejudiced. I know you think I am but I'm not. I just wanted things to be easier for you, Sofia. I wanted a marriage and a family for you, grandchildren for me." Her mom spoke without looking at her. Sofia crossed the space between them and took her mom's hands.

"Mama, if I have what I want, if Maddie and I can make this work this time, I promise you there'll be a wedding and kids and dogs and so much babysitting that you'll be sorry you ever wished for grandkids. I love her so much, and I never really stopped hoping that we'd get another chance. I really, really need you to find a way to accept this, to accept Maddie. She loves me but she's scared to be with me, Mama. And a part of that is because she thinks everyone will judge us and be hostile, and you know what, some people will. But I need to be able to show her that at least my own family thinks it's okay for us to love each other. If my own family won't accept us, what hope do we have?" She waited, with a tight feeling in her chest, for her mom to respond.

Her mom gripped her hands, holding them out in front of her. "She hurt you so much, Sofia. You loved her before and she left you, left you to suffer, and I can't help worrying for you. I care too much to want that to happen again. Someone has to be the voice of reason. You're too romantic, too full of love, to see straight. It's my job to protect my children."

"Mama, that's true. Sometimes wanting and loving someone so much means they have the power to hurt you, but it also means that the love is worth having. We both hurt each other—it was me as much as Maddie—and we had years apart because of it. Years that felt like living in the shadows. Now I feel like the sun has come out and I want to live in the sunlight with her. And I'm pretty sure she feels the same way. I just want you to stop fighting it, to love Maddie and be glad that we've found a way back to each other. Otherwise there's no future for me and you." Sofia was shaking with the effort she was making not to cry.

Her mom stood silently in front of her. Sofia waited.

"Your dad is so much better at this than me. And he had a lot to say to me when I got back from Paris. He reminded me that your abuela hated him for a long time because he wasn't the nice Cuban boy she had in mind for me. She told me to stop seeing him, but I didn't. We just got more devious about seeing each other behind her back. And when we had to confess we'd gotten engaged, we were both so terrified." She squeezed Sofia's hand. "But she was kind about it. We hadn't expected that. I think she'd realized by then how pointless it was to try to get in our way, how unhappy it would make us." She smiled. "And look at them now, he's her golden boy. Your dad reminded me that no amount of me disapproving is going to keep you and Maddie apart. I'm going to just drive you away from us and make you unhappy. And I don't want that."

Sofia couldn't stop tears from falling. Her mom wiped them away.

"You're going to mess up your makeup." She put an arm around Sofia's shoulders. "I'm sorry I've been a monster lately, cariño. I know you love her, you always did. And I can see that she feels the same way. Seeing you together in Paris made it so clear to me. But this business is harsh, and I didn't want you to get bruised by it. But if you've found a way to make sure that doesn't happen, and if you're sure about her..."

"I've never been surer of anything. I just need to wait for Maddie to realize she feels the same way."

They looked at each other for a moment, both in their own thoughts.

"Now, go do your interview and this big 'coming out' thing that you're determined to do. And your dad and I are going to watch later and be proud of your strength even if I think there's no need to tell everyone your business." The words sounded as harsh as ever, but her mom had tears in her eyes as she spoke, and Sofia believed that she meant it when she said she'd be proud of her.

"There's every need, Mom. This is my way of making up for every lie I ever told that made people think I was straight. And it's my way of helping make sure the people that come after me are less likely to have to do the same thing."

Felix stepped inside the house. He nodded at her mom.

"They're ready for you I think. They're a bit worried about how the breeze is going to affect the sound quality, but they think they can clean it up ready for the broadcast later."

Sofia took a couple of deep breaths and walked slowly toward the gap in the sliding doors. She paused in the doorway, Felix by her side. Brooklyn was smiling in her direction. The ocean behind her had a magnificent azure color, and there wasn't a cloud in the sky. The universe had blessed her big day with the best possible weather. She had to hope the universe would keep smiling on her for what came next. The small crew was in position, waiting for her. Felix put a hand on her shoulder, and she turned to him.

"I should have said this more often, but working with you has been a privilege. And you're going to nail this like the boss you are. People are going to be surprised, but they'll love the honesty and I think they'll understand. I'm sorry I wasn't more supportive, that I was one of the reasons why this was harder than it needed to be." He swallowed and Sofia smiled at the idea of even him getting all emotional. He'd been such a big figure in her life, and now she was going to live her life without him for a while. It would probably be good for both of them to have a break.

"Here we go." Sofia spoke to herself as she walked across the deck and settled on the chair next to Brooklyn. One of the crew began to fix a microphone to her shirt and another fussed with her hair.

"All set?" Brooklyn reached out and put a hand on her arm.

Sofia nodded, running her fingers through her hair nervously as the director cued them by slowly counting down from five.

Brooklyn faced forward and smiled.

"Welcome to *Pop Weekly*. I'm here with Sofia Flores at her beautiful beach house in Miami," she waved her hand to indicate the view, "and, boy, do we have some special exclusives for you guys tonight. We're gonna drop Sofia's controversial new video and Sofia's gonna drop a bombshell or two that absolutely none of us were expecting. Grab some popcorn, get comfortable, and get ready to be shook by all the tea we're gonna be spilling."

"You're making it sound so dramatic." Sofia raised an eyebrow in the direction of the camera.

"It's my job." Brooklyn laughed. "And it is kinda dynamite."

"I guess." Sofia smiled as she spoke. "It's also kind of ordinary for me."

Felix and her mom stood side by side in the doorway. Felix gave her a thumbs up.

"So, let's talk about this new video. You, in Paris, and a sexy plot line that's gonna blow people's minds. Earlier you described it to me as giving yourself the chance to show people something of who you really are. Let's start there. What did you mean by that?"

Sofia should have felt terrified by all of it. She was about to come out and admit to not just hiding, but actively lying, about her personal life for years. It could end up costing her half a million dollars and everything she'd ever worked for. But rather than feeling fearful, she felt calm and happy She was finally going to be herself—in public and private—and she wanted to make Maddie proud of her. It was important to start to live her own truth, but, more than that, she also hoped it was going to be the thing that meant Maddie would give them the chance at a life together, the chance she knew in her soul they both wanted.

❖

Mateo sat on the couch, his ukulele on his lap, strumming the strings happily. There was no tune, and if it had been anyone other than her son making that noise, she'd have stopped it by now for sure, but she was just happy he was happy. He'd been a lot keener on playing with it since Sofi had sung for them and spent time showing him how to play it. It didn't matter how many times she told herself they were better off away from Sofi and all her madness, the idea of Sofi and Mateo losing each other before they'd really gotten started was tough.

She had everything out of her kitchen cabinets and laid out on the counter so she could clean inside them. It was the latest in a range of unsatisfying activities she'd undertaken to try to take her mind off the way she'd been feeling since getting home from Paris. At first, she'd been upset, then she'd been angry, and now all she could seem to manage was a dull aching sadness that pulled at her heart and made her feel heavy.

"Seriously?" Ashley spoke as she came in through the door, pizza box in hand.

Maddie shrugged. "What's wrong with cleaning?"

"In the last forty-eight hours, you've cleaned every cabinet, every window, every inch of floor." She put the box on the dining table and crossed to the kitchen.

"You'd rather I was binge-watching romcoms on Netflix and crying into my wine?"

"I don't think those are your only two options."

Ashley had surprised her by trying to persuade her to stay in Paris and talk things out with Sofi, but Maddie had ignored her advice and come home. She was heartsick without her, but she was also sick of Sofi's empty promises. Of hoping and then being disappointed by her.

Maddie started to put the cans back into one of the cabinets. Ashley stood watching her silently. Maddie knew she wanted her to talk about it, but she couldn't. It wasn't just that she was disappointed in Sofi, she was disappointed in herself. She should have been more careful, less naive.

"You know she's canceled three more tour dates?"

"Yeah, I saw." Maddie didn't stop what she was doing. But the thought that Sofi might not be okay, mentally or physically, pricked at her consciousness and made her uneasy.

"And I saw something today that says she's back in Miami."

"Ash, don't."

Maddie had seen the same thing. Footage of Rosa entering and leaving Sofi's house, speculation that Sofi was inside. She had no idea if it was true. The first thing she'd done on getting home was send Anna a message withdrawing formally from the redesign project at Sofi's house. She'd suggested a couple of other designers and apologized for the "change in her circumstances." It hadn't been easy.

"What? I'm just saying that it seems like she's here. Fifteen minutes' drive away. I mean, if you felt inclined to go and speak to her rather than sulking, hurting, and assuming the worst."

"I'm not assuming the worst. I'm being realistic. She abandoned everything she said meant something to her the minute it looked like it might cost her the thing with Little Boy. What possible point is there in getting involved with someone like that? It would mean hiding, lying, worrying that I'm going to be bad for her career, and living with the certainty that she's always going to choose that career over me and my son."

"You don't know that."

"I do. I was there."

"Yet she's home and not wherever she's supposed to be touring right now."

"Amsterdam." Maddie hated that she knew Sofi's schedule.

She turned to face Ashley.

"Since when are you her chief cheerleader anyway?"

"I'm not. But I know you're crazy in love with her, and right now you're crazy unhappy. And I repeat, she's fifteen minutes away. I can't believe it's not worth a conversation. Honestly, Mads, you are stubborn AF. And I'm only not spelling that out in full because I know my nephew has excellent hearing."

Ashley began handing her stuff to put back into the cabinet. They did that silently for a minute.

"It doesn't matter if she's back, she hasn't tried to get in touch with me either."

"Are you joking?"

"No." Maddie couldn't look Ashley in the eye.

"You told me you asked her not to contact you. I think the words 'ever again' might have been mentioned. And, yeah, that was the day you walked out on her video shoot without giving her the chance to explain anything."

"I know." She picked up a towel and wiped off the counter.

She'd been angry, but even now, days later, she couldn't decide if she meant it. Her heart ached for Sofi, and she couldn't stop thinking about all the things they'd said to each other—all the things they'd done to each other—but what did it count for if Sofi wouldn't ever have the courage to stop hiding and give up all the associated madness. She didn't want that in her life. Mateo deserved better. She deserved better.

Ashley pulled her phone out of her pocket and peered at the screen. Maddie saw her frown and then smile a half smile before frowning again. "What time is it?" She turned to look at the clock on the kitchen wall which said seven twenty.

"Shit." She let out the curse word before fixing her face into what most people would have called neutral but what Maddie thought seemed deeply, suspiciously not-at-all-neutral.

"Can we watch some TV for a little while? Maybe have a glass of wine." Ashley crossed to the couch, looking around for the remote control a little frantically.

"I guess." Maddie could tell something was going on. "Who was that?"

"No one. Old friend. Haven't heard from them in ages. I guess I should be thankful I've never changed my number. I just didn't hear the message come in earlier. She located the remote, sat down, and started surfing through the channels. "I'll have white if you've got it, but come quick." Ashley patted the seat next to her.

Maddie grabbed an open bottle from the fridge. Took two glasses from the cabinet, and moved to sit next to Ashley. She watched as Ashley poured a large glass for herself and barely a finger of wine for Maddie.

"There's something I want you to watch," Ashley said.

"What's going on, Ash? You're being mighty weird even for y—" Maddie stopped talking as she saw the opening of Sofi's new video. The title, Sofi's name, a wide shot of Paris, followed by a close-up shot of Sofi standing in a pack of paparazzi holding her camera and snapping away. Her own name appeared in large letters across the screen beneath a caption that said 'Written, Designed and Directed by'. She took in a breath and watched in silence as Claudine exited a movie theater with her husband at her side and the photographers went crazy, jostling each other to get close to her.

Claudine.

In Sofi's video.

Claudine glanced across at Sofi, the camera following her gaze. Claudine, in all her glory, and most definitely not Guillaume. The realization made her feel hot and cold at the very same time.

"Fia!" Mateo jumped off the couch and walked to the TV, standing a foot away as Sofi was featured in close-up. *God, she is so beautiful.* Maddie couldn't stop the thought poking through. She watched the rest of the video with bated breath, alternating between trying to figure out how she had gotten things so wrong and how damn fantastic the whole thing was.

"Wow. That was amazing." Ashley spoke as the video ended with the camera zooming out from Sofi and Claudine's kiss in the window of the house in Muette.

Before Maddie could process anything, she was faced with Sofi sitting next to Brooklyn Beals on the deck of her house. It was like Maddie was having a strange dream.

"That video is lit. I love the song, but the video is something else. And I don't mind admitting I'm feeling a little flustered right now." Brooklyn fanned herself with her papers.

Maddie watched Sofi's face light up with happiness. It was a wonderful sight.

"But I guess, based on what you were saying earlier, this is both your coming out and your going away video." Brooklyn offered Sofi a wide easy smile.

"I guess it is." Sofi attempted a smile, but Maddie could see just how anxious she was. "But I'm so proud that this is the song and the video I'm going to be leaving behind for people to remember me by."

"Do you have any doubts about taking the time off? Six months is a long time in this business. Isn't there a chance that your fans might move on to someone else? I mean, leaving aside the risk you're taking in finally coming out, if you're not in the public eye, people can be very fickle."

"I'm aware it's a risk. All of it—the coming out, admitting the games Noah and I were playing, taking a long break."

Maddie watched as Sofi swept a hand through her hair, a nervous gesture she knew well. She couldn't believe what she was seeing and hearing.

"I don't feel great about canceling the tour—and I'm sorry if people are disappointed in me for that—but I really need this break. It's not just that I can't keep pretending—that's only a little bit of it— it's that sometimes other things, other people, come along in life that make you question everything, that make you realize that you want to live a different kind of life. And that's what happened to me. I think the majority of my fans will understand that and stick with me. I can't really do anything about the ones that don't." She shrugged.

"I don't want to put you on the spot, but that sounds a lot like you're doing all this for someone in particular."

"That is putting me on the spot," Sofi said. "What I will say is that sometimes you need to clearly see a future you really really want, to find the courage to change the things about your present that might be in the way of that future." She looked into the camera, and Maddie felt that the earnest gaze was all for her.

"Jeez, Maddie. This is every kind of incredible. Coming out, telling people about Noah, telling you she wants a future with you," Ashley said.

Maddie wanted Ashley to be right about Sofi's meaning, but she didn't dare let herself hope. But maybe Sofi had done this for her. It seemed like she had told Brooklyn everything.

"It's not for me. She doesn't even know I'm watching."

"She does."

Maddie turned to Ashley and frowned. "What?"

"The text. She told me which channel. And she asked me to make sure you were watching. I just didn't see it until after the program had started. I'm sorry."

Maddie's head was spinning. She looked from the screen to Ashley and back again.

Maddie had missed Brooklyn's question.

"Absolutely, I can't wait. It doesn't feel like I've had six days off in the last ten years let alone six months. I'm working with this really talented designer on doing up this house, I'm going to read, cook, learn to Jet Ski, and, hopefully, teach a buddy of mine to play the ukulele. I'm going to take some time to do the things that make me happy, with people who make me happy, and if I need more time, I'm going to take more time."

The feeling of exhilaration started in Maddie's feet and coursed its way up her body until it reached her chest and she felt like shouting with joy at the top of her lungs. Sofi had done this for her. And she meant for them to be together. She jumped off the couch and picked up Mateo, whirling him around in a dancing hug.

On the television, Sofi moved across the deck and seated herself on a stool. She picked up her guitar and checked the tuning. Maddie sat down again and settled Mateo onto her lap. She watched as Sofi closed her eyes. When she opened them and the camera moved in for a close-up, it felt to Maddie as if Sofi were looking right into her soul. She shivered and her chest fluttered lightly.

"This song is very special to me. It's about the importance of taking second chances. I wrote it for someone in particular, and I mean every word." She started to sing the opening verse, and Maddie felt the tears spring up from nowhere. She was happy, as happy as she could ever remember being, but she couldn't stop the tears from falling. Sofi loved her and she'd stopped her crazy career in its tracks for her.

They watched to the end of the song. Sofi had tears in her eyes as she sang the final line. She put down the guitar, brushed them away, and smiled at Brooklyn who had crossed the deck to embrace Sofi.

Ashley stood and picked Mateo up from Maddie's lap, settling him onto her hip. "We're going to play some Lego. Go get ready and go get your girl."

"I can't. There's going to be a houseful of people there. And a TV crew." Maddie gave Ashley a look that said she was being dim.

"There isn't. She's home alone."

"How do you know th—"

"The text message from earlier. She said it had been recorded this afternoon and she'd be at home alone all evening. Now, get ready and go and see her. I've seen enough romcoms to know that you have to dash over there, act all sorry, and fall into each other's arms."

Maddie shook her head. Ashley had turned matchmaker, and like everything else she ever did, she was frighteningly good at it.

Ashley's phone dinged. She switched Mateo to her other hip and reached awkwardly into her pocket to retrieve it. Something in the message made her smile.

"What?" Maddie asked.

"Too late."

"Too late for what?"

"Too late for dashing over there and possibly too late for costume changes."

"Ash. Speak English for me."

"She's outside, in her car. Asking me how you reacted, whether you might want to see her."

"Outside?"

"Yes." Ashley laughed.

Maddie felt her heart lift. She wanted to go upstairs and change, put on some makeup and tidy up her hair, but more than any of that, she wanted to hold Sofi, to kiss her, to tell her thank you, and to promise to love her until the day she died.

"I'll take him upstairs and we'll pack some stuff so he can spend the night at mine."

"But—" Maddie tried to object.

"No arguments."

Maddie stopped in the hallway. She ran her fingers through her hair and ran a palm down the front of her T-shirt as if to flatten out the creases. She held a hand out in front of herself and wasn't surprised to see it tremble. Sofia Flores had told everyone she loved women, promised she would take some serious time off, and just performed a beautiful song for her. Maddie had doubted her, but she shouldn't have. She had to hope Sofi being here meant she was willing to give her another chance.

The door opened and Sofia saw Maddie framed in the doorway. Even in frayed cut-offs and a long-sleeved T-shirt, she looked like a goddess. She'd waited for a reply from Ashley, her confidence draining away with every minute of silence, but the hesitant smile Maddie gave her as she moved toward her was reassuring. And beautiful. She got out of the car and moved around to lean against it, waiting for Maddie to reach her. She wasn't trying to be cool, she just didn't trust herself to be able to stand without something to lean on. Every nerve, every fiber, every blood vessel in her body wanted her to go to Maddie and claim her. But she took in a breath and made herself wait for Maddie to reach her. They had things they had to say first. And though she'd practiced what she wanted to say so many times, faced with Maddie, none of the words seemed like they would be enough.

They stood a couple of feet apart and simply looked at each other.

"I am so proud of you." Maddie spoke first. "That was just incredible. I didn't see all of it. Ashley didn't tell me until after it had started, but I'm just blown away." She stopped speaking, and a big smile appeared on her face. It was wonderful for Sofia to see. The sun was setting on the evening, but Maddie's smile reminded her of the sunrise.

"Damn, Sofi, it was amazing. And you were incredible. Brave, honest, real. I wasn't expecting any of it. I thought that you'd changed your mind about the video, and I got so disappointed, so mad. I'm sorry."

"I know." Sofia smiled. "The voice mail was pretty clear."

Maddie put her head in her hands. Sofia stepped forward and took them, moving them away from Maddie's face and then not letting them go.

"I should have believed in you."

"Why would you? Even I didn't believe in me. It was only in Paris that I understood what I needed to do, what I wanted to do."

"You're taking six months off?" Maddie's expression suggested she didn't quite believe it.

"Yeah. Maybe longer. We've canceled the tour, and I'm not doing any more promo work for the album or for the single. I can't be without you for four days, Maddie. I was crazy to think I could be away from you for four months." She was so happy to finally be able to say this to Maddie. "It's not that I'm tired, I just don't want to be without you, and I want a life where I've got time for you and Mateo, where you're the most important things in my life." It felt righteous to be able to say it. She waited for Maddie to respond. Sofia understood that she could still say no. Even now, even after coming clean about everything, there would be madness. They could ignore it and avoid it as best they could, but it would still be there.

"You think I can do anything but kiss you after you sang to me like that?" Maddie laughed and opened her arms, Sofia slid close and wrapped her arms around her.

Sofia gently picked up one of the hands that Maddie now had resting on her hips and lifted it to her lips—kissing the palm and then the fingertips softly. She heard Maddie take in a breath and then felt Maddie's thumb trace a path across her lips. Their eyes held each other and the intensity of Maddie's gaze left Sofia senseless. She slowly moved her hand to Maddie's back and stroked the soft, warm skin under her T-shirt. She pulled Maddie's face to hers and crushed her lips in a kiss, wanting to kiss her until they couldn't breathe, wanting to kiss away all the wasted time, the regrets, the fears. When she opened her eyes and looked at Maddie, the unmistakable need she saw on her face made her insides tighten. She stroked strands of hair away from Maddie's forehead and marveled at the feeling, enjoying the shiver that her touch produced in Maddie's body. Maddie tilted her head and pressed her lips to Sofia's once more, and when Maddie parted her lips slightly, Sofia tasted the woman who she was willing to give up everything for.

"I'm yours, Sofi, I always have been. I don't know how to love anyone else. I'm sorry I doubted you, but I love you and I will be by your side for whatever comes next. And I'm going to thank the universe every day for giving us this chance."

"And I'm going to release this song for you, for us, because you made a video that is frickin' awesome and because I wrote every word for you. Every word. I love you. I've always loved you, I've just been a bit slow at realizing the rest of what I needed to do."

As they kissed again, Sofia heard a bang on the window from behind them. They looked up to see Mateo's pajama-clad body pressed against the upstairs window. He was alternating frantic banging with frantic waving. Ashley appeared to pull him away hurriedly.

"I was going to ask you to stay over and tell you that Ashley had offered Mateo a sleepover, but, " she shrugged and smiled, "I think we've just been busted."

Sofia reached down and took Maddie's hand, leaning against her. "I'm happy with a play date." She leaned in and kissed Maddie. "I mean he's going to sleep eventually, right?"

Maddie laughed, her eyes sparkling. "He's spending the night with his auntie. Let's go say good night to them both. You can have your play date with him tomorrow. Tonight, at the risk of sounding like a bad songwriter, you're all mine."

Sofia could have floated into the house, she felt so happy. Which, considering the kind of week she'd just had, was kind of incredible. But then so was Madison Martin, the love of her life, the one who almost got away.

EPILOGUE

Maddie put her arm around Sofi's waist and pulled her a little closer, wanting the feeling of security that having Sofi's body pressed against her provided. It had been a long time since she'd been on a red carpet and the shouted questions and incessant flashes from the cameras had her senses overloaded. Sofi looked across at her and smiled reassuringly before returning her attention to the TV host standing in front of them both with a large microphone.

She had hold of Mateo's hand, and she felt him pull a little on it. She looked down to see he was swiveling on his heels, looking bored. He was dressed in a tuxedo jacket, purple bow tie, and his favorite Spiderman sweatpants. She couldn't help but smile. The outfit was all his own work. He'd seen them cooing over dresses the day before and asked if he could also play dress up. The wardrobe people had found the tux and bow tie. The sweatpants were, as they say, the model's own.

They were at the VMAs, and though Maddie couldn't quite wrap her head around it, it had been a year since Sofi had been scheduled to perform and not made it past the falling down stage. It had been a year in which Maddie had been the happiest she'd ever been.

The TV host had excitedly called them over as soon as they had finished having the formal photos taken.

"This is a big night for you two. Two nominations in the Best Video category. Does it ever get competitive in the Flores-Martin household?"

It was no secret that Maddie and Sofi were living together. Sofi had moved in with her six months ago. They'd been tempted by Sofi's bigger house, but Mateo was settled where he was and they decided they would wait and move there when they had more kids.

"Not at all." Sofi laughed. "We woke up today and were both so excited that it was like Christmas morning. To have the nominations and to have the VMAs here in Miami is just perfect. And I'm just happy to be here supporting Maddie. It's great that 'Not This Time' has been nominated because I'm super proud of that video, but if it wins, it's her award not mine. She conceived it, designed it, filmed it. I just turned up and did what I was told."

"Mostly did what she was told." Maddie leaned into the microphone with a raised eyebrow and a smile.

"And, Madison, you've also been nominated for the video you made for Kehlani's last single—which I loved by the way—so that must feel amazing too." The host moved the microphone to Maddie.

"Yeah, thanks. It is pretty dope. We had so much fun making that video. We filmed it here in Miami, in Little Havana and at Sofi's house, believe it or not, and it's a blast to see it get some recognition. Personally though, if I could, I'd vote for 'Not This Time' because it meant so much for us to be working together again after so long apart. It's hard not to be sentimental about it." She gazed at Sofi, not able to hide her feelings about them being here together, finally showing the world their love.

"And what are your plans for the future, Sofia? When you announced you were taking a break, you said six months, but it's been longer than that. How are you spending your time? Are you working on something new? I'm sure your fans would love to know there's something in the pipeline."

Maddie felt Sofi tense a little. They'd talked about what she might say if this question came up. The reality was that, for the first six weeks, they'd spent as much time at home, and in bed, as Mateo had allowed them to. And for the next six months, Sofi had cooked, got really good at Jet Skiing, played her guitar on the beach, and hung out with Mateo while Maddie worked. And only now was she ready to really jump into her next project.

"We make pancakes." Mateo tapped the host on her thigh as he spoke. "Every day. Me and Fia, after Mommy goes to work. Though sometimes she doesn't go and she eats pancakes with us. We have lots usually. I have blueberries and bananas with mine."

They all laughed. Mateo's intervention was perfect. And mostly true. Though Sofi had been doing a lot more than making pancakes.

Sofi caught her eye, a questioning expression on her face. Maddie nodded. She was so proud of Sofi, she wanted everyone to know.

"We've set up a new LGBTQ record company here in Miami and we just signed our first couple of artists. I'm so excited about them recording and bringing their music to the world and," Maddie squeezed her waist, sending encouragement, "letting them be their true selves as they record, promote, and try to make their careers successful."

"That's an exclusive for you," Maddie cut in with a smile.

"Wow, that's pretty unexpected, and kind of amazing." The host looked genuinely surprised.

"I've had a lot of years of recording and performing, and it's exciting to think that I can help bring new artists to the public's attention. And I can make sure they're valued for exactly who they are and not forced into trying to be something they're not."

"I was going to ask about that. I hope you don't mind, but there were stories at the time that speaking up about the pressures you felt about having to hide your sexuality cost you not just your recording contract but half a million dollars in contract penalties. It's kind of astonishing if it's true. Would you care to comment?"

"It didn't cost me the recording contract. They stood by me. We just agreed to pause things for a while." Maddie watched Sofi struggle to find the words. "And I had pancakes to make with this one so it all worked out well." Mateo hugged Sofi's legs as she spoke, and Maddie felt her heart melt a little.

"But, yeah, getting out of that PR contract with Noah, speaking up about Little Boy, it could have cost me a lot. In the end, though, we all decided to walk away and not get too punitive about it."

"But why choose that moment to speak up about everything? You were still at the top. It could have cost you a lot more than money."

"Not speaking up would have cost me so much more. My sanity, my happiness, this beautiful life I have now." Sofi sounded serious and a little emotional. Maddie couldn't help leaning in to kiss her cheek. Cameras flashed around them.

"And we both had the experience of letting that pressure, that caring too much about what people think, cost us our relationship the first time around," Maddie added. "But," she waited a beat, "not this time." She pointed a finger at the camera and pulled a face earning a groan from Sofi as the host laughed. "Sorry, couldn't resist."

"Good note to end on. Thanks, Sofia Flores and Madison Martin. Good luck tonight." She bent down to offer her palm to Mateo. "And thanks to you, adorable Spiderman in a tux." Mateo grinned and gave her an enthusiastic high five.

As the cameraman and host switched their attention to the next set of attendees, Maddie turned with Sofi and Mateo to Ashley and Rosa standing a couple of yards behind them.

"How was that?" Maddie barely got the question out before being wrapped in a big hug by Ashley. She let go of Maddie and did the same to Sofi.

"So proud of you both." She sounded a little choked up.

"Are you crying?" Maddie couldn't keep the smile out of her voice.

"God, no." Ashley lifted her eyebrows. "Okay, I might be." She smiled. "Can't I be proud of my big sis? Here on her own terms with the best looking man in this whole place, and a girlfriend that scrubs up pretty well too." She smiled at Sofi.

Rosa put a hand in the crook of her elbow as Ashley threw an arm across Sofi's shoulder and they all made their way as a family into the auditorium to find their seats. The chatter moved on happily to whether this was the first time Sofi had worn anything other than shorts this summer and whether she and Mateo should start a YouTube pancake making channel. Maddie couldn't stop smiling. Later, they might or might not win an award, but it didn't matter, none of it mattered as much as this. Happiness, family, and being in love. Maddie put a hand on Sofi's back and stroked it softly. Whoever said love wins was on to something righteous.

THE END

About the Author

MA Binfield is a hopeless romantic living in the UK. She loves escaping into books, drinking strong tea, traveling, lip-syncing cheesy disco songs, and growing vegetables. She is a frustrated linguist who is overly tall and has always wanted to be left-handed. MA is a passionate public servant who has finally found the time to write—and it's joyful. She's happiest by the sea.

Home is always where the heart is.

Books Available from Bold Strokes Books

16 Steps to Forever by Georgia Beers. Can Brooke Sullivan and Macy Carr find themselves by finding each other? (978-1-63555-762-6)

All I Want for Christmas by Georgia Beers, Maggie Cummings, Fiona Riley. The Christmas season sparks passion and love in these stories by award winning authors Georgia Beers, Maggie Cummings, and Fiona Riley. (978-1-63555-764-0)

From the Woods by Charlotte Greene. When Fiona goes backpacking in a protected wilderness, the last thing she expects is to be fighting for her life. (978-1-63555-793-0)

Heart of the Storm by Nicole Stiling. For Juliet Mitchell and Sienna Bennett a forbidden attraction definitely isn't worth upending the life they've worked so hard for. Is it? (978-1-63555-789-3)

If You Dare by Sandy Lowe. For Lauren West and Emma Prescott, following their passions is easy. Following their hearts, though? That's almost impossible. (978-1-63555-654-4)

Love Changes Everything by Jaime Maddox. For Samantha Brooks and Kirby Fielding, no matter how careful their plans, love will change everything. (978-1-63555-835-7)

Not This Time by MA Binfield. Flung back into each other's lives, can former bandmates Sophia and Madison have a second chance at romance? (978-1-63555-798-5)

The Dubious Gift of Dragon Blood by J. Marshall Freeman. One day Crispin is a lonely high school student—the next he is fighting a war in a land ruled by dragons, his otherworldly boyfriend at his side. (978-1-63555-725-1)

The Found Jar by Jaycie Morrison. Fear keeps Emily Harris trapped in her emotionally vacant life; can she find the courage to let Beck Reynolds guide her toward love? (978-1-63555-825-8)

Aurora by Emma L McGeown. After a traumatic accident, Elena Ricci is stricken with amnesia leaving her with no recollection of the last eight years, including her wife and son. (978-1-63555-824-1)

Avenging Avery by Sheri Lewis Wohl. Revenge against a vengeful vampire unites Isa Meyer and Jeni Denton, but it's love that heals them. (978-1-63555-622-3)

Bulletproof by Maggie Cummings. For Dylan Prescott and Briana Logan, the complicated NYC criminal justice system doesn't leave room for love, but where the heart is concerned, no one is bulletproof. (978-1-63555-771-8)

Her Lady to Love by Jane Walsh. A shy wallflower joins forces with the most popular woman in Regency London on a quest to catch a husband, only to discover a wild passion for each other that far eclipses their interest for the Marriage Mart. (978-1-63555-809-8)

No Regrets by Joy Argento. For Jodi and Beth, the possibility of losing their future will force them to decide what is really important. (978-1-63555-751-0)

The Holiday Treatment by Elle Spencer. Who doesn't want a gay Christmas movie? Holly Hudson asks herself that question and discovers that happy endings aren't only for the movies. (978-1-63555-660-5)

Too Good to be True by Leigh Hays. Can the promise of love survive the realities of life for Madison and Jen, or is it too good to be true? (978-1-63555-715-2)

Treacherous Seas by Radclyffe. When the choice comes down to the lives of her officers against the promise she made to her wife, Reese Conlon puts everything she cares about on the line. (978-1-63555-778-7)

Two to Tangle by Melissa Brayden. Ryan Jacks has been a player all her life, but the new chef at Tangle Valley Vineyard changes everything. If only she wasn't off the menu. (978-1-63555-747-3)

When Sparks Fly by Annie McDonald. Will the devastating incident that first brought Dr. Daniella Waveny and hockey coach Luca McCaffrey together on frozen ice now force them apart, or will their secrets and fears thaw enough for them to create sparks? (978-1-63555-782-4)

Best Practice by Carsen Taite. When attorney Grace Maldonado agrees to mentor her best friend's little sister, she's prepared to confront Perry's rebellious nature, but she isn't prepared to fall in love. Legal Affairs: one law firm, three best friends, three chances to fall in love. (978-1-63555-361-1)

Home by Kris Bryant. Natalie and Sarah discover that anything is possible when love takes the long way home. (978-1-63555-853-1)

Keeper by Sydney Quinne. With a new charge under her reluctant wing—feisty, highly intelligent math wizard Isabelle Templeton—Keeper Andy Bouchard has to prevent a murder or die trying. (978-1-63555-852-4)

One More Chance by Ali Vali. Harry Basantes planned a future with Desi Thompson until the day Desi disappeared without a word, only to walk back into her life sixteen years later. (978-1-63555-536-3)

Renegade's War by Gun Brooke. Freedom fighter Aurelia DeCallum regrets saving the woman called Blue. She fears it will jeopardize her mission, and secretly, Blue might end up breaking Aurelia's heart. (978-1-63555-484-7)

The Other Women by Erin Zak. What happens in Vegas should stay in Vegas, but what do you do when the love you find in Vegas changes your life forever? (978-1-63555-741-1)

The Sea Within by Missouri Vaun. Time is running out for Dr. Elle Graham to convince Captain Jackson Drake that the only thing that can save future Earth resides in the past, and rescue her broken heart in the process. (978-1-63555-568-4)

To Sleep With Reindeer by Justine Saracen. In Norway under Nazi occupation, Maarit, an Indigenous woman; and Kirsten, a Norwegian resister, join forces to stop the development of an atomic weapon. (978-1-63555-735-0)

Twice Shy by Aurora Rey. Having an ex with benefits isn't all it's cracked up to be. Will Amanda Russo learn that lesson in time to take a chance on love with Quinn Sullivan? (978-1-63555-737-4)

Z-Town by Eden Darry. Forced to work together to stay alive, Meg and Lane must find the centuries-old treasure before the zombies find them first. (978-1-63555-743-5)

Bet Against Me by Fiona Riley. In the high stakes luxury real estate market, everything has a price, and as rival Realtors Trina Lee and Kendall Yates find out, that means their hearts and souls, too. (978-1-63555-729-9)

Broken Reign by Sam Ledel. Together on an epic journey in search of a mysterious cure, a princess and a village outcast must overcome life-threatening challenges and their own prejudice if they want to survive. (978-1-63555-739-8)

Just One Taste by CJ Birch. For Lauren, it only took one taste to start trusting in love again. (978-1-63555-772-5)

Lady of Stone by Barbara Ann Wright. Sparks fly as a magical emergency forces a noble embarrassed by her ability to submit to a low-born teacher who resents everything about her. (978-1-63555-607-0)

Last Resort by Angie Williams. Katie and Rhys are about to find out what happens when you meet the girl of your dreams but you aren't looking for a happily ever after. (978-1-63555-774-9)

Longing for You by Jenny Frame. When Debrek housekeeper Katie Brekman is attacked amid a burgeoning vampire-witch war, Alexis Villiers must go against everything her clan believes in to save her. (978-1-63555-658-2)

Money Creek by Anne Laughlin. Clare Lehane is a troubled lawyer from Chicago who tries to make her way in a rural town full of secrets and deceptions. (978-1-63555-795-4)

Passion's Sweet Surrender by Ronica Black. Cam and Blake are unable to deny their passion for each other, but surrendering to love is a whole different matter. (978-1-63555-703-9)

The Holiday Detour by Jane Kolven. It will take everything going wrong to make Dana and Charlie see how right they are for each other. (978-1-63555-720-6)

Too Hot to Ride by Andrews & Austin. World famous cutting horse champion and industry legend Jane Barrow is knockdown sexy in the way she moves, talks, and rides, and Rae Starr is determined not to get involved with this womanizing gambler. (978-1-63555-776-3)

A Love that Leads to Home by Ronica Black. For Carla Sims and Janice Carpenter, home isn't about location, it's where your heart is. (978-1-63555-675-9)

Blades of Bluegrass by D. Jackson Leigh. A US Army occupational therapist must rehab a bitter veteran who is a ticking political time bomb the military is desperate to disarm. (978-1-63555-637-7)

Guarding Hearts by Jaycie Morrison. As treachery and temptation threaten the women of the Women's Army Corps, who will risk it all for love? (978-1-63555-806-7)

Hopeless Romantic by Georgia Beers. Can a jaded wedding planner and an optimistic divorce attorney possibly find a future together? (978-1-63555-650-6)

Hopes and Dreams by PJ Trebelhorn. Movie theater manager Riley Warren is forced to face her high school crush and tormentor, wealthy socialite Victoria Thayer, at their twentieth reunion. (978-1-63555-670-4)

In the Cards by Kimberly Cooper Griffin. Daria and Phaedra are about to discover that love finds a way, especially when powers outside their control are at play. (978-1-63555-717-6)

Moon Fever by Ileandra Young. SPEAR agent Danika Karson must clear her werewolf friend of multiple false charges while teaching her vampire girlfriend to resist the blood mania brought on by a full moon. (978-1-63555-603-2)

Quake City by St John Karp. Can Andre find his best friend Amy before the night devolves into a nightmare of broken hearts, malevolent drag queens, and spontaneous human combustion? Or has it always happened this way, every night, at Aunty Bob's Quake City Club? (978-1-63555-723-7)

Serenity by Jesse J. Thoma. For Kit Marsden, there are many things in life she cannot change. Serenity is in the acceptance. (978-1-63555-713-8)

Sylver and Gold by Michelle Larkin. Working feverishly to find a killer before he strikes again, Boston Homicide Detective Reid Sylver and rookie cop London Gold are blindsided by their chemistry and developing attraction. (978-1-63555-611-7)

Trade Secrets by Kathleen Knowles. In Silicon Valley, love and business are a volatile mix for clinical lab scientist Tony Leung and venture capitalist Sheila Graham. (978-1-63555-642-1)